"I CAN'T RUN A FARM BY MYSELF. BUT MAYBE . . . WE COULD DO IT TOGETHER."

He nodded. "Yeah, sure. I'll help all I can."

He'd misunderstood. "I'm proposing a partnership," she said solemnly.

He drew back slightly, clearly stunned by the suggestion.

"A business partnership," she added. She paused, giving him a chance to speak, but he didn't. "You and I would own the farm and work it together."

"I don't know if I can do that," he said hesitantly.

She felt a crush of disappointment that made her want to cry. In fact, the backs of her eyes felt the pinpricks of tears. She looked at her hands and willed herself to be calm and as emotionless as possible. "Because you don't want to leave the Triple H?"

"No, I wouldn't care about leaving."

She looked up at him quizzically. "Because I'm a woman?"

"No," he exclaimed.

"Then . . . what?"

He shook his head and color crept into his face.

"Please," she said. "I really want to know. Don't . . . don't worry about hurting my feelings. I just need to know."

"It wouldn't hurt your feelings. I'm just not the kind of man you become partners with."

Now, she drew back, because the notion was so wrong. "You are *exactly* the kind of man I'd want to be partners with . . ."

DOWN IN THE VALLEY

JANE SHOUP

ZEBRA BOOKS
KENSINGTON PUBLISHING CORP.
http://www.kensingtonbooks.com

ZEBRA BOOKS are published by

Kensington Publishing Corp.
119 West 40th Street
New York, NY 10018

All Kensington titles, imprints, and distributed lines are available at special quantity discounts for bulk purchases for sales promotion, premiums, fund-raising, educational, or institutional use.

Special book excerpts or customized printings can also be created to fit specific needs. For details, write or phone the office of the Kensington Sales Manager: Attn.: Sales Department. Kensington Publishing Corp., 119 West 40th Street, New York, NY 10018. Phone: 1-800-221-2647.

Zebra and the Z logo Reg. U.S. Pat. & TM Off.

First Printing: September 2015
ISBN-13: 978-1-4201-3709-5
ISBN-10: 1-4201-3709-3

eISBN-13: 978-1-4201-3710-1
eISBN-10: 1-4201-3710-7

10 9 8 7 6 5 4 3 2 1

Printed in the United States of America

Chapter One

July 2, 1881
Richmond, Virginia

The petite maid brushed aside a rogue wisp of hair from the back of Emeline Wright's slender neck and clasped the necklace. Miss Wright's chestnut brown hair wasn't exactly unruly, but there was a lot of it and it had a soft, natural curl, so there was always this tendril or that escaping the pins. Plus it blew ever so slightly from the airflow caused by the two-blade ceiling fan. Each suite on the floor had a ceiling fan, powered by a stream of water, a turbine and a belt—or so she'd been told. She stepped back with a, "If that's all, miss?" since it was one of the few lines she was allowed to speak to Miss Wright.

"Yes," Miss Wright replied, since it was one of the few words *she* was allowed to speak. "Thank you, Jenny," was added out of sheer defiance.

Jenny contained the smile that wanted to break through, curtsied and then left the suite, quietly shutting the door behind her before turning the key in the lock. She always felt a qualm about doing so, more than a qualm, really, but she unfailingly locked it because she was required to. An employee did not cross Mr. Peterson and keep one's job. It was rumored that one did not cross Mr. Peterson and keep one's life, although that might have been exaggeration.

As she started back to the east wing to see to her other duties, it occurred to her what an irony it was that someone as powerful and ruthless as Wilson Peterson was called Sonny. *Sonny* sounded sweet and harmless, while he was anything but. He didn't just own this place, The Virginia Palace, the largest, grandest hotel in Richmond; he had power. City officials existed quite cozily in his pockets and eagerly carried out his bidding.

Poor Emeline Wright. Even in the unlikely event she managed to get free of the hotel, it wouldn't matter. She could strip naked, run into a street full of people and scream at the top of her lungs all the things Sonny had done to her—and no one would say one single word against him after she was dragged back inside and probably beaten half to death.

The Palace was not just a hotel. The elegant, four-story stucco structure, fittingly built in the palazzo style, took up half a block. It housed a refined restaurant at one end and a lavish saloon, brothel and gaming facility at the other, where big money was made. Without question, Sonny had charm, and yet everyone knew he was little more than a thug at heart, having acquired every red cent of his fortune through deviousness and utter heartlessness. Take away his stature and confidence, and he was a plain-looking man, six feet tall, with wheat-colored hair. Not thin, but nor was he muscular. He hired muscle; he rarely had to use his own anymore.

Everyone, at least everyone within the confines of The Palace, knew about Miss Wright, as well. Like most every other possession Sonny had ever set his sights on, she had been wooed, lured and then trapped. Tenderly wooed, cleverly lured and then fatally trapped. Jenny had seen her arrive the first day of what Miss Wright had thought was to be a brief visit, all bright-eyed, kind and polite. How quickly things had changed, including Sonny's loving demeanor.

Once the trap was sprung, Miss Wright was informed they'd be married just as soon as she learned to behave as the perfect wife. It was simple, Sonny stated. If she chose, theirs would be an exceedingly pleasant life. If she resisted, as he suspected she initially might, she could expect her "training" to be harsh. No matter what, she would be his and she would make him proud, or she would pay the price.

Oh, and had he ever been right about her resisting. She had entirely too much spirit, but Jenny suspected that was one of the reasons he'd chosen her in the first place. After all, he could have had his pick of any number of impressive young ladies from Richmond. Docile, obedient creatures who'd been raised to be perfect wives. Instead, he'd chosen Emeline—a young woman attending college. A young woman without anyone in the world to come looking for her once she abruptly and unexpectedly withdrew from school and the society she'd chosen.

Naturally, Jenny and the other maids saw more than most. While Em was paraded around almost every day on Sonny's arm, presented as his lovely, fortunate fiancée, dressed in the finest fashions and glittering jewels, the casual observer didn't see the evidence of Sonny's "training." They saw. Some even believed that Emeline had finally learned a certain level of submissiveness, and that there would be a wedding announcement before long. In Jenny's opinion, what Miss Wright had "learned" was to become a master at subduing and concealing her emotions. She couldn't possibly be naïve enough to believe that Sonny bought the act entirely, but she'd performed flawlessly of late. There had been far fewer marks and bruises.

As a door opened just up the hallway, the door to Veronica

Peterson's room, Jenny dropped her gaze and picked up her pace, hoping to pass without having to acknowledge the woman. Veronica was Sonny's aunt and one of the most formidable, joyless people she had ever had the misfortune to encounter. Luck was with her, for Veronica's back was to her as she passed.

Indeed, Em wasn't naïve. She'd withdrawn so far within herself, she often felt nothing at all, but she wasn't naïve. After Jenny left the room, she rose from her vanity table and walked over to the full-length mirror. The pale blue gown she wore was form-hugging and beautifully made, the design straight from Paris. The bustle had all but disappeared and a short train had been added. It was highly flattering and yet there was nothing she would have liked better than to rip it off. To rip it to shreds.

Perhaps it was her lack of expression or the rigidity of her body, but she was suddenly struck by the memory of the porcelain doll she'd had as a girl, because she resembled that doll. The thought was so bizarre, she shivered. She blinked and the impression intensified. She was nothing but a doll, whose arms and legs could move, sometimes at her bidding, sometimes at his, but a lifeless, dressed-up doll just the same. *That* was what she had become.

"Barbara Jean," Em whispered as she recalled the name of the doll. How funny; she hadn't thought of the doll in years. She moved closer to the mirror, gazing fixedly into the eyes of her reflection. *No*, she was not quite a soulless doll yet, but she had to master her fear, find the right opportunity and get away from this place. There had to be a way to make it happen, especially since she'd managed to stash traveling essentials in a soft-sided bag in the basement. In it was clothing, a train ticket, and money—the exact same amount she'd possessed when she'd come to Richmond. She didn't want anything that belonged or had ever belonged to Sonny.

Everything she'd accomplished so far had been difficult and dangerous. In fact, purchasing the ticket to Green Valley, West Virginia, had been a risk she'd barely gotten away with. She'd been on a shopping excursion with Veronica, an infrequent and only recently granted privilege, when, in a milliner's shop, Veronica became involved enough in conversation with an acquaintance that Em was able to duck out of sight. Rushing to the railway station to purchase a ticket had been so nerve-racking that the station attendant had inquired whether she was ill.

She'd stammered that she was perfectly well, and, with badly shaking hands, she'd stuffed the ticket into her reticule and hurried back toward the milliner's shop, arriving just as Veronica emerged. Red-faced with fury, the older woman latched on to Em's arm with a brutal grip. "Where were you?"

"I just stepped out for . . . for air," Em replied shakily and much too quickly. She needed to calm herself. "I was feeling faint," she added. She was suddenly gripped with fear that Veronica would search her reticule. She should have hidden the ticket in her bodice or up her sleeve.

"I will never take you out again," Veronica swore as she led the way back to the carriage. "You can rot in that room for all I care."

In the carriage, Em kept her face turned away from Veronica and her reticule clutched at her side until the hotel was in sight. The tall arches that led to the portico had once seemed awe-inspiring; now the sight made her stomach ache with tension. Beyond the entrance was a lobby of grand scale with a marble floor strewn with thick, Oriental-style rugs, yet the path to the stairs was all marble and the sound her shoes made when she walked up was ominous and hollow. She hated the sound. She swallowed hard, knowing she was nearly out of time, and something else had to be said. "I only wanted a breath of fresh air," she said as tears sprang to her eyes.

"Not without my permission," Veronica uttered through clenched teeth.

"It won't happen again," Em replied quietly. Beseechingly.

Seconds of agonizing silence passed before the older woman gave a stiff nod. "We will neither of us mention it," she warned.

Em looked back out the window again, nearly lightheaded with relief that the crisis had passed. Not only that, but, with the ticket in her possession, freedom had finally become a real possibility. All she needed now was a window of opportunity.

"Emeline," a dry female voice said, startling her back to reality.

Em turned to find Veronica standing in the doorway. As Em started forward to retrieve her fan from the vanity table, Veronica raked her over from neckline to hemline, her gaze full of resentment. They walked without speaking, Em taking a slight lead as if she were in control of her destination. As always, Veronica followed nearly the entire way to the private salon on the second floor where Sonny and his guests had gathered.

The doors were opened for her and Em entered the salon, prompting heads to turn and a chorus of accolades regarding how lovely she looked. She smiled and murmured her thanks with all the hypocrisy she could muster.

"You're a lucky man, Sonny," one of the guests murmured, setting her teeth on edge.

As Sonny acknowledged the comment with a self-satisfied smile, Em took a breath and exhaled discreetly, forcing herself to relax. One day soon, very soon, she would be free of him, and once free, she would never allow a man to touch or control her again. It was a good thought.

Chapter Two

By ten o'clock, Em sat at her vanity wearing nothing but a white silk dressing robe. She brushed her hair distractedly until she froze at the sound of the lock turning. Dread seized hold, but she focused on her face in the mirror. Her eyes were *not* the eyes of a doll. She was not a doll; she was pretending to be one, but with a mind he knew nothing of.

Sonny stepped in carrying a drink, having left his jacket, vest and cravat behind, and nudged the door shut behind him. He sauntered toward her, set his drink down on the vanity and pulled the front of her robe apart. Watching her mirror image, he cupped her breasts. "You looked mighty fine tonight," he said, "but you look even better like this."

She watched his hands so she didn't have to see his face. *A doll feels nothing. Nothing. A doll feels nothing.*

He pulled her up and around to face him, untied the belt of her robe and looked hungrily at her body before he pulled her against him and his mouth closed in on hers. There was no tenderness in the intrusive, alcohol tinged tongue or the grip on the back of her neck. He tugged down the straps of his suspenders, his jaw set in anticipation, and she began unbuttoning his shirt with stiff, slightly trembling fingers. He liked things done in a specific way and she knew the order. She'd learned her cues. He stepped back and removed the long silver chain with the key to her room from around his neck and set it aside. Reaching for his drink, he said, "Middle of the bed. On your back."

He swallowed the last of his bourbon, emptied his pockets and moved toward her. As always, she had to fight her instinct to turn away or close her eyes. He climbed atop her, pinned her hands and bent to kiss her neck, but a knock on the door surprised them both. He got up and moved toward the door, scowling with irritation, while she sat and tugged the robe together to cover herself, thankful for the distraction. *But how foolish*, she silently chided herself, when he would be right back.

He jerked open the door.

"Sorry to bother you, Mr. Peterson," a man said quickly, "but we just learned the President was shot."

Sonny drew back. "What?"

"Shot," the man repeated. "Today. In Washington. The newspaper man, Harper, he received the telegram and came right over to tell you."

"Is he dead?"

"No, sir. He was taken back to the White House. Least, that's what the telegram said."

"Who did it?"

"Uh, some lawyer. Funny last name. The telegram's downstairs."

"I'll be right down," Sonny replied, already shutting the door.

He turned and looked at Emeline, but his mind was obviously busy evaluating all possible aspects of the matter. Her head was spinning, and not just because the news was shocking. Sonny was a creature of habit, and his routine had just been interrupted. "It's terrible," she murmured. As he began to button his shirt, she experienced a chill at the irony that President Garfield had been in office just about the same amount of time she'd been Sonny's prisoner, six months or so. Did it mean something? Her body and mind felt on sudden high alert. She was an animal ready to spring from a trap.

"I'll be back," he said, and then he turned and left, pulling up a suspender strap as he went.

The door closed and she held her breath, waiting for the sound of the lock, only it didn't come. She looked at the vanity table and saw the key. He'd left without it. She looked at the door again, expecting it to open once he realized his mistake, but there was only silence. She got up so quickly, the blood rushed to her head. She moved to the vanity, staring down at the items left behind, his money bound by a monogrammed silver clip, the key and his pocketknife. She reached for the knife with a trembling hand, knowing she had to go. Now. This very minute. *No!* He'd realize his mistake and be back, and to be caught leaving—

She withdrew her hand, but continued to stare at the knife. She tied the belt on her robe and a tear slipped down her face. She swiped it away angrily and picked up the knife. *Damn it,* this was her opportunity and she was squandering it. She started toward the door, but stopped short when she heard the soft squeak of the doorknob twisting. Staring at the brass knob, she stuck the knife behind her, clutching it so hard that the mechanism sprang the blade. He would demand to know why she had the knife, and what would she say?

The door opened, and Veronica, wearing a nightdress, leaned in and grabbed up the key from the dressing table. By the look of her sleep-creased face, she'd been rudely awoken. Em experienced simultaneous jubilation that it wasn't Sonny and dread that her chance was about to disappear. Her only hope was to place some kind of block in the crack of the door once it was closed. *The blade of the knife.* But already Veronica was shutting the door. "D-did you hear?" she called, stepping forward on wobbly legs.

The door opened again. "Hear what?"

Em closed the distance between them, careful to keep the knife from view. "The President was shot."

Veronica blinked in surprise. "All he said was to lock the door," she croaked, obviously dazed from being awoken so abruptly.

"It's terrible, isn't it?"

Veronica grunted and shut the door.

Shaking with equal measures of fear and adrenaline, Em leaned against the door and stuck the blade in the right spot to prevent the lock from catching. Her breath caught as the bar pushed against the blade. This was it. If Veronica realized what she'd just done, she'd force her way in and it would all be over. Em waited, half expecting the door to fly open and knock her backward, but it didn't. She managed a deep breath and then another. All she had to do now was to open the door and make her escape. But what if Veronica was still standing there? Or Sonny? What if it had all been a trick? A test of some sort? Memories of past punishments paralyzed her. "Stop it," she whispered.

She hesitated a moment more and then pulled the door open far enough to release the metal tongue. She tossed the knife onto the rug behind her and peeked though the crack. No one was visible. Slowly, she opened the door and looked out at the empty hallway. This *was* it. *This* was her chance. She had to move. Get to the side door, slip out, and get down and around to the cellar without being seen.

She took a step, but the floor creaked beneath her and she stopped, shaking violently. Her muscles wanted to seize, but she forced herself to start moving again and, once in motion, she kept going. Muffled voices and laughter from the rooms she passed reminded her that anyone could emerge at any time, and anyone who spotted her would immediately alert Sonny.

She reached the door at the end of the hall, opened it

silently and stepped out into a balmy night. Shutting the door behind her, she pressed her back against the wall and gulped breaths to help quell her dizziness. The warm breeze tickled her skin and urged her on, although her knees were dangerously weak as she started down the steps of the rarely used exit. She heard hoofbeats and carriage wheels from the street, and distant voices, but the cover of trees, in full summer leaf, shielded her from view.

She crept around the perimeter of the building and down the steep steps to the cellar. Her stomach lurched when the doorknob offered resistance, but then it gave with a squeak, and she disappeared into the dank, inky darkness and felt her way to the soft-sided traveling bag she'd stashed there. Her eyes were wide and unblinking as she untied her belt and slipped off her robe. She heard the soft scratching of rodents at the same instant she felt the brush of silk against her ankles, and felt a painful chill up her spine. As quickly as she could, clumsy with nerves, she dressed in the same traveling gown she'd worn on the day of her arrival and stepped into her shoes, not even bothering with stockings. She extracted her reticule from the bag, which held a purse with money, the exact same amount she'd possessed upon arrival, minus the ticket she'd purchased, a small brush and hair combs, a handkerchief and her train ticket.

As she started back out, it was with full awareness that she had to move quickly, but also warily, because if this opportunity was lost, there wouldn't be another. Again, she crept around the building to the rear edge of the hotel. It was the quietest street nearby and it was empty for the moment. She took a deep breath, exhaled and then began walking, clutching her reticule tightly. *Head down, keep moving. Walk, don't run. You can do this.*

She knew the least frequented paths away from here. She'd made mental notes of the shadowy alcoves and dark, side alleys on each and every excursion away from the hotel.

She'd thought long and hard about this moment. The hardest thing was not to run.

The prostitutes were housed in the north wing of the hotel, but with the addition of several new ones, a few had been temporarily installed in rooms on the far more elegant south wing, which was why Katie-Louise happened to be walking by Em's room a few minutes before eleven. The girls all called Miss Wright 'the princess' because of her looks, and because of the way she was treated, as if she had to be watched all the time, as if she might break or something.

The princess was slender, with perfect posture. Her hair was brown, which would have been nothing special, except that it was nice hair and went so well with her golden-brown eyes, which were more almond-shaped than round. Katie-Louise had round eyes. In fact, everything about her was roundish. Luckily, she had yellow hair, which a lot of men seemed to favor, a pretty face and the right opening between her legs, which allowed her to make a living. She'd be alright for a few years, and during that time she'd find herself a husband. That was her plan.

"How come you didn't take your top off?" Ned complained behind her. "You didn't show me your tits."

"Maybe I'll do that next time," Katie-Louise replied agreeably. "For a dollar extra."

"Aw, Katie-Louise, that ain't fair. It oughta be part of the package."

She gave him a look over her shoulder. "You can be so crude when you want to," she murmured as she noticed the door to the princess's room was standing wide open. Strange, since she was usually kept locked up tight—a princess in her tower. 'Course, she also got silk dresses made just for her and she got waited on hand and foot. She got to have dinner every night in the fancy, private dining room and she got Sonny Peterson. Not a bad life, in Katie-Louise's opinion. She would have traded in a flat minute.

"You oughta show me your tits and you ought not insult me after paying you, is what," Ned muttered.

"Fine," she gave in. "Next time I will. Alright, already?" They weren't allowed to go into the hotel lobby and so she turned the hall toward the back staircase, aware that Ned was still muttering complaints under his breath. The big baby. Stopping abruptly with an impatient huff, she turned to face him and lifted her top. Tugging it back down in place, she gave him a look. "Alright?" she demanded.

"Alright," he echoed, appeased for the moment.

She turned and walked on with a roll of her eyes. They started down the stairs to the saloon, but slowed in confusion at the sight of the roomful of people below. Everyone had a tense look, the talk was hushed and the whole crowd had converged in the less than half hour she'd been upstairs with Ned.

"Wha'cha think's goin' on?" Ned asked as he stopped beside her.

She shrugged and walked on, ready to be done with him. She made her way over to Nancy and Golden, who were leaning against the back bar taking it all in, their fans in continual movement. "What's happened?"

"President Garfield was shot," Golden replied solemnly. "He's probably going to die."

Katie-Louise's jaw dropped. "Why? Who shot him?"

Nancy shrugged. "Some crazy man."

"I wouldn't want to be president," Katie-Louise confided as she looked over the crowd. "They're always getting shot." Her lip curled to see Veronica Peterson standing across the way. The woman had a hard look about her, the same look men got on their faces when they wanted to cause pain rather than to receive pleasure. Or maybe causing pain was their pleasure, although that made no sense to her. They called her V.P. and frequently followed it with, 'is creepy.'

Sonny, on the other hand, was anything but creepy. She didn't even see how the two of them were related. He was standing at the head of the group like he was holding court—like he was the governor or something. She pictured herself standing next to him, dressed in a silver, satin gown. Sonny would give her that half smile of his, as if they were sharing a joke. It was a beautiful fantasy. "Where's the princess?" she asked without taking her eyes off Sonny.

"Locked away, as usual," Nancy replied. "You know, I kinda feel sorry for her."

"Sorry?" Golden scoffed. "What's there to be sorry for?"

"The door to her room was wide open," Katie-Louise said.

The others looked at her as if she'd just spouted pig Latin.

"You sure?" Nancy asked doubtfully. "You probably saw another room."

"I *know* which one's her room. It wasn't wide open, but it was open."

Nancy blinked. "Uh . . . if she's not down here—"

"Did you look in her room?" Golden asked. "Was she there?"

"I didn't look in, but it's open and it's never open." She paused. "Should we tell?"

"You better," Golden warned. "If she's gone missing again, there's going to be hell to pay, and you best make sure you ain't the one paying."

"Should I tell Sonny?" Katie-Louise asked, hopefully.

Nancy glanced over at Sonny and his group and then shook her head. "Viper lady. I'll wave her over." All three girls looked at Veronica in time to see the scathing look she gave them before starting toward them. "I hate that old witch," Nancy said under her breath.

"Me, too," the others agreed.

"What is it?" Veronica demanded when she got close enough. She always kept a certain amount of distance, as if they had something catching.

Katie-Louise crossed her arms. "The door to the prin—" Katie-Louise barely caught herself in time. "To Miss Wright's room is open."

Veronica flinched. "That's impossible."

Golden noticed that even though it was impossible, the notion sure made VP blanche. It almost made her smile.

"It was," Katie-Louise said with a shrug.

Veronica looked at the people gathered around Sonny, then turned and headed upstairs with a scowl on her face.

"Wouldn't surprise me if she didn't just soil her knickers a little bit," Golden said to the amusement of the others.

As Veronica stared at the sprung lock, cold tendrils of fear seeped through her system. She heard voices behind her and turned to see one of the whores, Betty or Betsy or something like that, coming toward her followed by a short, fat man, who was readjusting his trousers as he walked, low-class scum that he was. "Betty—"

"It's Bitsy," the young woman corrected without slowing her pace.

"Go tell Mr. Peterson I need to see him," Veronica snapped.

Bitsy halted in her tracks. "What?"

"You heard me. Now, hurry up."

Bitsy blinked.

"Go!" Veronica barked.

Bitsy huffed. "I'm going."

"Bitsy," Veronica called a moment later, halting the young woman yet again. "Tell him Miss Wright seems to be . . . missing."

Bitsy looked horrified at the prospect. "I'll tell him to

come up here, but I'm not telling him that," she said in a low voice. "*Uh*-uh," she added with a shake of her head.

"Go, then," Veronica hissed furiously.

Across the street from an establishment called Boxley's Bordello, Em pressed a hand to the stitch in her side and stared at the horses tied to the hitching post. She'd cleared enough distance from the hotel; now she needed a horse. Or better yet, *the horse and buggy at the end of the row*. She glanced around and then crept toward the hooded buggy. It was a two-seater, by no means new, but it was exactly what she needed. Inside the bordello, a piano was being played, and there was a bout of drunken laughter. She glanced around one more time and then climbed in and released the handbrake. "I need you," Em whispered to the animal before giving a flick of the reins.

As she rode away, she expected a hue and cry to go up, but it didn't. The sides of the buggy shielded her from view, which was a relief, and yet her posture remained rigid. It was possible the hunt for her had already begun and, if not, it would soon. She didn't want to think of Sonny's rage, but nor could she help it. She needed to formulate a plan, but mostly she just needed to get out of Richmond. She didn't dare go to the train station; it would be one of the first places searched. So, for now, she'd run. A plan would come later.

Sonny's eyes darted around the room. Behind him, Veronica clutched her hands in front of her. "I . . . I locked the door," she stammered.

He turned toward her, not bothering to conceal his wrath. "Did you check it?"

Veronica looked as though she wanted to say something

but couldn't quite form the words. Behind her, his men waited in the open door. "Get Morgan, get Hayworth, get everyone," Sonny ordered furiously. "My fiancée is on the loose again. I want her found and I mean fast."

The men nodded grimly and hurried off and Veronica was right behind them. Sonny walked over to the large, cherry wardrobe and yanked it open. He rifled through, growing more and more baffled because nothing seemed to be missing. He moved to the chest of drawers and began looking through the contents. He'd purchased each dress, each pair of shoes, each undergarment she possessed, and nothing seemed to be missing. If she had no clothing, where the hell was she, and what was she thinking? She knew he'd have to punish her now, harder than before. She knew that. He'd used his bare hands, a razor strop, even a cane and, apparently, none of those measures had worked. He'd threatened her with the branding iron last time and, now, what choice did he have but to follow through? What choice had she left him? "Damn you, Em," he whispered.

Chapter Three

After traveling for three days, pushing herself and the horse beyond exhaustion, Em gawked at the post marker. She was nearly to Charlottesville, which meant she'd been going northwest rather than due west as she'd intended. She was miles off course. There was no choice but to go into town for food and a rest. She was weak with hunger, not to mention filthy and smelly. So much for being invisible, she thought. People would *smell* her coming.

In Charlottesville, she left the horse at the livery and then went into an inn for a meal. She felt as if she was being watched from every direction. It was time to formulate that plan. When she left the inn, she went to the train station, extracting her ticket as she walked. The ticket was for Richmond to Green Valley, but her hope was that the stationmaster would allow her to use it anyway. If he refused—

No. She would cross that bridge when she came to it.

She entered the depot, which was empty of patrons. A spectacled, red-haired young man looked up at her from behind the barred window and blinked. "May I help you, miss?"

She walked to the window, placing the ticket on the counter. "I bought this planning to use it in Richmond, but then . . . it wasn't possible."

He looked from her to the ticket.

"Could I possibly use it here?"

He looked up at her sheepishly.

"Please," she pleaded. "There were circumstances. I am . . . I'm desperate to get home."

"Miss, the train's getting ready to pull out now."

She clutched at the counter, unable to breathe.

"Come on," he said urgently as he rose from his stool. "We'll catch it."

"Oh, thank you!"

He donned his cap and led her out a side door, taking long strides. She followed, nearly breaking into a jog to keep up with him.

"The stationmaster goes home at half past to eat his dinner," he confided as he walked. "And he's a stickler for the rules." He grinned and shook his head. "You don't even know, but your timing was perfect."

The train began to move and her heart experienced a jolt.

"Wait! There's one more," the young man called to a conductor.

The conductor reached for her hand and assisted her aboard the slowly moving train. "Almost didn't make it," he said. "Must be your lucky day."

She tried to reply, but her voice failed her.

"I approved her ticket," the young man called.

Em turned to wave at him, filled with gratitude. He must have seen because he reddened to his hairline and beamed a smile.

"Your ticket, please, miss?"

She grabbed the rail with one hand and offered it.

"I hope you didn't have a trunk that got left behind," the conductor said as he took it.

"No."

He glanced at her questioningly and then led her to the second-class accommodations. She sat in a hard, too-upright seat next to the window, unclenched her fists and pressed her hands to her stomach. Could it be that maybe luck was finally with her? As the train picked up speed, she felt a wild surge of hope. She was not home yet, but, if luck held, she soon would be.

Home. Rockbridge County. She'd never told Sonny about Rockbridge County. Early on, she'd started to. She told him of being born and raised in Lynchburg and that her parents had both died. And that was when the first of the moments, the warning moments, had occurred. "So, you've got nobody," he'd said, and there was something about the way he said it. A strange glint in his eyes.

So the truth of her existence had stayed secret. She'd chosen not to share that, at age eleven, she'd gone to live with her father's first cousin, Ben Martin, and his family. It was one of the few things she'd done right.

Now, if she could keep going, if she could just get back home to Green Valley, ironically the very place she'd wanted so desperately to escape. She longed to see Ben again, although she dreaded explanations. From the moment he'd shown up in Lynchburg to collect her all those years ago, he'd been both ally and friend. Without doubt, he was the only one of the Martins who could have ever been called either of those things. What would she tell him? The truth would hurt him and humiliate her. She leaned her head back against the seat and wondered if fabricating a story wouldn't be easier for both of them to live with.

As her fatigue and the rocking of the train lulled her toward sleep, she isolated sounds, the rumble of the engine, the clacking of the wheels on the tracks, the murmuring of voices of the other passengers. She jerked awake at the sound of the train whistle, and discovered it was dark outside. It was disorienting enough to set her heart to hammering. The train was slowing to a stop.

She sat up straighter, wondering if Green Valley had

really been called or if she had dreamt it. She started to rise and was thrown off balance as the train braked to a stop. And there it was—the Green Valley sign. She hadn't seen it in almost two years, not since departing for Spring Creek Normal and Collegiate Institute, ostensibly to pursue her education but really, to get out of Rockbridge County. Never, ever could she have imagined then how wonderful that sign could look. Her vision blurred with tears and her heart soared at the sight of it.

Home. She was home.

Her body ached as she stepped down from the train, but was filled with a buoyant joy. She'd made it. She'd really, truly made it. She walked several yards and then stopped. It was less than an hour's ride to the house, but she didn't have a horse and, moreover, she didn't want to be seen this way. Dirty, exhausted, dull with fatigue. Explanations would be hard enough without being seen in this sorry state. She thought of the boarding house a block away and started toward it. With sustenance, a good night's rest and a bath, she'd make a much better impression tomorrow.

The boarding house was just as she remembered it, white with pine-green trim and a porch filled with rocking chairs. She walked up the steps and raised her hand to knock on the door, but an auburn-haired woman inside noticed her and waved her in.

"Do you have a room available?" Em asked as she stepped inside.

The young woman blinked in surprise. "Emeline Wright," she exclaimed. "Well, as I live and breathe."

Recognition dawned with profound embarrassment. "Fiona. I'm sorry. I'm so tired, I didn't recognize you for a minute."

"We got plenty of room. Come on in."

Em pinned her arms to her sides in hopes it would help contain her odor.

"So, where you been?" Fiona inquired as she opened the registry. "I haven't seen you in, what? Two or three years, I guess."

Em nodded and gave a light shrug. "I went away to college," she replied hesitantly.

Fiona looked up. "Sure, but you been there all this time?"

"All of a sudden, it does seem like a long time," Em hedged.

"You want a meal?"

Em's stomach growled again and she pressed a hand to it. "Yes, please. And a bath."

"Then that'll be three dollars." As Em extracted the money from the purse and passed it over, Fiona couldn't help her curiosity. "Not that we're not glad to have you and all, but, uh, why aren't you going home?"

"I . . . I am. It's just—"

"Nope, nope, never mind. It's none of my business. To-morrow is soon enough, right?"

Em exhaled with relief and nodded.

"It's this way," Fiona said, stepping out from behind the desk. "So, can you believe this heat?" she asked as she walked. "Although I guess we all say that every year."

"It's very hot," Em said agreeably.

"Did you learn a lot at college?"

"I did," Em replied reluctantly.

"I think the only other girl from here to go to college was Mary Beth Hornby. 'Member her? She went to a teacher's college, but then she married Oscar Wells, so who knows if she's going to teach or not. Right now, the teacher is a man, name of Mr. Watson. He's a pretty nice fella, but he does have kind of shifty eyes. 'Course, maybe they have to be, watchin' kids all day. That's what Doll says. Doll's my aunt. I don't know if you ever met her or not. You want me to bring your supper to your room?"

The words filtered through the haze of weariness fogging Em's mind. "Yes, please."

Fiona opened the door to a room and walked in to light a lamp. "This alright?"

"It's perfect. Thank you."

Fiona started out again. "I'll bring your supper straight back and we'll get water heating for your bath."

Fiona walked to the kitchen plagued by the niggling feeling she had amends to make. As a girl, Emeline Wright had been snubbed, straight up and right away. It was because of the Lindley thing, of course, but, truth be told, also because she was so pretty. Had anyone ever given her a chance to explain? In fact, had anyone ever given her half a chance?

Jimmy, Em's own cousin, had been behind getting her ostracized. What was that chant she'd been teased with in school? '*Emmy, Emmy W, thinks that she's too good for you.*' It had gone on and gotten real mean, something about the Lindleys, but Fiona couldn't recall it now. Or was it that she didn't want to? She had a feeling in the pit of her stomach that Em was owed a big ole apology from her and everyone else. Only everyone else wasn't there.

"Whatcha frowning about?" Doll asked from across the kitchen where she was putting up food. Doll Summers, Fiona's aunt, stood 5'2", a plump woman with a round, but pleasing face.

"Nothin'. Just thinking."

"You should think something happier," Doll suggested. "A'course that's just my opinion, which doesn't count for much."

Fiona put slices of ham on a plate and added a generous helping of shredded cabbage and apples, a specialty of the house, as well as a thick slice of sourdough bread. When she returned to Em's room with the tray, she got another surprise when Em asked if she could either borrow or buy one of her dresses.

"I left everything behind and I need to burn this," Em said. "I have five dollars," she offered.

Fiona made a face, and not just because accepting five dollars for one of her dresses smacked of being morally wrong. A person could get a nice, new dress for five dollars. "I'll find you one to borrow, although I don't know how it'll look. You're about half my size." But even as she said it, Em got such a relieved smile on her face that Fiona couldn't help but return it.

A half mile away, at The Corner Saloon, aptly named since it sat on the corner of Main and Sixth, Gregory Howerton and two of his men took seats at the table unofficially reserved for him. The saloon was a large, two-story place with wide-plank floors and a hand-carved mahogany bar that looked too sophisticated for its surroundings. There was a second-floor balcony where scantily clad whores leaned upon the railing and surveyed the pickings below.

Howerton was a striking-looking man in his mid-thirties with hair that was prematurely graying at the temples. Behind his eyes lurked shrewd intelligence. He moved, spoke and looked like a man fully aware of his power.

"Here you go, Mr. Howerton," Alice said as she set a glass of premium whiskey in front of him.

Howerton picked up the glass. "Bring another round," he said. "In fact, bring the bottle."

"Hard day?" she asked sweetly.

"Just get the bottle," he returned coldly. Her smile vanished and she hurried off, which worked for Howerton since she reeked of sex, body odor and cheap toilet water. It was a noxious combination, or maybe it was the heat getting to him. Plus, the damn place was noisy. He looked around the smoky room, which was packed with his employees. "I should open a goddamn saloon. They drink every dime they make."

"That's a good idea, Mr. Howerton," James Beard spoke up.

"Shut up," Howerton returned. He downed his glass and then glanced over at Quinton Hayes, an employee of ten years. "What do you think, Quin? Is it a good idea?"

"Whatever you think, boss."

Howerton looked from Quin to James, his newest hire, who was way too nervous and talkative to last long unless he learned to shut it. "See that? That's when and how I want your opinion stated. When I ask and whatever I say."

James gave a terse nod. "Got it."

Alice bustled back to the table with the bottle. "Here you go," she said as she leaned in to refill his glass.

"Anyone not been screwed yet tonight?" Howerton asked.

Alice looked around at all the girls in attendance. "Not this time of night," she said apologetically. "Sorry."

"Well, go wash the smell off you. I'll be there in a few minutes."

Across the room, Tommy Medlin was nursing the last of his drink as he watched the poker game at the next table. His brother Mitchell was playing, as usual. And losing, as usual. "Need anything, pretty boy?" Josie asked, leaning down so Tommy could get a good look at her almost totally exposed breasts. Even one of her dark nipples was partially visible.

"No," he replied, barely glancing at her. "Thank you."

"Want some company tonight?"

"No."

"Full house," Mitchell sang out, slamming his cards on the table. "Read 'em and weep!" He leaned back in his chair and gave a loud whoop.

"Not so fast, Medlin," Clyde Johnson retorted. "Looky here."

There was a moment of silence as Mitchell looked at

Johnson's hand. "Well, son of a bitch," he exploded. "Who gets four aces? It sure as hell ain't never me!"

Josie rolled her eyes at Tommy as if the two of them were sharing a private joke. "You sure?" she whined softly, pouting for good measure. "I can be real good company."

"No, thanks," Tommy muttered. He'd spent enough money tonight and he needed to get out of here before any more of his pay was wasted.

Josie shrugged, but she sashayed away slowly, giving Tommy ample opportunity to change his mind. Instead, he reached for his hat, got to his feet and started to the door without drawing attention to himself. This was just about the time Mitchell was going to start pressuring him for a loan. Only with Mitchell, a loan wasn't really a loan. It wasn't ever repaid. Either he claimed not to remember having borrowed money in the first place or he disputed the amount.

Tommy had always been told he was slow, but he'd learned when to clear out of the saloon, and he'd learned to put most of his money away for safekeeping. His ma had taught him that. She'd tried with all her sons, but the others hadn't taken advice too well. It didn't much matter because at least half the Medlin boys were dead now. Pauly and Ted had been hanged for trying to rob a bank, and Franklin had been shot by his wife, Celia, when he tried to beat her once too often.

Celia had gotten away with it, too. She'd clunked him on his head with a cast iron skillet, and then shot him at point blank range, and then tore out of town without taking one blame thing, including a look backwards. The rest of his family had cursed Celia, especially his ma and Mitchell, but Tommy was glad she'd gotten away. Nobody liked being knocked around.

Tommy had a brother he hadn't seen in more than ten years and Mitchell, and they were all that was left of the Medlin line. Not that the end of the Medlin line was any cause for grief. Mitchell, the youngest of the brood, fancied himself the shining star of the family, but he had no idea that Tommy stashed most of his pay every week. Nor was he going to know, because Tommy had his act down pat. By Wednesday or Thursday, when most the men started grousing about not having any money left, he did the same. Mitchell spent most evenings too drunk to keep track of his own pay, much less Tommy's, so the plan had worked for years.

Sure enough, Tommy had just made it to the door when he heard Mitchell bellow his name. Tommy kept walking. Even if he had looked back, the smoke was probably too dense for them to see each other, but he wasn't taking the chance. As the saloon doors swung shut behind him, he put his hat on and went for his horse.

Chapter Four

In the morning, Fiona's jaw dropped at the sight of Em in her gray, pinstriped dress. How anyone could look good in that dress was beyond her. "Well, damn you," she declared good-naturedly.

"Thank you for letting me borrow it."

"Borrow it? I'd have to burn it now that I've seen you in it."

Em's smile broadened. "Fiona, you're being silly. You look wonderful. And happy."

"I suppose I am," Fiona conceded. "Come on. I waited to have breakfast with you."

"Oh, I'm sorry, I would have gotten up sooner—"

"No, don't be. I never eat early anymore. Too iffy in the morning lately, if you know what I mean."

Em blinked. "You mean—"

"We don't speak about it yet, a'course, 'cause it's too soon. But around Christmastime, there'll be another little Jones in the world."

"Congratulations," Em said enthusiastically. Then, "Jones?"

"Yeah, I married Wayne."

"Oh! Congratulations, again."

The dining room was empty as they walked in. "You sit

and I'll get us a plate," Fiona said. "I guess you like eggs and sausage?"

"I do. Thank you."

Fiona grinned. "You're so polite. I'd forgotten that about you."

Fiona walked away, and Em worked her way through the dozen or so tables to one in the back of the room, but before she sat, she heard an argument begin between two women. Fiona quickly returned with a tray, and the argument continued. It was a relief that Fiona wasn't involved.

Fiona transferred plates and glasses of milk onto the table. "I could'a guessed you'd choose this table."

Em eyed the plate of scrambled eggs, sausages and a biscuit hungrily. "Why is that?"

"Off by itself. You want some coffee?"

It took some effort not to appear taken aback. "If it's no trouble."

"'Course it's no trouble. You go ahead and eat."

Em did, because she was hungry. She'd barely eaten in the first days of running—and her body wanted to make up for it now. When Fiona returned with cups of coffee a few minutes later, half of Em's breakfast had been consumed.

"If you're wondering about all the fussin' and fightin', that's my mama and my aunt Doll. They love each other, believe it or not, but they are oil and water." She took a bite and then shrugged. "They try drawing me into one of their spats and I just hold up my hand and walk away. No way I'm getting in the middle. Ya'll work it out betweenst yourselves and leave me be."

"This was your mother's place?" Em inquired hesitantly.

"Still is. It'll be mine and Wayne's one day but, for now, he's working the mine, like everybody else."

"The mine?"

Fiona cocked her head. "You do know about them finding iron ore around here?"

"No."

"Lord have mercy, girl! There's this rich man, name of Gregory Howerton, and he's buying up everything. He's had this factory built, a big ole furnace is what it is, where they convert pig iron to steel. The railroads and the cities are changing everything. Come to think of it, Mr. Howerton's ranch is out near your uncle's place. Didn't he tell you?"

Em felt her face grow warm. "He may have mentioned it. I've been out of touch."

"I guess so. Anyway, there's a lot more people in town. I mean, a *lot*. It's probably doubled since you've been gone. You been home since you left for college?"

Em shook her head.

"I'm telling you, when you get near Main Street, you won't even believe your eyes. There's new stores and a big new restaurant called Wiley's. You heard of Harvey House Restaurants? Well, this is just like them. They even have Wiley girls, although, come to think of it, I don't guess they call them that. That's pretty funny, isn't it? So, what was college like? Did you really go to a college for men and women? All ya'll together?"

Em nodded, but she couldn't reply to one question before Fiona asked another.

"Was it worth it? I always wondered, what could they teach me that I need to know and don't already?"

"That's a good point," Em conceded.

Fiona sat back, suddenly looking burdened. "Em, I been thinking and, well . . . what I think is you weren't treated right. And I'm real sorry about that."

A painful lump formed in Em's throat. It was ridiculous how much the apology touched her. She nodded, unable to speak for a moment.

"People can be mean," Fiona continued. "And we were. I know that now. And all 'cause of that talk of how you'd struck up a friendship with the Lindleys." Fiona's hazel eyes still held a lot of curiosity. "It might not have even been true."

"My cousins made sure I became an outcast," Em said. "Especially Jimmy. But Patience wasn't much better."

"Yeah, that Jim's a mean one," Fiona agreed. "I learned that through Wayne." She picked up her fork and toyed with her eggs. "So, there never was anything between you and the Lindleys?"

The question struck Em as both painful and funny since no one had ever bothered to ask before. "No, there was something," Em said quietly.

Fiona almost cringed. "Oh?"

"I came to live with the Martins when I was eleven. It was in the late spring. I'd only been here a short time, a few weeks, I guess, when this girl, even younger than me, showed up on horseback in a panic because her little brother had gone missing. He was not even three, and the rain was starting again. I didn't fully understand the danger at the time, but there had been mudslides. She was pleading for help searching for her brother."

"I remember that spring," Fiona interjected. "The flooding and the mudslides."

Em could still picture the day. "My uncle was out in the fields, but my aunt and cousins were home. Jimmy told the girl to get off their property. I couldn't believe my ears. I yelled at him and ran inside to get my aunt."

"Let me guess; she backed him up."

Em nodded. "By the time I got back outside, the girl was riding off and Patience was tattling on Jimmy, saying he'd been throwing rocks at the little Lindley trash. That's exactly what she said. It made me feel sick to my stomach that I was even related to them."

"What'd you do?"

"I ran to the stable. At first, I just wanted to get away from all of them, but . . . I jumped on a horse and rode out.

Bareback. It wasn't planned; I just did it. Jim hollered at me to stop, but that only made me ride faster."

"One or two of the Lindley kids came into town, too," Fiona said, "begging for help." She paused and shook her head. "No one stepped up because there's just too much bad blood between the Lindleys and everyone else."

"Well, I didn't know anything. And I didn't know where I was going. I tried following the girl, but she was too fast. I ended up getting lost and scared out of my mind. Then the rain started and it poured. I saw a mudslide. It took *trees* with it."

Fiona nodded solemnly. "I've seen mudslides."

"I don't know how long I rode. I remember I was freezing and miserable and then I came into a clearing, right into the middle of this group of people. They all looked up at me and—" Em shook her head and blew out a breath, remembering the impact of that moment. "I'd never seen that kind of hatred before. I felt this . . . rush of cold fear, like I was going to faint. And, of course, I was wet and freezing, anyway."

Fiona's eyes were round. "It was the Lindley clan?" she asked breathlessly.

Em nodded.

"I would have fainted dead away," Fiona swore.

"One of them asked what I wanted and . . . everything seemed to happen at once. I saw the girl who'd been to our house and she was crying. She was looking at me as she said something to an older man. Suddenly, I either fell or maybe I was pulled down because I ended up on the ground, surrounded by all these people."

"Lord Almighty!"

"Then a man called out, 'Give the child some room to breathe. She come to help.' It was the older man the girl had been talking to. Now I know it was Xavier Lindley."

"Oh, Lord! He is the scariest man alive!"

Em shrugged. She knew what people thought, but he'd

never been anything but kind to her. "Then a woman asked me, 'Did you come to help, girl?' All I could do was nod. Then it was like something broke in her. Tears spilled down her face and she said, 'Well, it's too late. Poor little Bo got swept in a creek and drowned.' And that's when I saw him. People had shifted and I saw this little boy in his mother's arms. The mother was crying. She looked right at me, so torn up with grief, and then I started crying. It was as if everything caught up to me all at once, the fear of being lost, and that mother's pain, that beautiful little boy lying so still in her arms, the loss of my own father who'd just died. Everything. I started crying and I couldn't stop."

"Oh, Lord, Emmy Wright."

Even now, it made Em want to cry. She swallowed hard and had to wait for the lump in her throat to subside. "They wrapped me in a blanket and took me back to their house." As clear and sharp as some of her memory was of that day, there were parts where she only remembered disjointed bits and pieces. The main house of the Lindley compound was big and wide open, but the ceiling had seemed low. There were three or four hearths in the main room, and a fire burned in all of them. That was where the light came from— a flickering light that added to the strangeness of the moment. And there were dogs in the room, several of them. Her father had never allowed dogs in the house, so it had seemed bizarre to her.

At one point, Xavier took hold of her hand and remarked how cold it was. Then he'd rubbed both her hands to get the blood flowing. He'd said that amidst their dark sorrow, she'd been a beacon of light. Like an angel, he said. A little, wayward angel.

"Later," Em continued, "one of the boys took me back down to Ben's. My legs felt so weak, they put me on the horse in front of him and he led my horse behind."

"Which one? Do you know?"

Em couldn't respond for a moment. She tried never to think of Briar Lindley, much less speak of him. "Briar."

Fiona gasped. "I will tell you what! The Lindleys are dark, dirty criminals, but Briar Lindley is nothing short of one of the handsomest men alive, even with that wild, black hair halfway down his back. So, what happened then? Did he really just drop you off and leave?"

Em nodded.

"Did he say anything?"

Em hesitated. "Not much. Not that I remember." What she clearly recalled was that, midway down the big hill, he'd pressed a kiss to her temple, and said she really was an angel. That she'd be his angel.

"Was Ben mad?"

Em smiled sadly. "No. Not at all. He said he was proud of me. That it took real courage to follow my heart and do what I thought was the right thing. He was only upset because I could have gotten lost and died in the hills since I didn't know my way." Her smile dimmed. "Amy was a different story. I caused a rift between them because she wanted me to be punished and he wouldn't allow it."

"I guess you know about your uncle," Fiona said reluctantly.

Em prickled with alarm. "Know what?"

"He had a fit of apoplexy. It left him so he can't move or talk real good."

Em felt her breath vacate her body. "When?"

"Oh, gosh. Seven or eight months ago, I guess? I'm sure he didn't want to worry you." She paused. "You really didn't know?"

Em worked to hold back tears of shame. "No."

"Emmett looks out for him."

A surge of anger broke through the guilt. If Ben's illness had come on seven or eight months ago, that was before her trip and subsequent imprisonment in Richmond. She could have returned home to care for him. She would have returned home. "What about Patience and Jimmy?"

"Patience got married. You know that."

"Of course, but she's only across the county."

Fiona shrugged. "She never comes back to help that I know of. Not that I know everything."

"And Jimmy?"

"Moved off to Roanoke. He did come back a few months ago, but then he was gone again. For good, I heard."

Em was filled with a sudden, nervous energy. "I should go."

"Sure, I understand. Go."

"What do I owe you for—"

"Now, don't go and insult me. Be off with yourself. Get to Ben."

"Thank you for everything," Em said as she stood.

"Now that you're back, don't be a stranger," Fiona replied with a sheepish smile.

Em held out her hand and Fiona grasped it. "We're not strangers anymore," Em replied.

Chapter Five

It took nearly three hours for Em to make her way to the farm on foot, but she knew the way through wooded paths that shielded her from much of the sunlight and heat. The lightweight dress kept her relatively cool and she was grateful for it. She could have perhaps borrowed or leased a horse, but her funds were low and, knowing what she knew now, she and Ben might have need of them. Besides, she hated asking favors and being obligated to people. How many times had Amy declared that she was too proud? Maybe it was true.

Amy had taken ill during the last year Em was home and died suddenly. The doctor said it was brain fever, although there was no fever to speak of. By the time she passed, Jimmy had left school and was helping on the farm, but he hated it. Something he rarely failed to mention. It didn't surprise her that he'd moved to Roanoke, and she didn't count it as a loss. In fact, *good riddance*, she thought bitterly. Patience, two years younger than Em, had left school and married a young man her mother had stridently disapproved of a short time after Amy's passing. *Good riddance to her, too.*

When the house finally came into view, Em felt an onslaught of nerves. She'd written to Ben from college, but never from Richmond. Would he forgive her, especially given what he'd been through? He must have felt abandoned. The closer she got to the house, the more obvious the neglect became. Tall grass needed to be mowed, one of the barn doors was off its hinges and the cattle herd was nowhere in sight. The place looked abandoned. She'd begun to wonder if Ben was still there when the door squeaked open and he stepped out, moving awkwardly, as if he had a stiff leg. His hair had gone completely white and he looked thin and frail. Em stopped, shocked by his appearance. She studied his expression to determine how welcome she was, and her heart dropped when he appeared to grimace, but then she noticed his shoulders shaking and realized he was laughing. But the muscles of half of his face weren't cooperating.

She ran the rest of the way to him and threw her arms around him. One of his arms returned the hug and he said something that might have been welcome home, but she wasn't sure. She stepped back. "I'm sorry I didn't let you know I was coming."

He shook his head as if to say it didn't matter, smiled his one-sided smile again and gestured her inside with his good, right hand.

She stepped inside and tried not to gawk at the state of the house. Ben pulled out a chair for her, and she sat. He went to get her a glass of water and she felt bad about acting the part of a guest, but hesitant not to. She accepted the glass and downed the water as he walked around and sat.

"Ha ou air," Ben commented. *Hot out there.*

It was as if his mouth were full of something. The words were garbled but they were intelligible if she concentrated. And she would. They would get beyond this. His illness, her absence. She decided to own up to the truth, because she owed him that, no matter what embarrassment it cost her. "I need to tell you what happened to me."

He nodded, his gaze searching.

"Last winter, I met someone, a man from Richmond who had come to Bridgewater on business."

Ben nodded. "Ou wo me." *You wrote me.*

"Yes. I don't remember exactly what I told you then, but his name was Sonny Peterson. Is—" she corrected herself. She blushed and looked at the empty glass she held. "He was dashing and rich." She got up to fetch more water, and not just because it was easier to say what she had to say without looking at him. "He was very charming," she continued, keeping her back to Ben. "He showed me picture postcards of the most beautiful hotel . . . and then told me he owned it." She drank and sought the right words. "I was impressed," she admitted haltingly. "Oh, Ben, I thought I'd fallen in love and that he'd fallen in love with me." She turned back around because she wasn't going to hide from the truth. "I was so wrong. I was so wrong and so stupid." Her chin trembled and her eyes filled with tears, but she blinked and wiped them away.

"Wha hapn?"

"He stayed in Bridgewater for a few weeks," she replied thickly, "but then he had to go back. He owns The Virginia Palace."

Ben cocked his head, his expression intense.

"We wrote and he visited twice more and every time, all the time, he talked of my going to visit Richmond. He said he couldn't wait to show me around the city. And it seemed proper. He said his aunt would chaperone during my visit." She set her glass aside and walked back to the table. "One day, a train ticket arrived along with a letter saying his aunt had come and would escort me to Richmond whenever I could make it." She paused. "So I went. On February third."

He tensed.

"For a day or so, everything was perfect, but then—" She shook her head. "In the blink of an eye, everything was different." She clutched her hands together, knowing she had to finish. She had to say it. "He installed me in a room in the Palace and he kept me prisoner," she said in a low voice, blushing hotly. "He and his despicable aunt. I wasn't allowed to go anywhere alone and I was locked in my room when one of them wasn't with me."

Ben shook his head slowly.

"I couldn't write to you because I couldn't risk his learning where home is," she rushed on. "Besides, I knew you'd come for me, and I couldn't let you. He's so powerful, Ben, and so vicious. And I knew I'd get away eventually."

"Ow ou ge way?"

"A few nights ago when we learned the President was shot—" She broke off because of the shock on Ben's face. "You didn't know?"

He shook his head.

"He's still alive, or he was, last I heard, but the news provided a distraction. I slipped away and I've been running ever since. Straight back here." Ben slid his good hand over and she met him halfway. "I'm so sorry, Ben," she said, her eyes filling. "I'm so sorry I wasn't here for you."

"Nuh-uh-a." *None of that.*

How little his spirit had changed, and her ears were already adjusting to his speech impediment. "I'm so glad to be home."

He nodded in agreement. "Me, too."

Chapter Six

A few days later, Em had a clear picture of what had happened during her absence. Because of the discovery of iron ore deposits, dozens of mining operations and a vast variety of other businesses had sprung up around Green Valley, and the county's population had risen dramatically. She also understood how precarious Ben's financial situation was.

He was nearly broke, having sold the cattle and some of the land to appease Jimmy. Ben had refused to sell the farm outright, but he had sold what he considered Jim's inheritance, which he then handed over. Still, there was plenty of good land left, fertile land that could grow crops and support livestock. All they had to do was to figure out how to acquire the livestock and buy the seed and hire the necessary help, not to mention survive until the farm began paying for itself again. It was overwhelming to think about and, at the moment, they needed food and basic supplies, so that was what Em set her mind to. The rest they would figure out as they went along.

She hitched the wagon and started to town, and she hadn't gone far when she noticed changes in the landscape. There was a split-rail fence that went on for a good mile before she finally passed the entrance to the Triple H Ranch. She'd been told Mr. Howerton's ranch was close, but she hadn't expected it to be as close as it was. She couldn't see the main house from the road but the grounds were impressive. Mr. Howerton was the one who'd purchased land from Ben, and he wanted more. Ben suspected he wanted it all.

Em heard horses approaching. She stiffened as four riders, strangers, passed by, tipping their hats to her as they did. "Ma'am," one said.

"Mornin'," another muttered.

"You lost?" one asked in a slightly mocking tone.

She returned a simple, "Good morning," and kept going. Only after she was sure that they were not following did she relax her posture and her fisted grip on the reins.

Mitchell Medlin licked his lips and blew out a breath. "Who was that?"

"Yeah," Henry Joe Bluefield, known as Blue, said. "That was one fine filly."

"I don't know who she is," Joe Harris replied. "Never seen her before."

"Let's go, gentlemen," Sam Blake, the foreman, called. "We haven't got all day."

Curtis Dugan looked at the list, then narrowed his eyes at Em. "I cain't give ya'll nothin' else on credit. Your uncle ain't paid what he owes already. You need to settle up, first."

Ben had warned her about Dugan. He'd taken over the general store from his father and he didn't give much credit. She already detested the slight, sharp-featured man because of the way he'd treated Ben. "I'm not asking for credit," she replied, keeping her voice level and her face expressionless.

"I can pay for what we need now and we will get the rest paid." *You skunky little son of a bitch.*

He folded his arms. "Like I said, you need to settle your account."

"I heard you and I understand, but I can't do that today."

"Not my problem, sis."

"Are you saying you won't sell me what we need today?"

He shrugged. "Saying you need to settle up."

"Well, since I can't do that at the moment, I suppose I'll just have to make a trip into Lexington to get what we need." Before Dugan could reply, Em turned and looked around at the others in the store. "I'm going into Lexington, so if anyone wants me to get something while I'm there, just let me know." She turned back to face Dugan. "If you'll excuse me, I'm going to go ask around before I head out."

Dugan's face twitched with dislike. "You didn't fit in around here before and you don't now, neither."

A middle-aged woman tapped Em on the shoulder. "Miss, would you mind getting me some—"

"Fine!" Dugan exclaimed. He glared at Em. "You can get what you need for today, but you pay for it. And you better get that bill paid off soon."

Em was careful not to let the relief show on her face. They needed the supplies, and she didn't have time to go into Lexington. "You have my list," she reminded him.

Dugan was seething as he went to fill the order.

Em turned back to explain herself to the woman, but the conspiratorial wink she received was so unexpected, she almost laughed out loud. Not many people in this town had accepted her before, so the show of support was a delight.

"Can't stand that man," the woman whispered before walking off.

When the order was filled, Dugan insisted on payment before loading the big items onto her wagon. "Eleven dollars and fifty-eight cents," he barked.

She pulled out thirteen dollars, all she'd been able to scrounge up, and laid it on the counter. "And you can put the rest of it toward our account."

"Doesn't go very far," he snarled as he counted the money.

"The wagon is right outside," she said sweetly.

He gave her a final scowl before she turned and left, making her way next to the office of T. Emmett Rice, attorney-at-law and Ben's closest friend. Emmett was nearly as round as he was tall with a thick mustache that had turned silver in her absence.

"Thank God you're back," Emmett exclaimed when he saw her. He gave her a hug and stepped back, shaking his head. "We've missed you and Ben needs you."

"I know. I've been back a few days."

"I haven't been getting out there as much lately because I'm backed up with work. This town has grown and I can't keep up."

"I know how much you've done and I appreciate it more than I can say. But why didn't you tell me?"

"Aw, Emmy, I tried. Ben told me not to, but I know you. I wrote and got a letter back from the dean saying you'd withdrawn. With no forwarding address. Where have you been?"

She felt terrible. "It's a long story. I made a mistake that got compounded a hundred times over."

"Well, you're here now," he said with a smile that made his face look even rounder. "More beautiful than ever, and I would have sworn that wasn't possible. Aw, and she can still blush," he teased. "Come on. Let an old man buy you some dinner."

"I'd like that."

They walked to Wiley's Restaurant, and were seated and served immediately. Em looked around at the patrons, few of whom she recognized, and the waitresses, none of whom she recognized. "Where did they all come from?" she asked in astonishment.

"Discovery of a natural resource that mankind suddenly deems valuable changes everything," Emmett waxed philosophically. "Look at the gold rush in the west." He shrugged. "We've got ourselves iron in them there hills. Been there for thousands of years, or maybe more than that, but all the sudden, we've learned how to manipulate it to build ourselves fancy, big buildings and railroads, so it's got value. Great value."

"Still," Em mused. "How do people know? Where did all these young women come from?"

"It's my understanding that Wiley advertises throughout the whole country, and then brings girls to whichever location he needs them. He pays the girls seventeen dollars a month, plus they get their room and board. 'Course they work six days a week, ten hours a day. Not as bad as farming, I admit—"

"Speaking of which," she said slowly.

"Yeah," he said with equal reluctance. "That damn fool son of Ben's messed things up but good. He went and sold off most of the stock when Ben was first afflicted."

Em's jaw dropped.

"Ben softened the story, didn't he?"

She nodded. "Yes, he did. And what about Patience?"

"What about her? She's her mother's own child," Emmett said as he speared a cooked carrot. "She'd doesn't give a fig about anybody but herself. Never did."

"So Ben has an attack and Jimmy finds out—"

"Sent the telegram myself," Emmett stated. "And he showed right up." He grew somber. "You know, at first, I thought, maybe he's finally grown up. Maybe he's not the piece of crap I thought he was. Then I found out what he was doing. I don't know that I've ever been so mad."

Em nodded thoughtfully and they ate in silence for a few minutes.

"I see you've earned yourself a few blisters," Emmett commented.

Em shrugged. "There'll be more to come, I'm sure."

"The thing is," Emmett continued, growing more serious, "there's no money left, and you can't start over when there's no money left. Everyone had a couple of bad seasons, then that was followed by Ben's stroke, followed by Jimmy's theft. It should never end up that way after a lifetime of work, but that's the long and short of it."

"Then we sell off more of the land and work what we have left."

"Farming is a hard life. You know that. Someone like you, you could have anything. You could have an easy life. You cannot tell me that you really and truly want to live your life on the farm."

"Yes, I can. Oh, Emmett, all that time away and everything I experienced . . . the one thing I became sure of is that *this* is home. This is where I want to be."

"But, honey, the farm—"

"Is exactly where I want to be. I want to make it work more than anything."

"For Ben's sake?"

"Maybe. In part. But the rest of it is me. My wish. I swear."

Emmett sipped his coffee and his mustache wriggled in distaste. "Gone cold," he muttered, glancing around for a waitress. He caught one's attention and held up his cup. "Well, Howerton will buy more land. There's no doubt about that. And he's a fair man. Didn't even try to negotiate last time. I named a price, he paid it."

She nodded. "Good."

"Talk it over with Ben. Decide how many acres you'd want to offer."

"I will."

He pushed his plate away and leaned forward onto his elbows. "Did I say how good it is to have you back?"

"It's good to be back."

"Then let's have some pie."

Chapter Seven

"She had this pretty brown hair," Joe said. "And her face . . . just like an angel." It was after ten at night and he was lying in his bunk, staring up at the beams in the ceiling.

Shorty flung open the door of the bunkhouse and walked in, full of news. "Her name is Emeline Wright," he announced. "She's the niece of Ben Martin."

"I thought she went off and got married," Johnny Macgregor said.

"Nope, that was the daughter. This one went off to college."

"College," Mitchell said. "La-te-da."

"Bet she thinks she's something," someone muttered.

"Hell, she is something," Mitchell spoke up.

"Hell, yeah, she's something," Blue echoed.

Mitchell looked at Blue. "You don't have to go and repeat everything I say."

"I don't repeat everything you say," Blue snapped. His face was turning red, so he bent back to his task, repairing the hole in his brogans.

"So, she's our neighbor, is she?" Mitchell muttered.

Tommy Medlin was braiding rope and listening without comment until the tone in Mitchell's voice registered, and he looked up and saw the look on his brother's face. His fingers kept moving, but his mind had disengaged from the task. He was recalling another time he'd seen that look on Mitchell's face. He was recalling Kathy Cooper.

"Whatcha gonna do?" Kathy had asked Mitchell, real flirty like, one day when they were coming home from school. "Kiss me or something?"

Mitchell had been thirteen at the time, Tommy fourteen and Kathy fifteen, but petite. She'd looked younger than either of them, but she was no innocent.

"You'd probably like that." Mitchell laughed.

"I doubt it," Kathy retorted.

"Ever seen a boy's privates?" Mitchell challenged.

"I got brothers, don't I?" she snapped. "Bet you never seen a girl, though."

Mitchell smiled slowly. "Boys are all different, you know. Some are a lot bigger than others."

"You look at a lot of them?" Kathy teased.

"I seen enough, I guess. You want to see? I sure would like to see what you got under that skirt."

Kathy's eyes sparkled brilliantly, but they'd dimmed when she looked over at Tommy. "What about him?"

"He don't mind," Mitchell said.

"Well, I mind," Kathy snapped. "Tell him to get."

There was no need. Tommy was already headed off as fast as he could walk.

"He's slow, ain't he?" Kathy asked loudly, so that Tommy would be sure to hear.

Kathy Cooper had always had a hard look about her. Tommy had commented on it once to Mitchell. "Yeah, it's a look that says 'do me,'" Mitchell said. "'Give it to me hard.' That's what women really want, especially her."

Sometimes, the whores at the saloon had that look, too. Of course, he'd been with several, because who else was going to have him? But he didn't like anything except the buildup and the release. The women always smelled bad, like sex and stale smoke and booze, and they did everything by rote, the way he braided rope. He usually kept his eyes shut during the whole thing, but it was impossible to forget where he was and who he was with. Sometimes a man needed that kind of release, but he didn't like spending his money on pleasure that was over in two minutes. Afterwards, it always felt like a waste.

"You seen her, pretty boy?" Simon asked.

Tommy snapped back to attention. They were still talking about Emeline Wright. He detested being called pretty boy, but he'd long since given up trying to stop people from saying it. Now, he just acted like it didn't bother him. "No."

"Me neither," Simon said.

"Body like a goddess," Mitchell was saying. "Wouldn't mind getting into that."

"Like that would ever happen," Johnny scoffed.

"Hey, screw you, Johnny," Mitchell retorted.

"All of you shut up," Bart Shaw called from a top bunk. "I'm trying to go to sleep."

Tommy rose and left the bunkhouse, desperately needing fresh air and space. He put some distance between himself and the bunkhouse, reveling in how beautiful the night sky was. A magnificent shooting star stopped him in his tracks, and he had the fleeting thought that he should wish on it, but what would he wish for? This was his life and no shooting star, no matter how brilliant it was, would change that fact.

"This is nice," Ben said as he reclined in his rocking chair on the front porch.

His speech was no less impaired than the day Em returned, but her comprehension was nearly foolproof. The challenge had been to figure out what consonants he couldn't utter. There was nothing wrong with his mind or his sense of humor; it was just that some parts of his body had stopped working correctly. "Except you don't do it right," she teased. "You're supposed to *rock*."

He turned his head to watch her as she rocked and mended one of his shirts. "You know, you don't have to work every minute of the day."

"This isn't really work. It's relaxing," she said, stretching the truth beyond its limits.

"Is this really what you want, Emmy?"

"Yes, it is," she reassured him for at least the twentieth time.

"I don't know how we're going to do it," he said with a shake of his head.

"We're going to sell off one more parcel of land," she said. "Maybe from the northwest side."

"No, it's got the pond. Sell it, and you'll have issues with water rights and contamination and whatnot."

"Then which one?"

He was quiet a few moments. "I don't think we can make this a working farm anymore. It's too much work, and it'll take too much money."

"This is good land," she pleaded. "We can do something with it. Something profitable."

"Yeah. Sell it and let them mine it," he said wryly.

"Not that! I didn't mean that."

Ben studied her for a long moment. "I don't want this land torn up either," he admitted. "But it feels like we're kiddin' ourselves."

"Well, we're not. Maybe we do have our backs against the wall, but—" She shook her head, searching for the right phrase to explain her determination. "But all that means is we have . . . a different viewpoint."

He grinned.

"We *will* figure it out," she exclaimed.

"I bless the day you came into my life, Em. I probably don't tell you that enough."

She fought back a surge of emotion. "Me, too," she said thickly.

Ben looked out at the sporadic sparks of light, courtesy of the fireflies, knowing that soon they'd die out for the season. "A few years back, Amy's brother passed on. He didn't have any kin, other than us, so the land off thataways," he said, gesturing with his good hand, "came to us. I say we offer that to Mr. Howerton. It's over a hundred acres. It doesn't directly connect to his land, but . . . he probably figures he'll own it all eventually anyway," he finished with a wry smile.

Em drew breath to comment, but was distracted by a shooting star brighter than any she'd ever seen.

"Hurry and wish," Ben said, having seen it, too.

"I already did." Em laughed as she rose and walked to the railing, staring at the sky, although the celestial show was over.

"Then maybe all our problems just got solved," Ben teased. "I almost feel like they did."

Em bit on her bottom lip, thinking of how many of her problems had already been solved. She was here, safe, and away from Sonny. Plus, Ben was getting stronger, and the farm was slowly improving. They'd figure out the rest. She *felt* it.

Chapter Eight

"Wright, you say," the elderly lady murmured as she looked at the photograph.

"Yes," Sonny said. "Emeline Wright." He looked around the tearoom, wondering if he'd missed asking any of the ladies.

"She's lovely. And it does seem like a familiar face," the woman mused.

Sonny looked at her sharply. "Does it?" This was his second trip to Lynchburg, the first having been utterly unsuccessful. Em had managed what he had thought was impossible; she'd managed to disappear from Richmond and elude him for more than a month. He'd searched here and in Bridgewater, where he'd first met her, but so far, there had been no sign of her. It was frustrating as hell, but that only made him more determined to prevail. She'd put his reputation on the line, which was something he could not allow.

"I'm sorry," the woman said, handing the photograph back. "It does seem familiar, but I cannot place it, even with the name."

Sonny swallowed back his disappointment. "Thank you for looking."

"Why did you say you're searching for her?"

"A relative died and left her a sum of money. I'm the solicitor for the family."

"Ah! Well, if you'll leave your card, I'll certainly write if I remember anything."

"I'll do that, ma'am."

"And have some tea, dear. A good strong cup of tea makes everything better."

Chapter Nine

On Friday, the hands of the Triple H were excused early because of a good week's work and a looming thunderstorm. After collecting their pay, the majority of them headed into town, feeling celebratory. Gregory Howerton arrived just ahead of his men, although his horse had thrown a shoe along the way, which was why he was bent over inspecting his stallion's left front hoof when the others began arriving. He looked up at the group of men approaching and motioned for Tommy, who immediately broke off from the others and went toward him. "He's thrown a shoe," Howerton said when Tommy reached him.

"I'll take care of it," Tommy said, taking hold of the reins.

Howerton allowed the transfer and then watched as Tommy started to the livery without comment or complaint.

James and Quin had lingered behind as the other hands filed inside. "Sure you want to trust an idiot with that?" James asked with a smirk.

Howerton turned to him and fixed him with a cold stare. "Tommy's not the idiot."

James's smirk vanished. Howerton brushed past him and

Quin extended his hand in a *you first* gesture. "I can't seem to say anything right," James complained.

"Learn not to say anything," Quin suggested.

Emmett was stuck with a talkative client, so Em left the office and meandered up the street, looking into shop windows as distant thunder rumbled. She glanced up at the grayish-purple sky, wondering how soon the storm would hit.

She passed Eleanor Simmon's Dress Shoppe where the 'newest fashion from Paris' was, in fact, not terribly new. She smiled to herself, glad of it. She didn't miss, and she would never miss, the elegant gowns she'd left behind. Walking on, she noticed Joseph Schultz sitting at the entrance to the livery he owned and operated. He was seated on a tall stool at an even taller table, hunched over a saddle he was repairing. It was a sight she had witnessed many times, though not in a few years. He looked up and smiled to see her. "Emeline!"

His handlebar mustache had grown bushier since she'd last seen him. "Hello, Mr. Schultz," she said when she got close.

"It's good to see you, Miss Emeline. And as pretty as ever."

Her face warmed. "It's good to be home."

"Still can't take a compliment, I see," he teased. "All that learning in college and they didn't teach you that?"

"Truthfully, I'm not sure what I learned of any real value."

He grunted. "And in the meantime, been some big changes around here, eh?"

"Yes, indeed. I'm not sure what to make of them all."

"Where's my manners gone to? You probably don't know Mr. Medlin, here," he said, shifting on his stool to glance behind him.

Em followed his gesture and locked gazes with a man standing inside the livery. With his dark hair, well-proportioned features and compelling blue eyes, he was, without question, the most handsome man she'd ever clapped eyes on.

"Tommy," Mr. Schultz continued, "this is Miss Emeline Wright."

Tommy tipped his hat to her. "Ma'am."

"Mr. Medlin," she returned. Her voice sounded breathy and strained, which was ridiculous. For one thing, she had absolutely no interest in a man, any man, no matter how handsome he was.

Tommy pulled off his hat and set it on a post, avoiding her gaze, and Mr. Schultz went back to his mending. "If you're around any of his rowdy friends," Mr. Schultz said, "you'll hear him called 'pretty boy,' but his name is Tommy."

Em chanced another glance at Tommy Medlin and discovered he was frowning, his eyes downcast. How ironic that the most handsome man she'd ever encountered would also be shy. He picked up the horse's hoof and began filing the shoe with precise, practiced ease. "That's a beautiful horse," she commented.

Mr. Schultz grunted. "One of Howerton's prize stallions. The man's got a passion for thoroughbreds and the pocketbook to back it up."

"Ah, Mr. Howerton. I've heard the name."

"He tends to make himself known," Mr. Schultz replied. He looked up at the sky and then rose from his perch. "Best get inside, Em." The words were no sooner out of his mouth than rain began falling in fat drops. Em hurriedly stepped inside, as did Mr. Schultz, bringing the table, stool and saddle with him. "Going to be a drencher," Mr. Schultz commented as he reseated himself in the middle of the livery.

Em looked back at Tommy Medlin, whose blue eyes were immediately averted. "So, you work for Mr. Howerton?" she asked.

"Yes, ma'am," he said without looking at her.

It was strange to feel drawn to him. It was because of his shyness, she decided. "What's he like?"

"He's a rich man," Tommy said slowly.

She smiled in amusement until he looked up sharply. Embarrassed. "That much I'd heard," she replied, maintaining a warm smile. She suspected he thought she was laughing at him and she wanted to demonstrate she was not.

"He's all business, but he's fair," Tommy added.

"My uncle, well, he's actually a cousin, but everyone thinks he's an uncle. Anyway, he's had some dealings with him."

"How is Ben?" Mr. Schultz asked.

"He's . . . well. Still afflicted," she added quietly. "But it didn't affect his mind."

Mr. Schultz nodded. "I know," he said quietly. "And I know he's glad to have you back."

"No more so than I am to be back." It was funny; she'd forgotten how much she liked Mr. Schultz.

"Is T. Emmett Rice looking for you?" Mr. Schultz asked Em.

"Yes."

"Emmett," Mr. Schultz hollered. "She's in here."

Em glanced at Tommy, but he was intent on filing again, and then Emmett dashed into the livery.

"Coming down in buckets," Emmett exclaimed. "I didn't know where you got to," he said to Em as he propped his umbrella just inside the door.

"You were with a client."

"So she paid us a visit," Joe Schultz put in.

"Emmett, do you know Mr. Medlin?" Em asked.

"Can't say that I do," Emmett said as he walked toward the younger man, his hand extended. "T. Emmett Rice."

Tommy clasped it. "Tommy Medlin."

"He works for Mr. Howerton," Em said.

"Oh? Well, who doesn't anymore?" Emmett said. He patted the stallion's neck. "Betcha this beauty is one of his."

Tommy nodded. "Yes, sir."

"Well, Emmy, let's go have some supper. Shall we?"

Em looked at Tommy Medlin again, hoping her face was maintaining its natural color. She'd felt more than one flush of heat. "It was nice to meet you."

"Nice to meet you," he echoed.

She followed Emmett, who was going for his umbrella. "Bye, Mr. Schultz."

"You two have a good supper."

"Will do," Emmett returned, throwing up a hand. "Try and stay dry."

"I'm not sweet enough to melt," Mr. Schultz jested.

Tommy watched the interaction with fascination. They all made it look so simple. Why wasn't it simple for him? He felt a familiar hollow ache in his chest as he watched Emeline Wright retreat into the darkening evening. He wished he was with them, one of them, going off to have supper, talking to everyone they met in that simple, comfortable way.

"Pretty thing, isn't she?" Mr. Schultz commented.

Tommy nodded, although *pretty* wasn't nearly a good enough word. Her beauty made his mouth go dry.

"Got a good heart, too," Mr. Schultz went on. "Though it's gotten her in some trouble."

Tommy turned to the older man. "What do you mean?"

"I suppose you've heard of the Lindley clan?"

Tommy felt a tightening in the pit of his stomach. He'd done more than hear of them; he'd seen them blow into town. They were a wild bunch that intimidated most everyone they met, and liked it that way.

"Pull up a chair and I'll tell you the story of how a young girl became an outcast," Mr. Schultz said darkly.

Tommy glanced toward Wiley's Restaurant. The evening had grown dark quickly, so the well-lit restaurant glowed. He set his file aside and walked closer to learn what Joseph Schultz knew.

Chapter Ten

A fortnight later, Emmett climbed back into his buggy, left the Triple H and headed to Ben's place, confident he'd made the best deal possible. He didn't feel great about negotiating more of Ben's land into Howerton's vast holdings, but it's what Ben and Emmy needed to do.

He'd had a few doubts about Em's commitment to the farm at first, but he'd never seen anyone throw themselves into anything the way she'd done since returning home. She'd cleaned and repaired, plowed and painted. She'd worked blisters onto her hands and calluses onto her feet, and never once complained about it. He didn't doubt her commitment anymore.

Ben was on the porch when he drove in. "Been to Howerton's," Emmett called as he parked. "I told Em he wouldn't negotiate and then he went and gave me a price he's wil—" He broke off, realizing something was wrong. Ben's color was pasty and his mouth slightly open. Emmett jumped down and rushed to Ben, heavy with dread. "Ben?"

Ben's eyes took a moment to find his and then they lost focus altogether. His raspy breathing stopped. Emmett knew, because he was holding his own breath. As Ben slumped sideways, Emmett took him into his arms and eased him onto the floor. Ben was already staring up sightlessly. "Oh, Ben," he cried in a shaky voice. *Why now?* he wanted to yell. Why, when things were just starting to get better? A wave of grief descended, and T. Emmett Rice bowed his head and gave in to it.

The sun was low in the sky when Em came dragging back in from the day's work. She saw Emmett standing on the front porch and waved weakly, and even that took more energy than she had left. She led her horse into the barn and unsaddled him. By then, Emmett had followed her into the barn. "I was waiting for you."

She knew a lecture was coming. She was working too hard. Rome wasn't built in a day. She needed to learn to pace herself. He'd said it before and so had Ben, and she knew it was true, but the work needed to be done.

"Emmy—"

The tone of his voice startled her, and she turned to him, instantly reenergized with alarm. He was standing just inside the barn doors and the light behind him obscured his face from view. "What's wrong?"

Emmett walked farther in, to where she could see his face. "It's Ben."

It felt as if the breath was knocked from her lungs. She knew. From Emmett's expression, she knew, and yet she shook her head in denial.

"He had another attack. He's gone, Emmy. I'm sorry."

Em kept shaking her head because it wasn't true, not when she'd left Ben right after lunch and he'd been fine. He'd been joking about what to do with the money from Howerton. He said they should forget the farm and go see Paris.

"I'm sorry, honey," Emmett said.

"No," she whimpered. "No."

Emmett reached her and grabbed her arms to steady her. Her knees were already giving out, so he guided her to the ground and then held her as she lost all control and sobbed bitterly.

Chapter Eleven

Gregory Howerton surreptitiously glanced at Ben Martin's niece. He'd felt obligated to show up for the funeral, but the sight of her had been worth the effort. She stood, solemn and pale, next to Rice at the front of the small crowd. Not only was she a beauty, but she'd inherited all of Martin's property. He knew because it was the talk of the town and because he'd confirmed the rumors with Rice. Apparently, most townsfolk had expected Ben's property to go to his son. *That* would be the son, the robust, red-faced young man with the angry scowl on his face.

There seemed to be a lot of death, all of a sudden. Here they were burying Ben Martin and just this morning he'd learned President Garfield had finally died. After being shot, the poor man had gone from two hundred and ten pounds to a hundred and thirty due to one infection after another. His pain had been intense, his last days torturous. It was no way to die.

"Let us bow our heads in prayer," the preacher said in closing.

Good. It was almost over. The service ended and Howerton made his way toward Emeline Wright. He watched her interact with the others in front of him and found her to be sober, intelligent and poised. "I'm Gregory Howerton," he said when he reached her.

"Mr. Howerton," she said, accepting the handshake he offered. "Thank you for coming."

"I'm sorry to meet under these circumstances. And I'm sorry for your loss."

"Thank you."

"I hope we can meet again soon in happier surroundings."

She gave a subtle nod, and he moved on, allowing the next mourner to extend his condolences. Up close, Emeline Wright was stunning. There was also an intriguing restraint about her. She would require more study and observation, but, so far, she was looking like an excellent candidate for the role of Mrs. Gregory Howerton.

Just before dawn, Em pulled herself upright against the headboard, looking around as best she could in the dark. "Nightmare," she whispered, although the sheen of sweat on her skin and her pounding pulse were real enough. In the dream, she'd found herself back in the Palace as everyone searched for her. She'd gone from room to room, hiding wherever she could as Sonny ranted, wielding a red-hot branding iron. They'd been closing in on her when she'd jerked awake.

She shivered and got out of bed. Stepping into shoes and wrapping a shawl around herself, she went out to use the privy. She hadn't used the slop jar during the night and she didn't want to have to empty and clean it if she didn't have to. On the way back to the house, she was relieved to see darkness lifting. She went back inside for a blanket, swaddled herself with it and sat in a rocker on the front porch, waiting for the sun to rise.

Stupid.

The word seemed to come at her like an accusation, like a justly deserved punishment. She'd been stupid to get upset by a dream, and she'd been stupid to go to Richmond in the first place. Sonny had trapped her and then made it seem as if she'd asked for it. "You're not a fool," he'd scoffed later. "You knew I was providing a one-way passage from Bridgewater. You knew you weren't going back."

She didn't want to think about Sonny, *ever,* not for one more second in all the rest of her life, but the nightmare had etched his face in her mind's eye and it was still there. Lurking. Taunting. *Damn him! Damn him for what he did to me.* The humiliation, the whipping, making her beg to stay in order for it to end. Like a child, she brought her hands to her face, as if she could hide behind them.

After several deep breaths, she lowered her hands and tugged the blanket higher against the cold breeze. Occasional nightmares were inevitable, but it was foolish and harmful to dwell on the mistakes and misfortunes of her past. *She* was in charge of her mind and her life, and she would block out hateful, hurtful memories. She'd done it before.

In fact, she'd done it on the very first day she'd awoken on the farm to discover her most prized possessions had disappeared from her trunk. Her doll, Barbara Jean, was one of the lost treasures. She could still remember frantically digging through her trunk to find the doll, even though she'd been carefully placed on top. A pearl bracelet was missing, as was a delicate, red, cut-glass dish. Furious and devastated, she'd run to find Ben. Instead, she'd found Amy sewing in the parlor, and tearfully blurted out the whole thing.

"I don't know what you're talking about, Emeline," Amy coolly replied. "But I'm certain you were upset when you packed. Naturally."

"She's my only doll," Em pleaded.

"You still play with dolls?" Jimmy sneered, having just come in the room.

"You're too old for dolls," Amy stated. "This is not something to be upset over."

The anger Em suddenly experienced was like a face full of cold water. It instantly stopped the tears. "And my mother's pearl bracelet?" she demanded.

"You had best watch your tone, young lady," Amy warned.

"What's this?" Ben asked as he entered from the kitchen.

"Emeline forgot a doll at home," Amy replied, lifting her chin as if daring anyone to disagree with her.

"I didn't forget," Em cried, turning to Ben. "I put her right on top so she wouldn't get smashed."

Ben walked farther into the room, looking from Em to Amy and back. "And what was that about a pearl bracelet?"

"My mother's bracelet. It's gone, too. And there was a red dish. It was glass. Someone took them out of my trunk when I was sleeping."

Ben looked pointedly at Amy, and a muscle bulged in his jaw.

"Obviously, she's mistaken," Amy said.

Ben kept looking at his wife, and Em got the first of many warning pangs in her stomach. There was discord here, and she was squarely in the middle of it. Finally, Ben looked back to Em, and his expression was almost sorrowful. "Could you have left your doll behind? Because we could write and—"

Em shook her head stubbornly.

"Okay, Emmy," he said. "We'll look again and if we can't find her, we'll get you a new one."

"Don't be foolish," Amy snapped furiously as she stood and tossed her mending onto the chair behind her. "We don't have money to throw away on toys. And at her age!"

"She's just lost her father and been yanked away from her home," Ben retorted, barely holding on to his temper.

"Go outside," Amy yelled, looking directly at Em. "All of you. Jimmy, go tend to your chores."

"Patience isn't doing her chores," Jimmy whined.

Ben scowled at him. "Then tell her to get to it," he said warningly.

Em went outside, unsure of what to do, and Jimmy followed. "You're a damn troublemaker is what you are," he hissed at her. "I hope you die soon, like your father." He turned and stalked off before she could say anything, but he needn't have. The words had been so hurtful, she'd been rendered incapable of responding.

She'd never gotten Barbara Jean back. Or any of her treasures, for that matter. In fact, the only other time the subject came up was that first night at dinner when Patience had asked what the doll looked like. Amy had silenced her, silenced them all, and forbidden anyone to mention it again. It was one of many things Em had chosen to block from her mind.

Briar Lindley was another.

After the incident with little Bo Lindley, Jimmy had possessed all the ammunition he needed to ruin her, which he chose to do for the sheer fun of it. On Em's first day at school, Jimmy announced she'd had a 'thing' with the Lindleys. A few others, mostly Jim's friends, had seized hold of it, calling her a Lindley lover and white trash. Day after day, they tormented her with it, even making up rhymes that girls jumped rope to. *Emmy, Emmy W, thinks that she's too good for you, she loves the Lindleys, bold as brass, like them, she's just a piece of trash.* She'd sniped back, withdrawn and pretended she didn't care, but it had hurt desperately.

Occasionally, Patience would befriend her, but the younger girl always dropped her as soon as anyone so much as made a comment. School had been a lonely, isolated existence and home hadn't been much better. And then Briar had begun showing up. He always found her when she was roaming the fields or out riding. He seemed to sense when she was alone. She'd heard plenty about him by then, and there was a sense of danger about him, even though he never did anything but flirt and flatter. He had the darkest eyes she'd ever seen, nearly black, and he allowed them to roam all over her. At fourteen, as she was beginning to develop, she felt awkward and shy about the changes in her body, but Briar had openly, brazenly admired her. It was embarrassing, at first, but it was also pleasing and even empowering. His attention bolstered her self-confidence.

It was bitterly ironic that she'd been shunned for having a *thing* with the Lindleys when she didn't, but then she'd developed a friendship with Briar, and no one knew. Of course, she knew that as wild and reckless as he was, he would probably be dead within a few years, but at age fifteen she fancied herself in love with him. Until the rainy afternoon he'd shown up at the stable and discovered her lying on her side in an empty stall, her stall, Ben always teased, reading a dime novel on a cushion of fresh straw.

"I saw them leave," Briar said.

Em jumped, jolted by the sound of his voice.

"Why didn't you go?" he asked as he took off his hat and set it aside. "Or, do I already know?"

She started to sit up but, faster than she even knew what was happening, he was on top of her. She smelled alcohol on his breath and then tasted it on the tongue he shoved into her mouth. "Stop it," she said, turning her head.

Straddling her, he lifted up and took off his shirt. "I don't think so."

She felt a wave of raw panic because she was pinned by his legs. "What are you doing?"

"I want to feel your skin against mine, that's all," he said breathlessly as he began opening her shirt.

She resisted and tried deflecting his hands, pleading for him to leave her alone, but she couldn't stop him. She tried to scoot away, but couldn't. She thrashed and slapped, but he was doing what he wanted and ignored her pleas. In fact, the more hysterical she became, the calmer he got. She could only recall it now in strange, jerky flashes.

The moment he first put his mouth on her breast and sucked on her nipple.

The moment he shifted down her body and cupped his hand over her mound. "Soft," he rasped. She was crying by then, still begging him to stop when he inserted his finger inside her. He was looking at her, his mouth slightly parted, his jaw clenched, a low breathy sound coming from his throat. "Does that hurt? That's just one, baby. Just one. You gotta take all of me."

Consumed with panic, she kicked and clawed, which he managed to block for the most part.

"You do know that a wife's body is the property of her husband."

"I'm n-never m-marrying you," she stammered. "Never!"

"Sure you are."

"Everyone c-calls you s-scum and I n-never believed it—"

His face darkened. "Don't go making me mad, Emmy," he warned. He got to his feet and gave her a hard look. "A husband also has the right to beat his wife anytime she needs it."

She'd glared back, feeling more hatred and betrayal than she'd ever felt before. "I am not your wife and I never will be," she swore. "Never! I hate you! I *hate* you!"

* * *

How had she been so unlucky? Or was she cursed? Amy had secretly detested her and she'd probably cursed the day Em had come to stay with them. Had she also cursed her? Could hate do that? The rooster began crowing and Em was glad of it. She got up and went inside to dress and get to work on something. Anything.

Chapter Twelve

It took all Em's strength to unsaddle her horse after the day's work. She'd completed the repairs on the largest corral, a real accomplishment, but she felt it in every muscle. She leaned against the railing and pulled off her gloves, then started out of the stable. A long, hot soak was what she needed.

"Hey there, pretty lady," a man said.

She whirled around, startled by the unfamiliar voice and saw two men sauntering toward her. The expressions on their faces frightened her. "Wha—" Her voice failed her. "What do you want?"

The man in the lead position had unkempt, stringy brown hair. "Figured you might need some company," he said with a shrug.

Em backed up as they advanced on her.

"I'm thinking you must be awful damn lonely now that your uncle croaked and left you all alone," he continued.

"Get off my property!"

"Aw, now, why you want to go and be like that for? We come all the way over here just to give you some company and you're going to be rude?" He gestured to his partner, who then lunged forward at her with astonishing speed.

She tried to get away, but he was on her too fast. He grabbed hold and yanked her back around to face the other man. Her arm was pinned behind her so tightly, the muscles burned. One of her captor's hands was positioned around her neck, forcing her back against him, and she smelled his hot, sour breath. It was nauseating. Fear was nauseating her.

"She's shaking like a leaf," her captor taunted. "And look at them titties poking out."

"Means she wants it, no matter what she says," the leader replied as he came toward her. He grabbed hold of her breasts.

"Get off me!" she cried.

"Sweet thing, I'm going to ride you so hard your eyeballs'll dance." With a yank, he ripped her shirt open, sending buttons flying.

She screamed and kicked out at him, then made her legs go limp, but the man in back must have been expecting it, because he jerked her right back up.

"And after I get done," the leader said, "my friend here is gonna take a turn."

The man who held her was snorting with laughter, but his grip felt like iron. With a sinking feeling, she realized she was powerless to stop them. "Let me go or I'll kill you," she threatened anyway.

The leader began unfastening her trousers. "What's a woman doing wearing men's clothes, anyway? Have you forgotten you're a woman?"

"I think she did forget," the man behind her taunted. "Think we can remind her?"

"Let her go," a calm, male voice said from behind them.

The leader jerked his gaze over and glared at whoever had spoken. "What the hell are you doing here? Did you follow us?"

"Let her go, and back away," the voice repeated.

The leader considered the man who'd spoken. "You

gonna make me?" He suddenly snorted. "Oh, you're going to shoot me? You're going to shoot your own brother?"

"Not if you let her go. Just get on out of here."

Em couldn't breathe. Everything had happened so fast, she didn't know how to respond, although her entire body was shaking.

The leader sneered. "You can have a turn. Alright? Christ's sake, probably do you good."

In his distraction, the leader had backed up a step and Em saw an opening. She jerked her knee up into his groin with all her might and it doubled him over. It also alarmed the man holding her, and he tightened his grip. "You shouldn't a' done that," he hissed as his fingers dug into the sides of her neck.

"It's over, Blue," the stranger exclaimed. "Let go of her."

The leader looked murderous as he straightened and raised his hand to backhand her, but the sound of a shotgun cocking stopped him from delivering the blow. Grudgingly, he lowered his hand. "You're not going to shoot me, so put that thing down," he yelled.

"I won't shoot you in the head," the man said calmly.

"I don't think you'll shoot at all."

"I'm not going to let you hurt her."

"What is it to you?"

The man holding Em finally loosened his grip. He was obviously watching what was going on between the two brothers. Em jerked hard and got away from him, but the leader grabbed hold of her before she could get away and she was whirled about to face the house. And Tommy Medlin. Tommy Medlin had come to her rescue. His brother had come to molest her and he'd come to rescue her. Tommy's gaze was fixed on his brother. He also had a long-barreled shotgun aimed at him.

"Get out of here, Blue," Tommy warned.

The man who had previously held her looked nervously from Tommy to his brother.

"Blue ain't goin' nowhere," the leader replied.

Tommy turned his aim on Blue, and that was all it took.

"I'm goin'! I'm goin'!" Blue squealed as he backed up with his hands raised. "Don't shoot!" He turned and ran toward the entrance of the farm. "Come on, Mitchell. Let's get."

Em felt Mitchell release her, but before she could experience any relief, she saw the barrel of the pistol he was now aiming at Tommy. "So, what we gonna do, now, brother?"

Tommy didn't relinquish his stance or his concentration and moments of stressful silence ticked by.

Em clutched her shirt together. She was aware of the sound of her own breathing. She was afraid to move for the powder keg she'd possibly ignite. If it went the wrong way—

"I'll tell you one goddamn thing," Mitchell finally said as he lowered his gun and backed away. "Someone is gonna have hell to pay for this. You want to guess who?"

Em didn't move as Mitchell stalked off. Tommy turned to watch him go, but he didn't relax his stance or his aim until both men were completely out of sight.

Em's intention was to run into the house, but as soon as she tried to move, her knees buckled and she collapsed. Hot tears streamed down her face. *What was it with men,* she wanted to scream. She'd had it with being abused and manhandled. She'd had it! She couldn't take it anymore.

Tommy was suddenly there, kneeling beside her. "I'll help you."

She shook her head and refused to look at him. His brother had ripped her shirt open and she'd stood there exposed before all of them. His brother had touched her. That filthy swine had touched her and she felt soiled all over again. She *was* soiled. Why did men think they could ravage her anytime they wanted? It didn't happen to other women. It was *her.* There was something wrong with her.

"Miss Wright—"

Something in his tone penetrated and she finally looked at him. What she saw was decency and honor. He'd seemed so terribly shy before, but he'd come to her rescue. She'd been intrigued by him and then heard he was slow-witted. She didn't know exactly who or what he was, except for noble.

Tommy glanced back to make sure Mitchell and Blue weren't sneaking back and then he set down his gun and picked her up. "I won't let them hurt you," he pledged as he started toward the house.

She'd never been carried in a man's arms before. She'd been dragged. She'd been tossed over a shoulder. Always in an effort to get her someplace she didn't want to go. What a strange thing it was to be physically aided. To be *rescued*. Somehow, it made her feel more vulnerable than she'd ever felt before. Which made no sense.

Tommy set her down on the front porch and she felt herself sway, but he kept his hands on her arms and his blue-eyed gaze on her face until she was steady, and then he let go, drawing his hands back slowly. She opened her mouth to thank him, but the words were stymied by crushing emotion. Embarrassed, knowing the tears would not stop for some time to come, she turned and went inside.

Chapter Thirteen

Em jerked, hit her head against the wall, and came fully awake. For a moment, she was confused and disoriented by the fact she was sitting hunched in a corner of the parlor with a rifle across her lap, but then the night's events rushed back at her, leaving her shaken all over again. She set the gun aside and drew her knees up to her chest and hugged them. If Tommy Medlin hadn't shown up—

She hadn't thanked him. He'd saved her, and she hadn't even thanked him. Slowly, using the wall for support, she got to her feet. She was stiff and sore all over and still wearing the torn clothing from yesterday. It was time to admit that she couldn't do this. She couldn't make the farm work. Not alone. Not without Ben. She was too inept. Too helpless against vicious predators.

She picked up the gun and started to the kitchen, recalling Tommy's pledge the evening before. She halted and looked at the door, then started forward again. She unlocked and opened the door, and the cold, early morning air hit her squarely in the face. So did the sight of Tommy in the rocking chair, dozing, his shotgun still clutched in his hand. Guilt and gratitude swept over her, and she ducked back inside and went about the task of making herself presentable.

* * *

"Mr. Medlin?"

Tommy's eyes opened. He drew in a sharp breath and sat up.

"You stayed," she said. "I . . . didn't know you were doing that."

He got to his feet, unsure of what to say.

"It's so cold out here," she continued. "I'm sorry."

"You got no reason to be sorry," he assured her. "But I should be getting on." He tipped his hat to her and started off.

"Wait, please. I . . . I wish you'd have some breakfast. It's the least I can do."

He looked away from her, uncomfortable at the idea but not sure how to extricate himself.

"Please?"

He nodded. She went inside and he set his gun down and followed, feeling like a fish out of water. She was probably scared to be alone, which would make sense. So, he'd explain that Mitchell and Blue had to report to work, just like he did, and that she wasn't in any danger until evening. And then he'd come watch over the place again. But how should he say it? He was pondering that as he took off his hat and coat and hung them on the rack.

"Have a seat," she offered. "Please. Do you drink coffee?"

"Yes, ma'am." He rubbed his hands together to warm them as he went toward the table. He pulled back a chair and sat, noticing the pretty rag rugs on the polished floor. There was a lace tablecloth on the table, a fancy, cast iron stove and a corner, glass front cupboard full of glassware and dishes. He didn't belong in a home like this. He didn't belong at a table with Emeline Wright. She brought him a cup of coffee and a filled plate, because she'd already done the cooking. He watched as she went back to fill her plate, but looked away again before she caught him staring. He added sugar to his coffee and stirred.

"Was that really your brother?" she asked.

"Yes, ma'am."

She walked back to the table and sat across from him. "You couldn't be more different, could you?"

She hadn't picked up her fork so he hesitated, too. "I guess."

"Eat. Please."

He nodded and went to it, hoping she'd do the same. Instead, she picked up her coffee and sipped. "It's good," he said. "Thank you."

She finally picked up her fork and took a bite, which made it a little less awkward for him to eat. He didn't want to say so, but he had to go. He was already going to be late.

"What will happen with your brother?"

"I'll watch him. Or I'll come here if I lose sight of him again. Make sure he—"

"I meant with you," she said, stammering slightly. "Will he try to get back at you?"

He blinked in surprise at the concern on her face. "I can take care of myself," he stated simply. "I had five brothers."

"Five? Oh, my. I never had any brothers or sisters."

He took another forkful of scrambled eggs. "That's lucky."

"I never thought so," she replied, "but I guess it depends on who they are."

He didn't reply.

"Do you have any sisters?" she asked a moment later.

"No, ma'am."

"That's too bad. You would have been a wonderful brother for a girl. Protective."

Brother. He kept eating and he kept his gaze fixed on his plate.

"Are you the youngest?"

"No, ma'am. Mitchell's the youngest. Three of my brothers are dead now."

She frowned in confusion. "I'm sorry."

He set his fork on his plate, having finished. "Can I wash this?"

"No, I'll do it."

"I've got to report to work," he said apologetically.

She blushed. "Of course. Please don't let me keep you."

He stood. "Thank you for breakfast. It was real good."

Em rose and smoothed the front of her skirt. "I don't know how to thank you for what you did."

He nodded toward her shotgun, which was propped near the door. "You know how to use that?"

She glanced at it, too, and then looked at him quizzically. "Pull the trigger?"

For a split second, he grew anxious; then he saw she was teasing. Slowly, he gave in to a smile.

"I know how to use it," she assured him. "They just caught me by surprise."

Tommy's smile dimmed. "They're good at that." She paled right before his eyes and he felt terrible.

"You're right," she murmured. "They can just . . . anyone could just—"

He'd said something wrong, but he didn't know what exactly.

She sat back down and shook her head. "I can't do this."

"You can't do what?"

She looked at him. "Run this farm." She shook her head in wonderment. "I've been so stubborn, thinking if I just keep working . . . if I work hard enough . . . But I don't have enough money and Ben's gone and I . . . I don't know what I was thinking. I can't do this. How can I run this place when I can't even protect myself?"

"You could maybe get a loan," he said hesitantly.

She laughed. "Have you ever heard of a bank giving a woman a loan to get a farm up and running again? It doesn't matter, anyway. It's *not* just the money." She took a breath and stood again. "Thank you again for what you did. I am more grateful than I can say."

Had he been wrong to mention a loan? Money was a personal issue to a lot of people. "You're welcome, ma'am."

"Em, please," she said. "It's Emeline."

The thrill that passed through him was almost painful. He nodded and walked to the coatrack for his coat and hat.

"Mr. Medlin?"

He turned back to her. "Tommy."

"Tommy," she repeated quietly. "Should we tell anyone about what happened?"

He shook his head because telling would only get Mitchell in a lot of trouble and make him even madder, when there was still a chance he could talk some reason into him. "No."

"You'll be careful?"

It was strange and funny that she was worried about him. It was backwards, but it felt good, too. "I'll be fine. I'll keep an eye on them."

She nodded, and he left, astounded that he'd just shared a meal with Emeline Wright. Not that anyone would believe it if he told them—which he was definitely not going to do. He pulled on his hat, blew out a slow breath and walked to his horse.

Em sat back down, feeling painfully alone. She'd always either been told where she would go and what she would do, or else she'd had a plan. But not now. What was she supposed to do now?

Tommy Medlin was a puzzle. He was strong enough to stand up to his brother and protect her and yet so shy and reticent. He'd made her realize one thing, though; she could not continue as she had been. She couldn't live with a gun in her hand, nor did she have eyes in the back of her head. She had to sleep and work. If a man wanted to, he could sneak up on her again and she would have no real chance of defending herself. It was time to face facts. She thought of Ben and her eyes filled, knowing that she'd be disappointing him again.

The rule at the Triple H was, if you reported late for work, you worked double the time you'd missed when the workday ended. Tommy was almost an hour late. He didn't mind working the extra time, but if he did, he wouldn't be able to make sure Mitchell and Blue stayed away from Em. It was a dilemma he hadn't quite worked out when he reported to the foreman. "Go see Mr. H," Sam Blake told him.

Howerton was seated behind a huge, mahogany desk in his study, when Tommy knocked. "I'm supposed to see you," Tommy said when Howerton looked up.

"Where were you?"

"I had something to care of."

Howerton waved him in. "What?"

Tommy came further in. "I'd rather not say."

Howerton considered him thoughtfully. "You haven't shown up late since you started working for me. You don't drink much. You don't whore around. Doesn't look like you got in a fight. So, what was it?"

Tommy shifted on his feet, uncomfortable with the questioning. "I had to protect someone."

"Who?"

Tommy shook his head. He couldn't tell on Mitchell, but he wasn't comfortable lying to Mr. Howerton either.

"Protecting them from what?" Howerton asked. "Can you, at least, tell me that?"

"Some men."

"Who wanted to—"

"Hurt her. That's all."

"How'd they try to hurt her?"

Tommy looked uncomfortable. He'd already said too much.

"*Was* she hurt?" Howerton pushed.

"No, sir. Not really."

"Because you were there to protect her?"

Tommy hesitated, then gave a brief nod. "Can I go to work now?"

"You protected her from getting raped," Howerton guessed.

Tommy jerked slightly and then looked away from Mr. Howerton's penetrating gaze.

"Alright," Howerton said. "Get to work."

Tommy looked at him again. "I can't stay late, Mr. Howerton."

Howerton twirled the pen he held. "It's alright. You've pulled enough extra duty. Go on."

Tommy nodded and walked off.

Chapter Fourteen

Tommy walked back from the chow hall that evening alone and deep in thought. He'd seen Mitchell in the late afternoon and all his younger brother had said was, "Don't you even speak to me." Mitchell was irate, but he had to realize he'd been wrong. Deep down inside, he had to know.

What had most consumed Tommy, however, was the thought of the money he'd saved. So far, he'd filled a half dozen cigar boxes with nearly thirty-eight hundred dollars, all of it hidden beneath some rotting floorboards in an abandoned shed he'd found. It wasn't doing a bit of good, hidden away like that.

Mitchell and Blue suddenly sprang on him. Mitchell landed a hard blow to his middle, doubling him over, while Blue swung a short piece of two-by-four, hitting his head and knocking him out cold.

"What the—?" Mitchell hissed, turning on Blue. "You hit him with a board?"

"Just a short one." Blue tossed it behind him. "He's stronger than both of us."

"Let's get him out of here," Mitchell said, looking around nervously. He reached down and grabbed Tommy's shoulders. "Help me pull."

"Hey! What's going on?" Sam Blake bellowed from several yards away.

"Aw, shit," Mitchell said under his breath. "Nothing," he called back. "It's nothing. Tommy fell is all. He's fine, though. We got it." He glared at Blue and hissed, "Help me, you damn fool."

Blake hurried forward to reach them. "Move back," he ordered when he got close. He stared down at Tommy, zeroing in on the blood pooling around his head. He turned and shouted for help.

"Look, he's my brother," Mitchell objected. Several of the hands were already heading toward them. "I got this."

Blake ignored him. "Hurry up," he yelled at the men approaching.

The men converged, all talking at once.

"What happened?"

"Aw, shit. Look at the blood."

"What the hell happened?"

"Stop your blabbering and get him inside," Blake snapped. "And you two," he said, pointing at Mitchell and Blue and uttering a foul curse. "You stand right there."

The smell of guilt hung on Mitchell and Blue as strong as horseshit. After Howerton learned of the incident with Tommy and took one look at his banged-up face, he knew precisely who the men in Tommy's story were. Of course, when he came to, Tommy claimed he hadn't seen the men who'd attacked him, which was no surprise. Tommy was as loyal as Mitchell was not.

The solution was simple, separate and conquer. Howerton ordered Blue put in one room and Mitchell in another. Mitchell played cool and feigned total ignorance, but Blue blurted out the whole story in less than five minutes. It hardly took any pressure at all. "Miss Wright?" Howerton repeated, suddenly more livid than before. "You attacked Miss Wright?"

"We didn't *attack* her," Blue hedged.

"You didn't attack her because Tommy stopped you!"

There was such fury in Mr. Howerton's face that Blue didn't dare contest the point.

"How'd Tommy know you were there?" Howerton demanded.

"I don't know. I thought we'd ditched him in town."

Howerton glared at him. He was sorely tempted to kill the squirrelly little bastard right then and there. "You've got two seconds to get out of my sight."

The next morning, Howerton ordered Tommy into town to see the doctor. When he'd ridden off, Howerton had Sam gather the rest of the men. "Mitchell and Blue jumped Tommy last night," Howerton announced to the group of men, "because the night before that, Tommy stopped them from raping a lady. This is not acceptable."

Blue was shifting back and forth on his feet, too nervous to stand still.

"What happened is between Tommy and us," Mitchell interjected.

"That's where you're wrong," Howerton retorted. "You work for me, which means you answer to me. It means what you do reflects upon me, you ignorant fool. Now, you strip."

"What?" Mitchell exclaimed.

"Take off your clothes," Howerton repeated, enunciating clearly. "All of them."

"No, sir. Hell, no."

"Do it," Howerton bellowed. "The rest of you, go cut yourselves a switch. Now!"

The men all did as told, all but Sam Blake and Quin.

"Come on, Mr. Howerton," Blue whined. "Please. I swear

we won't never do nothing like that again. I swear it. We was just drunk and messin' around. We probably wouldn't even a' done nothin'."

Howerton looked at him with loathing. "You got a lesson coming," he stated, "and right now, that lesson stands to last for five minutes. But for every minute you stand there and argue with me or defy my order, you're going to get an extra five."

"What if we quit?" Mitchell demanded. "Then you can't touch us."

"You were my employee when you tried to rape Miss Wright. You were on my time when you attacked Tommy. And, by God, you are going to face the consequences. You want to quit, that is fine by me, but you'll do it after." He paused. "I won't warn you again about delaying. Five minutes can last a hell of a long time."

Furious, Mitchell began unbuttoning his shirt, and Blue followed suit, although his fingers were trembling so badly it was hard to get them to work. "Please, Mr. Howerton," he whimpered.

"Shut up," Howerton replied coldly.

The men were already coming back with thin, pliable branches cut from the surrounding trees. Some were slashing them through the air, making a whooshing sound.

Mitchell threw his shirt down and started unfastening his trousers. "Tommy doesn't want this."

"I'm sure you're right. Too bad for you I don't give a damn," Howerton replied hotly. "Tommy wouldn't even tell me who was involved in the rape in the first place."

"There was no rape," Mitchell yelled.

"He wouldn't even speak out against you once you busted his face up," Howerton said, shaking his head.

"That was Blue," Mitchell retorted.

Blue snapped his head up at Mitchell. "You said to!"

Mitchell glowered at him. "I didn't say to use a board, did I?"

Sam Blake lowered his head and shook it in disgust.

Blue, still shifting his weight back and forth, covered his genitals with both hands and began to whine.

"Tie their arms up," Howerton ordered. "No blows to the face. Everywhere else is fair game."

Mitchell gritted his teeth as his hands were tied and then pulled high into the air. He was buck naked and totally exposed. He'd no sooner heard the word 'go' then he felt scores of biting stings. He swore and screamed in reaction to the pain. Blue was flat out bellowing.

Howerton watched his men go at the thrashing, some out of duty and others with enjoyment and great abandon. "Call it when you think it's time," Howerton said to Blake, who was observing without expression.

Chapter Fifteen

Em threw her back into hoeing for two reasons. First, the hard work kept her from dwelling on her worries, and, second, she needed to eat, and the way things were looking, if she didn't grow it, she wouldn't be eating it. It was too late for planting much this year, but she needed a bigger garden in the spring, and it was best to start on it now. Even when she sold the land, she'd keep the house and a few acres, and she'd need a substantial garden.

At the sound of a horse approaching, she looked up to see Tommy returning. He wore his hat low and the brim cast his face in shadow, but he was back, and the gladness that washed over her was almost overwhelming. She let the hoe drop and smoothed down a strand of hair before she started toward the house, pulling her work gloves off as she went. He reached the house first, dismounted and pulled an awkward-looking pack off his horse.

She had nearly reached him when she saw his face. One eye was swollen completely shut. "Oh, no," she breathed. "Oh, Tommy!"

"It's alright," he said.

But it wasn't. She'd *known* he would pay a price. "We

should get you to a doctor. I'll hitch up the wagon and take you into town."

He shook his head. "I don't need to. I just needed to see you."

The words touched her to the extent that tears sprang to her eyes. "Come inside," she said in a thick voice. He walked beside her, carrying the pack. She reached the door first and opened it, saying, "I'll find some headache powder."

"I had some already."

"Oh. Good. Can you . . . will you sit?"

"Yes, ma'am. I mean, Em."

She poured them each a glass of water, carried their drinks back to the table and then sat across from him, besieged with guilt. His face was swollen, his nose cut and his right eye swollen shut. "I'm so sorry. I was afraid they'd do something."

"It'll heal. I've had worse."

"Is there anything I can get you?"

He shook his head and placed the pack on the table. "No, but I want you to have this," he said, scooting the pack toward her.

She leaned forward and opened the leather flap curiously. "What is it?"

"Just look," he replied shyly.

She pulled out a cigar box with twine wrapped around it. "Thank you, but I don't smoke," she teased with a straight face. He started to smile, but it hurt and he sobered. She slipped the twine off, opened the lid and her gaze flew to his. "What is all this?"

"It's mine. I saved it."

She looked down again and then back at him. "For how long?"

He thought about it. "I started working when I was thirteen."

Em shook her head in bewilderment. "Why would you do this? Offer me your money?"

"You need it."

She almost laughed—but she didn't, because he was in earnest. "H-how much is it?"

"About thirty-eight hundred dollars, although I haven't counted it in a long time."

"Why?" she asked breathlessly. "I don't understand. Why would you offer me your whole life savings? It is, isn't it? It's your whole life's savings."

He looked at a loss. "You need it," he repeated. "And you'll put it to good use. I figure you can hire some men to help you, and keep you safe, and you can buy seed or stock. Whatever you think's best."

She sat back, flabbergasted by the offer, and yet it was already beginning to sink in. She'd been without hope, and here he was, offering it up. On a silver platter in the disguise of an old cigar box. With that much money, she *could* hire workers. But who? How would she make sure they had the right experience, not to mention integrity? Ben wasn't around to rely on and so she'd be alone, the lone decision maker. And how safe would she really be surrounded by men who worked for her?

She brought her steepled fingers to her lips, reeling from the realization that she didn't know how to run a farm. She might well be stubborn enough and strong enough to do what needed doing—but how did she figure out what that was? She didn't even know how far thirty-eight hundred dollars would go. How would she ever really know if she was getting a fair deal on seed or stock? And what seed or stock would be best? "I can't accept this."

He frowned in confusion. "Why not?"

She lowered her hands to the table with a soft sigh. "It is the kindest, most generous offer ever, and I thank you from the bottom of my heart, but I just . . . I can't," she said with a shake of her head. He looked hurt, which hurt her, but she only had to look at his face to see the damage knowing her had already done. She couldn't risk his life savings. She wouldn't. "I think, if I knew more . . . if I was sure I could run the farm . . . if I knew I could pay you back, then—"

"I didn't ask to be paid back."

"This is your money," she declared, leaning forward. "I would never just *take* it. I'd accept is as a loan, maybe, if I really knew what I was doing, but . . . surely, you had plans for it."

"No. Not really. I was always told to save some of my pay and so I did. Then I figured out if I didn't get most of it put away, Mitchell would spend it."

"But haven't you thought about what to do with it? Haven't you ever thought about doing something or buying something special? Something you always wanted?"

"Just this. You need the money and I want to help."

For a moment, the selflessness of the response floored her and then her eyes widened as an idea dawned on her. A brilliant idea. An idea as brilliant as the shooting star she and Ben had witnessed. "Did you," she began slowly because she wanted to get it out right, "did you ever want your own place?"

"I never thought much about it," he admitted. "I always worked, so—"

"I . . . I wish you would," she said carefully, haltingly, "because, well, I can't run a farm by myself. But maybe . . . we could do it together."

He nodded. "Yeah, sure. I'll help all I can."

He'd misunderstood. "I'm proposing a partnership," she said solemnly.

He drew back slightly, clearly stunned by the suggestion.

"A business partnership," she added. She paused, giving him a chance to speak, but he didn't. "You and I would own the farm and work it together."

"I don't know if I can do that," he said hesitantly.

She felt a crush of disappointment that made her want to cry. In fact, the backs of her eyes felt the pinpricks of tears. She looked at her hands and willed herself to be calm and as emotionless as possible. "Because you don't want to leave the Triple H?"

"No, I wouldn't care about leaving."

She looked up at him quizzically. "Because I'm a woman?"

"No," he exclaimed.

"Then . . . what?"

He shook his head and color crept into his face.

"Please," she said. "I really want to know. Don't . . . don't worry about hurting my feelings. I just need to know."

"It wouldn't hurt your feelings. I'm just not the kind of man you become partners with."

Now, she drew back, because the notion was so wrong. "You are *exactly* the kind of man I'd want to be partners with," she replied emphatically. "Why would you say that?" He looked away and shook his head, obviously troubled, and she bit her bottom lip, wondering if it was wrong to push him. But the idea seemed so right. Unless there was something he wasn't telling her. "Won't you just consider it?" she said beseechingly. "I'll understand if you say no, but . . . this is good land."

He looked at her searchingly. "It is," he finally said. "So is Mr. Howerton's. It . . . it's great land."

"And I'm a hard worker," she said passionately.

"I know that."

"You've offered what you have," she said, gesturing to the money between them. "And I can offer what I have. This land. It was left to me. Ben saw to it that it was all left to me. Oh, Tommy, I so want to make this place work. I don't want to just sell it."

He nodded slowly. "I'd want to make it work, too," he admitted. "If I was you, I'd want to keep it and make it work."

"If I knew what to grow—"

"What—" Tommy's voice broke and he cleared his throat. "What did your uncle grow?"

"Wheat and corn. And we had cattle, but they got sold off."

"Tobacco might be good," Tommy ventured as he sat up straighter. "It takes good soil and it takes a lot out of the soil, so you can't grow it every year, but this is good land for it."

She nodded, hoping to encourage his suggestions. "What about cattle?"

"No. Mr. Howerton's too big to compete with. Sheep or goats maybe."

"Goats? What a funny idea."

"Their milk makes a good cheese. They eat less than cattle, a lot less, and no one else is doing it around here that I know of."

She sensed enthusiasm from him and it gave her heart. "Let's just pretend for a moment that we were going to do this," she said carefully, trying to hold back a smile. "Would we need many hands?"

"Some."

He was considering it. She could see it in his face. In the watchfulness of his gaze. "You know what would be perfect? If we could find people like us, willing to work now and have it pay off later."

He shook his head. "Maybe if there was no other work to be had, but there's a lot of work."

"Still," she mused. "We could provide room and board," she suggested. "And more pay than they'd ordinarily get, only later. What about that?"

"I don't know if it would work, but I guess we could try."

Her breath caught. "Really? Wait, did you mean . . . coming here?"

Moments of silence elapsed. "If you're sure you want to," he said warily.

"If I'm sure?" she repeated. She beamed a smile and clasped her hands together. "I am absolutely, positively sure! But are you sure?"

He nodded slowly and smiled. "I guess so."

She laughed in delight and stuck her hand across the table. "Partner?"

He took her hand in his and shook it. "Partners."

Howerton leaned back in one of the leather wingback chairs in his office with a book in his lap and listened as Tommy explained the situation. When he'd finished, Howerton shut the book on selective breeding he'd been perusing and set it aside. "You're quitting?"

Tommy nodded. "Soon as you can spare me."

"To go work the Martin farm? Because Miss Wright wants to hire you?"

"Not exactly. We're going to be partners."

"Partners?" Howerton repeated. "Partners, he says."

Tommy resented being mocked. "That's right," he replied with a flare of hurt pride.

Howerton got to his feet and walked to the bar in the back of the office. He picked up a bottle of scotch. "You want a drink?"

"No, sir. Thank you."

Howerton poured himself a drink. "Are you sure you understood her correctly?"

Tommy shifted on his feet. The truth was, he'd been wondering the same thing. "Yes," he said anyway.

Howerton turned back to face Tommy and took a drink. "Alright, Tommy. Go when you want to go. I've got enough hands. And, if you got it wrong, for whatever reason, maybe she wasn't clear enough, you come back. You've always been one of my best workers. Hell, you're probably the very best. Sam's going to hate to lose you."

"Thank you, sir." Tommy turned and started for the door.

"Oh, Tommy—"

Tommy turned back.

"You're going to learn about some punishment doled out to your brother and Blue," Howerton said. "It was meted out for my satisfaction. It wasn't because of you."

"Because of *you*," Mitchell hissed furiously.

Every part of Mitchell and Blue that Tommy could see was covered in raised welts. They were alone in the bunkhouse, because everybody else was working.

"They beat us! Every second, there was a dozen switches flying at me. For five goddamned minutes! Or probably more."

"I didn't know," Tommy replied.

"I didn't know," Mitchell mocked. "Moron! If you hadn't gotten in the way—"

Tommy started packing his few belongings and tried to block out his brother's voice. He stuffed his clothes into his beat-up leather satchel as quickly as he could, wanting to be clear of this place. He especially wanted to be away from Mitchell.

"What the hell are you doin'?" Mitchell demanded.

"I'm leaving."

"What are you talking about?"

"God damn it," Blue bellowed. "I'm hurtin'."

"Shut up," Mitchell yelled at him.

"I can't help it," Blue whined.

"I said, shut up," Mitchell yelled even louder.

Tommy picked up his bag.

Mitchell barred Tommy's path. "Just where do you think you're going?"

"Miss Wright," Tommy began.

"That *bitch*," Mitchell spat. "What about her?"

Tommy took several moments to answer, because he

didn't want to reveal how much the name-calling bothered him. "I bought half her farm," he said calmly. "We're going to be partners."

"What do you mean you *bought*?"

It was telling that Mitchell didn't question the partnership, only the money he'd spent. "I saved some money and I gave it to her. Then she asked to be partners."

Mitchell's expression was full of disgust. "You are just as stupid as I always said you were." Tommy made a move to leave but Mitchell grabbed his arm. "I ought to kick your sorry ass right here and now. Now, you go get every penny of that money back from that bitch—"

With a violent thrust, Tommy shoved him into the wall and pressed his forearm to his brother's throat. "Never call her that again," he bit out. He released Mitchell, but continued to glare threateningly for several seconds before he walked out.

"Goddamn," Blue said behind him.

Mitchell rubbed his aching throat. "Shut the hell up," he rasped.

Chapter Sixteen

Somewhere between the Triple H and the Martin farm, Tommy began to feel foolish and queasy with anxiety. Had Em meant for him to come back right away? All of Mr. Howerton's questions and doubts about whether he could have misunderstood her were plaguing him. Could he have? If he had, there was no way he'd go straight back to the Triple H, because how stupid would he look then? No, he'd have to find somewhere else to sleep, at least for the night.

She was beating a rug when he rode in. When she heard and turned toward him, shielding her eyes from the glare of the afternoon sun, he held his breath. A split second later, her relieved smile lifted the weight of uncertainty from him. "What did he say?" she called when he reached the house.

He dismounted. "Said it was okay."

"I'm so glad. I am so relieved."

He couldn't hold back a smile because she didn't know what glad and relieved were. "There's enough coverage so . . . he didn't need me to stay."

"It doesn't feel quite real," she admitted, still smiling.

"No, it doesn't," he agreed.

Her smile waned. "Um, about sleeping arrangements."

"I'll sleep in the barn."

"Oh, no," she replied firmly, her brown eyes flashing. "It gets cold at night." She stuck the handle of the rug beater under her arm and avoided his gaze. "What I was thinking is . . . you could sleep in Ben's old room," she said haltingly. "I know it *sounds* inappropriate, but it wouldn't be," she continued, speaking faster and blushing. "See, there's a bedroom downstairs and two rooms upstairs. I . . . I'm upstairs," she said, stammering in her nervousness. "I always was. I mean that was my room and it still is."

"I could sleep in the barn," he repeated. "I wouldn't mind."

She huffed. "Well, I would. You're the one who's making it possible for us to exist here. So if you're going to insist that someone sleep in the barn, it's going to be me."

He laughed at the preposterous thought.

"And if that won't do," she continued. "Then we'll just have to make do with both of us being in the house right now."

He thought about it. "People might talk."

She sighed and shrugged. "People are going to talk anyway. Besides, we don't get many visitors out here and we can *tell* people you're sleeping in the barn if anyone asks, which I doubt they will. And we can start on a bunkhouse. Right? We're going to need one, anyway. Sometime."

She was trying too hard and talking too fast. He'd been a wreck all the way there, but seeing her so nervous actually calmed him. "I guess so."

"Good." She turned to pull the rug down from the clothesline.

"I'll get that," he offered.

"Thank you," she said, stepping back. "So, it's settled?"

He pulled the rug down. "If that's what you think is best." He turned back to face her, and it looked as though she had something else to say, something that was weighing on her. "What is it?" he asked.

"As far as people talking . . . they do," she said. "I know that better than most."

He nodded, thinking he knew it pretty well himself.

"I don't think we should worry about it," she added nervously.

"I was only worried about you," he said.

She smiled. "I have a feeling that's what we'll do. You'll worry about me and I'll worry about you."

The smile he returned was one of wonder, since no one had ever worried about him. They started back to the house together, which was strange. It was strange to be acting like he belonged here. When he followed her inside, he smelled food.

"It goes there," Em said, pointing to the spot on the floor.

He walked over and placed the rug on the floor.

"And your room is through there," Em said, gesturing to a door and then quickly turning away to hide her blushing. She walked over to stir the contents of a pot, and he went to look in the room. There was a wide bed, a dresser, wardrobe and chest of drawers—but no personal possessions sitting around. Some butterflies kicked up in his stomach, knowing that she must have cleared them out for him.

By the time Tommy sat in a rocker on the front porch after supper, he knew this arrangement wasn't going to last. He didn't know what was going to happen or when, but this wasn't going to last. It was too good to last. This wasn't his life. A breeze blew, an enormous hawk circled overhead and a rooster crowed. Tommy wanted to absorb it all, every minute, so that he'd never forget.

He heard her footsteps and then the screen door squeaked as she opened it. He wanted to drink in every second, every sound and sight, so he'd be able to recall it when he went back to his real life. Mr. Howerton would be gracious about it and Sam Blake would be glad to have him back again. Some of the others would be glad, too, but Mitchell and Blue would make fun of him every day for the rest of his life. He didn't look forward to that.

"Let's try this," Em said as she stepped next to him. She had a small bowl and a rag in hand. "Close your eyes and lean your head back."

He happily acquiesced. He also slid his hands down to make sure his coat covered the bulge in his trousers that couldn't be helped. The sight of her was arousing, but even with his eyes closed, he was stirred by her nearness, her voice, her touch. The rag was cool, but her hands warm against the sides of his face. She had no idea how good it felt to be touched by her soft fingers.

She straightened, but remained standing next to him. She wasn't touching him, so it was surprising how clearly he felt her. He knew exactly where she was. In different circumstances, he could have put his hands around her waist and pulled her into his lap.

"Does it hurt much?" she asked.

"No. The medicine helped a lot."

"Good. I'm going to make some tea. Unless you prefer something else?"

"No. Tea's fine." As she walked back inside, it occurred to him that being taken care of was a new sensation. His ma hadn't been good at it, though she had doted on Mitchell. Not only was Mitchell the baby of the family, but he looked like her. Most of her sons favored her somewhat, but not Tommy. He must have looked like his pa, although he'd never laid eyes on the man or even seen a picture.

When Em came back, she gently lifted the rag from his eye, redipped it in the solution and then put it back on, saying, "The tea's steeping." She was exactly what a woman was supposed to be—soft and pretty, but also strong in her own way. She made up her mind about what was right and then she did it, no matter how hard it was.

She sat in the other chair and began rocking. "I'm so glad

you're here," she said. "Evenings have been lonely since Ben died."

"I'm glad I'm here, too."

"I'm sure you'll miss the others, though. After being around so many men."

"I'm glad I'm here, too," he repeated emphatically. She laughed and the sound of it made him happy. It was nice to be able to make her smile or laugh.

Her chair creaked in an easy rhythm. "Where are you from?"

"North of here. Harrisburg. We came to work the mines, but then we got hired on at the ranch."

"Do you miss Harrisburg?"

He removed the rag and sat up, because it was disconcerting not to see her. "No."

"I don't mean to invade your privacy. Please tell me if I do and I'll stop."

He put the rag back in the bowl. "I don't mind."

"I can talk too much."

He grinned. "I probably don't talk enough."

"Then we should balance each other out," she said with an easy smile as she rose to go check on the tea. Again, the screen door screeched as she pulled it open and banged twice as it shut behind her. He liked the sound. He liked it a lot. It was the sound of a home.

Chapter Seventeen

"What are you smiling at?" Tommy asked Em as they rode side by side, exploring the farm.

She looked at him and shrugged. "It's been a nice day," she replied.

"It has," he agreed.

In part, her cheerful mood was due to the unseasonably warm day, but the rest of it was that they were making plans for a future that was beginning to come into focus. They'd been together for more than a week, and each day had been good. Tommy was considerate and appreciative of everything. He was also the hardest worker she'd ever seen. He was up and working when she woke, which was always by seven, and she had to urge him to stop at the end of the day. He'd accomplished more in a matter of days than she had in the last month. Another benefit was that she'd been sleeping soundly since his arrival. He made her feel safe.

He reined his horse to a stop. "See over there?" he asked, pointing to the top of a wide ridge. "The tobacco barn should go up there."

"Why there?"

"Airflow. Tobacco's got to be kept high and dry."

"Ah." She maneuvered her horse in a wide circle, looking

around. They'd decided where to plant tobacco, wheat and corn, and where to locate the new barn and bunkhouse. They were going to build a kitchen that would attach to a dining room or chow hall, as Tommy called it, which would attach to the bunkhouse.

"What was that barn used for?" Tommy asked, pointing to an old barn in the hazy, blue distance.

She shook her head. "That was Amy's father's land. Her brother only recently died and left it."

"Left it?"

"To Ben. Although it was sold to Mr. Howerton not long ago," she added with a shrug. "Ben's land ended just beyond that little gulley."

"Let's go see it," he suggested, starting his horse forward.

It was such a glorious day, she didn't much care where they went. "Amy didn't want us going there," she said as they rode. "She acted as if it was cursed," she added ominously. "I don't think she had a happy childhood."

"Was she happy later?"

"No. I often wished that Ben had married someone else. For his sake. He deserved someone more . . . loving. She wasn't content with farm life."

"You'd think she'd be used to it, anyway," Tommy mused.

"Maybe she wanted to escape it. I don't know. All I know is that she hated her father's land. And we were told to stay away from it in no uncertain terms. Jimmy asked why once and she got angry and said it was dangerous. Something about the house burning down. Jimmy said something smart-alecky back to her and she slapped him across the face."

"The house burned down?"

She nodded. "There's nothing left but part of the brick foundation and a cellar hole and the chimney and part of a wall."

He grinned. "How do you know if you weren't supposed to go there?"

She grinned back. "How, indeed."

It was a half hour ride to reach the barn, which was badly overgrown. They looked around before finding a way in to the dim, cool interior which still smelled of hay and damp earth. Tommy glanced about and then headed up the ladder to the loft. "Be careful," she fretted, crossing her arms tightly. "The wood might be rotten."

"No, it's not."

She watched as he reached the top, stepped over and disappeared from view. She rubbed her arms, her eyes still adjusting to the light, and looked around at the implements hanging on the wall, vaguely disturbed that it still smelled so alive.

"There's some boxes up here," he called. "Clothes in them."

She looked up to where his voice had come from. "What sort of clothes?"

"Quilts, curtains, a coat. Moths got to it, though. It's all ruined."

Em walked to the ladder and looked up it, wondering if she had the nerve. She chewed lightly on a knuckle and then reached out for the ladder. Ignoring the anxiety that had her frowning, she started up, concentrating on one rung at a time, hand then foot. She made it to the top and crossed over, ending on her hands and knees. She was trembling all over, but determined to master her fear, and she'd already managed the hardest part. She knew the fear was because of her last encounter with Briar, and she wasn't about to let him control any aspect of her life.

Oh, but that day. She'd avoided him for months after the attack, mostly because she'd stayed so close to the house and to other people. But, that day, he showed up again and snuck up on her in the barn. Again. She'd grabbed a pitchfork and threatened him with it, but he rushed her and yanked it from her grip.

She barely averted his grasp, ran for the ladder and

scampered up to the loft—the only place she could go, since he stood between her and the door. Of course, he followed. Laughing, taunting, telling her how much he'd missed her, how much he'd had to jerk himself off because of her. She hadn't understood the reference, but got the gist and it made her feel sick with panic and revulsion.

In the loft, she searched frantically for a weapon, but there was nothing, and she was more trapped than ever. "Please, leave me alone," she begged as he closed in on her.

"Baby, that ain't never gonna happen. You are mine. You need to stop fightin' it."

"Please," she cried angrily.

"Believe it or not, once we get you broke in, you're going to like it."

She looked around in desperation, but there was nowhere to go.

"A year from now, when we're married, we'll be doing it every day. I won't have to chase you, neither."

The words were infuriating and she glared at him. "I will never marry you!"

"Yeah? We'll see about that," he said, and then he dashed for her.

Terrified and out of options, she ran three steps and leapt off the loft, grabbing onto a rope that hung from the ceiling as a fire escape and safety measure. In the wild swinging that followed, she saw Briar reaching for the rope. She scrambled down, burning her hands and thighs, barely hanging on. All she knew was that she had to beat him to the ground and get to the house before he caught her. Then the rope jerked hard because Briar had jumped on. Their combined weight proved to be too much and the rope snapped. She was close enough to the ground that the fall merely knocked the wind from her, but he fell farther and landed badly.

"My leg, my leg," he screamed, but she was already scampering backward. How he managed to get home, she never knew, because she ran into the house and up to her room and did not look back.

It was years ago, she thought now as she got to her feet. Unfortunately, she could still feel the swaying motion of the rope and the terror she'd experienced as she'd jumped through the air. She closed her eyes and clutched at the slanted roof.

"Em," Tommy called. "Don't move!"

A moment later, she felt his hands clamp around her arms and felt weak with relief. He pulled her shaking body against his, saying, "I've got you." He led her to a trunk and pulled her onto his lap. "What happened?"

Cradled against him, she realized his heart was beating as hard as hers. "I'm sorry."

Tommy didn't know what had spooked her, but something sure had. She'd swayed enough that he'd feared she would go over the side. That was one reason he was holding on to her so tightly. The other reason was that it was maybe the best thing he'd ever felt. It was so good, in fact, he was afraid to move or speak for fear she'd pull away. Their body heat mingled and her breast was pressed against his chest. He watched her chest heaving and it was a beautiful sight. Her fingers clutched his shirt, and that was beautiful, too. It wasn't that he liked her being scared. Or did he? He liked when she needed him. He liked being the one to rescue her.

"I'm sorry," she said again. "I shouldn't have come up here."

"You afraid of heights?"

She didn't reply at first. "Not exactly."

"What was it, then? What spooked you?"

"I had a bad experience in a loft," she admitted. She relaxed her grip on his shirt. "I must be hurting you."

"No, you're not." He didn't relinquish his hold because he didn't want the moment to end. He didn't want to let her go. "What was the bad experience?"

She sighed. "A man. A man was after me."

"He chased you up in the loft?"

She nodded.

His arms tightened around her. "Did he catch you?"

"Not that time. I jumped off, onto a rope that hung from the ceiling. Then he followed and it broke." She attempted to sit up again but he held firm. "I think I'm alright now."

Reluctantly, he relaxed his grip and she got to her feet as if testing the strength in her legs. She held her hands against her stomach and she looked pale. He stood and then moved aside. "Sit back down for a minute," he urged.

She sat on the trunk. "I'm sorry. I didn't know it would still affect me so much." She glanced at the boxes. "I was curious about what was up here."

"It's not much," Tommy said. He walked over to the top box and pulled out a moth-eaten shawl and tossed it to her. "Probably wasn't worth risking your life for."

"It wasn't my intention to risk either of our lives. And you're right, an old moth-eaten shawl is probably not worth it."

"What about a doll?" he asked, holding it up. Em gasped. Her eyes were wide, her mouth ajar. He quickly handed the doll over, puzzled by her strong reaction.

"I can't believe it," she cried. "After all this time. Oh, I *knew* she took it," she added vehemently.

"That was yours?"

"Yes!"

Tommy turned back and rummaged with more enthusiasm. A red cut glass dish brought a similar squeal of delight from Em, and then she joined him in the search for a pearl bracelet, which they didn't find. When they'd gone through every item in the boxes, he led her back along the narrow loft, keeping his hand on her arm. He started down the ladder just ahead of her, and then had her follow. She made it down without a problem and then he went back up for her things.

"You must think I'm crazy," Em said as they sat on the blanket she'd spread out beneath a large maple tree glorious with autumn-tinted leaves.

"No, I don't."

Em was still holding on to the doll she called Barbara Jean. "It's funny. I thought about her not long ago," she said. She turned the doll to face him. "Do you think she looks like me a little?"

The white-faced porcelain doll had a serene smile, pink cheeks, softly curled brown hair that had gotten smashed on one side and wide, almond-shaped eyes. Actually, the eyes resembled Em's a bit. "Maybe the hair," he teased.

She laughed.

"But you're prettier." He opened the knapsack containing the lunch she'd prepared and the scent of fried chicken made his mouth water. He pulled out bundles of wrapped food—chicken, bread and apples—and set them between them. He held up a dark green bottle, not sure what it contained.

"It's peach wine," Em said. "I hope it's still good."

He pulled apart tin cups stacked together and handed one to her, then poured wine into her cup. "Guess we'll see."

She tasted it and nodded. "*Mmm.* Still good."

He poured himself a cup. "So, who was the man in the loft?"

She lowered her gaze to her cup. "I'll tell you anything you want to know," she said slowly. "If you really want to know. I feel I owe you that." She looked up at him. "But sometimes it's better not to."

He studied her, recognizing that she wanted him to let it

go. But he wanted to know. He wanted to know everything about her.

"Will you make me a promise first?" she asked resignedly.

"What?"

"That you won't let it ruin things between us."

"What do you mean?"

"That you'll still be my partner."

What was she talking about? As if there were anything she could say that would change that. There wasn't.

"I like our plans," she said.

"I like our plans, too. I promise."

She looked back down at her wine. "It was Briar Lindley."

He made an effort not to react, and then he tasted the wine to buy a moment. It was sweet, too sweet, while the knowledge was bitter. There was always a heightened sense of danger when the Lindleys came into town. With their coal black hair and eyes and the sense of rebelliousness they exuded, you couldn't help but pay sharp attention when they were around. Their temper, trigger-fingers and impressive aim were all notorious. "Was that the story? About you and the Lindleys?"

She looked disappointed. "Do you really want to know about all that?"

He nodded. "Yeah. I do."

She sighed. "I'll need more wine first."

"You haven't even finished that."

She downed the contents of her cup, made a face and handed the cup to him.

"Is it that hard to talk about?"

"I bet you have stories, too," she hedged.

He refilled her cup. "Not really. Not any good ones."

"Are any of them hard to talk about? Hard to think about? Do any of them make you feel foolish and ashamed?"

"You don't have to tell me if you don't want to," he said, giving in. He wanted to know, but if it was that hard for her, he'd let it go.

"It's just that I'm always doing the talking."

He started to say, *you have more to talk about*, but refrained because it sounded flippant, and that wasn't how he felt. The truth was that he couldn't remember the last time someone had wanted to hear him talk. "I told you three of my brothers are dead."

She looked at him, surprised, and nodded.

"Two of them were hanged, one was shot by his wife . . . and they all deserved it."

"Really?" she asked softly.

He nodded.

She took a drink and wrinkled her nose. "It's too sweet, isn't it?"

He shrugged. "Maybe. A little bit."

"You said you had five brothers," she said, reaching for plates and doling out food for them.

"Yeah. The second to oldest, Seth, he was the one that got away." Her cheeks were already flushed from the wine, which made her look a little more like the doll she held.

"What do you mean got away?"

"Left home. Made something of himself. Or I hope, anyway." He took a bite of chicken, and it was good.

"Were you close?"

"I can't say I was close to any of them. I always felt . . . different. Like I didn't belong."

"Well, if you're not from the best of people," she said slowly, "then that's a good thing."

He grinned because he'd never thought about it that way. Maybe he should have since Mr. Howerton had made more than a few comments. Like *No way you came from the same parents*. "Right before he left, Seth told me I should clear out, too. He said the family was poison and that if I stayed, I'd die young. Probably with a bullet in my head or at the end of a rope. That was what he said, and it was before my other brothers died."

She was watching him intently. "Did you ever see him again?"

"No. Never saw him, never heard from him." He noticed she hadn't taken a single bite. "You should eat something."

"Do you want anything, Barbara Jean?" Em asked the doll. "What's that you say? You've been eight years without eating? Oh, my!"

"Eat," he urged.

"Suddenly, I'm not hungry. By the way, did I introduce you? Tommy Medlin, this is Barbara Jean Wright."

"Very pleased to meet you, Barbara Jean," he said, playing along.

Em held the doll to her ear and pretended to listen. "What?" she whispered. "He's what?" Em's eyes twinkled. "She says you're very handsome and very nice."

"Tell her I said thank you. And eat."

She set the doll aside, took a bite of the bread and frowned. "This is tasteless."

"It's not tasteless. You're about half drunk."

She made a face. "Not either." She picked out a chicken thigh and took a bite, then set it down.

"I like picnics," he said.

"Then we shall have more, and all of them with peach wine." She refilled her glass, far more interested in drinking than eating, and scooted back to lean against the tree. "Alright. Life story. You sure you want to hear it?"

He rolled onto his side, propping himself on an elbow. "I'm sure."

"My mother died when I was four and my father when I was eleven. That's when I came here to live." She paused. "I miss Ben so much. You remind me of him, in a way."

"Of your uncle?"

She nodded. "Did you ever meet him?"

"No."

"You would have liked him. And he would have liked

you. But he wasn't really my uncle; he was a cousin. It was his wife Amy who insisted that I call them Aunt and Uncle. Although I didn't really call him that unless she was around."

"When did Briar come after you?"

She drew up her knees and hugged them.

"You really don't want to tell me, do you?" he asked.

"I don't want you to think—"

"What?"

"Badly of me."

"I won't. Whatever you've done, I've done worse."

She looked at him searchingly. "How can that be true when rules are so different for a man than they are for a woman?"

Was she saying she'd seduced Briar Lindley? That she'd wanted him? His stomach knotted at the thought of it. "You don't have to tell me."

She looked off, sighed softly and then looked at him again, having made up her mind. "I was fourteen when he started showing up. It was always when I was out alone. We talked. Sometimes we went riding. It was perfectly innocent, but I kept it a secret because of . . . well, what everyone thought of the Lindleys. But everyone thought terrible things about me, too. Things that weren't true."

He was glad she was telling him because not knowing would have eaten a hole in his gut. "It's hard when everybody thinks something bad about you. Or calls you names."

"Pretty boy?"

He shrugged. "That's one of them."

"You have to admit, they have a point."

He grinned. "I'm not near as pretty as you."

"That's a matter of opinion," she said with a roll of her eyes. "What else do people think about you that's bad?"

He shrugged a shoulder. "That I'm slow."

Em frowned, genuinely aggrieved. "Everyone does not think that, Tommy."

He looked at the wine in his cup.

"Everyone does not think that," she repeated adamantly. "In fact, anyone who thinks that doesn't know you at all."

He was grateful she'd said so, and sounded like she meant it.

"We're two peas in a pod, aren't we?" she asked.

While he liked the thought, he couldn't bring himself to agree because they were a world apart. She was elegant enough for any society anywhere. Of course, they'd both been ridiculed plenty. "You were telling me about Briar."

She nodded slowly, resigning herself to the task. "One day, it was a few years after our friendship started, he showed up. Everyone else had gone into town and I was in the barn reading. It'll sound silly, but there was a stall I liked. Ben called it my stall. When we mucked out the others, he'd ask if we should change my straw yet." She smiled thinking of it, but then it vanished. "It had just begun to rain, I remember, and Briar showed up. I hadn't heard him. But he was there and he . . . jumped on top of me." Her voice broke and tears began streaming down her face.

Tommy sat back up, torn between wanting to hear and stopping her because it was causing her such pain.

"I couldn't get him off!"

"He forced himself on you?" he asked breathlessly. Her tears streamed harder, but she didn't move or speak. She was shaking and breathing in ragged little gulps.

She nodded jerkily. "But it was my fault," she whispered.

He shook his head. "No."

"It's true. I . . . stayed behind. I could have gone into town with the family. But I stayed behind."

"You didn't know—"

"I did, though. I had a *feeling* he'd show." She swiped at her runny nose with the palm of her hand.

"You couldn't have known what he'd do."

"No! Oh, God, no. I thought he was a good person that everyone else misunderstood. I thought he loved me." She wiped her face with her sleeve and took a few deep breaths, trying to regain control.

He handed her one of the cloth napkins and she dried her face.

"Do you know," she broke off and swallowed. "He said what he did was his right because he was going to marry me. His *right*," she hissed angrily. "I told him I would never marry him. That I hated him!" She quivered. "I would have killed him if I could," she said just above a whisper. She drank the last of her cup, and then held her hand out. "Bottle, please."

He handed it over and she refilled her cup with a badly shaking hand. He watched, fascinated by her changing reactions. The experience still had a lot of power over her. "What did that have to do with the loft?"

She let out a slow, shaky breath. "That was months later. He showed up again—"

"And you were alone again?"

She nodded. "And in the barn again. I grabbed a pitchfork, but he got it away from me. I couldn't get to the door, so I went up the ladder. Like a fool. Of course, he chased me into the loft. There was nowhere else to go, so I jumped onto the rope and tried to get down. But he jumped on, too, and it broke. We both fell, but he was really hurt. I think he b-broke his leg." She took a few deep breaths. "I never saw him again after that." She exhaled and rested her forehead to her knee, hiding her face. "My head hurts, now."

"Em?"

"What?" she said without moving. The sound was muffled, her nose clogged.

"He hurt you. He forced you. I don't think badly of you for that."

She shook her head.

"Em—"

"I don't talk about it," she said in a muffled voice. "I just . . . I don't talk about it."

"Are you sorry you told me?"

Reluctantly, she looked up and considered him for a moment, then shook her head. "No. I don't think I am."

"I'm sorry it happened," he said.

"I'm sorry it happened, too." She started to take another drink, then changed her mind and flung the remainder of her wine out. She looked at him with red-rimmed eyes, puzzled. "Can you die from a broken leg?"

"If infection sets in. Yeah."

"I wonder if he died," she said quietly.

Chapter Eighteen

Fiona brought the wagon to a stop in front of the farmhouse and climbed down carefully. Grunting, she bent to one side and then the other, stretching her back before walking up to the front door and knocking. It was opened at once by Em, wearing a coat and hat. She'd obviously been headed out, but she looked delighted to see her. "Fiona!"

"Surprise."

Em stepped back, opening the door wider. "Come in! It's so good to see you. And you're showing."

"That's a nice way to put it," she said as she stepped inside. Right away, she saw the home was neat and pretty with wallpaper and nice furnishings. "I caught you going out, didn't I?"

"Just to keep an eye on the sheep," Em replied. "Let me take your coat."

Fiona shrugged it off and handed it over.

"It's a new experience," Em added. "I'm trying to learn them."

"*Learn* them?"

Em walked over to the coatrack and hung it up. "Learn who they are, name them—"

"Name them?" Fiona burst. "You're going to eat them, aren't you?"

Em grinned as she took off her own coat. "Tommy laughs at me, too."

"Tommy? Lord, do tell. Come to think of it, you look all aglow. Have you gone and fallen in love or something?"

Em walked over to put the kettle on to boil. "Don't be silly. Have a seat."

"I'll stand a bit. It was a long ride. So, who's Tommy?"

"Tommy Medlin."

"The one they call pretty boy?"

Em turned back around. "He *hates* being called that," she said earnestly.

"Yeah, but he is, though. He's got to be the handsomest man I ever saw. But he's not quite right in the head, is he?"

Em frowned. "He's just shy."

Em's blushing and her frown said a lot more than that. "So, what else you got going with Mr. Tommy Medlin?" Fiona asked mischievously.

"Sheep and goats," Em replied, giving Fiona a look. "And in the spring, tobacco, corn and wheat. We're partners. Business partners. He provided the money to get the farm working again. He's already hired a few men to help and we'll probably hire even more."

"Well, isn't that interesting?" Fiona said playfully.

"How are you feeling?" Em asked, pointedly changing the subject.

"Fat and cranky. And my back hurts something awful. So, don't you think he's the handsomest man you ever saw?"

Em gave her a pained look. "Fiona."

"C'mon, now. Don't you? Just betweenst us girls."

Em turned and busied herself with the tea. "That has nothing to do with anything."

"Sure it don't. Hey, speaking of things that got nothin' to do with nothin'—" Em turned back around as Fiona pulled out a chair and sat, holding on to her swollen belly with one hand. "You know how my Aunt Doll and mama are always going at one another?"

"I heard them that one morning," Em replied carefully.

"Lord'a mercy, girl, it's all the blame time. Anyway, Doll's fed up. Swears she's leaving. You know what she said the other day? She said, 'Dalene,' that's my mama, she said, 'Dalene, I love you enough that I don't want to kill you with my bare hands, so I'm leavin' and that's that.' And that is a quote, I'm sad to say. Then, I thought about you and wondered if you could use some company out here. That's what I come to ask you. 'Course, knowing what I know now, this is even better because it sounds like ya'll need a cook. And that is perfect because Doll needs people around her. She drives me batty sometimes, but I love her dearly and she is a great cook. Mama's a real good cook, too, but two cooks in the same kitchen?" She shook her head. "You don't even want to know."

Em looked apologetic. "It's possible we could use her in the spring when we have more hands to feed, but we can't afford to pay her now."

"Oh, she don't need to be *hired*. She just needs a place to be and some fixings to work with. And look at this stove, will you? That is one nice stove. No telling what she could cook up on this thing. Will you think about it?"

Em blinked. "I don't have to think about it. If that's really the case, we'd love to have her."

"Really?" Fiona clapped her hands together. "Yippee! This just feels right. You know what I mean?"

"I do, but let's make sure it's what she wants. Because there is really no money to pay her right now."

"I'm telling you, she needs a place to be and people to be around. Room and board . . . and maybe the chance to kind of be in charge. Give her that and she's happy as a pig in slop."

"That really would be perfect," Em said, beginning to get excited by the notion.

"Will be perfect," Fiona corrected. "Yes, ma'am. So, on to more interesting matters. Like where exactly is Mr. Tommy Medlin?"

"He's in town getting supplies."

"Too bad. Don't you just want to stare at him?" she asked, dreamily. "Actually, you're both so pretty, you probably just sit and stare at each other all day long. It's a wonder any work gets done."

"Fiona!"

Fiona laughed. "Okay, I'll stop. Hey, I brung you some apple butter, so don't let me forget it when I leave."

Emmett had never considered that being handsome could be a burden, but the way the waitresses were ogling Tommy was downright disconcerting. No wonder Tommy had balked about having lunch here. The worst offender, a pretty, fair-haired gal named Colleen, was coming back their way. "Are you ready to order?" she asked, looking right at Tommy.

"I'll take the special," Tommy replied, avoiding her gaze.

"Make it two," Emmett put in.

Colleen flicked a tolerant smile in his direction. "You want corn muffins or biscuits?"

"Doesn't matter," Tommy replied.

"Bring them both," Emmett said.

"Alrighty, then." She glanced toward the kitchen and then looked at Tommy. "We don't see you in here much, Tommy."

He shook his head. "Don't get to town much."

Emmett cleared his throat. "I guess that's all," he said, hoping to spur the girl on. It worked, but she backed up into another waitress and turned beet-red, bless her heart. The poor girl had it bad for Tommy. "So, I got a few responses from that advertisement we placed," he said to Tommy, who was nearly as embarrassed as Colleen. He reached into his jacket pocket for some papers he'd folded and handed them over. "The one on top looks good. He's got a candor I like."

Tommy opened them and scanned the one on top from a man named Shaw. On Emmett's advice, they'd placed ads in nearby city newspapers for the sort of help they needed. They'd asked for experience at farming and a willingness to work for room, board and a set amount of pay at harvest time. "I didn't expect anyone to write," Tommy admitted.

"To be honest, neither did I," Emmett agreed. "Not anybody worth their salt, but"—he paused and shrugged—"I have to say a few of those look more than decent, and that Woodson Shaw fella looks ideal. He's not a perfect man. He used to drink too much and he got into some trouble and did time for it. Theft. He tells the whole story right there. He got fired from a job, felt he was owed some pay, so he broke into the place and took what wasn't his. He admits it. Sounds sorry for it. Did his time."

Tommy nodded slowly.

"I already wrote them all back," Emmett continued, "explaining the situation in more detail. Told them to send word if they want to come meet you and see the place."

"Thank you."

"You're welcome. How are things going?" Emmett asked, momentarily distracted by the waitresses clumped together discussing Tommy. They weren't even trying to be discreet about it. He wondered what their mothers would have to say if they could see them now.

"Good."

"How's our girl?"

Tommy grinned. "She's good. She named the sheep, though."

Emmett snorted a laugh. "In that case, I don't know that I'd be counting on eating lamb chops any time soon."

"I know it."

"Now, *you* haven't gone and memorized their names, have you?"

"Not that I'd admit."

Emmett laughed heartily as Colleen appeared with the tray of food.

"Here we go," she said sweetly as she slid plates in front of them.

"Thank you, miss," Emmett replied. "That was fast."

"We sell a bunch of specials," she replied. "So, they keep 'em coming."

"Well, it's hot. It's all I care about."

"Are you getting ready for Christmas, Tommy?" Colleen asked as she pulled the tray back.

"I haven't thought about it much," he replied.

"I hear there's going to be a big gala," she said nervously. "Did you hear about that?"

"No, ma'am."

"Howerton's throwing it," Emmett said to Tommy. "By invite only."

Colleen looked confused. "Don't the people who work for him get to go?"

"Colleen," one of the other waitresses whispered urgently behind her. "Simpson wants you."

Emmett glanced over and saw the manager of the establishment scowling at Colleen from the kitchen door. Mrs. Simpson didn't allow flirting from her girls.

"I don't work there anymore," Tommy said to clear up the matter, since she was obviously angling for an invitation.

Colleen's face fell. "Oh." There was a brief, awkward silence and then she walked off.

Emmett pursed his lips and tried to think of a way to lighten the moment and Tommy's discomfiture.

"I never thought about Christmas much," Tommy said as he picked up his fork.

"I figure we'll keep it simple this year," Emmett said. "A small family get-together. You, me, Em."

The smile that lit Tommy's face was real and instant. He nodded fervently. "That sounds good."

"And you don't need to get me a thing," Emmett added. "Now, next year, when you've made a big profit—"

The feed and grain store was Tommy's last stop in town. He was loading the last of the forty-pound bags when he heard footsteps behind him. Before he could even turn to see who it was, someone asked, "How's married life?" Of course, he knew Mitchell's voice. He turned to see Mitchell and Blue standing there smirking. "How's the little wife?" Blue asked.

"Hey, you know what everyone calls you two?" Mitchell asked. "Wright and Wrong. Get it? Wright, her name. And wrong, meaning you, of course." Tommy gave Mitchell a hard look, and Mitchell's expression went from amused to icy. "You really think you're something, don't you, brother?"

Tommy stepped around them and climbed into the seat.

"One of these days, someone's going to pull you both off your high horses," Mitchell called. "Wright and Wrong."

Tommy slapped the reins, putting the wagon in motion.

"Wright and Wrong," Blue sang out.

"Shut up," Mitchell retorted. "You don't need to repeat every goddamn thing I say."

"I don't repeat every goddamn thing you say."

"What'd you just go and do? Shut the hell up."

Chapter Nineteen

Em whimpered with fear as she hung on to the rope. The rope was hurting her hands, burning them; she couldn't hang on much longer. "Emmy," a deep voice playfully said over her head. She looked up as Briar leaned over the edge of the loft above. He smiled as if he had her just where he wanted her. "Go on, give it to her," he called to someone on the ground. Em craned her neck to see whom he was talking to and she experienced a painful chill to see Sonny standing directly below with a whip in hand.

"You're not stupid," Sonny mocked. "You knew I'd come. You knew I'd do this." The whip made a terrifying *whoosh* as he drew it back, prepared to strike, and she let go of the rope and began a dizzying descent.

"Em, wake up," a voice said. Tommy's voice.

She drew in a shaky breath as she woke. It was a struggle to sit because her muscles were so tight.

"It was just a bad dream," he said soothingly.

It was so dark, she could barely make out his form. "I'm sorry," she murmured. "I woke you?"

"It doesn't matter."

"I'm sorry."

"Em, I don't care. I'll go right back to sleep."

She reached out and made contact with his arm. A moment later, he took hold of her hand and then sat on the edge of the bed.

"You okay now?" he asked.

She didn't reply, because she didn't know what to say. Okay? She was anything but okay.

"What was it about?" he asked.

"I was hanging on a rope and then . . . I fell."

He squeezed her hand. "Listen to me," he said tenderly as he leaned in. "Briar Lindley is never going to hurt you again. I won't let anyone hurt you."

Her face tingled as tears threatened. "Oh, Tommy."

"What? Why are you crying?"

What could she say? She loved him. He was the most wonderful man and she loved and needed him so completely, but she couldn't say that. She could not and would not jeopardize their friendship and partnership, because she'd be lost without it. "Will you stay with me a little while?" she asked in a thick voice.

"Yeah, of course, I will. For as long as you want."

She withdrew her hand and scooted over, but he didn't move.

"You want me to get in?"

His voice was filled with such self-doubt, it made her ache. "Unless it would . . . make you uncomfortable."

He hesitated and then stood. He pulled back the covers and got into bed beside her, sitting very upright against the headboard.

"Will you just lie with me a little while?" There was a beat of silence before he moved down and lay flat on his back. She reached over and pulled the cover over him, then settled on her side facing him. Having him close made her feel so much safer.

It was quiet for several moments before he asked, "Would it be alright if I came closer?"

Rather than reply, she snuggled to his side, her hand on his chest.

He listened as her breathing evened out, and then he put his hand on her arm and stroked it gently. Then he stopped himself.

"It feels good," she murmured sleepily.

He lifted his left arm, the one she was lying against, and put it around her, and she snuggled even closer to him, as if it were the most natural thing in the world. She reached up and planted a soft kiss on his cheek and it sent a jolt through his body. Blood pulsed, his breathing became shallow. He was wondering how he could keep her from knowing when he noticed her breathing had also changed. She wasn't going to sleep anymore. "Em?" he breathed.

It was quiet, just the sound of their breathing. Then, "Yes?"

"You . . . don't want me to go?"

"No."

Slowly, he shifted toward her. She didn't stop him, so he pressed his lips to hers. Her breath was warm, her lips so soft. He pulled away and then kissed her again and again, loving the feel of them. Because she was responding. Kissing him back. He parted her lips with his tongue and then explored the depths of her mouth, anxious to taste her, to suck in her breath. Moaning softly, she wrapped her arms around him and ran her hands over the contours of his back, and it was the best thing he'd ever felt. Her tongue sought his, and her hips strained toward him.

He stood it for as long as he could, and then he got up and

pulled off his long johns, knowing she'd stop him if he was wrong. But he wasn't wrong, because she sat and maneuvered her gown up and over her head, confirmation that she wanted him, too. He climbed on top of her, and, bracing himself on elbows and knees, bent to kiss her again. His lips grazed the soft skin of her cheek and jawline and ear and then he nuzzled her neck. He lowered himself to her erect nipples and ran his tongue around one before drawing it into his mouth, the way he'd imagined so many times.

Her breathing was fast and labored. It was a good sound. He separated her knees and positioned himself between them, wondering if she'd truly allow a consummation. He was hard enough to enter her without guidance from his hand if she was willing. He heard her breath catch as he pushed at her opening, but she didn't say to stop. Her fingers tightened on his arms as he began filling her, but she still didn't say to stop.

She gasped and pushed against his chest, but, in that second, he pushed inside her. She cried out, but there were so many angels singing in his head, her voice was hard to distinguish. It was done, they'd become one. He was already withdrawing and reentering her, knowing that it was the best moment of his life. It was the moment that made everything else he'd ever been through worth it. They had become one and they would stay one—if only in his mind and heart.

He wanted to stay inside her and keep going forever, but it was too good and he wasn't accustomed to ecstasy. He didn't mean to cry out, he'd never done so before, but there it was. A deep, primal sound that split the night. Breathing hard, he moved over and stretched out beside her again. He was shaking, but so was she. He pulled her close and held her tightly, half afraid she'd disappear.

It took several minutes to start breathing normally and it took a while more to begin growing sleepy. They'd never said a word, he realized just before he dropped off, but they had made love. Made love. It was an interesting phrase. They'd started with love and made more, just as it was supposed to be. *November thirtieth, eighteen eighty-one.* It was the best night of his life.

Chapter Twenty

Em woke feeling the warmth of the sun on her bare shoulder. She blinked in dull surprise at the hour its brightness suggested, and then at her nakedness. She remembered what had transpired in the night, and sat up abruptly. What had she been thinking? It had been all her doing, or mostly her doing, and it might have changed everything. Things had been so easy between them before last night. And now? What would they be like now?

She dressed quickly and went downstairs, tying her hair back as she went. From the front window, she saw Tommy speaking with Emmett and another man. She hesitated a moment, wondering how guilty she looked, then grabbed her shawl and stepped outside.

"Emmy, come meet Mr. Shaw," Emmett called.

"I go by Wood," the man said when she got close. He extended his hand. "It's a pleasure."

"Nice to meet you," she replied as she shook it, chancing a glance at Tommy. He wasn't looking at her.

"Wood, here, is interested in becoming a part of your venture," Emmett explained.

"Oh?" She looked at Tommy again. This time, she received a nod of confirmation. "That's wonderful."

"And you understand there's no pay until we sell the first crop?" Tommy asked him.

Wood nodded. "I got it. Room, board and then ten percent of the profit."

"That's right," Tommy said.

"And for that, I act as foreman, as well as general help."

"Yes, sir," Tommy replied, nodding once.

Wood stuck out his hand. "Sounds good to me. As long as, knowing what you do, it sounds good to you."

Tommy sealed the agreement with a handshake.

Emmett looked highly pleased. "I told Wood that for a long time you had to have a name that rhymed with Em to work the farm," he said, winking at her. "Ben, Em, Jim and then there's me, T. Emmett Rice, not that I was ever much help in the manual labor department."

"And not that Jim ever did much work," Em added.

Wood grinned. "And I told him I'd change my name if need be. Maybe to . . . wind. I been told I have a lot of that."

They all smiled. "Naw, hardly necessary anymore," Emmett said. "Tommy, here, went and broke the pattern. And we're awful glad of it, aren't we, Emmy?"

Em was painfully aware of the heat blooming in her face. "Yes, we are," she replied, avoiding Tommy's gaze.

"I'll, uh, show you around," Tommy said to Wood. "You want to come?" he asked Em.

"No, I'm . . . doing something."

The three men started off, although Wood quickly turned back. "Nice to meet you," he called.

She smiled, although it felt empty. All of a sudden, she felt oddly let down. Things hadn't seemed strange between her and Tommy; they hadn't seemed different at all. In fact, there hadn't been the slightest flicker of recognition about what had happened in his blue eyes. Nothing. Had it meant nothing to him? Frowning, she crossed her arms tightly.

"That's quite a compound," she heard Wood comment, gesturing to the bunkhouse under construction.

"It's amazing what stubbornness and a couple pair of willing hands will get you," Emmett teased.

"Stubborn and willing," Wood said. "That's me, too. I should fit in right well around here."

"Wood's going to start in a couple of days," Tommy said when he came in for lunch. "As soon as he can pack his stuff and get back here."

"That's good," Em replied levelly. She set bowls of soup on the table and sat carefully. She was feeling sore in a very particular way, although she tried to give no indication of it.

"It's just what we wanted," he said. "Someone willing to work now and take his pay later."

He seemed uncomfortable, talking just to fill the silence. After all, Wood was not the first hire. Tommy had found two other young men and hired them under the same arrangement. One was a half-breed Indian no one else had been willing to take on and the other had an odd tick. Tommy saw beyond all that, and he'd been right. Simon 'Hawk' Godey and Jeffrey Redburn were hard workers and polite young men.

"Guess I'll be moving my stuff out to the bunkhouse," Tommy said.

Em looked up sharply.

"I wouldn't want him thinking anything," Tommy added quietly.

Her face heated and she looked back to her soup. The two of them busied themselves with eating, and it occurred to her that never before had it taken such complete concentration. "You weren't too concerned about Hawk or Jeffrey thinking something," she murmured, unable to stop herself.

"I was, too," he disagreed. "Besides, we got the cook coming, and she'll be sleeping in here. Right?"

Em didn't reply. She wasn't being fair or reasonable. What was wrong with her? What did she want him to say or do?

"When's she getting here?" Tommy asked.

She shrugged a shoulder. "Tomorrow or the next day." She paused. "Doll," she reminded him.

Tommy looked up with such a shocked expression that she almost choked on her bite. She pressed a hand to her mouth and finally managed to swallow. "That's her name." She laughed. "Doll Summers."

Tommy grinned. "Oh, yeah. That's going to take some getting used to."

"I doubt it."

He reached for a slice of bread. "Just out of curiosity, how will you know for sure when someone's talking to her? Somebody might say, 'Good morning, Doll' and just be *pretending* to talk to her. Or, uh, you sure look pretty today, Doll," he continued.

"Maybe you should meet her before you start planning all these comments. Don't you think?"

His blue eyes seemed especially penetrating as they met hers. "Nope."

Em shook her head, but she was relieved that the strain between them had disappeared. And all it had taken was a moment of humor. She'd have to remember that.

Chapter Twenty-One

Doll Summers had a round but still attractive face and tremendous energy. She also had definite views on most all subjects, although she frequently employed the disclaimer, "Just my opinion, now, which obviously don't count for much." She moved into the downstairs bedroom, rearranged it and added personal items until Em didn't even recognize it. "These are lovely," Em commented, referring to landscapes Doll had hung.

"Thank you, darlin'. Did those myself."

"Doll, they're wonderful. You could sell them."

Doll waved her hand in the air. "Go on with you, now. They're not that good."

"They are, too," Em disagreed. "I'd love to have one over the mantle."

"Well, we'll see if we can't do something about that," Doll said proudly.

Tommy's hand hovered above the doorknob to Em's room. He wanted to go in, but what if she didn't want him there now that Doll was downstairs? Slowly, he opened the door and saw her waiting for him. The candle flickering on the table made it easy to see her inviting expression.

He came closer, noticing that she was naked under the covers. Naked and waiting for him. He went to unbutton his shirt, but came in contact with his own flesh. He looked down and discovered he, too, was naked. He looked back up at her, astonished, but then forgot everything as she pulled the covers down. For a moment, he could only stare; then he moved on top of her. He'd been desperate for her for weeks, ever since they'd made love for the first time.

She stroked his hair as he drew her stiffened nipple into his mouth and sucked. Her sweet sigh urged him on. He put himself inside her and thrust deeply—then woke with a gasp, having ejaculated in his sleep.

Wood was snoring in the next room. Tommy stared at the ceiling and waited for his breathing to return to normal. He tried to recapture the dream, but it was already fading. He sat and swung his legs over the side of the bed, then rose and cleaned himself up. The floor was ice cold, but he walked to the window and looked out. His room faced the house, which was dark, of course, since it wasn't quite dawn yet.

He braced his hands on either side of the window and leaned his forehead against the cold glass. His breath fogged it, but only after he'd caught a glimpse of something on the porch. He moved over to peer out a clear pane, and squinted to make sure, and then he slipped on his clothes, shoes and coat. The icy ground crunched beneath his feet as he made his way to the house.

"What are you doing awake?" Em asked quietly when he got close.

"I saw you," he replied, keeping his voice low, so as not to disturb anyone. He climbed the steps to the porch.

She sat in a rocking chair, bundled in a coat and a blanket. "I had a dream."

He sat in the chair next to hers. "Me, too."

"You ever notice how bright the stars are on a night like this?" she asked, looking upward.

He nodded and blew into his hands. "Yeah. Pretty." Although the sky was beginning to gray up. Morning was coming.

"Wood's working out just fine," she said. "Don't you think?"

"I do. He fits right in. Doll, too."

"Remember when we wondered if we'd get anyone else to join us?"

He nodded. Of course, if no one else had joined them, he'd still be in the house. Closer to her.

"What was your dream about?" she asked. "Was it good or bad?"

"I don't remember exactly," he fibbed. "Yours?"

"The usual. I was running, hiding. Someone was after me."

"You're safe," he assured her. "I may be out there in the bunkhouse, but you're safe."

As she smiled in gratitude, he saw the first pink rays of the sunrise beyond her. When she rose and moved to the porch steps for a better view, he followed. They sat on the top step and she shared the blanket, wrapping it around his back. He held one side and appreciated her nearness.

"It's cold," she said. "You want to go in and have some breakfast?"

"Not yet. This is nice."

"It is nice," she agreed, hugging his arm.

It didn't last long enough. Already, the colors were dissipating in the lightening sky. The door squeaked open behind them. "What in the world?" Doll scolded. "It's freezing out there! Get on in here and let me fix ya'll something hot to drink."

Tommy grinned. "Good morning, Doll," he said without turning around. Em turned her face slightly away from him. Blushing, probably. She hated when she blushed, which was funny because he loved that about her.

"Good morning, yourself," Doll replied. "Must be frozen

through." Her voice faded as she walked away from the door. "Don't know what'chall are thinkin'."

Tommy stood, relinquishing the blanket.

"And good morning to you, sir," Em said with a slight bow to her head. She *was* blushing.

"I'd return the greeting, but I said it first."

Laughing quietly, she rose and walked inside and he happily followed.

Chapter Twenty-Two

Gregory Howerton dismounted in front of the Martin farmhouse and looked around in astonishment at the buildings that had been erected since he'd last been there. Where had the money and the manpower come from? He'd heard that Tommy, who was apparently acting as foreman, had hired a couple of 'rejects,' whatever that meant. Almost all current gossip reached his ear and he always listened, which didn't mean he gave it much credence. But *this* was proof there was manpower, know-how and money in play. Whose, though?

He turned as the front door of the house opened and a stout, middle-aged woman stepped out on the front porch with her sleeves rolled up and her blouse and apron dotted with flour. "Morning," she greeted. The greeting seemed wary, almost suspicious.

"Good morning," he returned. "Is Miss Wright around?"

"Maybe she is and maybe she ain't. Who can I say is calling, just in case she is?"

His smile was tight. "Gregory Howerton."

"Ah. So, you're him, are you?" She walked to the edge of the porch and extended her hand. "Doll Summers. I cook for the outfit."

The outfit? Howerton shook her hand, although he was taken aback by the unconventionality of a woman offering a handshake.

"Em's working in the bunkhouse," Doll said, pointing at the newly constructed building across the way.

"And Tommy?" Howerton asked, curious about his role.

"He's out working, of course."

He gave a tip of his head. "It was nice to have made your acquaintance."

"Right back at you," Doll returned.

Howerton walked toward the bunkhouse, impressed by the quality of workmanship he saw. He crossed the wide, covered porch in the center and stepped inside a vestibule, where the scent of pine assailed his senses. The lobby showed evidence of being used and enjoyed. There were comfortable-looking settees and chairs with brightly colored pillows on them. A table for four had a deck of cards waiting, and a checkerboard sat on a coffee table. There was a half cup of coffee and a pipe on one end table and plenty of lamps and rag rugs positioned around the room.

He heard the squeak of a chair to his far right and headed toward it, passing private dormitory rooms. Some doors were closed, others were open, revealing a roughly twelve-by-twelve space with a bed, bedside table, wardrobe and chest. It was an interesting design that allowed a man his own space. "Hello?" he called out.

"Down here," Em called back.

He crossed into an adjoining mess hall, where Em stood on a chair, hanging curtains. "Mr. Howerton," she said, clearly surprised to see him.

"Hello," he said, walking forward slowly as she climbed down from the chair. "I must say, I'm very impressed with what I see. You've been busy." The statement was truthful, if not completely forthcoming. The fact was, he had expected the venture to quickly fail and be available for purchase.

That was, if he didn't simply marry Emeline and absorb the property.

"Thank you. Yes, we have been busy."

"It's an interesting setup," he commented. "Who designed it?"

"Tommy."

Howerton blinked in surprise. He'd always known Tommy wasn't the idiot some assumed, but he wouldn't have guessed he was capable of this. "How is he?" he asked casually.

"He's well."

"Hard worker, isn't he?"

"Yes, he is."

"I met your cook a few minutes ago. She said you have several men working for you."

"Only four right now, but we'll hire more in spring."

"In time for planting, I suppose?"

"Yes."

"Planting what?"

She hesitated. "Tobacco, mainly."

"Is Tommy one of the four you mentioned?"

Em shifted on her feet, uncomfortable with the questioning. "Yes."

Howerton nodded, satisfied that Tommy was merely the foreman.

"May I offer you something to drink?" Em asked.

"Thank you, but no. I won't keep you from your work. I came to issue an invitation to my first Christmas gala." He paused to see if she'd jump right in and accept, but she maintained both poise and control. "It'll be next Saturday, the twenty-third."

She gave a slight nod.

"I plan on it being an annual event. Or, actually, two events, since there is a rather formal affair inside and a more casual affair for my employees in the showroom."

"The showroom?"

"For showing horses when we get some decent lines started. It's just been completed."

"How interesting."

"I hope you'll do me the honor of being my guest."

"Yes, of course. Thank you."

"Wonderful. I'll pick you up at half past six and we'll have dinner." Her expression went blank and she blinked. It almost felt as if she were panicking. *Why?* But perhaps there was a certain amount of pressure in being seen together at such an event. It would mark them as an item in the minds of all who attended. He should have considered it. "It should be a marvelous evening," he said with a warm smile to reassure her. He reached for her hand, brought it to his lips and kissed it. "Until the twenty-third."

As Howerton walked from the room, Em swallowed hard and took a step backward. She thought he'd said *guests. I hope you'll be my guests.* She'd accepted, not realizing he'd been talking about *escorting* her. The very last thing she wanted to do was to be with him, but how was she going to get out of it now without insulting the man?

She sank onto the chair she had been using as a ladder. *Damn it!* She'd thought he'd been talking about an invitation for all of them. They were neighbors, after all. Was Tommy even invited? She took a few deep breaths to calm her nerves because she was . . . "Overreacting," she murmured, rising again. She began pacing, her hands pressed to her stomach. It was a party, not an engagement. Yes, he was picking her up and, yes, they were having dinner beforehand, but that was all. "Oh, damn it," she swore again. How could she get out of it with grace?

* * *

Howerton walked toward his horse, but then remembered the invitation for Tommy. He turned to go back inside to leave it with Em, but then spotted Tommy riding in. He mounted and rode out to meet him.

"Mr. Howerton," Tommy greeted when he got close.

"Hello, Tommy. Good to see you."

"It's good to see you."

"Not wanting to come back, are you? Because you're missed at the ranch."

Tommy smiled, but shook his head. "I appreciate you saying so, but I can't do that."

"No, I guess not," Howerton agreed, glancing back at the bunkhouse. "The place looks good. Really good. I'm impressed."

"Thank you. We've worked hard."

"The reason I came by is, I'm throwing a Christmas party," Howerton said as he reached into his coat pocket. He pulled out an envelope and handed it over. "An invitation for you and a guest, if you wish."

Tommy took it, knowing it was the gala Colleen had asked about. And he was being invited even though he wasn't an employee any longer. It was almost like he was an equal, which was a thrill. "Thank you."

"See you at the party," Howerton said as he headed out.

Tommy opened the envelope and withdrew the invitation. The party would be held in *The Showroom*, whatever that was. He looked up, wondering if Em would go with him, and how he should go about asking her.

Doll was the first to broach the subject at lunch by asking Em what Howerton had wanted. Tommy felt his breath catch. He hadn't realized Howerton had seen Em.

"He's having a Christmas party," Em replied haltingly, staring intently into her plate.

Tommy tensed.

"And?" Doll pushed.

"And he asked me," Em stammered with a sheepish one-shouldered shrug.

"To go with him?" Doll clarified.

It looked as though Em cringed. "Yes."

Tommy stared at his food. It felt like he'd been punched in the gut.

"I didn't understand that he *was* asking me to go with him at first," Em continued, talking fast. "Not until after I'd accepted the invitation."

"You'll need a fancy gown, won't you?" Doll asked. "You have something or should we make you one?"

Tommy took a bite, determined not to show how thrown he was. Unfortunately, the food had lost all its taste. How stupid he'd been to think that Em might actually go to the party with him. Stupid and wrong.

"Pass the corn bread, will ya, Tommy?" Jeffrey asked.

"Sure," Tommy said quietly, reaching for the basket while studiously avoiding Em's gaze.

"That was one beautiful horse Howerton had," Doll said. "Man's got more money than God, doesn't he?"

Wood snorted. "Last I checked, God didn't need any money."

"Then he's the only one," Doll returned as she picked up her glass of milk. "Funny how fancy-pants Howerton didn't ask me to the party. Him and me jawjacking like we were."

"Go figure," Wood said wryly, barely holding back his amusement.

"Yeah," Doll said, giving him a look that dared him to laugh. "Go figure."

Chapter Twenty-Three

The weather was crisp as Tommy and Em drove into town four days later. The scent of snow was in the air, but, so far, there had only been an occasional flurry of snowflakes. Em stared straight ahead, not speaking because she resented Tommy's remoteness. This trip *should* have been the perfect opportunity to end the distance that had crept between them since Howerton's visit but, obviously, that was going to be up to her. Of course. He would remain silent the whole way there and back.

His petulance, if that's what it was, made no sense, since he'd had no reaction to the news that she was going to the gala with Howerton in the first place. She'd fretted and worried about it and then he'd had no reaction. But since then, he'd been aloof. She missed talking to him. She missed the ease between them. "Are you angry at me?" she suddenly blurted.

"No."

She frowned in discontent, wondering if she should mention the gala directly, but she set her jaw, stubbornly. Why should she when he had never shown any real romantic interest in her outside of that one night? And, if she were being brutally honest, *she* had been primarily responsible for what had occurred between them then. Besides, afterwards, they'd pretended it hadn't happened. She barely held back a sigh, because she was being foolish. He claimed nothing was wrong and he'd had no reaction to her going in the first place. Which meant, in very simple terms, he felt little or nothing for her in that way. She was just going to have to accept it.

"What's your dress going to be like?" Tommy asked.

She considered not answering him, not speaking to him at all. A little silent treatment would serve him right. "I don't know," she replied. "I'll see what there is."

"You have Doll's list?"

"Yes."

"Why don't you give it to me and I'll take care of it? You'll probably be a while at the dressmaker's."

At least it was conversation, which was what she'd wanted. So why didn't it feel as if they were connecting as they had before? Or had she imagined it? "Hold on," he warned as they approached some deep ruts in the road. She braced herself as the wagon began bouncing over them.

"Someone needs to fix that," he complained as he reached over and pulled up the blanket that had slipped off her lap. The gesture was so *him*, it made her want to cry.

"Thank you," she said quietly. He really was so good and kind and considerate—and he'd done nothing but come to her rescue in every way possible. So, what did she want from him? *All of it*, she thought bitterly. *I want his heart. I want him to love me.*

Riders came toward them. Em didn't recognize any of them, but obviously Tommy did. They greeted him by name, and he tipped his hat to them. "How's married life?" one of them said in a hushed tone as they passed.

Em looked at Tommy, wondering if the man was talking about the two of them, but either he hadn't heard the comment or he was patently ignoring it.

* * *

The reason for the man's question stared Em in the face as she happened to glance out the window of the dress shop and see Tommy engaged in conversation with a pretty waitress from Wiley's. What was her name? Carly or Cally or something like that. Em stared, unable to tear her eyes away. How had she not known?

"That looks wonderful on you," Mrs. Simmons, the patroness of the shop, commented.

Em managed to look away from Tommy and the waitress, although she felt slightly dizzy and more than slightly nauseous. She looked in the mirror at the gown. The bodice was ivory, the skirt a soft brown design with gold accents. It was fine. It was probably lovely, but she didn't care. She didn't care and she didn't want to be going to this party. "Thank you," she murmured. She looked back out the window again. Tommy and the waitress were still talking, so it wasn't simply a passing-by, how-do-you-do meeting.

"Will it do? Shall I make the alterations?" the dressmaker asked, stepping closer to pull the waist tighter.

"Yes, please," Em replied, distractedly. "It will do nicely."

When Em emerged from the shop, Tommy was leaning against the side of the wagon, waiting patiently. "I'm sorry it took so long," she said.

"It didn't take that long. Did you find something you liked?"

"Yes," she replied less than enthusiastically. "It has to be altered, though."

"Today?"

"No. I'll come back for it. But I was thinking . . . why don't we go see Emmett? Maybe have lunch together?" Was it her imagination or had he just winced at the suggestion?

Did he not want her to know about Cally or whatever her name was? Or maybe it was the other way around. Maybe he didn't want the waitress to know about her. Perhaps because she was the jealous sort who wouldn't believe they were simply business partners.

"I saw him," Tommy replied. "He said he can't get away today. Besides, I should get back."

He offered his hand to help her into the wagon and she had no choice but to accept it. She'd been hoping to see Fiona, but she wouldn't insist since he had work to do. Not that there wasn't always work to do. "Did you get everything?" she asked as they started off.

"I think so."

She smoothed out the lap blanket. "See anyone you know?"

"A few people."

She waited, but he wasn't going to tell her about the waitress because he didn't want her to know. Well, fine. If that's how he wanted to be, she'd go along with it, and give him a taste of his own medicine. The next time he asked her anything, she'd give him a nod, or a shake of the head, or a one-word answer. In fact, from now on, she wouldn't indulge in any personal conversation.

Of course, he wasn't asking. He could go hours or days without talking. Maybe weeks. He was a conversation camel. "So who was the girl I saw you talking to?" she blurted. *Damn it!* What was wrong with her? If she thought it, she had to say it? Why could she not keep her big, fat mouth shut?

"Her name's Colleen."

Colleen. So that was it. Em waited, but he didn't say more. She sucked in her bottom lip to keep from saying one more word. If that's the way he wanted it to be, that's the way it would be.

* * *

Tommy hated feeling cornered. He'd been cornered too many times in his life. His brothers had cornered him and pounded him for the sheer fun of it, and his ma had cornered him a few times when she thought he had information she wanted. Like the time she thought he knew where Celia had gone. She'd come at him, screaming and kicking and slapping.

Mitchell had cornered him a hundred times for money, the whores in the saloon tried to corner him every time he came in and Colleen had cornered him not a half hour ago. She'd spotted him in the street and come running. She told him she'd wrangled an invitation to Mr. Howerton's Christmas party and wanted to go with him. He'd tried to make a polite excuse as to why he couldn't make it, but she kept at it until he'd agreed to go just to shake her. He wished he hadn't done that, especially now that Em had seen them. That was stupid though, since Em was going with Howerton. To think, he'd actually been foolish enough to imagine she might go with him.

Wrong.

Chapter Twenty-Four

Sonny looked over the young woman with strawberry blonde hair. She was no beauty, but she was attractive enough. "Tell me about yourself, Abigail."

"Well, sir, I'm eighteen and healthy. I went to school through the seventh grade."

"And why are you here?"

"I need the work."

"Go on," he said.

"I was living with my brother, even after he got married, but he took sick and died last summer."

"Sorry to hear it."

Abigail nodded. "It was real hard on everybody."

"You do understand the nature of working here?"

"Sir?"

"You understand what whores do?"

She turned red. "Oh. Yes, sir. Of course I do. Yes."

"Have you been with a man before?"

"Well, um, not exactly . . . in the way you mean."

Sonny smiled at the prospect of breaking in a virgin. "Take off your clothes and let me see you."

She did as he instructed, shaking with nerves. "My s-shoes, too?"

"That's not necessary."

When she was naked, other than her shoes and stockings, he looked her over carefully. He rose and walked around to stand behind her. "I'm going to give you three important pieces of advice."

She nodded. "Yes, sir?"

"Pretend that you like what you're doing or what's being done to you, even if you don't. Do whatever the customer wants you to do, and charge him accordingly. And, most importantly, never attempt to cheat me."

"No, sir. I mean, I wouldn't."

"Good. Now, bend over and grab hold of the desk." She did and he focused on her ample, white backside as he unfastened his trousers, released his swollen cock and stroked it lovingly. Just thinking about breaking her in had gotten him hard. "Spread your legs apart." She obeyed and he positioned himself behind her and moved the head of his penis up and down her moist valley, enjoying her gasps. They were so virginal.

"I'm sure you know it hurts at first," he warned as he positioned himself to enter her. "But feel free to make all the noise you want to." He pushed in slowly, savoring her resistance and the deep sounds uttered from her throat. Grabbing hold of her hips, he began thrusting vigorously.

"No, no," she cried out. "Stop, please!"

His fingers dug in and he slammed harder, despite her rhythmic cries. After he came, he reached for his handkerchief and wiped himself off. "Remember what I said about pretending to enjoy it?"

She turned to face him, her arms crossed in front of herself. "I'm s-sorry. I . . . didn't know it would hurt so bad."

"The next time you tell me to stop, you're going to feel

the cane across your bare ass. Have you ever had a sound whipping, Abigail?"

"I'll do better," she swore.

He nodded. "I know you will. Go on," he said with a tip of his head. "Go see Nancy or George. They'll get you set up in a room."

An hour later, Sonny walked into the saloon to check on business and noticed George coming toward him with an intent look on his face and an envelope in his hands. "This came for you," he said. Sonny took the letter and noticed the return address was Lynchburg. He ripped it open as he walked to the bar. The writing on the expensive ivory parchment was feminine and somewhat hard to read.

> *Dear Sir,*
> *We spoke a few months ago in the teahouse.*
> *At that time, you were asking for information on a*
> *Miss Emeline Wright. Although I could not help you*
> *at the time, I told you the photograph in your*
> *possession looked familiar. Last evening, the answer*
> *occurred to me. The woman in the photograph*
> *strongly resembled Miss Rachel Thompson, who*
> *married Mr. Theodore Wright. The lady you seek was*
> *the offspring of that union. I have since learned that*
> *young Emeline was moved to Rockbridge County to*
> *be taken care of by relatives. I hope this helps and*
> *that you will be able to find her and award her the*
> *inheritance due her.*
>
> > *Cordially,*
> > *Mrs. Petunia Tippett*

Sonny smiled slowly and released a luxurious sigh. Finally, he was on the right track. He could feel it in his gut. *Yes,*

indeed, Mrs. Tippett, I will give Em exactly what's due her.
"Give me a drink," he ordered his barkeep. "That whiskey that just came in."

"Yes, sir, Mr. Peterson."

Sonny turned and surveyed his customers. It was a good crowd for this early in the evening.

"Here you go, sir."

Sonny lifted the glass to his lips and sipped, savoring the taste and the thought of Emeline back in his grasp. Oh, yes. Life had just taken a sharp turn for the better.

Em paced around her room, too restless to stay still. She walked to the window for the eighth time, drew back the curtain and looked out, hoping to see Tommy. He wasn't in sight, but Doll was making her way toward the bunkhouse kitchen; she was doing most the cooking there now. Em dropped the curtain back in place. Things were not right between Tommy and her, and it was all she thought about. Maybe the question ought to have been why she was so bothered when it didn't bother him.

It was possible that he didn't get bothered or all that emotionally attached to anything or anyone. She'd asked about his old home and he hadn't reacted at all. Of course, she didn't feel strongly about Lynchburg either. This was her home. She'd loved her father dearly, but his death had been part of her childhood and it didn't exercise the same power over her as Ben's. So what did that mean? Something? Nothing?

She leaned against the wall and then pushed off, too anxious to stand still. Was it possible she was being a spoiled brat who just wanted what she wanted? She wanted Tommy's full attention, and yet she was going to the biggest party of the year with Gregory Howerton. "Because I didn't understand," she muttered miserably.

The thing to do was to just get beyond the Christmas party. There was nothing else to do, really. It was tomorrow and after that, hopefully, everything would return to normal. Or had too much distance crept between them? That thought hurt terribly. She walked back to the window, pushed aside the curtain and saw Tommy walking out of the barn carrying the small stray cat that had adopted them. She pressed a hand to her throat because it suddenly ached. As if he sensed her watching, he looked up. Embarrassed at being caught staring, she jerked away from the window with a red hot face.

Chapter Twenty-Five

Gregory Howerton watched Emeline from across the table, thinking she was as lovely as any woman he'd ever seen, but far too restrained. Standoffish, even. Or was it that she sincerely had no interest in him? He'd thought at first she was being coy, playing hard to get in order to intrigue him, but he was beginning to suspect it went beyond that.

The evening had been planned down to the last detail. Not only was the ranch aglow with hundreds of candles and Chinese lanterns, but also a light snow had begun falling. Dinner was superb, and he had been charming, so what was wrong with her? Or did she have a cool, distant sort of personality? If so, that would never do. He needed life and passion. He needed a certain amount of fire.

"What does Triple H stand for?" Em inquired.

"Howerton, heaven and hell. It's all three. I also hope to have three sons one day. In fact, I feel quite certain I will."

She smiled and dropped her gaze back to her plate.

"And you, Emeline? What's your grand goal in life?"

She looked back up at him. "Making the farm work."

"Is that it? That's all you want?"

She blushed. "Well—"

So, she did have feelings and designs, after all. She had been playing coy. "Forgive me. I was being too personal."

"No, it's fine."

"How's the wine? Is it to your liking?"

"It's excellent."

"I have an extensive cellar. I'll give you a tour, if you're interested."

As soft snowflakes whirled down, Colleen giggled and scooted closer to Tommy on the seat of the wagon. She'd borrowed a rig and come to the farm to get him and now they were headed to the Triple H for the Christmas gala. All Tommy felt was empty and vaguely surprised at how little reaction he was having to Colleen as she pressed her breasts against his arm.

"I'm so glad it's snowing," she said, sighing happily.

He already felt tired from having to make pointless conversation.

"Everyone's going to be there tonight," she chattered on. "There's two different parties going on. One for the *la-te-da* people in town and one for us regular folks."

He frowned, not having been told this. That meant Em would be at the la-te-da party. Would he even see her?

"Do you dance, Tommy?"

"No."

"Maybe I could teach you."

"I don't dance."

"I don't mind," she said as she laid her head against his shoulder. "I'm just happy we're together."

He barely stopped himself from cringing.

It was more than an hour later before Colleen consented to dance with another man and Tommy was able to duck out of the showroom. She was a sweet girl, but it was a cloying kind of sweet that stuck in his throat. She was like creeping ivy that crawled around a tree and choked it to death. And he'd only been with her for a few hours. What he wished was that he was home with Em, sitting in the parlor, each of them working on something and talking. Or not. He missed that.

Tommy walked around the back of Howerton's sprawling home and looked into the gloriously lit ballroom from the cold, black night. Right away, he saw Em and Howerton dancing. She looked like royalty, especially in the arms of Howerton. Tommy hated Howerton's proprietary stance as he swept Em around the floor. He hated that Howerton's hand was on her back. He hated that everyone was seeing them together and commenting on what a perfect couple they made. The sight of them made him miserable, so why couldn't he just stop watching and go?

"I see the little wife's taken up with the man." Mitchell spoke up from behind him. "Although that little bitch in heat you came with looks mighty fine, too. Can't say I'd mind sampling some of that." He smacked his lips.

As Blue chuckled, Tommy turned and faced his brother. "You really are as low as they come," he said evenly.

"Yeah? So what? All us Medlins are trash," Mitchell shot back at him. "Always have been, always will be."

"Not all of us."

Mitchell snorted. "You think you're something because you got on at that farm? Hell, brother, she needed your money and she took it. She doesn't think nothin' of you, 'cept you're trash. Miss Ain't-I-better'n-everybody-else thinks you're wrong in the head. And you are! Wright and Wrong, that's what everyone calls the two of you."

Tommy walked away.

"Truth hurts, don't it?" Mitchell called. "Yeah, there she is rubbing up against the boss man. You think she's givin' you two thoughts?"

Tommy never stopped walking, but he heard every word. Not only did he hear, but the truth sank like a weight to the pit of his stomach and made it ache.

The brightness of the showroom took a few moments to adjust to. "There you are," Colleen exclaimed, rushing up to him. "I was looking all over." She took hold of his hand with both of hers, and it took every bit of restraint he had not to shake her off. "Let's go get some more hot mulled wine," she said cheerfully.

"I hope you don't mind," Howerton said to Em as he led the way to the showroom. "But I have to make an appearance."

"Of course I don't mind," Em assured him.

"I'd like for you to see the place, anyway. Was Tommy able to make it tonight?"

She was thrown by the question. Had she been expected to invite him? Her cheeks suddenly burned. "No."

"Really? He'd seemed enthusiastic when I invited him."

Em felt tingly and strange. "Oh. Maybe he is," she said weakly.

"Don't worry," he said with a smile. "I have no idea what my employees are up to either."

The words, or perhaps his tone of superiority, set her teeth on edge. "Tommy's not an employee," she stated.

"Oh?"

"He's my partner."

He glanced at her. "Really?"

"Yes. A full business partner. Everything that's been done that you've been impressed with, that's his doing."

"I see."

They'd reached the showroom and Howerton opened the door for her. It was a large, wide space and crowded and, while it lacked the elegance of the ballroom, it was filled with animated people having a wonderful time. Upbeat music came from accordions, fiddles and banjos, and the dancing was exuberant. More than a few of the ladies looked her up and down with an envious scowl, which made her uncomfortable and self-conscious. "If they knew you," Gregory Howerton confided in a confidential tone, "they'd be less hostile. But we're of different worlds and they know it."

The words barely registered since her gaze had fallen upon Tommy across the room. She watched breathlessly as he bowed his head to listen to Colleen. Of course! He was here with Colleen. He nodded and then, as if her will, or perhaps her shock, had drawn his attention, he looked up and directly into her eyes.

"Are you too warm?" Howerton asked with an edge to his voice. "You seem flushed."

She realized he'd seen her reaction to Tommy and was angry about it. "Yes, a bit," she replied. "If you don't mind, I'll get some air."

His eyes were suddenly full of disdain, a look she'd seen many times before. "If you're feeling ill," he said slowly, "I can have someone take you home."

Em lifted her chin. "How considerate. I'd appreciate that."

He took hold of her elbow with a tighter than necessary grip and escorted her out. Without speaking, they moved toward the line of waiting carriages. He instructed the lead driver to take her home and then opened the carriage door for her. "I saw that back there," he said in a low enough voice that the driver wouldn't overhear. "It makes me wonder if that sordid speculation about the Lindley men isn't, in fact, true."

The scorn in his voice was stinging. It made her furious with herself that she could still be so affected after the countless doses she'd endured over the years. "I won't even dignify that with a response," she replied in a tremulous voice. She ignored his outstretched hand and climbed into the carriage unassisted. "Good night," she said coolly, staring straight ahead.

He slammed the door without another word and the carriage started off. When they were on the road, Em tugged off a glove and bit on her finger in an effort to hold back the tears. She would maintain some composure until she was home and alone.

"Tommy!" Colleen called.

"I'll be back," he said curtly without breaking stride.

His chest felt heavy because Em had seen him and she'd looked upset. Then Howerton had taken hold of her and practically forced her out of the place. Was she upset because he was with Colleen? He followed after them, but people got in his way and slowed his progress. When he made it outside, he didn't see them, so he went around back to peer inside the ballroom.

"What are you doing, Tommy?" Colleen wailed as she chased after him.

"Nothing. I saw someone."

"Yes! Emeline Wright," Colleen interrupted. "I saw her, too. Everyone saw her! But you're here with me, Tommy. You don't just run off to see another woman when you're with someone!"

"She looked upset."

"Come on, Tommy," Colleen urged, pulling on his hand. "She's with Mr. Howerton. What would she have to be upset about? Let's go back inside."

Tommy caught a glimpse of Howerton as he lifted his glass in a toast. A lot of glasses were lifted into the air, Em's probably among them. He took a side step and then allowed Colleen to lead him back to the showroom.

Chapter Twenty-Six

"Happy Christmas Eve, ya'll," Doll called as she walked into the mess hall with a platter of freshly baked biscuits filled with ham. It was a holiday and, as such, breakfast was being served late and supper would be served early.

A round of returned greetings were spoken all at once.

"I'm assuming everyone is here for supper?" she boomed, holding up a hand.

Enthusiastic affirmatives were spoken again and all at once.

"Fine, fine. It's being served at five. I'll set some food out to snack on during the day and you can pick on the leftovers tonight if you've any room left. Now, you're not working, so you can all help. Wood—"

"Present!"

The men all laughed. Even Tommy smiled, and he was a wreck. He hadn't been able to think about anything other than Em since he'd seen her last night.

"You dole out chores, but there's potatoes to be peeled, beans to be snapped, pecans to be shelled, butter to be churned and it's likely I'll think of more as I go."

"We're at your service, general."

She grinned. "Ya'll can start after breakfast. And you

boys wash your own dishes today," she said as she started from the room.

"Yes, ma'am," more than one man replied.

"You making a pecan pie, Doll?"

"You just wait and see," Doll called over her shoulder.

Tommy considered following her and asking about Em, but he didn't want to draw attention to either of them. He'd just wait and bide his time. Surely, he'd see her soon.

"What's next?" Em asked that afternoon as she dried her hands on the towel.

"Did you put all two dozen eggs in?" Doll asked.

"Yes. And the milk and the cream and the sugar."

"Add that quart of brandy," Doll said as she slid mince pies in the oven. "Let's see, that's mince in here, pumpkin out there and now I'll start on apple."

Em poured the brandy and smiled to herself. Doll really did rule the kitchens like a general and she thanked God for it. "What next?"

"Rum. Pour about half that bottle in. About a pint." Doll placed her hands on her well-padded hips and studied Em. "Emmy, you alright?"

"You already asked me that."

"I know I did. Twice."

"More like five times. And, yes, I'm fine. I promise. I am very, very happy to be here."

"Well, where else would you be, silly? Add that whiskey next."

"I'm getting drunk just smelling this."

Doll chuckled. "Wait till you have some."

There wasn't an inch of space that wasn't covered with food preparations. "You do realize you're making enough food for an army."

"Well, honey, we got men with appetites to feed. Plus

Emmett and my sister, Wayne and Fiona, if she's up to it. Sweetie, taste these maple-sugar coated pecans and tell me what you think."

"Am I finished with the eggnog yet?"

"Yeah, that should be good. Stir it and stick it outside to get good and cold and you can start on the custard."

Tommy paced the floor in the bunkhouse. He'd gone all day without seeing Em and he couldn't stand it any longer. He had to see her and it needed to be before everyone was in the same room at the same time. He put on his coat and walked over to the house, hunched against the cold wind and blowing snow. There were three or four inches on the ground, at least, and it was coming down hard. He knocked briefly and then stepped into an empty kitchen. "Hello?" he called.

"Coming," Em called back.

He quickly shrugged off his coat and hung it up, then walked into the sitting room to see her coming down the stairs, looking relaxed and as pretty as ever. He heaved a silent sigh of relief that she seemed alright. "It smells as good in here as it does over there," he said.

"I know. She's got food cooking everywhere." Em stopped in front of him and her gaze dropped to the small wrapped gift in his hand.

"It's for you," he said, holding it out. "I thought you might want it for tonight."

She took the box with a smile. "Thank you."

She started toward the parlor, and he followed. "I wanted to give it to you when nobody else was around." She sat on the settee and he sat next to her, anxious for her to see what he'd bought. "Open it."

With an excited smile, she unwrapped the package to see a long, narrow bright green velvet box. She glanced up at him, surprised, and then opened it to find a strand of pearls.

Her smile vanished and her eyes filled with tears, which was an even better reaction than he'd imagined. "Oh, Tommy! You shouldn't have—"

His smile faded. He shouldn't have?

"You shouldn't have spent so much on me," she said, shaking her head. "But I *love* it. It's the nicest gift I've ever gotten."

His heart soared. "Better than Barbara Jean?" he teased.

She thought about it and then laughed. "I can't actually remember getting her."

"I saw those and they reminded me of you. Pretty, but not flashy. I didn't like the flashy ones. These had a light of their own."

The words so touched her, she couldn't speak for a moment. "Thank you," she managed in a thick voice.

"You're welcome."

She bit on her lower lip as she put the necklace back in the box. "I'm afraid the gifts I have for you are nowhere as special."

"Any present is special. Especially from you."

She got up and went to the pile of gifts on a table and selected one, then walked back and handed it to him. "This is the first. There is another."

He unwrapped a soft bundle and found a deep blue, hand-knit sweater and scarf inside. He looked up at her. "Did you make these?"

She nodded and sat again, smiling happily. "I had to when I saw the yarn. It's the color of your eyes."

"No one's ever made me something before. I'll wear it tonight."

"And I'll wear these," Em whispered, not having full control of her voice at the moment.

"Hey," he said tenderly. "Why are you crying?"

She shook her head. "I guess it's because I'm so happy to be here," she said, dabbing the corners of her eyes. "And I'm happy you're here. In a way, I feel like a little girl who doesn't want anything in her life to change."

"You didn't know I'd be there last night," he said gently. "And I'm sorry for that. I should have told you."

She shook her head. "I just . . . I shouldn't have gone. I misunderstood the invitation and then I felt stuck."

"I shouldn't have gone, either. Believe me."

She looked at him searchingly. "Really?"

He nodded. "I don't want things to change, either. I've never been as happy as I am here. I never even knew it was possible." She stretched her hand toward him and he took hold of it. Without thought to the consequences, he brought it to his lips and kissed it.

She drew breath to say something, but a rush of cold air blew in at them as the door was opened. Tommy released her hand reluctantly, disappointed that the moment had ended.

"Lord have mercy, ya'll," Doll exclaimed. "It's snowing like the heavens have broke wide open. I hope everyone makes it here. If they do, we'll have to put 'em up for the night. Not that I mind. It'll make for a nice Christmas. Now why don't you two bundle up and help carry some stuff over? Emmy, get the eggnog."

Em and Tommy exchanged conspiratorial smiles. "Yes, ma'am," Em replied.

Doll blew right back out again, carrying the last bundle of pies.

Tommy and Em stood. "Can I put that on for you?" Tommy asked, looking at the pearls.

"Please." She handed the necklace to him and turned around.

He opened the strand and put it around her neck, then leaned closer to fasten the clasp. Being that close to her warmth and her scent stirred his blood and he fantasized about kissing the back of her neck. He managed the clasp and then placed his hands on her shoulders, wanting desperately to turn her around and kiss her. Unfortunately, they heard the kitchen door open again.

Em turned to him, and pressed a kiss to his cheek. "Thank you," she said as she lovingly touched the pearls.

His gaze caressed her beautiful, flushed face and then he pressed a kiss to her cheek.

"Hello, you two," Emmett greeted as he stepped into the room. "It's blowing up a blizzard out there."

Em looked at him with excitement burning in her golden brown eyes. "Is it too bad for a brief ride?"

"I left the sleigh right out front, pointed in the right direction if you're tough enough to brave the snow. You might have to cuddle under the blanket a little bit."

Tommy looked from one to the other of them, wondering what they were talking about.

"You have one more present," Em reminded him. "You want to go see?"

Tommy reached for his new scarf, which he wrapped around his neck. "I can handle the snow if you can." Em laughingly hurried to get her coat, full of delight, and he followed. "You're not going to tell me what it is?" he asked as he put his coat back on.

"Not a chance."

Tommy maneuvered the sleigh easily. He'd never driven one before, but it wasn't hard and the ride was thrilling, especially with the strangely light sky above and the cover of snow from the ground giving a surreal glow to the world. When they were approaching the road, he asked how much farther they were going. Not that he cared. The night was glorious and he was with Em. He would have happily gone on forever.

"Not far. Just . . . there!" she said, pointing with a gloved finger. "Stop!"

He stopped the sleigh and stared at a carved, wooden sign propped against the fence. He had to squint to make out the lettering.

WELCOME TO THE MARTIN-MEDLIN FARM.

He was shocked. The sight of it, the significance of it, stole his breath and rendered him speechless.

"We wouldn't be here without you," Em said, leaning in and hugging his arm. "Ben would be really proud of the place and the work we've done. In fact, I just know he is."

Tommy looked away from her and swiped at his nose and eyes with his gloved hand. He nodded, unable to speak.

"It's really pretty in the light," she added. "We'll have to come see it tomorrow."

Tommy nodded again, knowing he would be there at first light.

Chapter Twenty-Seven

January 8, 1882

Howerton cocked his head as he watched a group of men working their way through the saloon with enough style and authority to draw attention to themselves.

"Who the hell's that?" James asked no one in particular.

"Go find out," Howerton returned.

James looked from Howerton to Quin, uncertain whether the boss was kidding or not. Neither was smiling, so he got to his feet, picked up his drink and sauntered to the bar.

Howerton leaned back in his chair and watched James strike up a conversation with the strangers. One of them pulled out a photograph and James looked at it. Immediately, James looked over at him, alarmed. Howerton's eyes narrowed as he pondered whom they might be looking for. His view of the dialog was suddenly obstructed by one of the whores who was pulling a man's arm as he laughingly resisted. "Move," Howerton barked. They did, but by that time, James was already headed back to the table.

"They're looking for Miss Wright," James whispered urgently when he sat back down. "I didn't tell them nothin' 'cause I didn't know if you'd want me to."

Howerton picked up his glass, noticing the strangers were all focused directly on him. "They know you lied, you idiot. You can't lie worth a damn." He downed his drink and set it down hard. "Pour me another."

The leader of the group made a beeline for their table. "I wonder if you can help me," he said to Howerton. "I'm looking for a friend," he said, offering a photograph. "Maybe you know her."

Howerton took the photograph in hand. It was of Emeline Wright, dressed in an elegant gown of very recent fashion. He looked up at the man. "Why are you looking for her?"

"I think I mentioned . . . she's a friend."

Howerton handed the photograph back. "Who forgot to tell you where she was?"

The man smiled, but no warmth touched his eyes. "I'm close, aren't I?"

"I wouldn't know. I've never seen her before."

It was the man's way of ending the conversation, of course. Sonny recognized the tone, having used it hundreds of times himself. "Well, thank you for your time." He tipped his hat and walked back to the bar, looking around as he went. Surely someone would be interested in exchanging a little information for coin. It just had to be handled discreetly. Already he sensed an order not to speak with them going around. As if that would stop him.

"Yeah, I know who she is," Mitchell confirmed a few hours later. "So what?"

Sonny held up a twenty-dollar piece. It was late, almost everyone was gone, and the few who were left were drunk. He had no time or energy left to waste on nonsense. "Then what's her name?"

"Emeline Wright," Mitchell replied. He was practically salivating at the sight of the gold piece. "Whatcha want her for?"

"That's none of your concern." Sonny's expression, which had turned victorious only a moment before, now grew chilly. He withdrew the money.

"Okay, okay," Mitchell said. "Never mind. I can take you to her. She's with my brother, matter of fact. I mean, he works for her."

"Where?"

"On her farm. It was her uncle's place, but he died not too long ago."

A farm? Sonny couldn't picture it. "Are you sure?"

"Damn sure."

"Because you get the money after I get possession."

Mitchell frowned. "How do I know I'll get it then?"

Sonny pocketed the money. "You'll get it. Now, tell me what you know."

Chapter Twenty-Eight

Doll looked up from the list she was making as someone knocked on the front door. She rose from the kitchen table and went to get it. She opened the door to a man in his twenties with blue-gray eyes and a scraggly beard, hat in hand.

"Morning, ma'am," he said. "Is Miss Wright here?"

"She's here," Doll replied. "She lives here. Who are you?"

"Can I speak with her?"

Doll sensed rather than heard Em behind her, but when she turned, the expression on Em's face troubled her to the extent that she looked back to the stranger with an accusing glare.

"It's alright," Em assured Doll as she moved to the door. "This is Tommy's brother."

Doll huffed in disbelief. "My left foot," she muttered under her breath.

"We'll talk outside," Em said to Mitchell. She stepped out and shut the door behind her, giving Doll a look.

"What do you want?" Em asked as she crossed her arms.

"I come to apologize. To you and my brother. I'm real

sorry about what happened. I've had a lot of time to think about it, and I want to make it up to both of you."

"I want nothing to do with you, but you should talk to Tommy."

"Yeah, I want to. Where's he at?"

"They're building a barn. That way." Em pointed.

He shifted on his feet. "Truth is, I don't have a lot of time today. Maybe I'll come out tomorrow or the next day."

"He's leaving in the morning. They all are. Going after cattle and they'll be gone a few days. If you want to talk to him, you should do it today."

Mitchell nodded. "I will, then. Thank you, ma'am. And, like I said, I'm awful sorry about before. I wish I could take it back." He put his hat on, tipped it to her, and walked in the direction she'd pointed.

Em watched him go, baffled by how little similarity there was between him and Tommy. She heard a wagon approach and turned to see Wayne Jones approaching. She waved at him and ducked inside to tell Doll he was here.

Sonny lowered his binoculars, having seen Em through them. Apparently, farm life agreed with her because she looked more beautiful than ever. Mitchell Medlin was headed back to report with an irritating, shit-eating grin on his face. The man was pure scum. "Well?" Sonny demanded, when he got close.

"You'll want to get her tomorrow," Mitchell said.

"Why is that?"

"'Cause all the men, including my brother, are going to be gone. They're leaving for a few days."

"What time?"

"First thing in the morning."

"Good."

"I'll take my money now," Mitchell said.

"You can take half now and half after I've collected her."

"Hey, now, I got work, Mr. Peterson. I cain't be sneaking off—"

"Half now, half tomorrow. The rest is your problem."

Tommy had made a wide circle around the man he'd spotted spying on the house, and now he silently closed in on him. He'd been up at the tobacco barn when he'd spotted the man as he lay in wait.

A hunter who had, on occasion, been hunted, Briar Lindley heard him approach and sprang up with his gun drawn. The man before him was unarmed, so he slowly lowered his. "Shouldn't sneak up on a man," he warned.

"You shouldn't be here," Tommy returned.

"Just who the hell are you?"

"Tommy Medlin."

"Oh, of the Martin-*Medlin* Farm?" Briar mocked.

"That's right. And you're Briar Lindley."

"Yeah. That's right, too. Ain't that nice? We know each other."

"I know what happened before and it's not going to happen again."

Briar considered him. "I don't think you're married to her or nothin'. You're sleeping in that fancy new longhouse down there. So, what the hell is it to you what I do?"

"I'm her friend."

Briar smiled broadly. "Her *friend*? Ain't that sweet."

"You try to get near her again, I'll kill you," Tommy said evenly.

Briar grinned and then holstered his gun. "You'll kill me? *You'll* kill *me*? Mister, the only reason you're still breathing, is 'cause you ain't slick. You know what I mean? I hate a slick son of a bitch. Now, you're misguided, but you ain't slick."

"Stay away from her," Tommy warned again.

Briar's smile dimmed. "I *have* stayed away from her!"

"What are you watching her for?"

"That's my business. So, how you think you're gonna kill me?" Briar challenged.

"I don't know."

The man's honesty and lack of bravado impressed Briar against his will. "What? You protect her? Is that your job?"

"That's right."

"You love her?" Tommy didn't answer, but Briar saw a moment of uncensored pain in the blue eyes. "Yeah, you love her." He reached for the telescope and then studied Tommy a moment more. "Be careful, Tom Medlin. She creeps under your skin and you can't shake her. Not for nothin'." He walked forward with a slight limp, but stopped when they were shoulder-to-shoulder to make a point. "My pa forbade me to go near her again, so I won't. Has nothing to do with what you say." He waited until he got a nod, confirming that Tom Medlin had understood, then he walked on.

At supper, Em noticed how preoccupied Tommy was and assumed it was due to the impending cattle drive and possibly the visit from his brother. She wanted to know how the meeting had gone, but resisted asking. After all, when he wanted to, he'd tell her about it. She was the first to leave the chow hall after supper. No one else seemed inclined to break up the revelry. Midway back to the house, Tommy caught up to her, although they didn't stop walking. It was too cold to stand still, especially with the wind blowing.

"We're going in the morning," he reminded her.

Since the drive to get twenty-five head of cattle for use

on the farm was practically all that had been discussed for days, she nearly laughed. "Oh, you are?" she teased instead. "Tomorrow, you say?"

"It's only a couple days' ride there, but the drive will take longer getting back," he replied, ignoring her attempt at humor.

"I promise not to forget any of the chores or the animals."

"It's not that."

They walked up the steps and he opened the door for her. It was a relief to step into the warmth of the house. "Everything will be fine here," she assured him after he'd shut it. The only light came from the woodstove in the kitchen, the fire in the parlor and a single gas lamp on the wall. "When you get back, all the buildings will be standing, and all living things will still be . . . alive. Don't worry."

He pulled off his hat, clearly bothered by something. "I want you to be careful," he said solemnly.

Her smirk vanished, because he was sincerely concerned. "I will."

"Keep a gun near you."

She cocked her head, wondering why he'd worked himself into such a state. It had to have been the visit from Mitchell. "I will. I'll be fine."

He shifted on his feet. "I wish you could come with us."

She felt a rush of warmth and affection that made her chest constrict. "Me, too." She smiled and shrugged. "Next time."

He nodded, but seemed reluctant to go.

"You be careful, too," she said, reaching out and lightly touching his chest with both hands. It was a momentary touch through her gloves and his coat, but it still felt personal.

"I will," he pledged. He put his hat back on. "I'd best let you get to bed."

"You, too," she said, equally reluctant to let him go. "You'll be getting an early start."

"Keep the gun close," he said again.

This was definitely about Mitchell. Even though he'd come to make amends, Tommy hadn't fully bought it. "Is there . . . anything you want to talk about?" she asked. "Because you can."

"I know."

Apparently, he was not ready to discuss it and she was not going to push. "Anytime you have anything to talk about—"

"I know," he repeated. He leaned in and kissed her cheek. "You just take care of yourself. We'll be back as quick as we can get back." He reached for the doorknob. "'Night."

"Good night," she returned wistfully, wishing she had the courage to pull him back and keep him there. But he was already shutting the door behind him. For several seconds, she couldn't move. She just stared at the door, wishing it would reopen.

"Honey? Emmy?" Doll said, waking Em from a heavy sleep.

Em turned over and pulled herself upright. Doll was holding a candle and wearing a coat. "What's wrong?" Em asked in a husky voice.

"Wayne's come to fetch me. Fiona's having the baby."

"Oh!"

"She seems to think she can't do it without me."

"Go," Em exclaimed. "Of course. She needs you."

"I'll be back maybe tomorrow, maybe the next day. Or I'll send word."

Em nodded. "We'll be fine here. Just take care of Fiona."

"Alright, honey. Go back to sleep."

Doll turned and headed from the room, the light of the candle illuminating her way. Darkness was left in her wake, especially as the older woman descended the stairs and crossed to the kitchen. Em watched and then listened to the front door open and close and then she listened to the quiet. She lay back down and tugged the covers more snugly around her, but sleep eluded her.

Chapter Twenty-Nine

By the time Em got up and moving the next morning, everyone was gone and the quiet was unnerving. She'd gotten used to having people around. She tried to go about her usual activities, but everything she did seemed louder than usual—the clanking of the skillet, the scrape of a chair. She never would have noticed the sounds had Doll been talking and the men around.

She made a small batch of biscuits and fried a slice of ham, wondering about Tommy's anxiousness the night before. Maybe she should have pushed to learn how the meeting had gone. When he got back, she would. She carried her plate to the table and sat to eat, only to discover she had no appetite. She picked at the food and then decided to leave it and go feed the animals. She'd be hungry later—and activity would ease her mind.

She rose, but the sound of heavy boot steps on the porch made her freeze. She glanced at the gun next to the door, seized by alarm, but the door was thrown open before she'd had a chance to move. Her worst nightmare stood outside. She went rigid with fear, couldn't breathe. The expression on his face was one she remembered well. On the surface, he was calm, but beneath that, he was seething. He was perfectly in control, until such time that he chose to abandon it. Her knees threatened to buckle. It was only her grip on the table in front of her that prevented it.

Somehow, he'd found her.

He stepped inside and shut the door behind him without taking his eyes off her. "I offer a palace and you choose a pigsty."

She let go of the table and took an unsteady step backward.

"A farm," he mused thoughtfully as he came forward. "And an uncle who raised you from the time you were a girl. You never mentioned it." He reached the table and looked at her plate. "You weren't hungry?" he asked conversationally.

She couldn't think for the panic that gripped her. "I have to feed the animals," she said breathlessly.

He pulled off his gloves as he came around the table toward her. He stopped, tossed the gloves on the table and reached for the biscuit on her plate. "You don't need to feed the animals today."

He took a bite and Em glimpsed men outside the window. How many did he have with him?

Sonny tossed the biscuit onto the table. "Thinking of running again?" He began unbuttoning his coat. "You can if you want, but there's a public whipping in it for your trouble. I don't mind if you don't."

A painful shiver traveled the length of her spine and tears sprang to her eyes. "Why? Why go to all this trouble?" she bit out. She was having trouble speaking. Having trouble making her jaw work.

"You didn't leave me a choice," he replied in a reasonable tone. "I didn't get to where I am by allowing anyone to make a fool of me. I believe I explained that to you before. Don't you remember?"

He was going to kill her, she realized. Maybe he'd only hurt her, at first. But she'd gone too far. He was going to kill

her. Her mind raced for ways to fight him. She couldn't get
to the gun, but what about a knife? Or the candlestick. The
heavy pewter candlestick on the table. If she could grab hold
of it, she'd hit him and then run out the back. If she could
make it into the woods, she might have a chance. She knew
the woods. She knew hiding places.

Sonny slipped off his coat and set it on the kitchen chair.
"As you can probably imagine, I'm curious as to how you
managed it."

She took a step away from him, and yet the candlestick
had to stay within reach. "Do you want to sit down?" she
asked, stammering slightly. The expression on his face turned
so menacing that she quickly added, "W-while I tell you?"

He flexed his hands, and she felt herself shaking. "I . . . I
slipped something in the door to stop the lock from catching."

He nodded. "My knife. It was a clever move. And then?"

"I went out the side door."

"Wearing what?"

He was pressing closer, sucking up all the air around him.
She couldn't keep herself from edging away from him,
around the table. "My robe. I had something stashed in the
basement."

His eyes narrowed. "So you'd been planning for some
time."

She nodded stiffly. There was no point in denying it.

"Who helped you?" he demanded coldly.

She shook her head. "No one."

"Where did you go?"

"I just . . . I ran and then I took a horse. I just ran."

He grabbed hold of her throat so quickly, she didn't even
see it coming. Instinctively, she wrapped both hands around
his wrist. "I don't think you'll run again," he swore as his
fingers tightened.

He was going to kill her. He'd come all this way to kill
her. She reached behind herself with one hand, desperately

feeling for the candlestick, but black dots were already dancing before her eyes. She touched cold metal, but she couldn't close her fist on it.

He released her abruptly, a disgusted look on his face. "You're crazy if you think I'm going to make it that easy on you."

She grabbed hold of the candlestick and swung with all her might. It made a sound *clunk* as it made contact with the side of his head. Blood gushed from the wound, his face went stark white and his eyes lost focus, but he remained on his feet. Then he dropped onto his knees before crumpling in a heap.

She let out a shuddering breath as the candlestick slipped from her grasp. She whirled around and looked out the window, trying to determine the best course of action. Her instinct was to slip out the back door and run, but if she did, they'd probably see her. They'd catch her and, if Sonny were dead, they'd kill her. If he were alive, *he'd* kill her.

Hide!

She backed into the parlor, keeping her eyes on the front door and window, and then rushed to the back door to open it a little ways. Make them think she'd left. Lifting her skirt, she hurried to the steps and crept up them, knowing where to hide.

In her room, she opened the window and climbed out on the roof. It had a steep pitch, but she'd hidden out here as a child and gotten away with it every single time. She'd managed it then and she would manage it now. The tricky thing was to shut the window behind her, but she did it. Staring up at the cloudy morning sky, she scooted inch by inch toward the chimney. It would be something to brace herself against and it would be warm. In that spot, she couldn't been seen from the ground or the window.

* * *

Sonny opened his eyes and tried to make sense of the table leg in front of him, not to mention the pounding in his head. He groaned as he sat up slowly and looked around. *Em.* She'd clocked him and gotten away. Fury overtook his pain and he pulled himself up and stumbled out to the front porch. The sight of him started a commotion and, within moments, men were mounting excited horses and taking off in different directions to hunt for Em.

Sonny walked back into the house to clean himself up.

"What is it?" Wood asked Tommy as they rode. "What's got you so antsy?"

Tommy reined in his horse and Wood did likewise. "You can handle this by yourself."

"Sure I can, but why?"

Tommy shook his head. "I don't know. It's Em. I've got a bad feeling."

"And you want to go back and check on her?"

Tommy nodded. He'd had a knot in his belly, and it had been tightening for an hour. He couldn't help worrying that Briar Lindley would swoop in and hurt her again, despite the man's claim that he wouldn't. How much of a stretch was it, really? He'd hurt her before, he was spying on her. He was aware of the happenings on the farm enough that he'd figured out sleeping arrangements. He would see she was alone.

"Then go," Wood said. "I can handle it."

Tommy handed over the pack with the money. "Thanks."

The display of trust sent a jolt of gratitude straight to Wood's heart. "We'll be back in a few days," he said gruffly. He spurred his horse on and rode away before any emotion was obvious on his face. The fact was, he'd done eighteen months in prison for theft. He'd been honest about it, too, first with T. Emmett Rice and then with Tommy. He'd faced plenty of rebuffs, rejection and prejudice since his release.

But they'd given him a chance. Then they'd given him authority and a home. They'd helped to restore his pride and now he'd been given the ultimate display of trust. He wouldn't let them down. Not for all the tea in China.

Sonny watched the search.

"Don't see her anywhere, sir," one of the men shouted.

"Search the house again and the grounds. Maybe she didn't go far."

Mitchell Medlin topped a ridge and turned his horse around, frustrated by the mounting conviction that he wasn't going to be paid the rest of what he was owed. He hadn't shown up for work this morning, which meant he had to come up with one hell of a story for Howerton. He'd thought about saying that he was trying to protect Miss Wright because of rumors he'd heard about her getting taken. He could say how he felt guilty for what he'd done before. Howerton would buy that. Of course, the bitch had to go first.

His elevated vantage point offered a great view of the farm—and of Emeline Wright on the roof. A slow smile crept over his face. He drew breath to shout out her whereabouts but, on second thought, he headed down to the farm instead. He'd collect his money first and maybe a nice bonus, too.

Sonny was on the back porch awaiting word when he noticed Mitchell Medlin riding toward him. He tensed, knowing from the man's expression, he was going to report something of value. "Spotted her," Mitchell announced.

"Where?" Sonny barked. He was in no mood for games.

Medlin dismounted. "You still owe me money, Mr. Peterson."

Sonny took some money from his pocket and flung it on the ground. "Where is she?"

Mitchell looked down at the money. It was more than what he was owed. "She's—"

"She's on the roof!" a man yelled from the hill.

Mitchell looked behind him, resentful that someone had said it first. He looked back at Sonny and nodded. "On the roof." He stooped to pick up the money from the ground as quickly as he could.

Sonny gave him a look of disgust and then jerked around and headed inside. "She's on the roof," he bellowed to the man searching the loft. "Get her!"

Em heard the shout, but there was nothing she could do. She saw the men coming for her and fear robbed her of breath. A man stuck his head out the loft window and saw her. "She's here alright," he reported.

She inched away, despite the fact there was nowhere to go. The man was already scrambling out after her and the others were arriving back at the house. She was surrounded.

"Come on, miss," the man called to her. "Before you fall and break your neck."

If only she could somehow drop to the ground *without* breaking anything and get to a horse.

"There's a half dozen men down there," the man reasoned. "Just come on in."

There were several men below and they were watching her and following her every move. Already, one was carrying a ladder from the barn.

"Come on, miss," the man said. He'd crawled close, almost close enough to touch her.

"Please. He'll kill me," she pleaded.

"No, he won't. He came a long way to get you. He only wants to take you back home."

She shook her head and scalding tears ran down her face. *I am home. Tommy!*

"Come on," the man said. "I'll help you."

It was over, she realized. No one could help her.

She was pulled back through the window to face Sonny. He stood, absolutely expressionless, until he raised his arm and backhanded her across the face. The force of the blow sent her reeling sideways against the wall. "Get her up," he demanded.

The man who'd pulled her off the roof, pulled her upright, although he avoided her gaze.

"Wait outside," Sonny ordered.

The man obeyed, and Em listened to his retreating footsteps with dread.

"You stupid bitch," Sonny said as he unbuckled his gunbelt. He pulled it off, removed the holster with his gun still it in and tossed it on the bed. He doubled the belt over and advanced on her. "You just refuse to learn."

Chapter Thirty

Tommy rode in to the farm fast, sensing trouble. There were fresh tracks from multiple horses, which he didn't understand. It wasn't Briar Lindley who'd been there; this was something else. "Em," he yelled as he dismounted. His hand closed over his pistol as he hurried to the house. He pushed open the unlatched front door and saw the blood on the floor. A chair was overturned and various items were in disarray. In the parlor, there were more drops of blood. "Em," he called again, although he knew in his gut she wasn't there.

He glanced in Doll's room, which looked untouched, and then bolted up to the loft. The scuffle had continued up here, or had it started here? There was blood on the wall and drops on the floor. The bed was made, but the covers had been mussed. His eyes narrowed to see the smears of blood on the bedspread. He'd almost missed them because of the color and pattern of the spread. The window was open and he moved to it and looked out, hoping to see something that would explain what had happened here. All he could tell was that the tracks led to the road.

Moving fast, he got back to his horse and followed the tracks until one set veered off toward the Triple H. The majority had gone straight down the road, but one had gone this way.

* * *

The riders came to a fork in the road and stopped. "I think it's this way to the station," one of the men said, jerking his thumb to indicate the road heading northeast.

"Which way?" Sonny demanded of Em, who was riding on his horse in front of him.

Em pointed, confirming the man's suggestion.

"Ya!" Sonny yelled, spurring his horse toward the opposite road.

Em felt a sharp thrill, but then she realized what a small and insignificant victory it was since both roads eventually led to town. This path simply took longer. She'd known he wouldn't trust her word.

"When I get you back to Richmond—" Sonny said, under his breath.

He didn't have to finish the statement. She knew. He would beat her again and again. He would burn his brand onto her. He would break her. He had nearly succeeded before; he would not settle for coming close again. She couldn't let it happen. Once they were in town, she had to make a scene, no matter what he did to her. She could not allow herself to be dragged onto the train. Once that happened, it was over. If he got her back to Richmond, she would be trapped for life—however long a life he allowed her.

Tommy rode alongside Howerton and ahead of a quickly amassed posse. He'd ridden onto the Triple H and barged into the house without even thinking about what he was doing. He'd found Howerton and blurted the story.

Howerton's eyes narrowed as he listened. "Mitchell," he'd said to Quin. "Get him! And lock him the hell up until we get back." He waved Tommy onward and followed close behind. "He claimed he was looking out for her, because he'd heard Peterson and the others were closing in."

"Who?" Tommy demanded, frowning darkly as they stepped back out to the porch.

"A man named Sonny Peterson and his men. I made it my business to find out who Peterson was after he started asking about her in town."

Tommy battled a wave of fury. "When was this?"

"A few nights ago. You know anything about him?"

"No."

"He owns a big hotel in Richmond. The Virginia Palace. Emeline was with him before she came back home. Apparently, she left without telling him and he's been searching for her ever since."

Richmond. That meant, "The train," Tommy exclaimed. He mounted his horse and rode out. Behind him, Howerton shouted for men to arm themselves and follow them on the double.

As they cantered through town, Sonny's grip tightened around Em, all but cutting off her air supply. He pressed his lips to her ear. "Make a scene and I will cut you," he swore, popping open a vicious-looking switchblade with a serrated edge so that she could see it. "I can stick you so it takes days to die. It's a waste, but I will have made my point. You get me? You had better not give me any more problems."

Always before, she'd felt excitement and relief when the train station came into view; now she experienced cold terror. The train was waiting and it represented a one-way passage to hell, and there was absolutely nothing she could do about it. When they stopped, she was pulled from Sonny's horse and surrounded by the pack of men. In no time, Sonny had one hand around her waist, and the other around her arm as she was hustled forward. They moved directly onto the train and she couldn't stop it, although she couldn't help balking, knowing that she was being marched to her execution.

"Move," Sonny hissed.

Tommy jumped off his horse and forced his way onto the train, pushing past the agitated conductor despite the man's shouted objections that the train was about to leave the station. Howerton was right behind him and he would deal with the man.

"What the hell?" one of the male passengers demanded as he stood.

"That's one of his men," Quin said from directly behind Tommy.

Tommy saw the man reach for his gun, but he drew his faster.

"Keep them in their holsters, gentlemen," Howerton called out as he closed in from the other direction. "And you might just live through today."

Sonny's men didn't need to count to see they were outnumbered. Still, it was close quarters. Numbers didn't count for all that much when you had talent with a gun. The train jolted.

"If you don't have a ticket, you'll have to get off," the conductor cried yet again.

Quin picked one of Sonny's men up by his shirt collar. He'd seen him in the saloon with Peterson. "Where are they?"

The man spat out a curse.

Quin drove the man's head into the window, breaking the glass. "You were saying?"

Tommy pushed on.

"Let's go," Howerton said as Tommy moved past him. "They'll be in a private compartment. Let's start trying them."

"Would you care to sit?" Sonny asked in a dead-sounding voice.

Em felt as if she were heavily weighted. She'd been forced into a compartment with Sonny, and the train was preparing to leave. She started to sit, but he backhanded her before she knew what was happening. She hit the floor and tasted blood again.

"Or perhaps you'd rather lie down," he said.

She tried to twist into a protective ball, but he brought his foot straight down on her buttocks. Then, he reached down and yanked her up to face him. She knew her face was bleeding, because she saw the blood that spattered on his white shirt. Taking hold of her arms, he shook her with all his might and when his energy was spent, he tossed her backward onto the seat. He stood, considering her, and then reached for his handkerchief, which he tossed at her. "Wipe your face. It offends me."

He walked to the door in two long, purposeful strides, yanked it open and called to the conductor at the end of the row. "I want water. To wash with. And salt."

"Salt, sir?"

"You heard me. Why aren't we moving?"

"There was a small problem, sir," the man reported nervously, "but we'll be on our way presently."

Howerton pushed open the door to the last car in time to see Peterson demanding to know why they weren't moving. Quickly, Howerton turned back to Tommy, who was looking in the compartments of that car. "It's him," he said with quiet urgency.

Tommy looked just as Sonny withdrew into his compartment.

Em shrunk into the backmost corner of the seat as Sonny came toward her.

"Let's discuss what I should do with you," he said. "I really do want your opinion."

Tears blurred her vision as he popped the blade out and twisted the knife back and forth, as if he was inspecting the lethalness of the blade.

"I need you to see things from my perspective," he said.

She crossed her arms in front of herself.

"I'm not going to kill you," he said reassuringly. "Then I'd have your body to get off the train. No. You won't cause me that kind of trouble again. What I am going to do is to carve—"

There was an urgent rap on the door that silenced him.

Sonny glanced at it, then considered Em again. "The water is for you to clean the blood off your face and out of your hair. Because you will look presentable when we exit this train. Now, the salt. That's a different matter. That's part of your punishment."

He turned and started for the door, and Em experienced a heady rush of relief, which was immediately tempered by the realization that the reprieve was merely momentary. Dizziness descended fast and hard as she puzzled over when and where she had experienced that very thought before. Oh, yes. *At the Palace.* The night she'd gotten away from him. Or thought she had. The switchblade was still in his hand, although he held it behind him as he opened the door. She thought about charging him, but she no longer had the strength. He'd won. He'd already won.

"Back up," a voice ordered.

Tommy. It was Tommy's voice. "He has a knife," she cried.

In a surreal moment, Sonny charged, but Tommy fired. Sonny lurched backward and fell, having been shot in the throat. Blood poured from the wound and his body jerked in death spasms. Then it went still. Too quickly. It was a trick. It was all a trick. Em stared, knowing she'd been cast into a dark dream world, a nightmare world, where everything was moving slowly, jerkily, wrongly and Sonny was about to get up and come at her again.

Tommy had stepped in the door and he was looking at her. Howerton pushed in behind him. "It was self-defense," Howerton said urgently. "He pulled a knife on you." Howerton noticed her and cringed. "Aw, shit," he said under his breath. He clapped Tommy's arm, murmuring that he'd get the conductor and left again.

Tommy holstered his gun and started toward her. Using her arms to help pull herself up, she managed to stand just before he reached her. He drew her into his arms and held her tightly. It meant she was safe. She was finally safe. "I'm sorry," she whispered. "I'm . . . suh . . . sorry. I—"

"I've got you now," Tommy said as he stroked her hair. "You're safe."

She stared at Sonny's body, in case it was a trick. But he wasn't moving. "Sorry," she whispered again.

"*Shh,*" he said as he rubbed her back in a gentle circle. "Just breathe. Listen to me, now. Just breathe."

"I'm sorry," she whispered. She didn't mean to keep saying it, but she couldn't stop.

"It's my fault. I shouldn't have left."

She shook her head and began to cry because he was the one man in the world who wasn't at fault.

"Tommy," Howerton said from the door.

Reluctantly, Tommy shifted to glance at the stricken-looking conductor standing there. He nodded and then pulled back to gaze at Em, holding on to her arms. "I've got to talk to this man now. We'll get through this and I'll take you home. Alright?"

She tried to nod although her neck felt too stiff.

"I won't let you out of my sight," he added.

She tried to nod again. Why couldn't she move right? Maybe because she was so cold. Her body was stiff with it. He put his arms around her and led her from the car, trying to shield her from the carnage, although she needed to see it. She needed confirmation that Sonny was dead. He pulled her even closer as they stepped down from the train, and then they made their way into the office of the stationmaster. She was led to a chair and Tommy pulled one right next to it. She watched him, every second, because the only time she was safe was when he was near.

Howerton was suddenly there with a blanket. He wrapped it around her, despite the fact she was in a coat. But it was cold in the office; it was freezing. She couldn't stop shaking.

The stationmaster was talking, asking questions—and Tommy was answering, while looking at her every few seconds. The stationmaster asked more questions, his agitation increasing. "You'll have to talk to the marshal," he said more than once.

"That's fine," Tommy replied, "but I've got to get her home now."

"Why don't you send the marshal to me first?" Howerton suggested from the doorway. "I saw the whole thing."

The stationmaster knew who Howerton was. He pursed his lips and nodded. "You can all go for now."

* * *

"We should go see the doctor," Tommy said to Em as they left the train station. He still had his arm around her, and hers were around him as well. She was clinging tightly, but she was still shaking.

"You can't," Howerton said from alongside them. The rest of the men were waiting ahead. "He's out on a call. I sent someone for him, but they don't know when he'll be back."

Tommy stopped, wondering what to do. She needed to see a doctor. "We could go to Emmett's," he suggested.

"I want to go home," she said pleadingly. "Please. I just want to go home."

He glanced at Howerton, who gave a discreet shrug.

"Alright," Tommy said to Em, who sighed in relief. He looked at Howerton. "Thank you."

Greg Howerton nodded.

Tommy led her to his horse. "Shall I lift you up?"

She nodded her head.

He let go of her and she took a minute to prepare herself.

"I can go get a wagon," he offered.

She sucked in a breath and put her foot in the stirrup. He lifted his hands to catch her or support her if needed, but she made it up. He mounted behind her and spurred the horse on, anxious to get her home.

From a short distance away, a dozen men of the Triple H Ranch watched in admiration. As Howerton mounted, he heard someone say, "You know, I used to think Pretty Boy was slow." He was about to retort, when Sam Blake beat him to it.

"That's because you're an idiot," Sam said. "And his name is Tom Medlin. Not Pretty Boy. We call him Tommy, not Pretty Boy. You got me?"

Howerton smiled with satisfaction and rode out.

Chapter Thirty-One

Back at home, Tommy bundled Em in blankets and started a fire in all the hearths. He left her to go tend to the animals and when he came back, it looked as though she hadn't moved an inch. He fried eggs and made toast, which she refused. He ate and cleaned up the place and tried to get her to eat again, which she again refused. "At least drink this," he said, easing a glass of warm milk with a little sugar and a healthy dose of brandy in it into her hands.

She took it and sipped, and he went to warm a pan of water. Returning, he saw she'd had most of it. He sat and gently cleaned the dried blood from her face. She winced a time or two, but didn't say a word. As he helped her upstairs, he wondered what Sonny Peterson had done to her beside hit her and choke her. That much he knew from the cuts and bruises. Still, he'd never seen a more vacant stare, and she hadn't stopped shaking. Her breathing, too, indicated she was in a lot of pain.

In her room, he stood at a loss for a moment. But this was up to him. She needed him. "Let's get your dress off," he said. "You need to just . . . rest." She didn't reply or react, and so he reached for her top button, half expecting her to brush his hands away, but she didn't. One by one, he unbuttoned her and then eased the dress down around her, cringing at the bruises on her arms. He squatted. "Step out," he said. He felt the pressure of her hand on his shoulder as she stepped out of the dress.

He stood back up, wondering how much he should undress her. To buy a moment, he carried the dress to her wardrobe and hung it up. Returning to her, he asked, "Do you want me to help you out of this?"

She looked down at herself and frowned, as if just realizing where she was and what he was doing. "I can do it," she murmured.

He turned and went after the nightgown he'd seen in the wardrobe. When he turned back to her, she was getting into bed. His gaze went right to the bruised welts on her back, and his jaw clenched at the sight. She grunted as she pulled the covers around her.

"You should put your nightgown on. It's cold in here."

She didn't respond, so he walked over and set it in front of her. "It's right here. I'm going to turn around and you're going to put it on. You need it on." He turned and, a moment later, he heard the bed springs creak and then a soft rustling. Then he heard her lie back down. When he looked at her again, she was curled on her side, her eyes squeezed shut, her clenched fists pressed to her forehead. "Get some rest," he said tenderly, smoothing her hair back.

Her eyes flew open. "Don't leave!"

"I'm not," he assured her. "I'm not leaving again." He stood a minute and then went for a chair. He pulled it beside the bed and sat next to her. "I'll be right here."

When Howerton and the other men got back to the ranch, there was a commotion. "What happened?" Howerton demanded.

Mark Hanks looked grim and remorseful. "Johnny Macgregor's dead. Blue shot him, or maybe it was Mitchell Medlin. I don't know. But they got away."

Howerton seethed.

"I only went to take a piss," Hanks wailed. "I was gone two minutes. Next thing I know, there's shooting."

"Shot Johnny in the face," Clyde spoke up.

"Blue was probably lying in wait for one of you to take a break before he made his move," Sam stated. "You're going to have to let it go, Hanks. It's not your fault."

"What about tracks?" Quin asked. "We could go after them."

"Ulrich and Green went," George Smith replied. He was in command of the operation when Sam was gone. "I told them to track the sons of bitches and then report back. Not that it'll surprise me a whole hell of a lot if they come back with Blue and Mitchell facedown over their mounts. Won't bother me none, either."

Sam nodded.

Howerton swore viciously. He rubbed the spot at the base of his skull that was throbbing. "Where's Macgregor's body?"

"Laid out in the shed," George replied. "It ain't pretty."

"Did he have family that anyone knew of?"

Sam shook his head. "No, he didn't."

Howerton was grateful Sam knew the men. Sam Blake was a good foreman. "I should have hanged them after they attacked Emeline Wright," he said.

Sam shrugged. "Tommy stopped that. And we couldn't have guessed this. They are some bad eggs, though."

"I feel like shit," Hanks said.

"I know you do," Sam replied, clapping him on the shoulder. "I imagine you will for a while."

Howerton started for the house. "We'll all feel better when those two are dangling at the end of a rope."

* * *

Em woke in the middle of the night and saw Tommy sleeping on a mattress on the floor beside her bed. Obviously, he didn't want to lie beside her. And why would he? He must think she was dirty and tainted. She'd told him about Briar and now he knew about Sonny. She felt cold inside and out. Dead. Sonny had always made her feel dead. He always would. She reached down and touched Tommy's hair. A dark curl fell into her fingers, and she began to cry. He stirred and she withdrew her hand.

"Em?"

She turned over, away from him, holding her breath so a sob wouldn't escape, but it felt like her damned tears were going to drown her.

"It'll be alright," he whispered.

She didn't answer, because she didn't believe it.

Chapter Thirty-Two

In the morning, Em didn't want to get up and face the day, in large part for fear of the disgust she'd see in Tommy's eyes. But he insisted, and it wasn't disgust in his eyes; it was more of a wariness. She certainly would have understood disgust. Her face was bruised, one eye blackened. Her neck bore Sonny's handprint.

Besides sore, she felt jumpy and strange. Even knowing that Sonny was dead, she still felt watched. Every noise startled her. The only time she felt safe was when she was with Tommy, and so she hovered close to him. At lunch, she made an attempt to eat, but she felt as if she couldn't swallow.

"You gotta see the doctor today," Tommy said as they cleaned and put away the dishes. "I thought I'd go get him and—"

"No. I'm fine. I'll be fine."

"Em—"

"I'll be fine," she repeated stubbornly, but she moved too suddenly and pain shot through her that made her breath catch.

Tommy dried his hands and then turned her to face him. "I saw the bruises. And that shaking your body's doing, that's 'cause you're hurt, worse than bruises. I can see it's hard for you to breathe. That's probably because you got broken ribs. They should be seen to."

"You could do it," she pleaded. She was frustrated to feel a tear run down her face when she'd sworn to herself she'd stop crying.

He wiped her tears away tenderly. "I'd do anything for you. You should know that. But we have to get the doctor here. 'Fraid I have to insist on this."

"Tommy, I don't—"

"If we didn't take care of something that causes a problem later, I'd never forgive myself."

"I don't want to be alone," she admitted.

"Either you can go with me—"

She shook her head.

"Then I'll go to the Triple H, it won't take any time at all, and I'll bring back someone to stay with you while I go into town."

"But I'm fine! Why can't you just believe me?"

"We're getting you seen, and that's that," he said as he stepped back. "I promise I won't be long." He went for his coat and hat, looked back at her from the door, and then left.

She listened to him ride off, then turned and went into Doll's room. She got the blanket off the back of a rocking chair and wrapped herself in it, but the motion caused sharp pains in her lower back and side. For a few seconds, she thought she would vomit, but she breathed in shallow pants until the sensation lightened, then sank into the chair, staring at the door.

Tommy knocked on the front door of the ranch, and a matronly housekeeper answered with an unexpected, "Hello, Mr. Medlin."

It took him by surprise that she knew his name. He took off his hat. "Is Mr. Howerton here?"

"Come on in, Tommy," Howerton called.

Tommy stepped inside, noticing the smell of lemon oil.

Howerton stood in the back hall with a cup of something hot in his hands. "You want some coffee?" he asked.

"No, I'm fine."

"Janice, get him a cup. Cream and sugar?"

Tommy nodded at the smiling housekeeper.

"Come on back," Howerton said. "How is she?"

Tommy came toward him, and then followed toward the office. "Not so good."

"I can imagine. Bastard beat the living hell out of her. God, I hate a woman beater." They turned into his office. "Have a seat."

"I need the doctor and she shouldn't be left alone."

Howerton sat at his desk. "I'll send someone for the doctor. Anything he should be told?"

Tommy sat, as well. "I think she may have some broken ribs. I don't like the sound of her breathing."

Howerton nodded thoughtfully. "I'll send someone right away. But, uh, there's something you should know."

Tommy tensed. He suspected he was going to be told there was a warrant for his arrest. "What?"

Howerton drew breath, but hesitated as Janice walked in with a tray of cookies and a cup of coffee, which she offered to Tommy. "Thank you, ma'am," Tommy said.

"Janice, send Ace to town for the doctor. He's to go to the Martin Farm and see Ms. Wright."

"Yes, sir."

"Tell him to leave right away and to tell the doc to get a move on. As a personal favor to me."

Janice nodded and left, and Howerton sipped his coffee.

"Thank you," Tommy said.

"You're welcome. It's what neighbors do."

Tommy took a drink to buy a moment, and the coffee was delicious. The best he'd ever tasted.

"I should have said the Martin-Medlin farm," Howerton said with a half-smile. "You know, when you left that day—"

Tommy nodded, remembering well. "Yeah, I know. I had some of the same thoughts."

Gregory laughed, then sobered. "But about this other thing."

Tommy experienced a pang of anxiety, imagining the next words to be *you're going to be arrested for Peterson's murder.*

"Your brother escaped."

Tommy blinked. "What?"

"I thought he might run, so I had him guarded by a couple of men, but Blue waited until one went to take a piss and he snuck up with a gun, and either he or Mitchell shot the guard."

Tommy's eyes widened. "Shot him dead?"

"Yeah."

"Who was it?"

"Johnny Macgregor."

Tommy ducked his head and exhaled forcefully.

"We're going after them," Howerton continued. "I've got men tracking them now."

Tommy shook his head slowly. "I'm sorry about Johnny."

Howerton nodded. "Yeah." He took another drink and studied Tommy thoughtfully. "You and Mitchell, you don't have the same father. Am I right?"

Tommy shrugged. "It was never talked about."

"You don't," Howerton stated. "Different men, different blood. And the strength of the bloodline mostly comes from the father."

Tommy didn't know what to say to that.

"Mitchell is bad news," Howerton added.

Tommy nodded. "I know."

"Blue's just a pussy who blindly follows. It's too bad for him he fell in with someone like Mitchell. But he did. And

he snuck up on Johnny with a gun. I don't know which of
the two pulled the trigger, and I don't care. They've both
done enough and they're going to pay. I know you wouldn't
have chosen any of this, but that's the way of it. Mitchell
made his bed."

"I thought you were going to tell me I was being arrested."

Howerton drew back. "No. It was self-defense. You're
fine on that score."

Tommy finished the cup of coffee and set it down. "I appreciate everything you've done," he said as he stood.

Howerton smiled a cockeyed smile. "You owe me, but
I'm good with that."

Tommy nodded and left, hat in hand.

The doctor examined Em and then walked out to speak to
Tommy, who was waiting in the kitchen. He was leaning
against the counter, arms crossed, a worried frown on his
face.

"That was quite a beating she took," the doctor commented.

"I know," Tommy replied grimly. "I saw some of the
bruises."

"Well, you couldn't have seen them all, so let me just
tell you, there's not too many inches on her that are not
black-and-blue."

"What about her ribs?"

"Bruised. Not broken." He paused. "You ever been a care-
giver before?"

"No," Tommy replied. "But I don't mind. Just tell me what
to do."

The doctor shook his head. "Nothing really to do, but let
her heal. You do the lifting and heavy work the next few
days. She'll mend. She's young and she'll mend just fine. I

left a bottle of laudanum for the pain, but she should only use it for a short time. Especially in her state of mind."

Tommy nodded. "What do I owe you?"

"I stopped by the ranch and Howerton said to put it on his tab."

Tommy shook his head. "No, sir. We pay our own bills."

The doctor grinned. "He said you'd say that, too. But he remembered a favor or two you did for him. Fixin' his horse's shoe or something?" He gave a little salute. "Good day, Mr. Medlin."

Chapter Thirty-Three

Four days later, Tommy helped Em on with her coat, watching how she moved. They were going out so he could tend to the stock, and because she had a fear of being left alone. She wasn't speaking much, never complaining, but he could tell by the way she moved and breathed where and how much she hurt.

He came around and pulled her coat together in front and her gaze locked with his. He lowered his fingers to her top button as he worked it. He didn't usually do this, nor did he need to, but he had been pushing some boundaries, and, so far, she'd let him. He moved on to the second button. "Wood and the others'll probably be back tomorrow," he said. He noticed the flush of her cheeks before she stepped back, nodding. She finished her buttons, so he went for his coat. "Gloves, too," he said as he put his coat on. "It's cold."

"Tommy."

He looked at her. "Yeah?"

"You came back," she said curiously. "Early." It was as if she'd just realized it. "Why?"

"I had a bad feeling."

She blinked in surprise. "Did you really?"

He nodded and came closer again, wondering if he

should tell her about Briar's spying. But she was so fragile. And he wasn't letting anyone near her again. If knowing would do more harm than good, which it would—

"I was worried about you, too," she said quietly. "Before you left. About the talk you'd had with your brother."

He cocked his head sharply. "What? What talk?"

Her eyes widened in surprise. "The day before you left. You were working on the tobacco barn?"

His expression darkened.

"And Mitchell came . . . t-to apologize."

"You saw him?"

Em nodded stiffly. "He said he came to apologize, so I told him where you were. He said maybe he'd see you the next day, and I told him you were leaving. That he shouldn't wait. I thought he was going right over to the barn."

Tommy felt prickles of anger all over his body because, somehow, Mitchell had been part of it all. He'd taken part in setting Em up for Peterson.

"He didn't see you?" she asked. "He didn't . . . come find you?"

Tommy shook his head. "No. Why didn't you say something?"

She looked crushed. "I should have. I should have said something. I thought maybe you'd had words and you needed time. I thought you'd tell me when you were ready."

He reached out and took hold of her arms. "Hey, it's alright."

Her eyes filled. "I should have said something and maybe—"

He brushed her hair back. "You can't think that way. What's done is done. The man that hurt you is dead and I'll settle things with my brother. He's done some bad things, and Mr. Howerton's going after him. Him and Blue." He paused. "He'll be arrested and tried, but even if he walks, he'll pay. I'll make sure he pays."

"I don't want you hurt," she began.

"And I won't see you hurt," he pledged, pulling her into his arms. "Not ever again."

After supper, Tommy left her to wash and shave, because he was going to lie beside her tonight if she allowed it. Since the others would probably be back tomorrow, there might never be another opportunity. He knew he'd never make love to her again. That had been a one-time thing, a mistake on her part. She called him a partner, but he wasn't. Not really. No matter what the sign said. That had just been a nice gesture. A grand gift. A partner implied equality, and he wasn't her equal. She belonged with men like Howerton and Sonny Peterson, not him. But she needed him now, which gave him the opportunity to lie beside her and hold her.

When he went back to the house and climbed the steps to the loft, Em was curled up on her side. The room smelled softly of powder and her. He moved forward, knowing she wasn't sleeping. He knew her breathing when she slept. He pulled back the covers and sat. She didn't say anything, so he stretched out beside her and pulled the covers over him. He remained still for a few moments, waiting for his heart to slow its pace before he put an arm around her. Instead, she rolled over and hugged her body to his side.

Instinctively, he wrapped his arms around her. He started to reassure her that she was safe, that he would always be there to protect her, but he didn't want to say anything that wasn't true, and he still wasn't a hundred percent sure he wasn't going to be arrested for Peterson's murder. It hadn't been murder, it had been self-defense, like Howerton said, but Sonny Peterson had been a powerful man, and the law seemed to apply itself differently to powerful men. As their body heat melded, her trembling subsided.

"I don't know what I'd do without you," she said softly.

"You don't have to do without me," he replied, secretly praying it was true. "I'm not going anywhere."

"Promise?"

He kissed her forehead. "Everything will be fine. You're going to be fine."

It was quiet for a while except for an owl hooting in the distance.

"Before I met you," Em murmured, "right before, I was sitting outside with Ben and we saw this shooting star. It was . . . so amazingly beautiful."

He smiled. "I saw it, too."

"Really?"

"I swear."

"Ben and I had been talking about the farm. Then we saw the star and he said he felt like all our problems had just been solved."

"I remember wishing for a different life. It was just for a second and then I told myself nothing would ever be different for me."

A hush fell between them before she spoke again. "That was quite a star, wasn't it? We both got our wishes."

"Well, I did," he said. "I don't know that *all* our problems have been solved," he said with a smile.

She sighed and held him closer. "It feels like it," she whispered.

He nodded and smiled, because it did feel like it.

Briar lowered his telescope and took another long swig from his flask. There was a full moon, so there was no doubt about seeing Tom Medlin go inside the house. Maybe they were married, after all. Goddamn. It should have been him.

It was crazy how things had worked out. If Em hadn't

tried to help when little Bo died, his pa would have never known anything about her. Of course, *he* might not have known about her either and that was the day he'd decided she'd be his. Things had been going fine, too, until that damn rope snapped, followed by his leg. It had been a bad break, sending the bone right through the skin. "Goddamn, son-of-a-bitch break," he muttered bitterly.

He'd never fully recovered from it. He had a limp and his leg ached something fierce before it rained or whenever it was cold. His pa had been furious when it happened because, somehow, pretty little Emmy Wright had become a saint in his eyes.

"You won't touch her again," his pa had ranted. "Am I understood?"

"I'm gonna marry her," Briar shouted back at him. He was in pain at the time because his leg was being set.

"How? By us putting a goddamn shotgun to her head? No, by hell, we will not! If you was gonna marry her, you shoulda done it before you messed with her. Now you went and hurt her and you got hurt back. It's over!"

Unfortunately, the whole story had come out when Briar had shown up with his leg busted. Pa had made him repeat every bit of the explanation before his leg was seen to. When Briar revealed Em's declaration that she'd never marry him, the matter was sealed for Xavier. "She didn't mean it, Pa," Briar cried. "She loves me. And I love her!"

"You go near her again, I'll break your other leg," Xavier Lindley swore.

When the break healed, as much as it would ever heal, Xavier arranged for him to marry one of the Davies girls. Marriage would help calm him down, Xavier declared. "Besides, it's high time you produced some young'uns."

Briar had fought it, but his pa had prevailed. As usual. So he'd married Annie, the prettiest of the bunch, although she was nowhere as pretty as Em. She was nowhere as sweet or as smart, either. Annie had given birth to two sons so far. She'd also gotten fat as a cow.

That's where he wanted to be, he thought as he lifted the scope back to his eye. He wanted to be right where Tom Medlin was. Inside Em, unless he missed his guess. "Shoulda been me," he wailed into the night.

Chapter Thirty-Four

Blue snapped twigs and tossed them into the campfire.

"You don't have to snap 'em in half," Mitchell complained.

"I like snappin' 'em." Blue snapped another and tossed it in the fire.

Mitchell glared at him and took a pull from his flask. "We got to get to a town."

"Hey, Mitchell. You think they'll put our pictures on Wanted Posters?"

"Hell, no. We ain't that important. They'll look for us a bit, 'cause of ole Johnny, but Howerton will want to get back to business quick as he can."

"I wish you hadn't shot him," Blue said.

"He had it coming."

"People will think it was me," Blue muttered.

"Will not. You're too big a pussy to kill somebody and everybody knows it. Naw, your style is to bash somebody's face in with a two-by-four when they don't see it comin'."

"That wasn't all me," Blue blustered.

"That wasn't all me," Mitchell taunted.

"I wouldn't even be here if wasn't for you!"

"Stop your whining."

"That's goddamned gratitude for you," Blue sulked.

"Yeah, well, I didn't plan this," Mitchell yelled. "I didn't plan any of it."

"You think I did?" Blue yelled back. "I'm freezing my ass off. I'm probably wanted, too. Posters are probably being printed right now that say 'Wanted, Dead or Alive.'"

"I'll tell you whose fault it is," Mitchell ranted. "It's that *bitch*, Emeline ain't-I-too-good-for-anybody-else Wright. Every bit of trouble I've got into is 'cause of her. And I'll tell you something else. I'm gonna get her back, if it's the last thing I do. I'm going to screw her and then I'm gonna kill her."

"Are you crazy? We can't go back there," Blue said nervously.

"Who said anything about *we*?"

"What do you mean?"

"What you mean, what do I mean? I don't need you coming along and getting in my way."

"They catch you, they'll hang you. Sure as shit."

"Yeah, well, I don't plan on lettin' them catch me."

Blue studied Mitchell in the firelight, wondering how serious he was.

"Damn, I'm hungry," Mitchell complained.

"You had the bigger squirrel."

"'Cause I'm bigger," Mitchell snapped. "A bigger man needs more food."

Blue sighed. He was tired of the bickering. They were both miserable, and griping didn't make it a bit better. "Maybe we'll come to a town tomorrow."

"And maybe we won't come to a town for a week," Mitchell countered.

"You don't have to bite my head off."

"Shut up."

"I rescued you!"

"Did I ask you to? Huh?"

Blue couldn't believe his ears. He wasn't going to get the

least little bit of credit. "You're a piece of work, Mitchell Medlin."

"Think about it, though. If you hadn't shown up with that gun, shaking like a little titmouse, then what would have happened? I'd have gotten docked some pay or I would have had to work a couple of Sundays or something."

"Or maybe you'd a' got beat again," Blue added.

"For what? They couldn't prove a damn thing. Probably nothing would have happened. I would have said, 'Hey, I was only there to try and help Miss Wright. 'Course there was too many of them bad guys and I couldn't do a damn thing. It's not like that's a crime.'"

Blue shook his head. Only Mitchell could turn something like this around to be somebody else's fault. "You didn't have to shoot Johnny."

"I already told you, he had it coming. If he was sitting right here, right now, he'd say the same."

"I doubt that."

"I doubt that," Mitchell mocked, talking like an idiot.

"You better stop doing that," Blue warned.

"Or what?"

Blue glared at Mitchell, trembling with frustration.

"Build up that fire," Mitchell ordered. "Before we freeze to death."

"Mr. Howerton," someone called from the door of the showroom. "Bud Ulrich and Lynn Green just rode in."

Howerton backed away from the sleek, black stallion being offered for sale. "Give me a minute," he said to the owner before heading out. He didn't have to go far, as Ulrich and Green were walking toward him.

"They went into the hills," Lynn Green reported when they met up.

Howerton considered the news. "They'll probably starve

and freeze for a while and then be stupid enough to go into town and get caught."

"We can find them," Bud spoke up. "They ain't that careful."

"I'm not wasting any more manpower on a hunting expedition for the likes of them," Howerton replied. "Posters are up in every town within a hundred miles, and a reward has been posted. They'll surface. They'll either die in the hills or they'll surface."

"Yes, sir," Bud replied.

"Rest up today and report to Sam in the morning."

"Yes, sir," both men replied.

Tommy carried wood into the house and shut the door with his foot. "Thank you much," Doll said without turning from the stove, where she was stirring a large pot of something that smelled savory. "Ham and beans for supper and some of my good corn bread," she said. "How's that sound?"

"Good," Tommy replied as he began stacking the wood in the box. When he finished, he walked closer to Doll. "How is she?" he asked quietly.

"We're getting there," Doll replied softly with a wink and nod. "She's sitting in there knitting."

"I'll say hello," he said as he started for the parlor.

"Don't hardly need my permission," Doll quipped under her breath.

Em sat in her favorite chair, staring out the window. The knitting rested in her lap. She heard Tommy as he walked in and looked over at him with an instant smile. "Hello."

"Hello." He sat on the settee facing her. "How are you?"

"Fine."

She didn't look fine. She looked pale and thin, and she had circles beneath her eyes.

"Doll and I might go see Fiona and the baby tomorrow," she said.

Tommy frowned worriedly. "I think we're gonna get another storm."

She looked back outside. "I thought it looked like it."

"You think it's going to snow some more, Tommy?" Doll called from the kitchen.

Em looked back at him and grinned, which made his heart lurch. "'Fraid so," Tommy replied, not taking his eyes off Em.

"Me and Emmy were thinking about going to my sister's to see Fiona and the babe."

"It may not be the best day tomorrow," he called back.

"Well, tomorrow or the next day or the next. We'll get there, eventually."

"I can't wait to see the baby," Em said wistfully.

Doll joined them, wiping her hands on her apron. "He's a fat, healthy thing. And, Lord, what a pair of lungs."

"Who's he look like?" Tommy asked.

"He's got some red fuzz on his head, but that's about all of Fiona he got."

"I'll bet she's happy," he said.

She nodded. "She is. Tickled pink."

He looked back at Em. "You want to go down to the barn with me? Get some fresh air?"

She wrinkled her nose. "Too cold."

"It is that," Doll agreed as she headed back to the kitchen. "Although the icicles hanging everywhere are awful pretty."

Tommy stood, because he still had plenty of work waiting.

"We'll get over to the chow hall for supper," Doll called. "That's about all the fresh air we need, I think."

Tommy was relieved to hear it. Em had been taking all her meals in the house since the attack. Em also rose and tugged her shawl close as she started back toward the kitchen with him.

"Apple cobbler or bread pudding tonight?" Doll asked. "What do you think, Tommy?"

"Cobbler."

She chuckled. "How'd I know you were going to say that?"

"Because it's his favorite," Em said, knocking into him playfully.

At least Em was trying to get back to normal. Surely that meant she'd eventually get there. "I'll see you at dinner?" he said to her.

She nodded.

He put his hat on and started for the door. "You good on wood, now?" he asked Doll.

"Wood the man or wood to burn?"

He grinned. "To burn."

"Yep. We're set."

"Did Wood make you mad, or something?" he asked.

"Not recently. Though I'm not opposed to telling him when he does."

Tommy chuckled. "I didn't think you were." Tommy glanced back at Em and found her watching him, which made him feel good. She mouthed 'bye,' and he left, still picturing her sweet lips.

Chapter Thirty-Five

March 18, 1882

Midway to the chow hall kitchen, Em smiled as a breeze caressed her skin. It was mid-March, the world was turning green again, daffodils were sprouting and the farm was running smoothly. It was only a small operation, and probably always would be, but that was perfectly fine with her. *A butterfly*—that's what she felt like. She'd been cocooned all winter, silent and afraid, but now she was free. Sonny no longer haunted her. She didn't know when she'd stopped thinking about him and dwelling on the past, but she had. She was free.

"You coming to help with dinner?" Doll asked as she walked from the cheese shack to the bunkhouse. The 'cheese shack,' a name Wood had come up with, was actually a newly built summer kitchen, but there hadn't been a need for it yet, other than to make goat cheese, which Doll lovingly toiled over.

"I am, and then I'm leaving." She was taking the soft, white cheese to Mrs. Simpson, the manager of Wiley's Restaurant to see if she wanted to purchase it. It would be the first time she'd been into town by herself in months, since before Christmas, and she was looking forward to it.

Doll pulled open the screen door to the chow hall and held it for Em to walk through. "I just hung four more bags, so you tell 'em we can provide all the cheese they want and they'll never taste better. You make sure she tastes it."

"I will."

In the kitchen, Em peeled potatoes as Doll chopped onions. "Sure is a pretty day," Doll commented. "But I don't know that it should be this warm, this quick. I can't say I'm looking forward to the summer heat."

Em grinned. "It's a beautiful day," she agreed. *And I am looking forward to summer*, she thought. And to fall and winter and everything else.

"Don't you be giving away any of my secrets, now. That nosy Mrs. Simpson doesn't need to know a thing about how we make that cheese."

"I don't even know your secrets."

"You know enough and I'll bet she asks," she said, putting the knife down and sniffing hard. She blinked, and rubbed her stinging eyes with the backs of her hands. "Just you wait and see."

Em reached for the knife and another cutting board. "Your secrets are safe with me. Not that I know them, but even if I did."

"Right back atcha." Doll moved over to the stove and melted lard, then put the vegetables in a pan to fry.

"*Mm-mmm,*" Wood murmured as he walked in. "I'm hungry."

"Well, when aren't you?" Doll replied. "Why are you back early?"

"Because I'm hungry," Wood said, edging closer to see if there were any tidbits to snack on.

"Emmy, I set some pies out to cool earlier," Doll said. "Get them for me before you go?"

"Sure." Em wiped her hands on her apron and complied cheerfully.

Wood watched her go. "She looks good today."

"And she's going into town," Doll said meaningfully. "Now, if you want to help, finish slicing those taters. After you wash them hands. No telling what you been touching."

Chapter Thirty-Six

Mrs. Simpson unwrapped the white cheese and cut a small chunk. "Soft, dry," she commented. She smelled and then tasted it. "Very good."

Em realized she was holding her breath, and let go of it. It wasn't that they needed the money, but Doll had toiled over the cheese; she'd be sorely disappointed if Mrs. Simpson rejected it.

"Back in New York," Mrs. Simpson said, "we made a goat cheese pie with tomatoes and onions. Delicious. So, how much can you bring me every week? And how much per pound? Let's settle on it now."

Em walked out of Wiley's feeling positively high, and headed toward the General Store. Besides staples, she was going to buy tobacco, since Tommy and Wood had been sampling and comparing brands.

"Miss Wright?"

Em stopped and turned to see two of the waitresses from Wiley's who'd followed her out. "Yes?"

"Can we speak with you for a minute?"

"Certainly."

"I'm Dixie and this is Meredith," a solidly built brunette said. "We're friends of Colleen."

Em's smile suddenly felt a bit strained. Not only at the mention of Colleen, but because of the way the women stood and looked at her as if they disliked her. When they didn't even know her.

"I don't know if you know this or not, but we sign a contract with Mr. Wiley not to get married for a year after startin' work," Dixie continued.

Em blinked, wondering why they would tell her this. "I . . . didn't know that."

"We're friends with Colleen," Meredith said. She had light-colored hair and a strangely asymmetrical face.

"We already said that," Dixie reminded her, sotto voce.

"Anyway," Meredith said, sending an insulted glance at Dixie, "her year isn't up yet, but sometimes rules shouldn't matter. You know what I mean?"

"I'm not sure," Em replied hesitantly. The only thing she was sure of was that she didn't want to hear this. She just wanted to buy her goods, get back home and share the good news with the others, especially Tommy.

"Tommy Medlin wants to marry Colleen," Dixie stated.

Em's jaw went lax. It felt as if the wind had been knocked out of her.

"And Colleen loves him, too," Meredith spoke up again. "He is all she talks about."

"But Tommy feels like he can't, because of . . . you know, obligations and all."

"It's the farm," Meredith added. "He doesn't want to disappoint you, ya'll having a partnership and all."

Em felt sick to her stomach. How did they know all this? Had Tommy told them? How else could they possibly know?

"He takes responsibility real serious," Dixie said.

Em experienced a clutch of annoyance that the two of them would have the gall to tell her what Tommy was like. *Her* Tommy.

"They're together right now," Dixie continued. "Tommy and Colleen. Talking about it."

Em nearly took a step backward. She felt sick.

"We were thinking, if you could just talk to him and maybe encourage him—"

"Release him, so to speak."

Em's fingernails dug into the palms of her hands. *Release* him?

"Like we said, he doesn't want to disappoint you. But—"

"But if he knew it was fine by you to marry Colleen, he'd do it in a minute."

"Just your blessing. That's all he'd need."

"He feels kind of held down."

"He should be able to have a life, too."

As if she'd tried to prevent Tommy from having a life, which was exactly what they were insinuating. What a load of sheep shit. He was happy at the farm. He'd told her he'd never been happier. Of course, that had been months ago. And she had been a recluse and a burden since. "I never thought otherwise," she said weakly.

"He's awful proud and shy," Dixie ventured. "So, you'd have to be careful, I guess, in how you brought it up."

The women had inched closer to Em, too close, and she felt a pressing need to get away from them. "Thank you," she said stiffly, "for telling me," she added.

"You'll think about it?"

"Yes," Em replied, and she turned and hurried away, too close to tears for comfort.

* * *

Dixie and Meredith waited until she was out of sight before they turned to each other gleefully. "My God," Dixie exclaimed. "Did you see her face?"

"I thought she was going to faint!"

"Me, too."

"I almost feel sorry for her." Meredith's eyes twinkled mischievously. "Almost."

"Not me," Dixie said, lifting a brow and folding her arms. "Women like her get everything."

"Yeah, but she's in love with him. You can see it."

Dixie's expression hardened. "Who cares? I'll be so glad if she loses him. I swear, I'll do a jig at the wedding right in front of her."

Chapter Thirty-Seven

Colleen spread a blanket under a huge oak tree and in view of the lake. Tommy watched as she sat and then looked up at him, full of expectation and he couldn't tell what else. He moved forward and sat, feeling awkward. Why was she here? He didn't have time to waste like this and yet he didn't want to hurt her feelings. She'd driven a long way out to see him.

"It's so pretty here," Colleen said. "Would you stay at the farm if you was to get married?"

Get married? What was she talking about? "I don't think I'll be going anywhere," he replied. It sounded choppy and he felt even more foolish than before.

"I know the farm couldn't run without you. But haven't you ever thought of getting married and starting a family of your own?"

This was undoubtedly the most uncomfortable he had ever been. "Not really."

"Tommy, will you kiss me?"

A soft pout was playing on her lips and her dress was so low cut he could see her breasts heaving when she breathed. She was pretty, so why didn't he feel the least inclination? "I don't know if that would be a good idea."

"One kiss, Tommy. Please? I come all this way."

He hesitated and then leaned over to kiss her.

As he got close, she wrapped her hands around his neck and went flat on her back, bringing him down with her. She grabbed hold of his hand and brought it to her breast. "You can touch me. I want you to."

His instinct was to back away, because it was too fast and forced, plus she wanted too much from him, but her breasts were straining toward him. He cupped one and a part of him wanted to go along with her wishes. His body was responding even without his emotions being in play. But then she reached down and began tugging up her skirt, and he heard his ma's warning inside his head. *She will lift her skirt up and say 'put your thing inside me and move.'* The memory stifled all desire in him and he pulled back. "I'm sorry. This just isn't right."

"I'd marry you, Tommy," Colleen pleaded.

A sickening kind of panic took hold, but no words came to his rescue. He sat up.

"And have your children," she continued. She sat up, too, and readjusted her clothing to cover herself. "I've been hoping you'd ask me, but . . . you're so busy," she finished weakly. "But wouldn't you like to have a wife who'd cook and keep house for you? Somebody you could come home to at the end of the day and *be* with? Because I'd do that."

He looked away from her. She was a pusher, like his ma. "I haven't thought about it that much," he hedged, not wanting to hurt her.

Colleen chewed on her bottom lip nervously. "Will you do me one favor?"

This was pure misery. "I'll try."

"Close your eyes and picture something for me."

He closed his eyes. He felt foolish, but he'd said he would.

"It's the end of the day and you come home," she said softly. "And your wife is there, waiting for you. Dinner's all made. Let's say it's . . . wintertime and snowing outside."

His lips parted slightly, because he *saw* it. He saw the house, the polished wood floor, the fire burning in the hearths. He imagined the savory scent of food and the familiar face and figure of his wife as she untied her apron and set it aside. She smiled, glad to see him, and it affected his heart like it always did.

"And your young son comes running in to tell you something and he throws himself up into your arms. Oh, Tommy, he looks just like you."

Tommy smiled, picturing it.

"He's so beautiful and healthy and strong," she continued.

Tommy breathed out slowly. His son did look like him and his daughter, his precious little baby girl, looked just like her mama.

"Now, imagine it's later on," Colleen went on. "Time for bed," she said in a low, seductive voice. "The children are asleep in their rooms. Can't you just imagine how sweet they look when they sleep?"

It was true; they did. They looked like angels tucked in their beds in the loft.

"After you check on them, cover them up, you come to bed."

He could see it. Em was waiting for him, looking up at him with those beautiful golden eyes of hers. She wanted him as much as he wanted her. She lifted back the covers, offering herself to him. Just like in his dream.

"And I'm waiting there for you," Colleen finished.

Tommy opened his eyes, knowing he couldn't hedge anymore. It wasn't right. "I can't marry you, Colleen."

Her face fell. "Why not?"

He shook his head. "I just can't."

Tears sprang to her eyes. "But why?"

"Because I love someone else."

Colleen's expression changed, hardened. "But does *she* love you?" she demanded. "Will she marry you?"

Tommy drew a breath, but didn't speak.

"She won't, Tommy," Colleen implored. "She won't. And you'll end up all alone."

Tommy got to his feet. She was telling the truth, but it didn't matter. He couldn't marry someone else just because the woman he loved didn't love him back. Not in the way he loved her.

"Tommy, please," Colleen wailed.

He felt terrible. Colleen cared about him and he was hurting her. He'd never imagined he'd be in this position.

"I'd be a good wife!"

"I know you will be. But it can't be to me. I'm sorry." He offered his hand to help her up.

She accepted his hand and got to her feet. "You're making a mistake," she said in a shaky voice.

He wondered what else he could say.

"Will you think about what I said?" she begged. "Just think about it?"

"There's no use," he replied gently. "I'm sorry."

Em made herself go though the motions. She purchased supplies and then headed back home, navigating the road without truly seeing it. She could only picture Tommy and revisit scores of insignificant moments they'd spent together. Working, talking, planning. But they hadn't been insignificant. They'd been little building blocks of communication and trust. And all for what? She'd taken him for granted, just like everyone else in the world had. And now a woman who was smart enough to appreciate him had snagged him.

Tommy, her rescuer and best friend, wanted to marry someone else. "Maybe it's not true," she murmured. And yet how else could those girls at Wiley's have known what they did?

Em brought the wagon to a stop and pressed her fist to her chest. Her heart felt heavy and swollen. Maybe it was;

that would explain her not being able to breathe very well all of a sudden. *Stop it*, she commanded herself. *You'll go on. You'll be calm. You will talk to him, and if he truly wants to be free of you—*

She shook her head as tears blurred her vision, but she forced herself to finish the thought. *If he wants to be free, you will let him go.* She swallowed hard, wiped her face and drove on.

Everything looked normal when she arrived back home. The men were returning from the field, although Tommy wasn't amongst them. Of course, that wasn't unusual. He often stayed behind and worked longer than anyone.

Doll came scurrying out. "Well?"

"She wants to buy all we can make," Em replied as she climbed down from the wagon on weak-feeling legs.

Doll pursed her lips in order not to burst into the wide smile that threatened. "Means she's got good sense. And what's that, may I ask?" She pointed to the case of sarsaparilla. "I don't recall ordering that."

"It's a treat," Em said, trying to keep her voice light. Everything looked and felt perfectly normal, except for her.

"Wood," Doll bellowed. She reached for one of the 20-pound bags of sugar and headed back to the kitchen. Wood passed her and she gave her thumb a backward jerk. "Emmy brought sarsaparillas. Get 'em."

"Went well, then, did it?" Wood asked with a grin.

"Good enough that I got you this," Em replied, handing him a tin of snuff.

Wood whooped and kicked up his heels. "And it ain't even my birthday!"

She grinned, despite the sick tension she felt. "Is Tommy around?"

Wood was walking around the wagon, his back to Em. "Sure, he's around. Want me to find him for you?"

Was it her imagination or was there something odd about Wood's tone? "Is he busy?" she asked reluctantly.

"He's with someone, I believe." He looked back at her sheepishly. "You okay, there, Emmy? No offense, but you're looking a little green around the gills."

"I'm fine," she said quickly, stammering only slightly. She started to walk off, then stopped and turned back to him, because she had to know. She could not stand one more instant of not knowing. "The person Tommy's with, is it Colleen?"

He hesitated, hating the answer. "I believe it is."

Her faced heated; she felt so foolish. Apparently everyone knew about Tommy and Colleen except her. She'd been so stupid. So foolish and remiss.

"How 'bout I get him for you?" Wood offered again.

"No," Em replied. She held up another tin of snuff and then tossed it to him. "Just give him that when you see him."

Colleen was relieved to see her horse. She couldn't stop the tears from running down her face, but they didn't relieve the hysteria she felt building. A terrible outburst was coming and she wanted to be well clear of the place before it did. She mounted her horse without the hand up Tommy offered.

"Will you be alright?" he asked.

She gave a stiff nod, because she wasn't capable of speaking without blubbering like a baby. He handed up the blanket she'd brought and she took it and then kicked her horse into motion.

"Went that well, did it?" Wood asked as she rode away.

Tommy looked back at the older man as he approached. He shook his head, unable to express how bad he felt.

"I was coming to find you," Wood said. "You should probably go see Em."

Tommy tensed. "Why?"

"I don't rightly know but she seemed strange and she was asking for you." As Colleen turned onto the road and disappeared from sight, he scratched behind his ear. "I, uh, didn't know the two of you had something going on."

"Who?"

"You and Miss Colleen."

"We don't," he stated firmly.

"Oh?" He nodded slowly. "I see. My mistake."

Tommy started off. "I'm going to find Em."

"Yeah, you should do that," Wood called, giving in to a relieved grin.

Chapter Thirty-Eight

Tommy opened the door without knocking and found Em pacing. She saw him and quickly turned and dabbed at her eyes and nose. He closed the door behind him. "What's wrong?"

"Nothing," she replied too quickly.

"Em?"

"Nothing," she said again, turning back to face him. "Really, nothing. I'm fine." She shrugged.

"Wood said you wanted to see me."

She crossed her arms. "No. I just asked where you were. That's all. Not that I was checking up on you. I just asked. It was nothing. Oh, I b-brought you a tin of snuff. Wood's got it."

Whatever was bothering Em wasn't nothing. She was chattering and stammering the way she did when she was nervous, and she'd been crying. Something had happened in town. He walked to the table and sat. "Tell me what happened," he said calmly.

Seconds of silence ticked by.

"Aren't you with someone?" she asked.

"Yeah, I'm with you."

"I meant Colleen."

"No, she left."

She looked away to collect herself. "Are you—"

"What?"

She had to know. She had to ask him. Rigidly, she moved to the table and sat across from him. Stiffly. "I heard you were getting married."

Tommy frowned. "Where did you hear that?"

He hadn't denied it. So it was true. She felt sick. "Wiley's," she said weakly.

He struggled to understand what she was talking about and why she looked so devastated, as if he'd disappointed her beyond belief. "Wiley's?"

"Dixie and Meredith told me."

"Who?"

She shook her head. "Friends of Colleen. They followed me and told me." She spoke as if the words were hard to get out and, suddenly, a silent stream of tears ran down her face.

He sat up straighter and drew breath to speak, but she beat him to it.

"I'm not . . . crying because I'm sad," she rushed on. "It's because I'm s-surprised and so . . . happy for you."

Tommy shook his head. "I said no."

Her breath caught and she blinked. "What?"

"I said no."

Color flared in her face and the tears stopped at once. Em wiped her face with both hands. "What are you talking about?"

He was befuddled by her reactions. "She asked me to marry her but I—" Tommy could tell this wasn't what she'd been expecting. She was shaking her head slightly and breathing faster. Her hands clutched the sides of the table. "What were *you* talking about?"

"You're saying she asked you?"

Tommy nodded.

"*She* asked *you*," Em said again.

Her disbelief was beginning to get insulting. Did she think he was so undesirable that no one would want to marry him? "Yes, Em. She asked me. Colleen asked me to marry her. Made a halfway decent case of it, too."

Em swallowed. "I only meant . . . that's not what they said."

He stared, waiting for her to continue.

"Dixie and Meredith said you'd asked, or that you wanted to, but that you were—"

Once again, he didn't know what she was talking about. "What?"

"They said you felt too obligated to me and to the farm. They asked me to speak to you. To release you."

Release? As in to fire him? "I don't know what they were talking about."

The dinner bell started clanging, but neither of them moved an inch.

"So . . . you don't feel held down by me?" Em asked quietly.

"Held down?"

She nodded. "They suggested you felt held down here. By me."

"How are you going to hold me down? You're not big enough."

Only a small breathy laugh escaped her as she leaned back in her chair, but she was still trembling, and there was relief on her face. Sheer, joyous relief. "Oh, Tommy. I just had the worst afternoon."

He tried to collect his thoughts, but his mind was racing. "Didn't they like the cheese?"

"No, they did. They want as much as we can make. You were right about that. You were right about everything."

Right. The word struck hard and emboldened him. "So why was it a bad afternoon?"

"Never mind," she replied, averting her gaze. "It's over now."

Breathing had suddenly become harder to do. "Did you have trouble with the wagon?"

"No."

"The ruts in the road?"

She shook her head.

"So why were you crying?"

"It's nothing. Really."

There was suddenly so much vigor coursing through him, he couldn't sit still. He got to his feet and strode to the cupboard. "It was what they said? Those girls at Wiley's?"

"Let's just forget it," she said, pushing back from the table and rising. She smoothed her skirt.

"Em!"

She turned to him, blinking in surprise. "What?"

"I asked you a question."

She blushed harder. "I guess so. Alright? Yes. Now, can we please forget it?"

She'd been upset because she didn't want him to marry Colleen. Was it possible?

"I felt foolish that I hadn't seen it," Em continued, trying to make light of it. "It just took me by surprise. That's all. I shouldn't have let it upset me. I guess . . . the excitement of the day," she concluded weakly.

She looked so vulnerable. Didn't she know how he felt? Was that even possible? "People don't cry because they hear something that surprises them," he said slowly.

She folded her arms again, clearly uncomfortable. "Sometimes they do," she argued. She turned slightly away from him. "We should . . . probably go to dinner."

"I don't want to marry Colleen," he stated. "I never wanted to marry her." She bit on her bottom lip and avoided his gaze, and he suddenly knew that she'd been crying for him. He walked to her, taking deliberate steps. She looked at him again and, this time, her gaze didn't waver. He moved in for a kiss slowly enough to allow her time to stop him, but she didn't. In fact, her face was turning up to his, her eyes full of longing. The moment before contact seemed like a small eternity, but then his lips covered hers and the feel was as perfect as he remembered.

She put her arms around his back and pulled him closer, and he knew everything had just changed. His hands dropped around her waist and he caressed the tender curve of her back and pressed her tighter against him. It was perfect. She was perfect. He suddenly knew that the strength of their love could undo all the damage of their pasts. He pulled back to look into her eyes and the love he saw in her face bolstered his courage. "You're the only woman I want to be with. I thought you knew that."

She slowly shook her head. "But that's how I feel, too."

The power of the words robbed him of breath.

"I love you," she said.

He closed his eyes and exhaled from the sweetness of the words. He'd waited all his life to hear them.

"When I thought it was too late—"

He leaned in to her, hardly daring to believe what he'd heard. "I never thought any woman would want to marry me."

She shook her head and tears sprang to her eyes. "Were you ever wrong."

Wrong. *This* was the way he was wrong? He didn't know whether to laugh or cry. "Marry me."

She smiled with her eyes. "I wouldn't marry anyone else in the whole world but you."

He knew he wasn't dreaming, but it didn't feel real either. Her arms were wrapped around him, there was utter certainty in her face, and nothing in his life had ever felt so right. Was it him shaking or her? Or both? All he knew was that his entire life had just changed. The entire world had just changed. He kissed her again. "I love you, Em." He could say it out loud, now. He could say it as much as he wanted to. "I loved you from the first second I saw you."

"Me, too. In the livery. Me, too!"

They both laughed, thinking of it. All the misunderstandings and the time they'd wasted. She'd always loved him, too? That meant the night they'd made love hadn't been a mistake. She'd loved him, too. Why hadn't he recognized it, especially when he'd *felt* it that night. He remembered thinking they'd started with love and made more. He'd thought it, so why hadn't he believed it the next day?

Doll marched toward the house to give Tommy and Em a piece of hell for being late for supper again, but Wood caught up to her and grabbed her arm. "Wait a minute," he urged. "I got a feeling."

"You got a head full of cabbage, is what you got," she snapped. "Now, how many times have I said—"

He held up a finger. "Just hold your horses, woman."

Doll watched as he crept up to the porch and peered in the window. Then he turned back, grinning from ear to ear, and waved her over.

"Don't go spying, you old fool," Doll said loudly as she stomped up the front steps. Damnation if she was going to sneak up on anybody. "What is it?" But he didn't have to answer. One look through the window, one glance at Tommy and Em locked in a lover's embrace, and Doll flew back from the window as if she'd been stung. Without warning, she hit Wood squarely in the chest. "Well, why didn't you say so?"

Wood placed both hands over the spot she'd pounded, but he couldn't stop grinning.

"Come on," she snapped, starting back down the steps. "Let's get."

They were halfway back to the chow hall when Doll let out a rich chuckle of delight. "It's about time, ain't it?"

* * *

"I don't want to wait," Tommy declared.

His eyes were glistening an impossible blue. He was so beautiful, inside and out; she didn't deserve him. "Me, either."

"Let's go tell everyone. You want to? I want the whole world to know."

She was nodding and smiling. She felt the strain of her smile and yet she couldn't wipe it from her face. It was absurd and wonderful. They walked hand in hand to the chow hall and Doll turned to them, scowling. "I only got one thing to say," she began.

Em's smile faded.

Wood stood, looking stern. "And I'm going to back her up on it."

Jeffrey stood, too, and then smacked Hawk on the arm. Hawk shoved one more forkful into his mouth and stood.

"What?" Tommy asked, confused as to what they were all so put out about.

Wood grinned. "Congratulations!"

"It's about time," Doll exclaimed, slapping the side of her leg.

The room erupted in laughter and Em laughed with them and shook her head. "I didn't know what we'd walked into."

"But . . . how'd you know?" Tommy asked.

"Son, you don't know the risk I took for you two," Wood said.

"Oh," Doll objected. "Go on with you now, you old fool."

"Ya'll didn't heed the dinner bell," Wood continued as he sat. Hawk and Jeffrey had already resumed eating. "And Doll lit out after you."

"Picturing your scalps in her hands," Hawk interjected, holding his clenched fists in the air.

"Oh, pipe down," Doll scolded the men. "And you two, sit. Don't listen to this nonsense."

Tommy waited for Em and then sat next to her.

"Aren't you the perfect gent?" Jeffrey teased with a wink. "Tommy looks like a ten-year-old boy who done got his first crush on a girl."

Tommy chuckled. "It's kind of what I feel like, too."

"Leave him be and eat," Doll snapped. "And you, Hawk, you're doing dishes."

"I don't think she appreciated that scalp comment," Wood said under his breath.

"I ain't deaf, Wood," Doll bellowed.

Wood looked sheepish. "Am I drying?"

"Hush and pass the food."

"Wait a minute," Tommy complained good-naturedly. "I didn't even get to say it."

"Well?" Wood asked.

"Em and I are getting married. She's going to be my wife."

Em felt tears close in. "I'm honored you asked," she said in a thick voice.

He looked at her. "I'm the one who's honored."

"Hell," Jeffrey said. "I'm honored to know you both."

Again, there was laughter and it was good. Doll sniffed and swiped a tear from her cheek.

"Better eat now," Wood said, heaping Em's plate with a helping of greens. "Before Mama gets at you."

For Tommy, the evening passed too quickly. After dinner, everyone helped clean up and then they played cards. Neither he nor Em could concentrate, which amused the others. Jokes went around and around and he didn't mind a bit. He'd never been the center of attention before in a good way, and now he was there with the woman he loved. The woman who was going to be his wife. He still couldn't believe it.

He walked her back to the house and they talked. He'd never been a talker before but suddenly he couldn't shut up. He wanted to know everything she thought, everything she felt, everything she wanted, and he wanted to share just as much. When they finally kissed good night and parted, he walked back to the bunkhouse feeling a foot taller than before.

"You look happy," Wood commented when he shut the door. The men were playing a round of poker.

"You need to play, Tommy," Jeffrey stated. "'Cause you sure as hell don't have a poker face tonight."

Tommy took a seat at the table. He didn't particularly want to play, but he was too keyed up to sleep. "I still can't believe it."

"That's funny," Jeffrey said. "It didn't surprise anyone else."

Tommy looked from face to face, wondering if they were kidding.

Wood shrugged. "It's been pretty clear to see . . . for everyone but the two of you, apparently."

"That I loved her, you mean?"

Wood nodded. "And that she loved you."

Tommy couldn't believe his ears.

"It's always hard to see when it's you," Hawk said.

"How would you know?" Jeffrey teased.

Hawk gave him a dark look.

The banter continued, but Tommy didn't hear much of it. No one else was surprised that Em loved him. To him, it seemed nothing short of a miracle, but they didn't see it that way. It was hard to process exactly what that meant, but it was something like they thought he was worthy of her. "I don't think I've ever felt this good," he said.

"Lucky?" Wood asked.

Tommy grinned. "Yeah."

Wood reached over and rubbed his arm. "Maybe some of it will rub off on me. I could use it."

Em paced around her room, unable to still her mind, and each round ended up with her at the window, staring out at the lights emanating from the bunkhouse. She heard footsteps and turned to see Doll appear in the doorway dressed in a faded pink robe.

"What is it, honey?" Doll asked.

"Nothing." Em shrugged. "I can't sleep."

"Well, you're going to worry a hole through the floor and fall through."

"I'm sorry. I didn't think about the noise I was making."

Doll waved her hand and walked over to sit in the chair next to the bed. "Come take a load off," she said, tapping the bed, "and tell me what's bothering you."

Em walked to the bed and sat. "Did you ever think something . . . I mean, a thought occurs to you and then you can't get it out of your mind?"

"What thought?"

"I've been . . . unlucky," Em said quietly. "A lot."

"You think?"

"Oh, I have," Em stated matter-of-factly.

"Well, I know most of your story. Right? Is there much I don't know?"

Em shook her head.

"Some unfortunate things have occurred," Doll said reasonably, "no doubt, but you might ought to reconsider your thinking."

"What do you mean?"

"Your folks die, which is a sad thing, but then Ben takes you in."

Em nodded.

"Just think for a minute about how many children aren't so lucky," Doll added. "Some go to families that misuse them. Or they go to orphan asylums."

Em looked down at her hands. "My aunt detested me."

"And your cousins weren't much better. But you had Ben and he had you, and you survived."

Em looked at Doll searchingly. "Do you think it's possible for one person to curse another?"

Doll made a face. "As in a voodoo kind of curse?"

Em shrugged and nodded. "Maybe because they hated them?"

Doll pursed her lips as she pondered the matter. "I don't think so. And I'll tell you why. Aren't we all children of God? I mean, for one person to have that sort of power over another, it ain't natural. No, I don't think that's possible. 'Course, that's just my opinion, which obviously don't count for much. You're talking about your aunt?"

Em nodded.

"What put it into your head?" Doll fretted.

"Things happening. I don't know."

"Sonny Peterson?"

Em hesitated. "And other things."

"Well, honey. Peterson was one determined man. Determined to have you. But he doesn't have you, does he? He's dead. The man you love and who loves you killed him. I'd say that was lucky."

Em thought about it.

"I know that man hurt you, honey. I know you've survived your fair share of rough treatment, but that's all behind you now. You have a good man who loves you, and he'd no more allow somebody to hurt you—"

"But that's just it. He's *so* good." Her voice cracked and she cleared her throat. "I don't want to be stupid, but—"

"Em," Doll rejoined, shaking her head.

"No, listen! What if it's too good? What if I don't deserve him?"

"You're talking nonsense."

"I'm not! Tommy is—"

"He's a good man with a good heart and he's not hard on the eyes. Yes, you're a lucky woman. Say it," Doll coaxed. "For goodness' sake, speak the truth and shame the devil."

"I know I'm lucky to have him in my life."

"And he is lucky to have you, too." Doll reached out and took hold of her hand. "You've had a lot of excitement tonight. That's all it is. And maybe you've got a wound or two inside that's not completely healed. But you've got time, Emmy. You've got time and you've got the man of your dreams and he loves you and you love him."

Slowly, Em smiled. "Thank you."

"Tomorrow, I'm going to have Wood and the boys start on a room for me at the far end of the longhouse."

Em opened her mouth to object.

"No," Doll said, beating her to the punch. "You and Tommy will have this as your home, and I'll have the cutest little place you ever did see out there. It'll be attached to the longhouse so I can come and go to the kitchen without having to go out in any bad weather."

"Doll—"

"It's what I want, so that's that." She stood. "Now, try and get some sleep."

Em stood and threw her arms around the older woman. "Thank you."

Doll patted her back. "You worry too much, Emmy. No more thinking tonight."

Em pulled away. "Yes, ma'am."

Doll smiled, patted her cheek and then left.

Chapter Thirty-Nine

April 4, 1882

Fiona couldn't help smiling at how beautiful the chapel looked. It was filled with flickering candles and colorful wildflowers. Tommy looked so handsome, it was hard not to gawk. He also looked nervous. "Tommy looks a wreck," she whispered to Doll, who sat next to her.

"He's only worried Em will disappear or something. You wait and see. The second he lays eyes on her, you won't see an ounce of fear."

Fiona had known the music would be nice, because Beulah Barnes could play the piano like nobody's business. She knew, too, that the reception would be nice, because they'd been preparing food for days. The only thing that had surprised Fiona so far was the turnout. They'd expected fifteen or twenty people at the most, and there was double that. "The Wedding March" began and everyone stood. "Tommy sti—" Fiona uttered. She'd started to say that he still looked scared to death, but his expression changed the second he spotted Em. Now, he looked like he'd been touched by an angel.

Fiona turned to look, and it was almost embarrassing the

way her eyes filled at the sight of Emeline. She'd known
Em would look beautiful, but there was a radiance about her
tonight as she walked down the aisle on Emmett's arm. Her
gown was ivory satin with a softly rounded neck and a train.
She wore pearls around her throat and carried a bouquet of
pink roses interspersed with baby's breath. Fiona hugged
Doll's arm. Doll could only nod because she was crying, too.
Wood, standing on Doll's other side, discreetly handed Doll
a handkerchief.

At the front of the church, Emmett lifted Em's veil and
eased it back for her. He kissed her cheek and stepped away
with a discreet wink at Tommy.

Tommy and Em looked at each other and smiled.

"They look so perfect," Fiona whispered. "Have you ever
seen anything so perfect?"

Doll shook her head and dabbed at her wet face.

"Friends," Reverend Thompson began in his sonorous
voice. He was an interesting-looking man in his early forties
with a head full of snow-white hair that he wore down to his
collar. "We are gathered together this evening in the sight of
God to witness the holy matrimony of Tommy and Emeline.
A wedding is a celebration of a man and a woman entering the
Divine Mystery of Oneness. It is nothing less than the procla-
mation of a couple's love for one another in a reverent manner,
just as Jesus expressed his reverence and love for God."

"Lord, I hope he don't go on for an hour and a half," Doll
said under her breath.

Fiona stifled a giggle, since she'd been thinking the very
same thing. She glanced over and saw Wood grinning like
an idiot.

"Who presents this woman?" the reverend asked.

"I do," Emmett spoke up. "On behalf of the best friend I
ever had, Ben Martin, who loved her more than anything.
Not that I don't love her, too, because I do."

The reverend smiled. "The first 'I do' of the evening."

There was a soft ripple of laughter, followed by a settling of sorts, which felt right.

Fiona saw Em glance at Emmett with a grateful smile.

"In First Corinthians, the Apostle Paul describes love. 'Love is patient, love is kind. Love is not envious, jealous or boastful. It is not arrogant or rude. Love does not insist on its own ways. It is not irritable or resentful. It does not rejoice at wrong and wrongdoing, but rejoices in right and truth. Love bears all things, believes all things, hopes all things, endures all things. Love never ends. So faith, hope and love abide these three. But the greatest of these is love.'" The reverend paused. "And now for the good part." He paused. "Tommy, do you take Emeline to be your lawfully wedded wife? Will you devote your life to loving her, honoring her and taking care of her? In sickness or in health, for richer or poorer, in good times and in bad, for as long as you both shall live?"

"I will," Tommy said clearly. "I do."

"Emeline, do you take Tommy to be your husband? In sickness or in health, for richer or poorer, in good times and in bad, for as long as you both shall live?"

"I do," she replied.

"And will you devote your life to loving him, nourishing him and honoring him?"

"I will."

The reverend nodded. "Turn and face each other and state your vows."

As they faced each other, Fiona knew she had never seen two people more in love. It also occurred to her that the reverend had taken possession of Em's bouquet so smoothly, they must have practiced the move.

"I, Thomas Medlin, take you, Emeline Rachel Wright, to be my lawfully wedded wife," Tommy said. "To have and to hold from this day forward, for better for worse, for richer for poorer, in sickness and in health, till death do us part . . . and even then some."

"He memorized it," Fiona whispered, tearing up all over again.

"I, Emeline Wright, take you, Thomas Medlin, to be my lawfully wedded husband, to have and to hold from this day forward, for better for worse, for richer for poorer, in sickness and in health, to love and cherish, till death us do part." She smiled. "And even then some."

Doll's shoulders were shaking with silent sobs and she was dabbing the hanky at her face furiously.

"The ring," the reverend said.

Tommy slid a ring on Em's finger and then looked at her. "With this ring I thee wed."

She smiled in utter happiness.

"For as much as Tommy and Em have consented together in holy wedlock," the reverend said, "and have witnessed the same before God and this company, I pronounce them man and wife. Those whom God has joined together, let no man put asunder."

When the piano music started up and Tommy and Em walked back down the aisle amid a burst of applause, both of them were smiling joyfully.

A trio of stringed instruments played at the reception. "That's a nice touch," Fiona said to Mr. Howerton, acknowledging the contribution. He'd also provided champagne. "It was very generous of you."

"I've been fortunate in my life," he replied graciously.

"To Mister and Missus Thomas Medlin," Emmett called out, raising his glass of champagne. The toast was repeated as glasses were lifted into the air. Toasts continued and Howerton found himself watching Tommy and Emeline with a curious envy. They had the most tangible love for each other

that he'd ever witnessed, and it had nothing to do with
money, prospects or social standing. It was just what it was,
a love so pure, it seemed meant to be. He watched Tommy
whisper something to Em. She smiled and said something back,
placing her hand on his shirtfront, and the intimate gesture
made Howerton feel an acute ache of loneliness.

"Say something, Wood," someone called.

"I'm not much on making speeches," he hedged.

"Oh, come on."

"I'll just say this," Wood began. "Tommy and Em are two
of the finest, most caring, generous people I ever had the
privilege to know."

"Here, here," someone said.

"They deserve each other," Wood continued. "They deserve
the happiness they've found." He looked at the couple and
lifted his glass. "To Tommy and Em."

As the words echoed enthusiastically, Howerton contem-
plated the word *deserve*.

"You know what we need to do, don't you?" Wood said
laughingly as he drove the wagon home after the reception.

Doll, sitting next to him, gave him a suspicious look.
"Much as you've had to drink? Get to your bed and sleep.
That's what."

Hawk and Jeffrey, riding in back were in no better shape.
They, too, had celebrated and imbibed boisterously. "What?"
Jeffrey asked. "What do we need to do?"

"Have ourselves a shivaree," Wood replied to the hoots
and laughter of the others.

Doll turned and cast a stern eye on the lot of them. "My
left hind foot you will."

"Aw, come on," Hawk complained. "It's all in fun."

"You know what else is fun?" Doll retorted. "Eating. You

ever want to eat in my kitchen again, you'll hush up that foolishness."

"Just a little one," Jeffrey wheeled.

"Come near one of my pots and pans, I'll take a pan to your sorry skull," Doll said, straightening back around imperiously.

In a wagon several yards behind Wood and the others, Tommy drove and Em sat closely next to him, both euphoric from the day. Ahead of them, their friends joked and laughed. Behind them, tin cans and shoes were being dragged behind the wagon, some nonsense about good luck, warding off evil spirits or something of the like.

When the wagon ahead rounded a bend and disappeared from sight, Tommy reined the horse in, stopping theirs. Em looked at him quizzically. "Just for a minute," he said.

She smiled. "Is that . . . *quiet* I hear?"

"Yeah, but just for a minute." He reached out to stroke her face tenderly and then he wrapped a strong hand around the back of her neck and coerced her into a kiss. "My beautiful wife," he said as he pulled back.

She felt a shiver of anticipation.

He noticed the tremor. "Are you cold?" he asked, rubbing her shawl-covered arms.

She was glad the darkness hid the extent of her blushing. "I'm fine," she assured him. As he faced forward again and started the wagon moving again, she hugged herself to him, loving him so much, she ached with it.

The yard was quiet as they drove in, until Wood appeared, having just exited the outhouse. "Night ya'll," he called playfully. "Real sweet dreams."

"Woodson Shaw," Doll hissed from around back.

"Oh, I'm coming," he said as he headed toward her. "I

was just saying good night. Can't a fella wish his friends a good night?"

Tommy was grinning as he climbed out of the wagon. Em gathered her flowers, the box of chocolates and bottle of champagne Gregory Howerton had given them and stood, ready to be helped down, but Tommy whisked her into his arms instead, stealing her breath. "A man is supposed to carry his bride inside," he said.

She laughed softly and clung to him as he made his way to the house.

He climbed the steps, opened the door with one hand and went inside before he set her down. "Welcome home, Mrs. Medlin."

Tears blurred her vision because it was their home now where they would live the rest of their days. "Why, thank you kindly, Mr. Medlin. And how long do you anticipate staying this formal?"

"Not too long," he replied teasingly as he took the items from her one by one and then set them aside. He took hold of her hand and led her back to their bedroom.

Despite her heart pounding and her body trembling with excitement, when he let go of her hand, she slowly and seductively removed her shawl. His eyes glistened, although they looked dark in the dim light of the one lamp left burning. He pulled off his jacket and set it aside. "I need some help," she said softly, turning around.

He came closer and began the work of unbuttoning the far too many slippery pearl buttons down the back of her gown. His head was slightly bent, his hair accidentally caressing the skin of her shoulder as he worked his way down the row. It was almost more than she could bear, and she exhaled slowly aware of how ready she was for him. He was almost finished unbuttoning her, enough that she could wriggle out of the garment, so she turned to face him. "Make love to me."

"Oh, I'll make love to you," he said huskily. "Every night for the rest of our lives, if you'll let me."

He pulled her gown down slowly and she helped, carefully stepping out of it. Then he pulled off his shirt, wrapped her in his arms and kissed her. Piece by piece, the rest of their clothing came off and was discarded as they kissed and stroked, turning around and around in a dizzying dance of lovemaking.

When they found themselves in the middle of the bed and he lay atop her, her gaze was locked on his, full of love and longing. He pushed inside her slowly, but the pressure of her fingers on his back and the expression on her face left no doubt that it was what she wanted and more. Their movement and intensity increased and still they needed more. They needed to entwine body and soul.

Her climax, when it came, pushed him over the edge and it was explosive enough that they fell apart afterwards to catch their breath. They couldn't stay apart long, though. As the moon cast an almost theatrical light into the room, they faced each other, cuddling close. "What was your favorite part of the day?" she asked.

He pulled her hand to his lips and kissed it. "Besides making love to you?"

Her laugh was rich and throaty. "Yes, besides that."

"Seeing you walk into the church."

She smiled and closed her eyes.

"You're not going to sleep yet, are you?" he objected.

"It's late, you know," she murmured sleepily.

"I know. I've just never been so happy."

"Me, too," she whispered.

"What was your favorite part?"

She opened her eyes again. "All of it."

He chuckled. "That's not fair."

She thought about it. "Seeing you. Seeing you see me. It was the best thing ever. One second you were nervous, the next . . . I don't know. You were looking at me with such purpose. And you never once looked away."

"Neither did you."

"And I liked what Emmett said," she added.

"So did I."

"And all the flowers and candles." She paused. "I liked when we danced."

"I like this," he said. "Laying in the dark with you. Holding you. Talking."

"Me, too." She sighed, then turned and snuggled back against him.

"I like being married," he said.

Her smile widened. "That's good since we're going to be married forever and ever."

With those final, sweet words, Tommy wrapped an arm around her and they both gave in to sleep.

Chapter Forty

"Hey," Mitchell called to Blue. "You know this fella?"

Blue looked and then blanched at the sight of the poster in Mitchell's hand. It was a Wanted poster of them, and there was a two hundred and fifty dollar reward being offered. "You out of your mind?" he hissed. He looked up and down the street, but, luckily, no one was paying them much heed.

"You're such an old woman." Mitchell laughed, thoroughly enjoying himself. "No one's even noticed this thing and it's been hanging right here."

Blue swallowed nervously. Mitchell wasn't even talking quietly. He'd get them arrested with his bravado. His eyes bulged as Mitchell rolled the poster up and stuck it under his arm. "What are you doing?"

"Don't go and wet your pants, Henry Joe Bluefield. Jesus Christ Almighty. Look around. We're just two men standing on a street shootin' the bull. You see anybody giving us a second look?"

It was true. No one was looking at them. Plus, the beards they'd grown made it hard to tell it was their faces on the poster.

"Let's get a drink," Mitchell said, starting for the saloon.

"You don't need to be carrying that thing around," Blue complained.

"Why not? I'm gonna save it as a souvenir," he called over his shoulder.

Blue followed, still looking around for any indication that they'd been recognized. Being wanted was a miserable thing. He'd thought it might be a little bit glamorous, but it wasn't. It didn't bother Mitchell in the least. In fact, Mitchell was experiencing a hot streak at cards. He'd won so much, they hadn't had to work for a month. Of course, that wasn't an altogether good thing, since Mitchell was even more full of himself than usual, which was saying something. Also, they were drinking too much and feeling lousy for about half the day until they started drinking again.

They entered the dim saloon, got a drink at the bar and then wandered over to a back table. There wasn't much happening this early in the day.

"Was that two hundred and fifty apiece or together?" Blue whispered.

"Why? You thinking of turning us in?" Mitchell chuckled. "Together," he stated. "Or a hundred apiece. See, they're trying to make it a better deal to get us together." Mitchell unrolled the poster part of the way and studied it. "You know what would be funny?"

"What?"

"To send this to Howerton along with a letter saying, 'I see you got the law after us, but it doesn't look like they're finding us, does it? Know what else, *Gregory*? We're having a grand ole time. And working for you sucked.'"

Blue took a drink. It burned his stomach, so he took another.

"Know what else would be good?" Mitchell continued. "Get some paper and draw a picture of ole Johnny, dead on the floor, half his face gone. I think I'll do it. Send them both to Howerton."

"Can you draw?"

Mitchell shrugged. "I could get close enough."

Mitchell finished his drink. "Need a bottle over here," he called.

The barkeep brought it, although he wasn't in a hurry about it. Mitchell paid, and the barkeep walked away. "Much as you pay for a bottle," Mitchell muttered, "they oughta pour it for you." He poured another glass, then slumped in his seat and leaned way back in his chair. His hat was still on his head and it cast his face in shadow. "I'm thinking it's time," Mitchell said slowly.

"Time for what?"

"To go pay a visit to Miss Ain't-I-too-damn-good-for-anybody. That's what."

"Aw, forget it."

Mitchell nudged his hat up, his expression incredulous. "Did you say *forget* it? Forget it, he says! I ain't gonna forget nothin'. Because of her, I was whipped like a dog. Because of her, I was humiliated. *Used* in an unnatural way. Because of her, I spent weeks freezing my ass off in the mountains. 'Cause of her, my brother grows a pair and then starts thinking he's better than me. Yeah, I'll forget it. When hell freezes over, I'll forget it."

Blue squirmed in his seat. "But you're having luck now."

"So what? That ain't gonna change. Has nothing to do with getting even with Emeline Wright."

"I don't want to get caught," Blue said, leaning in closer to the table.

"There you go with that *we* crap again. I got news for you, Blue. I don't want you to go. You know why? 'Cause you're an old woman. You panic. You get scared and you panic. You're a pussy."

"Am not!"

Mitchell smirked. "It's not your fault, Henry Joe. Your pa was probably a pussy. It's all you knew."

The way Mitchell said it like it was fact was so infuriating that tears sprang to Blue's eyes.

"Oh, don't go crying, now," Mitchell moaned.

"You ought not talk to me that way. It's not right."

"I don't know what you're getting all worked up about. The whole thing will take me a week. At the most, nine or ten days and then I'll be back and it'll be like nothin's different, 'cept I'll feel a whole lot better. The only thing that will be different is Emeline Wright will have disappeared off the face of the earth. No trace. No word. My brother can just wonder for the rest of his life."

Blue scooted his chair back and stood, trembling with fury.

"Where you goin'?" Mitchell asked.

"You can go to hell," Blue said in a low voice.

"Oh, don't go being a girl."

"Screw you. I'm no girl. I'm no pussy."

"Yeah, whatever you say, Henry Joe."

Blue knocked his drink over, spilling it on the table, and then walked away.

"Oh, come on, Blue," Mitchell called behind him.

Blue kept walking. A man could only take so much.

Chapter Forty-One

Doll carried a plate of breakfast over to the house and found Em sitting at the table, her head in her hands. "This is the third morning in a row you didn't show up for breakfast. What's wrong with you?"

"I don't feel well," Em said without looking up.

"I can see that." She set the plate on the table. "Maybe some food—"

Em moaned.

"When did this start?" Doll asked.

"Just the last few days."

Doll pursed her lips. "Does it ease up as the day goes on?"

"A little."

"How long since you bled?"

Em jerked her head up with a gasp.

"Good Lord, honey. You hadn't even conceived of the notion?" She paused, but Em didn't move or speak.

Em's eyes filled. "That I'm . . . pregnant?"

Em was so shocked, Doll didn't know what to make of it. "Isn't it good news?"

"If I'm . . . *pregnant*?"

Doll pulled back a chair and sat. "Why are you so surprised?"

Em shook her head. Since it hadn't happened with Sonny,

something she'd been grateful for, she'd suspected she couldn't conceive. "How can I know for sure?"

"You just have to wait. If you don't get your cycle—"

"I did miss it," Em interrupted as she thought about it. It was the end of May, which meant, "maybe even two."

Doll grinned. "You didn't waste any time. That's for sure."

Em felt like laughing and crying. "I don't want to tell Tommy if it might not be true."

"If you've missed two cycles, you'll begin to show in a month or two."

Em's jaw dropped. "I can't wait a month to tell him."

"Then tell him. Tell him that I suspect it. Lord, it will make his day!"

He would be so happy. He'd be a *father*. And she would be a mother. She couldn't quite envision it.

"Let's see," Doll mused. "It's nearly June and you've missed two—" She closed her eyes and counted on her fingers. "It'll probably be a Christmas baby."

A baby. A Christmas baby. Em shivered at the strangeness of it.

"Somewhere around then."

A wave of nausea rose in Em and she clapped her hands over her mouth.

"I'll fetch you a bowl," Doll said, rising. "This is part of it, sweetheart," she said cheerfully as she went to the cupboard. "It's just part of it."

Tommy soaked in a tub outside the back door and under the stars, pondering the logistics of building a lavatory that would attach to the house. "An inside outhouse," he muttered. He grinned, thinking he'd have to share that joke with Wood and the others. Gregory Howerton had an indoor flush toilet and a six-foot tub. It was an intriguing thought.

Tommy climbed out of the tub, dumped the water and dried off. Holding the towel in front of himself, he hurried inside to their room, where Em was reading in bed. "Forgot clean clothes," he said as he slipped the towel off and got under the covers.

She grinned. "Oh, my."

"I don't think anyone saw me."

"Too bad for them," she replied mischievously. "Did the bath help your back?"

"No. Just my smell." His back was sore from bending over all day to transplant the tobacco seedlings. "What are you reading?"

"A new book," she said, showing him the cover.

The Portrait of a Lady, he read. "Is it good?"

She wrinkled her nose. "I'm having trouble concentrating. Why don't you turn over and I'll rub your back."

He grinned and turned over, and she put her book aside and straddled him. She began to rub his skin and knead his muscles. "That feels good."

"How was it with the new help?"

He had to refocus his thoughts. "Malcolm works hard but Edward's kind of lazy. I don't know that he'll last. I don't know about the other one yet." He moaned. "There," he said when she reached a particularly sore spot. "Yeah, right there."

She used both hands to work the muscle kink. "I feel it."

"It's just slow work. Plant by plant."

"It probably feels like it'll never get done," she empathized.

"I learned a long time ago, you just keep at it and it'll eventually get done."

She pounded gently on his back with the sides of her hands.

The feeling took him by surprise, but then he relaxed into it. "How'd you learn to do this?" The answer was obvious, although it didn't dawn on him until after he'd asked. He turned halfway over, lifting her body in the process. "Sorry."

She leaned forward and kissed him. "Turn back over."

Instead, he rolled onto his back. "I don't know," he said suggestively, lifting his hips and pressing himself against her.

"This is a pretty nice position right here." He suddenly noticed something different about her. "Are you feeling alright?"

She nodded.

He reached up to feel her forehead to see if she was feverish, because her color was high.

"I felt sick this morning," she said quietly.

"Sick how?"

"Well—" She climbed off.

He started to object and pull her back, but she looked strange, as if she had to admit something. He watched her warily.

"I've been feeling ill for the last several days, mostly mornings."

"Why didn't you say something?"

"I thought it would pass. But then Doll said something."

"What?"

"It's what she asked," Em said haltingly, blushing hotly.

He was growing worried, because she had something to tell him and it wasn't good. "Which was?"

"She suggested I might be pregnant."

For a moment, he couldn't process the statement. "Pregnant?"

Em nodded.

It sank in and he exhaled so hard he got dizzy. He sat up. "Why does she think so? Do you think so?" he asked, reaching out for her.

She smiled and nodded.

He beamed a smile. "I thought you had bad news. A baby?"

She nodded.

He pulled her into his arms, then immediately relaxed his grip, because he'd been too rough in his excitement. He looked down at her stomach.

"Doll thinks it will be a Christmas baby."

He looked at her searchingly. It was incredible enough

that he had her in his life, but now there would be a child. "Do you ever get scared at how perfect it all is?"

Her smiled faded. "Yes," she admitted.

A second later, he laughed in sheer delight. "A baby! We're going to have a baby!"

Smiling again, she fell into his arms and they clung to each other.

Chapter Forty-Two

The fields were shaping up nicely in the perfect weather of early June. Wood straightened and wiped his forehead with his sleeve as Tommy walked by him. "Kind of early to call it a day, ain't it?" he teased.

"I'm going to go check on Em," Tommy replied.

"You know you got about six or seven more months of this, don't you?"

"Then the baby will be here," Hawk joined in. "And he'll have two of them to fret over."

Tommy knew he was probably being silly, but he felt a nagging pull of worry. Unwittingly, his gaze raked the landscape to the west, to the area where he'd come upon Briar Lindley spying on Em. Maybe Briar was at it again. Maybe *that's* what this feeling was. Because it felt like Em was in danger. He hoped it was only her being sick and him being overprotective. He reached the house and started up the steps.

"Kind of early to call it a day, ain't it?" Doll called from behind him.

He turned and saw her walking toward him with a teasing grin on her face. He shook his head and went inside.

Right away, he saw Em in the parlor. She was in the rocking chair, sitting very still. "Are you okay?" he asked as he got close.

"No," she replied, hardly moving her mouth.

He fought back a grin. It wasn't funny that she was sick, but the reason for it was wonderful. And the fact that he was just being overprotective was a relief. This wasn't danger, it was morning sickness. He squatted in front of her. "Can I do anything?"

"No. You've done quite enough."

He lost his battle and smiled.

So did she, and then she groaned. "Don't make me laugh. Go away."

"Alright, I will," he agreed, standing. "I just had to check on you." He bent and kissed her head and she groaned again. "Sorry if I made you move there," he said, backing away.

Doll peered into the parlor as Em rose and made a hasty exit through the back door, her hand pressed to her mouth. "Now, you know this is just a part of it," Doll lectured. "You need to stop worrying so much."

He started to agree, only the feeling returned more strongly than before. Frowning heavily, he turned and went into their room for his revolver, a six-shooter.

"What is with you?" Doll called.

"You ever see a man, a dark-haired man in the distance, kind of spying on the place?" he called back.

"No. Who you talking about?" Her eyes widened to see him with the gun. "And why do you have a gun?"

"It's probably nothing. I'm just worried about Em. That's all."

"Honey, she's *pregnant*. Her being sick is a part of it. It'll pass. Trust me when I tell you that she doesn't feel bad enough that she wants you to shoot her."

He gave her a look.

"What are you thinking?" she insisted.

He could only shake his head, because how was he supposed to explain a bad feeling?

"You're being silly!"

"I probably am."

"Well then, get on with you," Doll said as she stalked to the front door. "Goodness' sake. We just all need to be about our business."

He heard Doll leave and then he listened to the quiet, taking a breath to calm his nerves. Maybe she was right, but the foreboding wasn't going away. Not to mention that, the last time he'd felt it, he'd been right. Em *had* been in danger. If he hadn't heeded the warning, she might not even be here now. He wondered if maybe he shouldn't just stick close today.

Blue grimaced as a muscle cramped in his leg. He stood, having squatted for too long. He'd spotted Emeline Wright twice this morning, but both times, an older woman had been around. He patted his pockets for reassurance that he was prepared. His fingertips closed in on the small bottle of chloroform he'd taken from a doc at gunpoint before he'd left Roanoke. He was going to use it to incapacitate Emeline Wright, so he could get her back to Mitchell. Of course, first, he'd make Mitchell admit what a feat he'd pulled off. Then he'd get an apology, not to mention a promise of more respect. "Pussy, my ass," he muttered.

The Martin Farm looked good. He'd seen cattle and horses, and there was both wheat and tobacco growing in the fields. There was an impressive bunkhouse and a new barn. Blue grinned at the thought of rubbing Mitchell's nose in it, but that would be later. For now, his plan was to sneak up on Em the second he saw her alone. He'd douse a cloth with chloroform and force it over her mouth and nose before she knew what was happening. She'd never even have a chance to scream.

His breath caught as she came out the back door, walking briskly toward the outhouse with her hand pressed to her mouth. He patted his pockets again and then reached for his gun. Not that he'd use it on her. No, siree. He wanted her alive. She was his ticket to respect.

Midway through the yard, she stopped and doubled over.

"Come on, lady," Blue whispered. "Come on. Keep going."

As if she heard his wish, she stood back up and continued on. She reached the outhouse, but she didn't go in. Instead, she reached a hand out and leaned against it.

"Go in, damn you," he whispered. He'd begun to shake with nerves and anticipation, and the longer she delayed, the more nervous he'd get. Finally, she opened the door and went inside. He looked around to make sure the old woman wasn't lurking about and then he crept forward. He kept his eyes glued to the outhouse door. Once he reached it, breathing hard, he stuck his gun in his belt and fumbled for the cloth and the bottle of chloroform.

"You okay, honey?" a woman hollered.

Blue flattened himself against the side of the outhouse. Whoever the woman was, she was a damned nuisance.

"Yes," Em called back a moment later. "But being pregnant is *not* enjoyable."

Pregnant? Blue reeled from the newly acquired knowledge. Delivering Miss Wright to Mitchell had been one thing. But Mitchell would kill her, sure as shit, and killing a pregnant woman was just plain wrong. It meant the baby would die, too. Blue shook his head, knowing he couldn't be a party to that.

Damn it, but he'd made a long ass trip for nothing. He sighed heavily as he stuck the bottle and cloth back into his

pocket. On second thought, breathing was a whole lot easier
now that the decision was made. Maybe he hadn't come a
long way for nothing; maybe this was his stand. Yeah, that
was it. This was his stand. He could have grabbed her, but
he'd chosen not to. Because that was the right thing to do.
Now, he just needed to get the hell out of here. He peeked
around the outhouse and didn't see the woman who'd yelled.
He took his gun back in hand and backed up a step. The
getting looked good, so he took off.

"Hey!" a man called.

The voice startled Blue. He whirled back around, saw a
gun pointed at him and pulled the trigger.

Tommy, standing in front of him, gasped and dropped to
his knees, lowering his gun. A red hole appeared above his
eyebrow.

Blue couldn't breathe. He'd shot Tommy! He jumped as
Emeline Wright screamed. He shook his head because he
hadn't meant to do it. Em ran to Tommy and he collapsed into
her arms. Another man was running toward them now, shout-
ing at him. Crazed with panic, Blue took off in a dead run.

He made it up the rise, into the thicket and pushed
through to where his horse was tied. His knees felt springy
as he mounted, but he managed it and took off. Mitchell
would have mocked the tears streaming down his face, but
he couldn't stop them. He'd killed Tommy. He hadn't meant
to, but he'd killed Tommy.

Hawk squatted and placed his fingers above Tommy's
mouth and nose. "He's breathing," he exclaimed as he
squeezed her shoulder. "I'm going for help!"

Em felt so strange, as if everything was suddenly moving
in slow motion. *It's because it's not real,* she reasoned. This
was a nightmare. It had to be a nightmare! Or was it the curse?
She thought she'd escaped it.

"What's happening?" Doll cried from the house.

"Tommy's been shot," Hawk yelled. "Ring the bell!"

Doll dropped the bowl she was holding and green beans scattered as she turned and ran flat out for the bell. She reached it, panting for breath, and tugged the rope fast and hard.

"I'm going for the doctor," Hawk yelled to her. He was already on his horse and he was a good rider.

"Stop at Howerton's," Doll called back. "He may have someone he can send!"

Hawk gave a cursory nod and spurred his horse on, and Doll kept ringing until she caught sight of the men returning. She pointed frantically. "Tommy," she cried. "It's Tommy! Hurry!"

Em was bent over Tommy with her fingers pressed to his forehead, but blood seeped from beneath them.

"Let me see," Wood said as he bent closer.

She resisted, shaking her head.

"Let me see, honey," Wood repeated, grabbing hold of her wrist and forcing it back. "Oh, God. What happened?"

Tears streamed down her face. "It was B-blue! His b-brother's friend. He s-shot him!"

"Let's get him inside, boys," Wood called. "We got to get a doctor here and fast!"

"Sam," Howerton bellowed across the corral.

Sam turned, as did several other men.

"Tommy's been shot," Howerton said. "Send some men after the doctor. Find him and get him over there!"

"Yes, sir!"

Howerton never stopped moving. He reached his horse and mounted. "Tell me what happened?" he said as he and

Hawk rode out. "You said he was shot in the head, but he's still alive?"

"Was when I left."

"I need a damn doctor on staff," Howerton fumed. "By God, from now on, we'll have one."

They didn't speak all the rest of the way to the farm. They dismounted and rushed inside the house, moving toward the sound of voices in the bedroom. Hawk hung back at the door of Tommy and Em's bedroom, but Howerton continued in, and everyone moved aside and allowed him close.

Tommy's eyes were closed, and there was a bandage above his right brow. Em was sitting on the bed next to him, white-faced, leaning forward slightly, holding one of his hands in both of hers. There were smears of blood on her face and her dress was stained with it.

"He's still got a pulse," Wood reported grimly.

"Mr. Howerton sent men after the doc," Hawk said.

"We're obliged," Doll said, glancing up at Howerton.

"Who did it?" Howerton asked.

"A man who used to work for you," Wood replied. "Name of Blue."

Howerton flinched. "You sure?"

"Yeah, we're sure. Em saw him. He wasn't two feet away from her."

"He was after me," Em said in a flat voice. She didn't look away from Tommy. "Tommy came up on him."

"How long ago?" Howerton asked brusquely.

"Half hour," Wood estimated with a shake of his head. "Not even."

Howerton leaned over to lay a hand on Tommy's arm. "I'm going to get the son of a bitch, Tommy," he said, squeezing lightly. "You hang on!" He glanced at Em. She'd been crying, but she wasn't now. "Your wife needs you." He turned on his spurred heel and left.

Hawk followed the man outside. "Mr. Howerton?"

Howerton turned back. "Yeah?"

"It may not be my place to tell you, but Em's going to have a baby."

Howerton blinked.

"Tommy's going to be a father," Hawk said.

Howerton nodded. He looked and saw some of his men riding in, Sam and Quin in the lead. "I don't trust Doc Simmons to be able to handle this," he said to Hawk. "Get to town and see Rice. Have him send a telegraph to every doctor and hospital in traveling distance. We need someone with experience at this kind of thing."

Hawk nodded.

"I'll pay. Whatever they need. Tell Rice."

Hawk nodded again. "Yes, sir."

"Did you ever know anyone to survive that kind of wound?"

Hawk hesitated. "No," he admitted.

"Me, neither."

"But I know Tommy," Hawk said. "I know his heart. He wants to be here and that's something."

"Is it? When you've been shot in the head?" Howerton mounted and rode out without looking back.

"Anything we can do?" Sam called, when he reached them.

"No. Tommy's alive, but barely. Blue shot him."

"Blue?"

"That's right. And we're going after him."

"I'll go get some men," Sam said.

"*We'll* go get the men," Howerton corrected. "This is going to end."

Emmett hurried toward the telegraph office, concerned about the hour. Sure enough, Jules Gunderson, the telegraph operator, was locking up for the day. "Wait," Emmett called.

"Hello, Emmett," Jules Gunderson greeted. His cheerful smile faded quickly. "What's wrong?"

"Tommy Medlin was shot."

"What? Who did it?"

"Who doesn't matter so much, since Mr. Howerton's gone after the scoundrel. Tommy's still alive, so I need to send a telegraph out to every doctor and hospital in this part of the country. Can you help me?"

"Yes, of course. Is he hurt bad?"

"He was shot in the head."

Jules's jaw dropped, and then he quickly unlocked the door and went right back inside. "Has Doc seen him?"

"He's on his way there now. And I mean no offense to the doc by this, because he's a good man, but we're hoping for some sharp mind with new ideas."

Jules reached the machine. "Where was he hit?"

Emmett pointed to just above his right brow.

"Tarnation! Does he have a chance?"

"Of course, he's got a chance! Let's do this."

"What do you want to say?"

As the clock struck twelve, Em slipped out of her ruined dress and then stared at it, her gaze riveted on the bloodstains. She opened her hand and dropped the dress, then walked to the nightstand, poured water in the basin and placed her hands inside. Despite the fact that her hands had been repeatedly wiped off, the water turned pink. It was too much and she lost control and sobbed bitterly. *Please,* she prayed. *Help us. Please. Please!* Tommy was lying motionless in bed, but she suddenly imagined him in a casket, and cried even harder. *Please, God. Please. I need him. I need him. I'll do anything. I'll give anything. Just give him back to me.*

Chapter Forty-Three

Em heard knocking and wearily dragged herself from the choppy sleep she'd managed in the last few hours, but it was the sharp stench of urine that shocked her into full wakefulness.

"You up yet, honey?" Doll asked.

Em jumped out of bed so fast, she was overcome with dizziness and nausea, and had to sit back down again.

"I was afraid of that," Doll said. She'd cracked the door open and saw the wet bed. "I mean I knew it would happen. Because it has to happen. That's why I said—"

Em dropped to her hands and knees and reached for the chamber pot under the bed. She barely got it there in time before she vomited.

"Oh, honey," Doll said.

Em retched, but there was very little in her stomach to come up. She quivered and heaved again. The next thing she knew, Doll was there by her side, handing her a cool cloth and pulling her hair back. "I hate those dry heaves," Doll said.

Em closed her eyes, felt scalding tears and heaved again. Why couldn't she stop? There was nothing in her stomach. She hadn't eaten yesterday.

When it finally subsided, Doll helped her up and into a robe. "You go use the outhouse," Doll said. "Then you get dressed. I'm going to clean up in here and we're going to move Tommy to his old room."

Em shook her head. "No."

"Yes, Emmy, because it's best. We can all watch over him that way. Him being in here is no better for him and it makes it worse for you. It's what I said yesterday and I'm right. Now, that is that."

"No, I—"

"Em, honey, you've got to take care of yourself and that baby. We're all of us here for Tommy. He's going to come out of this and look at you and ask how his baby is, and you want to be able to tell him the baby is just fine." She took a step backward. "Now, go pee."

"Don't do anything yet," Em pleaded. "I have to think."

"You go think," Doll agreed pleasantly. "Go on, now. We got more to do than we can shake a stick at."

Em stepped outside and the day was glorious yet again. The temperature was mild, a soft breeze was blowing, and she resented it. Which was foolish. It wasn't as if foul weather would have made the day easier. She used the outhouse, which reminded her of the last time she'd used it. What had Blue been doing skulking around? And why had Tommy been there with a gun? Why had it all happened? It made no sense.

She left the outhouse and made her way to the spot where Tommy had fallen. She stood rooted there, staring down at dark blotches of blood left behind, then started back to the house, wiping the tears from her face as she went. Doll was right. There was a lot to do and she'd spent enough time feeling sorry for herself. It was time to put her full concentration into getting her husband well.

* * *

The eleven-man posse topped a hill and saw Blue perhaps a half-mile ahead, riding hard and kicking up dust. "Ya," Howerton yelled, spurring his horse on. They overtook Blue in short order and circled him, forcing him to stop, their guns leveled at him.

"I didn't mean to do it," Blue cried.

"Throw down your gun, Blue," Sam ordered.

"I didn't mean to shoot him!"

"If you don't throw down—" Howerton threatened.

Blue tossed his gun, then stuck his hands high in the air.

Jackie Johnson dismounted and retrieved the gun. "You only have the one?"

"Yeah."

"If we find another, I'm going to shoot your kneecap clear off," Johnson warned.

"I only got the one! I swear it."

"Get off your horse," Howerton ordered.

Blue kicked his leg over and slid off the horse, still trying to keep his hands in the air. "I swear, Mr. Howerton, I did not mean to shoot Tommy."

Mark Hanks was seething. "Yeah? Well what about Johnny, you son of a whore?"

"I didn't shoot Johnny!"

"Liar!" Hanks accused.

"I ain't lying! I only took the gun to threaten him with, just so he'd let Mitchell go. That's all."

"That ain't hardly all, Blue," Sam spoke up. "Not when Johnny ended up dead."

"I didn't mean for that to happen and I didn't shoot him!"

"You're saying Mitchell shot him."

Blue didn't speak for several seconds. "I'm saying I didn't shoot him. That's the God's honest truth. But that's all I'm saying."

The men began dismounting, all but Howerton, Sam

Blake and Bud Ulrich. Ulrich pulled a thick coil of rope from his saddle and rode toward the nearest usable tree.

"Hey, now. I deserve a trial," Blue cried, shifting from foot to foot. "You can't just go and hang me. It ain't legal and you know it."

"It's not legal," Howerton agreed. "I know it and I don't give a rat's ass," he railed, yelling the last of it.

"Where's Mitchell, Blue?" Sam asked.

Blue shook his head rapidly. "I ain't telling you that."

"Oh, I think you will," Howerton said.

"Why'd you go after Tommy anyhow?" Lynn Green asked. "*Tommy*, of all people. He never hurt you or anybody. Not in his whole goddamned life."

"I wasn't after Tommy. I was after Miss—"

Howerton seethed. "I cannot believe you were stupid enough to just say that."

"I wasn't going to hurt her," Blue added quickly.

Howerton leaped off his horse. "Move!"

Blue was forced forward at gunpoint as the rope was thrown over a tree, knotted and prepared. "You can't do this," Blue whimpered.

Howerton holstered his gun. "If I'd done it when I should have, Tommy would still be alive and well and so would Johnny."

Sam sighed. "I got to ask," he said, leaning over in the saddle to holster his gun. "Why? I don't get it. What could you ever have against Mrs. Medlin?"

"Mrs. Med—" Blue's jaw dropped.

"That's right," Sam said. "Emeline Wright married Tommy. The man you shot and probably killed."

"Probably?" Blue stammered. "Is he still alive?"

Johnson and Green grabbed hold of him and Hanks tied his hands behind his back.

"Don't matter if he's alive or dead," Johnson replied. "You shot him in the head. You die."

Blue gritted his teeth as Hanks yanked the rope as tight as it would go, cutting into his skin. "It doesn't have to be that tight," he bit out.

"Scurvy son of a bitch," Hanks fumed.

"Sam asked you a question," Howerton said. "Why did you go after Miss Wright? Time and time again?"

"I never had nothin' against her! It's Mitchell. First, he wanted her and now he hates her. Hates her guts. Thinks it's all her fault, what happened."

Sam frowned thoughtfully. "You said you weren't going to hurt her," he mused. "So . . . what? Were you taking her to Mitchell? So he could do it?"

Blue didn't answer.

"The man asked you a question," Johnson warned.

Blue shook his head. He was breathing fast. "You're gonna hang me? I ain't tellin' you nothin'."

"You might want to consider that we can make it last a long, long time," Howerton said calmly. "You're not going to have your neck snapped, if you were hoping it would go fast."

"I wasn't hoping that. I wasn't hoping anything. I can't believe this crap!"

"Answer the question," Howerton warned. "You were taking her to Mitchell. Yes or no?"

"Yes! He was always calling me names, saying things."

"But you knew he'd hurt her," Sam said. "Probably kill her."

Blue looked away from Sam's gaze.

"Which makes you just as guilty, Blue," Sam continued. "Don't you see that?"

"Give it up, Sam," Howerton said. "He either doesn't get it or he doesn't give a damn. Let's do this."

Hanks slipped the noose over Blue's neck. "Any last words?"

"Yeah. Screw you," Blue replied angrily, his voice shaking.

"Mitchell probably sent him, which means he's close," Green suggested.

"Is that true?" Howerton asked Blue.

Blue breathed rapidly through his nose and stared down at the ground.

"That true?" Hanks asked, jerking him backward by the noose.

Blue remained silent.

"Nothing to say?" Howerton said calmly. "Take him up."

Ulrich had formed a lariat around the far end of the rope and snubbed it around his saddle horn. Now, he walked the horse forward. Sam looked away as Blue was hoisted into the air.

"Don't tell me you think we're wrong," Howerton said to Sam.

"No." He paused. "Doesn't mean I want to watch it."

Other than a rogue flinch or slight grimace here or there, no one else showed any emotion as Blue's face turned purplish and his body began to convulse. A painful whistling, wheezing sound came from him and he wet himself.

"Bring him down," Howerton ordered.

Sam looked at Howerton sharply. "What are you doing?"

"We've got to find out where Mitchell is, don't we?"

Blue collapsed on the ground, gasping for air. Howerton waited until he'd recovered enough to hear him. "This can go relatively fast or we can make it last all day long. Where's Mitchell?"

Blue didn't answer.

"If you can speak, you'd better do it," Howerton warned.

"I don't know where he is," Blue rasped.

"Where was he when you last saw him?" Howerton demanded.

"Come on, Blue," Lynn Green spoke up. "You don't want to die like this."

Blue glared at the man.

"Haul him back up," Howerton said.

"Wait a minute," Sam snapped. He dismounted and strode

forward, squatting beside Blue. "You think it takes principle to keep silent? Think about it! Mitchell would have raped Miss Wright, if not for Tommy. Mitchell killed Johnny Macgregor. There's a debt needs paying, Blue, and I think you know it. And I'll tell you what else; if we don't stop him, there's no telling what he'll do next. And if you don't tell us where he is and he hurts someone else, that's part your fault. I'd give that some thought, since you're fixin' to meet your maker."

"He was the only friend I ever had," Blue rasped. A tear slipped out of the corner of his eye.

"I know you thought so," Sam replied gently. "But he wasn't really much of a friend, was he? What you'd say earlier? He was always belittling you, calling you names? Would you have gotten into all this trouble, if not for him?"

"Doesn't mean I'm going to betray him. I ain't no Judas."

"All we asked was where you last saw him. You're just sharing a fact, not really betraying him."

"I'd listen to the man," Howerton said. "Otherwise, you're going to die a hard death."

Blue's lips quivered. "He'd know it was me."

Sam shook his head. "He won't."

"Swear it?" Blue whispered.

"I swear," Sam replied. "And you know I'm a man of my word. None of us will tell him. If he asks, we'll lie. That's if he's even still there, which really isn't too likely."

"I feel like crap."

"You've got call to. You've done a lot of bad things. But telling us where a murderer is, who's got every intention of murdering again, it's not one of them." Sam paused. "Where is he?"

"Roanoke," Blue replied weakly.

"Is that true?"

Blue nodded.

"Thank you."

"This ain't right, hanging me like this."

Sam was silent for a moment, then he stood. "Yeah, it is."

Howerton gave the signal, Ulrich backed his horse and Blue's body went back into the air. For several seconds, not much happened, then the wheezing, choking sound began again. Not only did his face turn blue again, it engorged. His tongue protruded and his body convulsed harder than before. A terrible stench filled the air.

"He shit his pants," Hanks complained.

"And he's getting a hard-on," Johnson observed with an amazed frown.

Sam turned away, thinking it couldn't last too much longer, and he was right. Howerton pulled out his pistol and shot the man dead. The sound ricocheted, and then there was silence. "Let him drop," Howerton ordered. "We're pushing on to Roanoke."

Chapter Forty-Four

Tommy started toward the house, feeling the eeriness of an inexplicable change. He focused on the middle-aged man sitting on the front porch. He vaguely recognized him, and yet couldn't place him.

"Hello," the man called.

Tommy stopped, realizing it was Ben Martin. He shook his head in confusion, because Ben wasn't supposed to be there, although he couldn't recollect exactly where he'd gone or why.

"Sit awhile," Ben invited. "How's the tobacco coming?"

Tommy continued on to the porch and sat in one of the rocking chairs, hoping to regain his bearings. He wasn't thinking clearly. Something wasn't quite right. "We're getting it in the fields."

"Slow go, ain't it?"

"Tedious," Tommy agreed.

Ben grunted. "All those tiny, little seeds. Preparing the first seedbed and planting, and then plowing the fields, how many times?"

"Four. Wood thought three would do, but it's our first crop."

"Bright Leaf?"

Tommy nodded. "Yes, sir."

"Lot of work. Gonna be worth it, you reckon?"

"Hope so." He paused. "Does Em know you're here?"

"Oh, I think she knows. She knows you're here, too."

Tommy felt a chill come over him because Ben was *dead*. That's why he'd moved on. Suddenly, Tommy was recalling Blue and the gun. "Am I dead?" he exclaimed, feeling strangely weak.

"No," Ben said, leaning forward, his expression somber. "No, you are not. And Emmy needs you, so I'm here to keep you company and keep you from going any further."

"What do you mean . . . further?"

"That's not important right now." Ben sat back. "What's important is that you relax for a spell. Got any big news you want to share?" he asked with a sly grin.

"The baby, you mean?" Tommy replied, wondering how Ben knew everything that was happening.

"Well, yes! Congratulations! It's wonderful news."

"If I'm not dead—"

"You're not."

"Then how am I seeing you?"

Ben pursed his lips. "I'm visiting, is all. I don't remember you being such an inquisitive fella."

Tommy shook his head. "We never . . . we never met."

"No, you're right about that. But we saw one another. Heard of one another. And now we have Em in common."

"I have a good life with Em."

"I know that."

"I want to be with her."

Ben nodded. "Know that, too."

"Where is she?"

"She's fine, Tommy."

"I didn't ask if she was fine. I asked where she was."

Ben studied him a moment and then gave a resigned

shrug. "She's over there," Ben replied, nodding toward the bunkhouse.

Tommy got up and walked toward the bunkhouse. Halfway there, he saw movement in the window of his old room and changed course to see who was there. He reached it, peered inside and saw Em sitting next to someone in bed. Doll and Wood were there, too. He leaned further over to see who was in bed and received a bone-jarring shock to recognize himself. An overwhelming crush of dizziness and movement overcame him and he braced himself against the window and closed his eyes. "Em——"

Em drew back with a gasp and studied Tommy anxiously. He still appeared to be unconscious, but he'd just uttered her name. She hadn't imagined it, had she? "Did you hear it?" she asked, looking up into Wood's face.

The man's smile answered for him. "I heard it, honey. God as my witness, I heard it!"

A glass of water was trembling in Doll's hands. "I think it may have been the best thing I ever heard," she said. She drew a deep breath. "Tommy," she bellowed.

Em jerked at the unexpected outburst.

"Good Lord, woman!" Wood chastised. "Don't go and give him a heart attack. Or us neither. Like we don't have enough problems."

"Sorry," Doll replied. "Thought it was worth a try."

"Let's try to get a little water down him," Wood said, shifting over to lift Tommy. Em took the glass from Doll and brought it to Tommy's lips as Wood worked to open his jaw.

"Won't he choke?" Em worried.

"I don't know, but we have to try, I think. Just a little."

Em held her breath as she poured a little water into Tommy's mouth. He swallowed and there was a collective sigh of relief. She poured a little more and he gagged, spewing the water.

"Now, now, now, take it slow," Wood coaxed nervously. "Just a little dribble at a time."

"You want me to do it?" Doll offered.

Em shook her head and tried again. It was nerve-racking and she'd begun crying again, which was a damn nuisance. "I'm fine," she said. "I swear, I'm not really crying."

"You're entitled," Wood said gently.

Tommy choked again and Doll reached out, unable to help herself. "Slow, now."

"Might want to be starting on supper pretty soon," Wood suggested tenderly.

She straightened indignantly. "I suppose I might be," she replied snappishly before walking off in a huff.

"She doesn't mean to hover, you know," Wood said.

Tommy had a little fluid in his mouth, but he wasn't swallowing. "He's not taking it," Em said.

"He will. It's just slow, is all. We got to be patient."

She lowered the glass. "Why did this have to happen?"

"It didn't have to happen. It just happened. And we just have to handle it. We're strong enough and Tommy's strong enough to come through this. Now, you got to believe that."

She nodded.

"You know, you're getting some salt in that glass," he teased. "Come on back and give him another swallow."

Tommy found himself standing in front of the house again. Ben still sat in the same spot. "Satisfy your curiosity?" Ben asked.

"I'm going to die, aren't I?"

Ben frowned. "Now, you listen to me, Tom Medlin. You cannot think that way. Not for a single minute. You hear me?"

"I don't understand," Tommy said, beginning to get angry and frustrated.

"Do you have to understand everything?"

"I want to live!"

"And you have got to hold on to that and keep holding on to that. It is essential. It's important."

"I know what essential means," Tommy muttered as he sat back down, although when he'd walked onto the porch he didn't remember. "I'm not slow."

"I never thought you were. In fact, nobody ever really thought that, Tommy. It was kind of a joke your family played on you. They had a mean streak to them for the most part. Isn't that right?"

"They had a mean streak, but they thought it."

"Nah. What they realized was that they could make *you* think it. And, son, that is everything. What a man thinks about himself determines everything else in his life. What he goes for or chooses not to. What he believes he's entitled to. Or thinks he doesn't deserve."

Ben began rocking, and Tommy pondered his statement.

"It's a pleasant thing, rocking," Ben said. "Emmy likes to rock."

Tommy leaned back and noticed a water stain on the ceiling of the porch he'd never seen before. It was in the shape of a rabbit. "I want to hold our baby," he said. *And make love to Em again. To hold her in the night.*

"You keep right on wanting. That's what'll make the difference. Hear me?"

Tommy nodded. He wanted to believe it. "I hear you."

Chapter Forty-Five

Only by the grace of coincidence did Dr. James 'Jack' Werthing become privy to the telegraph sent by T. Emmett Rice of Green Valley, Virginia. For a matter of eight long days, Jack had taken over the responsibilities of administration of Philadelphia Hospital so that his friend and mentor, Dr. Miles Kay, could enjoy a brief vacation. Miles had returned to work earlier in the week, but as Jack cleared his desk and prepared to leave for the day, he noticed an application for employment he'd failed to pass on.

Jack, an attractive, fair-haired man, considered putting it off until tomorrow, but then grabbed it and headed back to Miles's office. He liked a clean desk and he liked starting the day with a fresh slate, which was why administration had been such an unpleasant experience. The hospital was understaffed and overpopulated. The insane ward of the hospital housed over a thousand patients at the moment and the administrative challenges never stopped. For the chief administrator, there was no such thing as a clean desk or finishing the day's work.

Miles was in a meeting, so Jack handed the application to his newly hired assistant, Randall Miller. "I forgot to pass this on."

"I'll see that he gets it, Doctor Werthing."

Jack couldn't help noticing how frazzled the young man seemed. He gave him a smile of encouragement as he turned to go. "Have a good evening."

"Doctor Werthing?"

Jack turned back. "Yes?"

"May I ask your opinion on something?"

"Of course."

Randall reached for a telegraph and handed it over. "I'm supposed to discard what's not important, but—"

Jack took the telegraph and perused it. Frowning, he read it more closely.

"Should I discard it? Or might we post it somewhere for the other doctors to see? I believe Doctor Kay will say to discard it, short of staff as we are, but—"

Jack looked up at the assistant, wondering if he knew his history. "I'll take it."

"You don't mind?"

He saw only relief on the young man's face, no guile. "Not at all. As a matter of fact, I was involved with a case that bears rather a striking similarity to this one."

"Really?" Randall Miller asked as if genuinely surprised.

Either the man was a good actor, or he really didn't know. Jack merely nodded and held up the telegraph. "I'll take care of it," he said, turning to go.

"Thank you, sir," Randall called.

Jack gave a quick nod and a smile and then left the hospital at a brisk pace, anxious to get home and share the telegraph with Charity.

Sitting in front of the oval vanity mirror, Alma Werthing adjusted the pewter comb in her dark hair. She noticed another gray hair, plucked it out with a frown, and then pondered whether the mauve shirtwaist was a flattering color on her or not. She had not decided when she got up to go check dinner preparations. Walking down the hall, she heard the familiar sounds of sniping. She stopped, sighed deeply and then continued into the room where an altercation between her daughters was in full swing.

"Don't you dare call me a ninny," Alexandra huffed.

"Mother," Eugenia warned. "Tell her to get out of my room. She flounces in here and—"

"I do not flounce!"

"Stop it, both of you," Alma snapped.

"I only wanted to *borrow* the lavender gown she *never* wears," Alexandra said, glaring at her sister. "You're so selfish!"

"And does she knock?" Eugenia asked, scowling back. "No. She *flounces* in, demands to have her own way—"

"Mother, she's not being reasonable," Alexandra declared.

"Get out," Eugenia replied hotly. "And wear your own things! It's not as if you don't have enough. You are so spoiled! And you call me selfish?"

"Alexandra," Alma snapped, gesturing at the door.

"But she never wears it!"

"Go," Alma warned.

Alexandra stomped from the room, saying, "You just wait until you want to borrow something of mine, Eugenia."

Alma scowled at her eldest and then stepped from the room and shut the door, perhaps more forcefully than necessary. The girls were sixteen and nearly eighteen, and therein lay the problem. She'd had them entirely too close together. Other people's children were not so competitive and quarrelsome.

Jack was pouring himself a glass of sherry when she walked into the informal parlor. "You're home," she remarked.

"I am," he replied more cheerfully than usual. "How's everything?"

"The girls are at one another again."

He sipped his drink. "I heard."

She walked closer and kissed his cheek. "How was your day?"

"Busy. Yours?"

"Fine."

"Is Charity home yet?"

Alma felt a flush of irritation. "No," she replied sharply. Her ire increased when he looked disappointed. Obviously, there was something he wanted to share with his sister that she was too dim-witted to understand, but did he even try to include her in what he found so interesting? "I'm going to check on dinner."

"Good, I'm hungry."

Alma bit her tongue as she left the room. The man never even bothered to notice her frustration or her hurt feelings. *Oh, but if Charity had hurt feelings—*

At that moment, across town, Charity Werthing pulled off her soiled apron, having failed to save either mother or premature infant. There had simply been too much blood loss.

"You did all you could," a nurse commiserated.

Charity nodded slowly and walked away to wash up before facing the woman's husband. When she left the hospital a half hour later, she felt drained and distracted, so much so that it was a surprise when the house came into view. She went to her room to change and then joined the family at dinner, although they were nearly through with the meal.

"There you are," Jack greeted.

"Good evening," Charity said to everyone. "Sorry I'm late."

"Natalia," Alma called.

"You look tired," Jack remarked, gazing at Charity.

"I am," she replied.

Natalia, a new maid Alma had recently hired, appeared at the door.

"Bring Miss Werthing her soup," Alma said.

"No, just a plate, please," Charity said to the maid. "I'm not very hungry."

"A shame," Alma said tightly. "The soup was excellent."

Charity poured a glass of wine and sipped. She could tell the girls had been arguing again. Alma was on edge, as well.

"May I be excused?" Alexandra asked.

Alma raised her highly arched brows. "If you choose to be excused before dessert is served, do not bother asking for it later."

"Well, do we have to wait for Aunt Charity?"

Natalia was already back with a filled plate. "Please don't hold up dessert for me," Charity said to Alma.

"Fine," Alma replied. "Natalia?"

"Yes, ma'am," the maid said as she slid Charity's plate in front of her.

"Did you lose a patient?" Jack asked quietly.

"If you don't mind," Alma spoke sharply, looking at her husband. "Not at the table. How many times—"

"Of course, my dear," Jack replied easily. "Apologies. Actually, I think I'll skip dessert." He scooted his chair back. "Join me in the study later?" he said to his sister before he rose.

Charity could feel the daggers from her sister-in-law's eyes. The pettiness was so wearing. She took a bite of the meat.

"It's roast duck," Alma informed her. "I wasn't entirely pleased with the sauce. Oh, but she didn't put any on yours."

Charity swallowed the bite. It was rather dry. "It's fine."

Natalia was back with a tray of dessert.

"Natalia," Alma said. "Bring Doctor Werthing a bowl of sauce, as none was offered her."

"Yes, ma'am. I'm sorry, ma'am."

Charity tried to catch the maid's eye to indicate that it was of little importance, but she'd already gone.

"Gingerbread cake," Eugenia rejoiced. "My favorite."

"I would like a change in the gardens next year," Alma announced. "What would you think of a Chinese pavilion, girls?"

The girls both shrugged. They were enjoying their cake and not terribly interested in the subject.

"Or is a little conversation too much to ask for?" Alma asked testily.

"It sounds very interesting, Mother," Alexandra replied.

Alma scowled, having heard the petulance in Alexandra's voice. "Do you care for rock gardens, Charity?"

Charity didn't reply until she swallowed her bite, nor was she about to rush in order to answer an inane question. "Honestly, I prefer rambling gardens with fountains."

"Sounds like what we already have," Alexandra remarked.

"Which, by the way," Alma said, looking at Charity, "you spend very little time in."

"True," Charity conceded. "Unfortunately. Too little time in the day."

"People's lives to save and all," Eugenia said breezily.

Charity glanced up at her, but Eugenia's gaze was on what remained of her cake. The comment had just bordered on sarcastic. Alexandra's fork was pressed to her lips, where the merest smirk played. The pettiness was sorely wearing.

"So, about the lavender—" Alexandra wheedled.

"Mother," Eugenia said through gritted teeth.

"Enough," Alma warned.

"Well, if I can't borrow it, which is totally unreasonable, I need something new for Josephine Walker's coming out."

Need, Charity thought. Her nieces hadn't the vaguest notion of what the word meant, which had very little to do with the family's wealth. After all, she and Jack had grown up in this very home with all the trappings of wealth, and neither of them had ended up flighty or frivolous. The credit for that went to her parents and to their passion for education and community service. If she ever had children, which, admittedly, was unlikely at this point in her life, she would raise them so very differently. Of course, it was easy to be critical when you were not in the position of having to prove anything. She needed to remember that.

Charity stopped in the open door of her brother's third-floor study, where he had his nose stuck in a book. "What's so interesting?" she asked.

He looked up. "Come in and read this telegram," he said, reaching for it and handing it over.

She took it and began reading. Partway through, her jaw went lax. "Forehead, just above the right eyebrow," she said, looking up at him.

He nodded, his expression intense.

"Where exactly is Green Valley?" Jack rose and came around the desk with a map in hand, which he laid out.

"You've looked it up already. You want to go."

"Of course! Don't you?"

She realized it was true. She'd felt exhausted and melancholy until the last two minutes. "We should send word first. Make sure the man is still alive."

"I think we have to assume he is."

"You're right. There's no time to waste."

"Here," Jack said, pointing to Green Valley on the map.

It wasn't so terribly far. "After all we went through with Father—"

"I know. Perhaps we'll be able to put it to use."

She looked up at him. "I'd like that."

His eyes sparkled. "So would Father."

After the long, emotionally draining day, the statement hit with an unexpected force, and she had to blink tears away.

Jack sank into the chair beside her. "Tell me about it."

She shook her head. "She was just a patient, like all the others."

"Charity," he said softly.

She sat, too. "Her name was Lorna Collins and she went into premature labor. I lost her and the child."

"I'm sorry."

"She was lovely and she wanted to live. Her husband," she said with a sigh. "He was shattered."

Jack reached over and squeezed her hand. "I know that's hard."

Charity sat back. "And earlier in the day, there was a confrontation when a woman was denied admission."

"A prostitute?"

"She said not," Charity replied without conviction.

"Let me guess. You stepped in—"

"Knowing it would do no good," Charity added bitterly. "The rules," she exclaimed. "That we only serve married women of good character—"

"Seems as though we've had this conversation before."

"Fine. I won't get started again."

"They're not going to change the rules because you don't like them."

"They should change the rules when the rules are wrong. When I think about all the work it took to get to this point—"

"You don't regret the choice?" he asked with an earnest frown. "I know it took diligence and hard work and all, but—"

She nearly reminded him how much easier his path to becoming a physician had been than hers, but she refrained. At least she lived in a day and time when it *was* possible for a woman to pursue medicine. Before the Women's Medical College of Pennsylvania had opened its doors some thirty years ago, it wouldn't have been. "No, I don't regret it. Of course not. It was just a difficult day." She handed the telegram back. "We should leave in the morning."

"I agree."

"It makes you wonder," Charity said slowly.

"What?"

"Is it merely coincidence this came to our attention or is it . . . more?"

"Fate, perhaps? You know, if you hadn't become a physician, you would have made an excellent philosopher," he said with a teasing grin as he rose. "I've got to go to the hospital tomorrow first thing to make arrangements."

She made a face. "While you're there, demand to know why they refuse to hire female physicians."

Jack groaned. "Go pack, already."

Chapter Forty-Six

Jules Gunderson hobbled toward Emmett's office, excited to share the news. One of his legs was shorter than the other, although he'd learned to adjust. A company in New York had begun making special shoes for conditions like his, and he'd spent good money to try a pair. It amounted to nothing more than a platform fastened onto the bottom of the shoe of his shorter leg but, still, it made sense. Unfortunately, his balance had been thrown off by the correction and his back had begun aching in a different way than it usually did. The doc had told him he ought to tough it out and adjust, but he hadn't. He'd spent his whole life lopsided, he'd informed the doc, and he had already adjusted to that.

Emmett looked up as Jules walked in and braced himself for news. "Some doctors are headed this way from Philadelphia."

Emmett bowed his head. "Thank God."

"It's a brother and sister team," Jules said. "Both of them doctors. Doesn't that beat all?"

Emmett stood and reached out to shake Jules's hand. "You made my day, sir. Do we know when they arrive?"

Jules handed him the telegram. "Tomorrow."

* * *

Mitchell tried to maneuver the bottle of whiskey to his mouth without spilling any, which was impossible since he was lying down and it was too full. He spilled a little, grinned, and then rose up on an elbow for a swig and to watch a pudgy whore named Missy pleasure him.

There was a quick rap at the door before it opened and a petite prostitute named Dee-Dee stepped in and shut the door behind her.

"Come to have a turn?" he asked.

"Some men are looking for you," she cried.

His grin disappeared and he tried to sit, but Missy clung on. "Get off," he ordered, smacking her hip hard.

"Hey," she objected, climbing off him.

He gave her a sour look as he reached for his pants.

"They have a picture of you and everything," Dee-Dee fretted, wringing her hands. "They called you by a different last name. Said it was your name."

Hopping on one foot, he got a leg in. "Anybody tell them I was up here?"

"Not yet, but Joshua will."

Mitchell moved to the window as he fastened his pants. Keeping his back to the wall, he peered out sideways and saw Bud Ulrich across the street. "Son of a bitch!"

"Who's after you?" Missy asked.

"Shut up. I gotta think." He went back for his shirt and quickly put it on. "Is there a back way out of here?"

"No, but my room's on the back side," Dee-Dee replied. "You can sneak out onto the roof and jump down."

Mitchell sat and hurriedly pulled on his boots. "Yeah, alright."

"You gotta pay me," Missy reminded him.

"I didn't even come," he complained.

"That's not my fault."

He reached into his pocket for the money and threw it at her.

She huffed. "That's rude. It ain't my fault you're wanted, Mitchell. Or whatever your name is."

"Shut up," he snapped. "You just keep your trap shut about where I am or I'll come back and find you." He put on his gun holster and buckled it.

Dee-Dee was standing at the door beside herself.

"Let's go," he told her.

She opened the door, looked both ways and then dashed out. He followed, but didn't make it far before a deep voice boomed, "Medlin!"

He stopped and turned around to see the shotgun Lynn Green had aimed at him.

"He's up here," Green called.

"You came all this way 'cause Howerton wants to yell at me for being late that one day? That's pretty pathetic." He took a step backward.

"Take another step and I'll blow your brains out," Green warned, tightening his aim. "I'd rather see you swing than shoot you, but I'll do it."

Mitchell's throat closed for a second. "What the hell you talking about?"

Mark Hanks ran up the stairs two at a time, his pistol drawn.

"We know you killed Johnny," Green said. "Let's go."

"I didn't kill Johnny. Blue killed Johnny. Hell, I tried to stop him."

"You're nothing but a lowdown liar," Hanks said as he walked forward with his pistol aimed at Mitchell's head. "Now, get your hands in the air, scumbag."

Mitchell put his hands up. "You're making a big mistake. I didn't kill nobody."

"Miss, you'll be wantin' to move along," Hanks warned.

"Come on, Dee-Dee," Missy said breathlessly. "Get in here."

Hanks took possession of Mitchell's gun and stepped back. "Move."

Mitchell walked toward Green. "This is a misunderstanding."

"Like hell," Hanks retorted, pressing his gun into the center of Mitchell's back.

"Plan on walking me over to the marshal, do you?"

"Nope," Hanks said.

Mitchell halted abruptly. "Dee-Dee, run and get the marshal! They're gonna try to hang me!"

Hanks and Green forced him down the stairs, where patrons and whores alike gawked, but no one attempted to intervene.

"Somebody needs to help me," Mitchell called out as they neared the front door. "These men are making a mistake. I didn't do what they think I did."

"Move," Hanks hissed, pressing his gun against Mitchell's spine.

Outside, Howerton was striding toward them, followed by a half dozen men from the Triple H.

"Hello, Mitchell, you worthless son of a bitch," Howerton greeted.

"You got it all wrong, Mr. H," Mitchell stammered. "I didn't kill nobody. 'Fact, I was only trying to help Miss Wright when—"

"Shut up! Blue spilled everything before we hanged him."

Mitchell recoiled. "Hanged him? He was a waste of space. Why'd you go and hang him for?"

"He counted you as his friend," Sam Blake seethed. "You son of a bitch."

"We're going to go mount up," Howerton announced. "And we're going to ride out of here."

"Oh, yeah?" Mitchell asked nervously. "And then what are we gonna do? Have ourselves a picnic and talk about old times?" He had to buy time for Dee-Dee to get the marshal. The jail was something like four doors down, so it shouldn't be long. However, the men of the Triple H had all converged and they were forcing him along.

"I was thinking we'd find a good, strong tree," Howerton replied calmly. "Wrap a rope around your neck and suspend you by it until you're dead. That's what, you worthless—"

"Sir," a man's voice interrupted sharply.

Mitchell felt so glad to hear the marshal's voice that he tingled all over.

Resignedly, Howerton turned to face the man who had spoken, a man approximately his own age but with salt-and-pepper hair.

"I'm Marshal Owens," the man stated.

"Marshal," Howerton replied.

The marshal looked perfectly calm and he hadn't drawn his weapon, although his deputies were behind him and theirs were drawn. "I understand you think this man committed a crime?"

"He shot a man who worked for me," Howerton stated. "Shot him in the face. And I don't think it; I know it."

"Well, that'll have to go before the magistrate, sir."

"The hell it will."

"No, sir. It will. That's how we do things in Virginia."

"We're *from* Virginia," Howerton stated.

"Then you should know."

"They got it all wrong, Marshal," Mitchell spoke up, shifting on his feet. "I didn't kill nobody."

Howerton turned to Mitchell. "You know why Blue was hanged? Because he shot Tommy."

Mitchell blinked. "What would he do that for?"

"Because Blue was after Miss Wright," Sam spoke up. "For you. Only she ain't Miss Wright anymore. She's Mrs. Tommy Medlin."

"You're lying," Mitchell scoffed.

Howerton shook his head. "Blue went to abduct your brother's wife, Tommy moved in to protect her and Blue shot him."

"Well, I didn't tell him to do that! And you can't prove that I did, 'cause I didn't! Why would I want my own brother shot dead?"

Howerton turned back to the marshal. "This piece of shit is someone you really want to protect?"

"It's the law," Owens stated. "It's got nothing to do with what I want."

Howerton looked at the five or six deputies. His men still had them outnumbered, but he wasn't about to let it play out like this. "The law. Right." Howerton stuck his gun back in his holster, cueing the others to do the same.

"As luck would have it, the magistrate is in town," Owens said. "He should be able to get to this right away." He looked at his deputies and gestured to Medlin. "Take him. Lock him up."

Owens's deputies took Mitchell Medlin and led him away.

"If he's a murderer," Owens said to Howerton, "and it can be proved, we'll hang him."

"Forgive me if I don't hold my breath," Howerton said.

"Done," Owens replied. "But I live by the law, sir."

"That man tried to rape a woman, he attacked his own brother and he killed one of my men," Howerton said. "I'll be damned if I'll see him walk."

Owens considered the man and then turned to look at the onlookers who'd gathered. "Y'all get back to your business. There's nothing to see here." As people began dispersing, Owens looked back to Howerton, tipped his hat and walked away.

Chapter Forty-Seven

The magistrate was a hefty, sixty-year-old by the name of Roy Gilleywater. The top of his head was bald; the hair around the sides and back was fuzzy and gray, as was his beard and mustache.

The courtroom was stifling. Most people fanned themselves, but Gregory Howerton sat perfectly still, staring at Mitchell Medlin.

"Let me make sure I got this right," Gilleywater said. "The only witness to the crime is dead . . . and might possibly be the one who did the shooting."

Howerton didn't flinch, although it was obvious the magistrate was going to let Mitchell Medlin walk. They'd all given their statements and it wasn't enough.

Gilleywater shook his head. "No. No evidence, no trial. No, sir. Let's move on to the next case. Have I got one?"

"I'll get them in here," Owens said. He glanced at Howerton. "I thought this would take longer."

"I can go now, right?" Mitchell asked.

Gilleywater squinted at him. "I'll tell you something, Mr. Medlin. I got a bad feeling about you. It's lucky for you that a bad feeling doesn't amount to a pile of dead chickens in the eyes of the law."

"A pile of dead chickens?" someone whispered behind Howerton.

"Yes, you can go," Gilleywater said. He banged his gavel.

Howerton stood and watched Mitchell walk toward the door, glancing from side to side. The son of a bitch looked plenty nervous. With good reason.

"I need my gun back," Mitchell said to one of the deputies. "And I need protection."

"Your gun's at the jail," the deputy replied. "And protection ain't our job, unless the marshal says so."

"Mr. Howerton?" Owens said.

Howerton turned to him.

"In my experience," Owens said, "a man who blatantly disregards the law and commits a crime, usually does it again. Luck doesn't hold out forever."

Howerton nodded slowly. "I have a strong feeling his won't hold."

"You can't just take him and hang him. You know that."

"I heard the magistrate, same as you."

"I know you're disappointed."

"I'm not disappointed. I'm thirsty. Excuse me." Howerton left the courthouse and made his way to the saloon, watching Mitchell scurry ahead.

"What now?" Sam asked, falling into step beside him.

"I'm going to have a drink," Howerton replied.

"I'm gonna head to the telegraph office and see if I can get word about Tommy."

Howerton nodded.

"You planning on taking him?" Sam asked.

"What do you think?"

The sun streaming in through the windows of the jail illuminated dust particles in the air as Vince Owens sat at his desk, ignoring the stares of the few deputies in the room.

"You know those men are going to find a way to kill him," Gene Ashcroft commented.

Vince tugged on his shirt collar. He'd hadn't slept well last night—the weather was too damn hot—plus he had a headache. "Not right under our noses, they aren't."

"So, whatcha wanna do?"

Vince squeezed the bridge of his nose gently and pressed upward. That's where the ache was. Right across his brows and into his temples. "Go sit on Medlin. He'll probably be in one of the saloons."

Ashcroft nodded.

Owens looked up as he thought of something. "Grady hasn't been here," he mused.

Ashcroft nodded. "Yeah."

"Not since Medlin came into town. Right?"

"That's right. Not since his pa's accident. Why?"

The youngest of the deputies, John Jewel, had been listening to the conversation without comment. "What'd you ask about Grady for?"

"I want you to go get him," Owens replied. "If he's willing, I want him to work his way into the saloon and strike up a conversation with Medlin."

"Why? In case Medlin admits what he did?"

"Gilleywater still won't try him," Owens said as he opened his desk drawer and rummaged in search of headache powder. "Running off at the mouth is not evidence."

"Well then, what?" Ashcroft asked.

Vince found a packet of powder and looked up at him. "You're right about those men. They not only want to get their hands on Medlin, they plan on it." He downed the contents of the packet and made a face. "Thing is, I've got to be able to sleep at night. I don't much care for Mitchell Medlin, but if he's not guilty of what they say, we've got to keep him safe. We're going to have to outlast his friends."

"And if he is guilty?" Ashcroft asked. "What if Grady does his magic and Medlin admits everything?"

"Then I'll be able to sleep, no matter what."

Jewel nodded. "I'll go get Grady."

"Tell him to come see me first."

"Yes, sir."

Both Ashcroft and Jewel left at the same time, just as one of Howerton's men entered.

"Yes, sir?" Vince asked.

The man came forward and offered his hand. "I'm Sam Blake."

They shook hands.

"Have you got a moment?" Sam asked.

"I do." Vince motioned to a chair. "You want to have a seat?"

"Thank you." Sam moved to the chair and sat. "I thought I'd give you the whole story about Medlin. What I know of it, anyway. If you'd care to know, that is."

"Matter of fact, I would."

"He and his brother, Tommy, got hired on when the ranch was first being built. I oversee things at Mr. Howerton's ranch."

Vince nodded.

"Mitchell and Tommy," Sam said, shaking his head. "You can't imagine how different they are. I guess that's really who I want to tell you about. Tommy Medlin. And when the trouble all began. That's the real story here."

"I'm listening," Vince said sincerely.

Mitchell slumped in his chair, but his relaxed stance was a far cry from how he truly felt. Howerton and his boys were eyeing him hungrily from across the room. "Damn vultures," he said to no one in particular.

They were just waiting for him to leave or get drunk off

his ass. They'd have a long wait, because it wasn't happening. He wasn't going to get drunk and he wasn't leaving without an escort back to the jail. His plan was to sleep there until the Triple H boys got fed up and left town. Or maybe he'd sneak away when they weren't paying attention. They weren't nearly as clever as they thought they were. He'd dodged them all this time. A couple of tables over, some men started playing a three-handed game of poker. Mitchell had played with one of them before. The man's name was Jim something or other. "Mind if I sit in?" Mitchell asked.

The three either ignored or didn't hear him.

"Hey, Jim—"

Jim turned. "Yeah?"

"Mind if I sit in?"

"Sure, I guess it's okay," Jim replied. His eyes flicked to the group of men watching Medlin. "Long as there's not going to be any trouble."

Mitchell also glanced at Howerton's table and then got up and joined the others. "Nah, no trouble. Name's Medlin," he said by way of introduction. "Mitchell Medlin."

"You're the one all that fuss was about," an older man put in as he shuffled the cards.

"Yep."

"What happened with that?"

"The magistrate let me go 'cause there wasn't no evidence." The cards were dealt.

"Evidence of what?" Jim asked. "What was it about?"

"Murder," Mitchell replied with a smirk.

The third man, a good-looking fellow with curly dark hair, looked up sharply. "There wasn't no evidence or it wasn't true?"

"There wasn't no evidence because it wasn't true," Mitchell replied, picking up his cards.

"This here is Fred Wells," Jim said, pointing to the old man, "and that's Grady Douglas."

"How many?" Fred asked Mitchell.

"Two."

"Jim?"

Jim considered. "Give me three."

"Grady?"

"Two."

"And the dealer takes one."

"Hey, Mitchell," Jim said. "Why are them men watching you like a hawk?"

"'Cause they're sore losers."

"Tell you what," Jim said, shaking his head, "that would make me jittery as a junebug."

Grady glanced over at the men.

"They don't bother me," Mitchell said.

Grady narrowed his eyes at Mitchell. "Is there gonna be trouble with them? 'Cause we don't need that."

"No, there's not gonna be no trouble. You see the deputy by the door?"

All three men glanced over.

"Well, hell," Mitchell complained. "Why don't ya'll look at once?"

"What about him?" Grady said.

"He's watching so they don't get me," Mitchell replied. "The marshal don't like men taking the law into their own hands."

"So, let's play," Fred said.

Sam Blake made his way to Howerton's table and sat. "Tommy's still alive," he reported. "He hasn't woken up yet, but he is still alive."

"Who said?" Howerton asked, as he passed Sam the bottle.

Sam poured himself a drink. "The telegraph operator. Gunderson. Fella with a short leg." He drank. "He said some doctors from Philadelphia are coming."

"Good."

"Shot in the head," Lynn Green said, "and still alive. How's that possible?"

"I don't know," Sam replied, "but you know what occurred to me a little while ago? We never did tell Mitchell that Tommy's alive. Did we?"

"No," Ulrich spoke up.

"You can see how torn up he is," Howerton seethed.

"About Blue, too," Bud said.

Howerton picked up his glass and downed his whiskey.

"You know that money you gave me for incidentals?" Sam said to him.

Howerton looked at him. "Yeah."

"I spent it."

"All of it?"

"I may get some of it back, but, yeah."

"What for?"

"After I sent the telegraph and got one back, I went over to the marshal's office. Had a chat with him."

"And?"

"I gave him the money."

"Why?"

"To snare a killer, I hope." He looked over at the poker game. "See that fella with the curly hair? We've staked him."

Howerton glanced over and then poured more whiskey in his glass. "Hope he can bluff."

* * *

Lisa Owens walked into the jail carrying a plate covered by a striped dishcloth. "I made your favorite," she said dryly, "although I doubt it's as good as it was."

"I'm sorry, honey, but I've got to keep my eye on a situation," Vince explained.

"I know that since Johnny Jewel came by the house and told me." She handed Vince the plate. "Is there any particular reason one of your deputies can't keep an eye on this situation?"

"It's a long story," Vince replied as he pulled off the towel. "That smells like heaven."

"It smells like beef tips and gravy," she retorted. "Eat."

He did. "So good," he said, shaking his head.

"Your daughter won the spelling bee at school today," she said, pulling up a chair in front of his desk. She leaned forward and took a pinch of one of the yeast rolls on his plate.

He playfully slapped at her hand. "Hey, that's mine."

"And just what were you going to eat, if I hadn't brought this?"

"You know I'd rather have my supper at home with you and the kids," he said from behind his napkin, since his mouth was full.

"I made blueberry pie, and I didn't bring you a piece, either. So you better just wrap this situation up."

"Done," he replied with gusto.

She shook her head, but finally grinned. "Katy spelled equinoctial."

He took a forkful of greens. "Never even heard of it."

"Me neither," she admitted. "Can you believe that? Only in the sixth grade, and she spelled equinoctial."

"How'd Andrew do?"

"He was out in the second round."

Vince shrugged. "Spells like his old man." When he finished the plate, he sat back with a sigh. "That was good."

"You eat too fast."

"You make it too good. Can't help it." He covered his mouth and belched.

She rose and began gathering up plate, fork and napkin. "How late will you be?"

He rose and started around the desk. "I don't know." He kissed her temple. "Save me a piece of pie?"

"Can't promise anything."

"Come on. I'll walk you home."

"Oh? You can spare five minutes to walk your wife home?"

He grinned. "I can, at least halfway."

She shrugged and started toward the door. "Alright," she said. "A woman takes what she can get."

Vince walked her home, kissed his children good night and left again, going directly to the saloon Medlin had chosen to patronize. His men had gone back and forth between saloon and jail all afternoon reporting. Mostly that there was nothing of significance to report. When he walked in, the place seemed both louder and smokier than usual. These days, more men were smoking than chewing, and it was hard on his eyes after a long day. "Anything?" he asked Ashcroft.

"Only that Grady's made a new friend," Ashcroft joked.

Vince looked over at Howerton and his men. They took up three tables. "Looks like they've settled in," he observed.

Ashcroft's mouth kicked up. "For a long time, they all stared at Medlin and he acted like he didn't notice. 'Course he kept scooting around in his seat and glancing sideways at them. Yeah, he didn't notice. But they've kept their distance. Nobody's yelled nothing or threatened."

Vince looked back at the poker game. "He doesn't seem mindful of them, now."

"Nope. Sure doesn't," Ashcroft agreed.

* * *

Grady poured more whiskey for everybody. Medlin had a big thirst, but he wasn't sloppy. And he was winning most every hand.

"I never did shoot a man," Jim said.

"That's a good thing," Grady replied. "It's not exactly something that makes you feel good."

Mitchell looked up from his cards. "How would you know?"

Grady didn't reply.

"Who'd you shoot?" Mitchell pushed.

"It's nothin' I want to talk about," Grady stated flatly, "and it's your call."

"Most men," Fred said, slurring his words a bit, "we don't have it in us."

"Bull," Mitchell scoffed. "Most men sure as hell do have it in them."

"Depends on the situation," Grady said.

"Damn right it does," Mitchell agreed.

"It's not always even a crime," Grady said. "Not really."

"Yeah," Mitchell agreed again. "Least, there's times it shouldn't be."

"Fellas, I'm out," Fred said. "Medlin done wrung me dry."

Mitchell grinned. "Thanks for that, by the way."

Fred shrugged. "Win some, lose some."

"You mean, win some, lose a lot." Mitchell laughed.

Fred waved his hand at Medlin, got up and left.

"I think I'll get us another bottle," Jim said, patting his pockets.

"Here," Mitchell said, handing him money. "What the hell."

"Thanks, Medlin."

Mitchell tossed his cards down. "That hand got screwed."

Grady gathered up the cards.

"So, who'd you shoot?" Mitchell asked, leaning forward onto his elbows.

"I'm not saying, so you can stop asking," Grady returned as he began to shuffle.

"I'll tell you," Mitchell offered.

"I don't care," Grady stated.

"Come on," Mitchell urged.

"What the hell you want to know for?"

Mitchell shrugged. "Curious."

Grady sighed and shook his head. "I'll just say this. Did you ever know somebody who just wouldn't leave you alone? Who just rode you and rode you. Always running off at the mouth."

"Yeah."

"There you go. Enough said."

"Enough said," Mitchell repeated.

"It's not like I didn't warn him," Grady added.

"People should know when to keep their big mouths shut," Mitchell agreed. "It was the same with me. Only my guy . . . he didn't plan on my buddy showing up with a gun."

"Walter, the man I shot," Grady said in a low voice. "He had a gun. He'd a shot me, if he could have drawn fast enough."

"Johnny, too," Mitchell said in a low voice. "He sure as shit would have. Probably wouldn't have killed me. Probably would have shot me in the foot or something."

Grady shook his head. "Not me. Man would have shot me dead. Thing is, I warned him."

"Me, too," Mitchell replied. "I said, 'You'd best stop poking fun of me, asshole.'"

Grady made a face. "That was quite a buddy, to shoot him for you. I never had a friend like that."

Mitchell shook his head. "He didn't shoot him for me.

Didn't have the balls. I took the gun from him, took aim, bye-bye, asshole. Cain't say I didn't warn him."

"This looks deep," Jim said, as he returned with the bottle. "Whatch'all talking about?"

"Nothing at all," Mitchell said easily, leaning back in his chair again. "Shootin' the shit." He grinned and winked at Grady. "Get it? Shootin' the *shit*?"

"I'm out," Grady announced, pushing his chair back.

"No! C'mon, stay," Mitchell said, slapping the table. "Night's young."

Grady stood. "Not for me. It just got old." He turned and walked away.

"Well, screw him," Mitchell complained. "We're going to need more players," he said. "Who wants some?"

Grady walked to the marshal, who was standing near the door. "He did it."

"He said so?" Vince asked, frowning.

Grady nodded. "Said a buddy of his showed up with a gun, Medlin took the gun and shot a man, name of Johnny. I didn't get a whole lot of details."

"That confirms what I heard," Vince said. "Any doubt that he was telling the truth?"

"No," Grady replied. "It's true and he's not a bit sorry."

"What do we do now?" Gene asked.

Vince was quiet a moment. "Go on home," he finally replied. "I'll see you tomorrow."

"I'm half drunk, so I am going," Grady said. "It'll be another week or so before I can report back, you know."

"I know," Vince replied. "How's your father doing?"

"He busted the leg good, but we got a lot of people stepping up to pitch in."

"I appreciate your help on this."

"I didn't mind." Grady glanced over at Medlin's table and saw that two other men had moved in and begun playing. "He's a cold one."

"You're sure?" Gene asked Vince. "About going?"

Vince nodded. "I think I'll be able to sleep just fine, no matter what happens. What about you?"

"Oh, yeah," Gene said. "I'll sleep like a babe. You coming, Grady?"

Grady saw Sam Blake heading their way. "In a bit. I'll see you."

Gene left as Sam joined them. "Learn anything interesting?" he asked conversationally.

"Like that he did it?" Grady asked. "Yeah, he did it."

"I know he did," Sam replied evenly. He looked pointedly at Vince.

Vince gave him a significant nod. "It's late. Think I'll be going home now."

Sam offered his hand. "We'll probably be heading out soon, so—"

"Safe journey," Vince said, accepting the handshake.

Grady reached into his pocket for the little bit of money still there. "There's not much left," he said. "He was winning."

"Keep it," Sam said. "Far as I'm concerned, it was money well spent."

Grady nodded and left, shoving the money deeper into his pocket, and Sam looked at Mitchell, who hooted at another victorious round. "His streak's about over," he murmured under his breath.

Mitchell felt victorious. He'd won at least two hundred dollars, and Howerton and the others had called it a night. Of course, the night *was* gone. It was almost two in the morning as he left the saloon. "Walk me to the jail," he said to the two men he'd been playing with at the end.

"The jail?" one exclaimed.

"Yeah, the jail."

"Why?"

"I'm sleeping there. For protection."

The man shrugged. "I'm going that way, anyhow."

"Not me," the other man said. "'Night."

Mitchell looked up and down the street. He saw neither hide nor hair of his foe, so a one-man escort would do. Halfway there, he stumbled on a rock in the road and realized he was drunker than he'd realized. Luckily, the jail was close.

"'Night," his escort muttered as they reached the jail.

"Yeah, 'night." Mitchell went to walk inside but ended up falling into the door because it didn't open as he'd expected it to. He tried the doorknob again. *Locked.* He peered inside, but it looked deserted, which made no sense. A lawman had been watching him all night, making sure Howerton and the others kept their distance. Why would they abandon him now? He swore under his breath.

He looked around. He thought about hollering for the man who'd walked with him, but the fellow's name escaped him, plus, he'd already walked on. Besides that, the man was drunker than he was and probably worthless in a fight. *Dee-Dee,* he thought. He could probably jimmy the lock of the door of the saloon and get in easily enough. He'd reached the end of the building and stepped down into an alleyway when he was grabbed and hurled against the wall with such force, the wind was knocked from him.

"Hello, again," Mark Hanks said.

Before Mitchell could react, his gun was yanked away and six others were pointed at him.

"I told you," Mitchell wheezed. "You got it all wrong."

"Shut up," Howerton said. "We've wasted enough time on you."

A gag was shoved into Mitchell's mouth. His hands were forced behind his back and bound by rope. Despite the gag, he yelled. It was muffled, sure enough, but loud.

The barrel of a gun came down on his head, stunning and silencing him, and blood trickled into his eye as he was led away. He could barely keep his legs under him.

Chapter Forty-Eight

Emmett waited, hat in hand, as the passengers began to disembark from the train. One by one, he eliminated them as possibilities. A fair-haired woman paused in the door of the train, looking around for someone. She was so attractive, he stared longer than he should, but she was no doctor. She was tall and slender and moved with the sort of elegance that came from a highly privileged upbringing.

Emmett noticed a squatty-looking, middle-aged man and woman making their way toward him. They looked disenchanted and ill tempered, but perhaps he was judging too quickly. He cleared his throat as the couple drew close. "Dr. Werthing?"

The man appeared to be insulted and walked on without even the courtesy of a reply.

"I'm Dr. Werthing," a man said behind him.

Emmett turned sharply and was astounded to see the lady he'd noticed earlier standing next to the gentleman who'd spoken, obviously her brother.

"I should say, we *both* are Dr. Werthing," the man said with an easy smile.

They were both handsome as could be with wheat-colored hair and gray eyes. Their posture and carriage made Emmett

want to stand up straighter; in fact, they made him want to
be taller. Their clothing was stylish and highly fashionable.
Philadelphia doctors were obviously a different breed from
the homespun variety he'd known. "T. Emmett Rice," he said,
offering his hand.

"James Werthing, but call me Jack. And this is my sister,
Charity."

"Hello," she said, offering a slender hand.

He shook it. For a moment he was stymied by her presence. She looked at him very directly, as if drinking in every
nuance of his person. "I'm so glad you've come," Emmett
said, finding his voice. "Let me take you on out to the farm
so you can see Tommy."

"The trunk," Charity said to her brother.

"I'll see to it," Jack said. "Won't be a minute," he said to
Emmett, and he hurried back toward the train.

"I've never met a woman doctor before," Emmett commented as he put his hat back on his head. "Is it a common
thing in the East?"

"I don't think it's common anywhere yet," she replied
pleasantly. "But give us time."

"Well, the world's changing every day," he returned.

"The man who was shot. Is he family?"

"In a way, he is," Emmett replied. "It's an interesting story."
Already Jack Werthing was coming back, leading a young
man who carried a trunk. "I'll tell you and your brother about
it on the way."

Em finished what she could of her dinner, then rose and
picked up her plate.

"Leave it," Doll said.

"Thank you." Em started back to Tommy's room, but Doll
caught hold of her arm, stopping her.

"Nuh-uh-uh," the older woman chastised, shaking her

head. "No, ma'am. You haven't left that room for ten minutes straight. Go take a walk."

Em opened her mouth to object, but Doll practically shoved her out the door. "Go!"

"Doll, I don't wa—"

"And don't you come back before you've had a decent walk," Doll interrupted. "Or, so help me, I'll send you right back out again."

Em gave in with a frown and a sigh. She walked outside and rolled her shoulders, wondering what luck Howerton and his men were having finding Blue. She wanted to know what Mitch's friend had been doing on their land. She needed to understand.

She walked until she reached the road. Staring at their sign, she recalled the moment Tommy had first laid eyes on it. And when he saw the sweater she'd knitted for him. When he flung the scarf around his neck. When he put the pearl necklace on her and then laid his hands on her shoulders. She became so immersed in the memory that she didn't realize someone had come up behind her until she felt a presence there. She turned to see who it was—only no one was in the road. A tremor of shock passed through her and goose bumps broke out all over her body. "Ben?" she whispered, suddenly certain it had been he she'd felt.

Tommy looked at Ben. "Why doesn't she see me?"

"She doesn't see me, either," Ben explained. "She just felt me for a moment."

"But why doesn't she feel me?" Maybe it was stupid, but he felt hurt. No one loved her more than he. Why didn't she know he was there?

"I have more practice," Ben replied teasingly with a wink.

Tommy shook his head, aggravated. "It's not funny."

"You're jealous of a damn ghost, son. It is kind of funny."

Tommy drew breath, but didn't know what to say to that. Nor did it matter since Ben had started back to the house.

"Besides," Ben called over his shoulder. "You and I aren't in the same place at all. I told you that. I'm just visiting for a spell."

The man made no sense, but it didn't matter. Em started back to the house, as well, and she looked so tired. More than tired, she looked completely drained. It made him sad. In fact, he could feel her fatigue.

"Tommy!" Ben called sharply as he whirled back around to face him. "You can't do that!" He started back toward Tommy, but Tommy felt as if he was being drawn backward at the same rate of speed. Ben stretched out an arm toward him. "Keep fighting!"

Tommy knew something was happening. He felt weaker than he ever had before in his entire life. It was as though he was fading, disappearing.

"Tommy!"

Em heard Jeffrey's call of distress the second she opened the back door. Her heart gave a painful jolt and she ran full out.

"Oh, no, no," Jeffrey cried. "Damn it! Help, y'all! I think he's—"

"Tommy!" Doll yelled.

Em saw Wood and Hawk rushing toward Tommy's room from the opposite direction, looking as panicked as she felt. She was going so fast, she nearly careened into the door-jamb. Tommy was too white and too still.

"Oh, Jesus," Jeffrey wailed. "He . . . he—"

"No," Em breathed. She bolted forward, and the others moved out of her way. She sat on the bed and gathered Tommy up in her arms. "Tommy!"

"Jesus himself must just have heard you, son," Wood

exclaimed breathlessly, yanking back the curtain. "I see 'em coming! Hawk, run and get them!"

"The doctors?"

"Yes, the doctors! Go!"

"Stay with me," Em begged, her lips moving against Tommy's ear. "Please, please, please stay with me." She was only vaguely aware of Hawk yelling. Of Doll's hand on her back. Of the palpable fear in the room. *I love you.* She had to put her full heart, her entire being, into willing Tommy to live. Love was supposed to be the most powerful force on earth, even more powerful than death. *I love you. I love you. I love you.*

"I see them, Emmy," Wood reported. "They're coming. Running like it was their own kin!"

"Don't leave me," Em whispered, blocking everything else out. She rocked slightly and he moved with her. He didn't feel dead because he *wasn't* dead. He wasn't dead and he wasn't going to die. She loved him too much and he loved her. *Love is the most powerful force in the universe. More powerful even than death.* She could will him back from this. He had saved her. He had made her life worth living. And she would save him. Her love, *their* love, would save him. "Love is the most powerful force in the universe, more powerful even than death," she whispered in his ear. "Believe it. Believe it!"

"Emmy, honey," Doll said. "Move back."

Em's grip tightened. She heard footsteps and she knew she had to let go, but she couldn't do it. She had to keep holding on. She had to keep him alive. "I won't let you go," she whispered. "I won't."

"Em, let the doctor in," Wood insisted, pulling at her.

The words penetrated. Trembling, nauseous with fear, Em released her hold, and two people, a man and a woman, pressed in, the man on her side of the bed, the woman on the far side. Em rose and stepped back.

"He just went," Jeffrey blurted. "One second he was breathing and the next—"

The man reached inside a black leather bag and pulled out a stethoscope. The woman felt the side of Tommy's neck and shook her head slightly. Em crossed her arms in front of herself. She didn't want to faint, but she was dangerously light-headed. She felt Doll brace her. "You stay strong, now," Doll said in her ear.

The man put the instrument on Tommy's chest. "There's a beat," he said after listening for a moment.

They were the three best words Em had ever heard and she nearly collapsed with relief.

"Stay strong," Doll urged, giving her a hard squeeze.

The man withdrew and the woman began rubbing Tommy's chest aggressively. Back and forth, rocking his prone body. "Em—" the woman said. "Come talk to him."

Em felt jerky and strange as she went back to Tommy's side, perching on the edge of the bed to stay clear of the doctors' efforts. "I'm here," she said, taking hold of his hand and pressing it to her heart. "Keep fighting."

"Has he revived at all?" the woman doctor asked.

"No," Doll said, "but once we heard him say Em's name."

"I'm Charity Werthing," the woman said as she continued to rub Tommy's chest. "And this is my brother, Jack."

"Physicians from Philadelphia," Emmett reminded them from the door.

Em closed her eyes and tried to find Tommy's mind to connect to. *These people have come to help. Hang on. Please hang on.* She was aware of the conversation going on. Doll was saying, "We're grateful you've come. This man means everything to us."

"Have you gotten him to take any liquid?" Jack asked.

"Not much," Wood replied. "We tried."

"We can help with that," Jack said.

Em looked over as he withdrew a coil of flexible tubing from his bag.

"How?" Doll asked.

"Intravenously," he replied.

"It means entering by way of a vein," Charity explained as she sat on the bed and positioned Tommy's arm on her leg.

"Is that something new?" Wood asked nervously.

"No," she replied quickly. "Although there have been improvements of late. It's perfectly safe," she added reassuringly.

"Actually, it was fifty years ago or so that the concept was conceived," Jack said conversationally as he walked around to the other side of the bed. "A doctor by the name of O'Shaughnessy made a breakthrough in the midst of a cholera epidemic after analyzing blood samples of victims and discovering that dehydration was primarily to blame for the majority of deaths." Jack pulled a bottle of clear liquid from his bag, shook and then studied it.

Charity doused a cloth in alcohol and used it to clean the skin of Tommy's inner arm. "Intravenous replacement of the deficient salt and water saved thousands of lives, and that's what we're going to do for Tommy."

The smell of the alcohol assailed Em's senses and she watched Charity's nimble hands with dread fascination.

"So," Wood said, "that'll keep him from wasting away until he wakes. Is that right?"

"That's exactly what we hope to accomplish," Jack replied as he handed his sister tubing with a sharp, needle-like end on it.

"So that's just water?" Jeffery asked. "You're gonna put water right into his vein? That don't hardly seem right. I thought it was only blood runs in veins."

"But blood is made up of certain components, including water and salt," Jack replied.

Charity seemed to ignore all the talk as she lightly slapped the inside of Tommy's arm repeatedly. "I've got a good vein," she said under her breath. A second later, she stuck the needle end of the tubing into Tommy's arm. "Trocar's in."

Jack attached the tubing to the bottle and the liquid snaked through it to Tommy's arm. "Will you hold this, please?" he asked Wood.

Wood quickly stepped up and took the bottle and Jack began setting up a stand. He took the bottle back from Wood and attached it to the stand, and every eye was riveted.

"You have any thoughts on how we can revive him?" Wood asked.

Jack took a breath before replying. "To be perfectly honest, in large part, the brain is a mystery to us. Tommy could wake up in an hour or tomorrow or next week."

Or never. No one said it, but the word hung in the air.

"He's got the best heart," Wood said, "and a wife he loves like you can't even believe, and he's going to be a father. He's so looking forward to that."

Charity wrapped a bandage around Tommy's arm to keep the tubing in place. "A man's will to live counts for a lot."

Jack cleared his throat quietly. "The fact of the matter is, our father suffered a similar injury."

Shock reverberated around the room. "He was shot in the head?" Doll burst out.

Em looked at Charity, her mouth agape.

"Yes," Charity replied evenly, compassion evident in her blue-gray eyes. "In almost the exact same location as Tommy."

Em's throat felt painfully tight, but she had to know. "Did he live?"

Charity hesitated. "I'm sorry to say he didn't."

Em didn't feel as if she were crying, and yet cold tears trickled down her face.

"But he was thirty years older than Tommy," Charity added, reaching across to lay a hand on Em's arm.

"He was also wounded in the shoulder, which worsened the situation," Jack said. "There was too much blood loss."

"Jack and I learned a great deal caring for him," Charity added.

Em nodded stiffly and wiped her face.

"It's why we knew we had to come when we read Mr. Rice's telegram," he added.

The room was uncomfortably silent for a moment.

"Perhaps," Jack said, breaking the silence, "if we could examine Tommy in private. We'll catheterize him, and—"

"They'll what?" Jeffrey muttered.

He'd only been heard because the room had gone so quiet. "I think I know," Hawk said quickly. "Let's go." Jeffrey quickly followed him from the room.

Emmett cleared his throat. "You got coffee on, Doll?"

"Don't I always?" she asked testily as she walked out.

Wood seemed reluctant to go. "That's to, uh—"

"The catheter drains his urine," Jack replied. "Someone must have spent quite a bit of effort keeping him clean."

"We didn't mind," Wood replied quickly. "We didn't mind at all. When Doll said he's important to us, that was an understatement."

"This will make things easier," Charity spoke up. "It's also better for him."

"I see," Wood replied. "Well, then." He cleared his throat and then left.

"You can stay, of course," Charity said to Em. "We routinely ask others to leave to preserve the patient's dignity."

Em nodded. Both doctors were on the right side of the bed, so she remained on the left as Jack Werthing inserted a tube into Tommy's penis. She looked away, clutching his hand tightly. She loathed having his privacy and dignity invaded. He didn't deserve it. He didn't deserve any of this. Was it her? Her and her curse? Had she done this to him?

Next, they examined the head wound.

"It's clean," Charity said.

"The bullet is still inside," Jack noted.

"Will you try to get it?" Em asked, her stomach tight with dread.

"No," Jack replied without hesitation. "Not at this time, anyway. Brain surgery usually does more harm than good. We'll see if he comes back around in the next day or so and then assess what the effects of the bullet are."

There was a light rap at the door.

"Yes?" Charity called.

Doll opened the door. "I have food ready and your rooms and all. Whenever you'd like. No hurry, but whenever you're ready. And if there is anything you need, anything at all, you just pick up that bell on the table and ring it."

"Thank you," Jack said. "We're finished here, for now, so we'll be right there."

Doll looked at Em worriedly, and then shut the door again.

Jack inspected the tubes once more and then looked at the clear bottle of liquid. "He's taking it," he said with satisfaction.

Charity leaned over to look at something at her feet. "The catheter is working, too," she reported.

"Do you have any questions, Mrs. Medlin?" Jack asked.

Em shook her head numbly.

"We'll do all we can for him," he said. "We can see how important he is to all of you. In fact, I've rarely seen a comatose patient so immaculately—"

Charity shot him a look. "Yes, he's so smoothly shaved and clean," she said.

Em nodded shakily. "We didn't want him to wake to . . . to h-hair on his face. He always shaves."

Charity nodded and smiled.

"Hawk does it. Every morning. He hasn't cut Tommy once."

"Well," Jack said. "I suppose we'll have something to eat and settle in. Charity?"

"I'll be there in a minute," she replied. He nodded and left the room before she spoke again. "How's the nausea?"

"I've never had so much," she admitted. The doctors didn't need to waste time and concern on her, but she could tell Charity wasn't one to give up. In different circumstances, they might have become close friends.

"That's perfectly normal. May I examine you in the next day or so?"

"Honestly, I'm fine."

"I'm sure you are, but I am here. We'll do everything we can think of for Tommy, but it won't take our every minute. Are you eating enough?"

Em shrugged a shoulder. "I'm not hungry, but everyone's watching. What I eat, when I eat," she added drolly.

Charity grinned. "Annoying, is it?"

Em blushed. "I shouldn't say that."

"I understand. You have quite a family."

Em nodded. "Yes, we do. It's because of him," she said as she lovingly stroked his arm. "Everything is because of him."

"Emmett shared some of Tommy's story with us," Charity confided. "He sounds like an extraordinary man. And strong." She paused. "Strong enough to survive this. It is possible."

Em pressed her lips together and fought tears.

"The sleep he's in, the coma, it's a mysterious thing. As mysterious to us as the brain or even the soul. We don't yet understand it, not as physicians. But as a woman—"

Em looked at Charity.

"—I believe that this state Tommy's in, this coma, is

nature's way of protecting him. He may appear to sleep, but his body is trying to heal."

Em's eyes filled and spilled over. "Thank you," she whispered.

Charity nodded. "So, I'll examine you tomorrow. Make sure everything is fine?"

"I'd appreciate that."

Charity looked at Tommy again and then rose and left.

In the silence that followed, Em lifted Tommy's hand to her lips and kissed it. "You'd like them," she said softly. A shiver came over her because of her blunder of tense. "You will like them," she corrected herself. "You will, I mean." She kissed his hand again. "You will."

Em woke the next morning dazed from a deep sleep. She got up, fighting the urge to vomit, and dressed hurriedly, agitated by her clumsiness, which was all consuming because of her panic to get to Tommy. She left the house, not even bothering to brush her hair.

"Emmy? You okay?" Doll asked, when she walked into the mess hall.

Em didn't bother to answer, because she didn't know. She only knew she had to get to Tommy. She stepped into his room and froze, shocked by how much better he looked. Some color had returned to his face.

Doll came in right behind her. "Don't it beat all?"

Em went to him, sat beside him and smoothed back his hair with both hands. She leaned down further and kissed his cheek. It felt warmer.

"He looks almost like his old self," Doll said, "'Cept he was never one to lay around."

Em felt a surge of hope. She leaned down and kissed his lips, and they felt warmer. Sighing deeply, she touched her forehead to his.

Chapter Forty-Nine

Three mornings later, as a rooster repeatedly crowed, Jack walked to the house and knocked. A few moments later, Charity answered, dressed and ready for the day. "Good morning," she greeted him.

"Care for a walk?"

"Of course." She gladly stepped outside and they started toward the fields at a leisurely pace.

"I've got to go back," Jack said.

That was so like him. No equivocation. "I know."

"If we weren't so understaffed—" he commented. She drew breath to reply and he stuck his hands in the air. "Do not start."

She grinned. "Fine. I won't."

"You'll stay?"

She nodded. "Yes."

Jack stopped. "You know this isn't likely to have a good outcome," he said quietly, even though no one was in hearing distance.

"I know. But these people—"

"I know. I like them, too. And they will be devastated."

"I am glad you saw that telegram, Jack. And I'm glad you shared it with me."

"I'm glad I saw it, too. I just wish we could have made more of a difference."

"It's not over," she stated. "I'm not giving up. Tommy has so much to live for."

"If he didn't," Jack agreed, "I think he would have passed over already."

She felt tears prick the backs of her eyes, and so she looked at the newly planted fields. She'd never given farming a moment's thought, but she saw the beauty and wonder of it now. "Oh, Jack, there's so much life here. Look at it!"

"Charity—"

She looked at him.

"You're an excellent doctor," he said. "I don't know if I've said that enough."

She smiled, touched by the statement.

"You will return, won't you? When this is over?"

She cocked her head. "Of course. Why wouldn't I?"

"I need you for balance, you know. Intellect versus pure female emotion."

She gave him a look. "*Hmm.* I'm trying to think how many times you've lectured me on letting my emotions control my work."

"I never used those words," he rejoined. "I don't think you let your emotions *control* your work; I think you allow them to influence your work. Heavily. And that is, and will always be, the argument against admitting female physicians to work in hospitals. Which is not a subject I want to reopen. What I meant is that there's too much nonsense in that house."

"Well, it's your home and they're your daughters. Perhaps they haven't been challenged enough," she ventured carefully. She'd made it a practice not to voice her opinion on Alma or the girls to him or anybody. She'd always understood the marriage. It had been expected, planned, a union of families, the children of friends and fellow physicians coming together as they should. Everyone had been willing to play their parts. More than willing. Jack and Alma Werthing would have a charmed life. It had been decided. Only it hadn't turned out quite so idealistic.

Jack, too often, was unsatisfied and Alma knew it. Alma, almost always, was unfulfilled and Jack knew it. And the girls were spoiled.

"You're right about that," he admitted. "The thing is, you're not only my sister, you're my closest companion. We understand one another. We have the same sense of humor. For purely selfish reasons, I don't want to lose that connection."

"Nor do I," she assured him. "I value it as much as you do."

He smiled and offered her his arm, and she took hold as they walked on. "These people," he murmured, "are very caring and supportive of one another."

"Yes, they are."

"And you see the ease with which they go about their lives because of it."

She nodded. "We were fortunate to grow up in a good home."

"But didn't you feel you had to meet expectations? To live up to the potential you were born with? Sometimes it felt as if we deserved no credit for our accomplishments or talent or even hard work. There was never this—"

"Ease?" she suggested.

"Yes. And joy. There was never the simplicity and acceptance you feel here. Of course, there's also sorrow for what's befallen Tommy, but you get a sense of how it was before. I almost wish it wasn't time to get back to the city and to real life." The bell clanged, indicating breakfast was being served and so they stopped. "But it is."

Chapter Fifty

Gregory Howerton walked into Tommy's room and stopped short, alarmed at how markedly thin and pale Tommy looked. He took off his hat, grabbed the back of his neck and squeezed the knotted muscles. His gaze was drawn to the tube coming out of Tommy's arm. Hooked to the far end of the tube was a bottle of what looked like water. Another tube emptied into a bucket halfway under the bed. Urine. Somehow Tommy's urine was being drained from him. Tommy's lifelessness was disturbing. The damn tubes stuck in him were disturbing. It wasn't how a man was supposed to live or die.

"May I help you?" a woman asked.

Howerton turned and blinked in surprise at the woman standing there with a pile of freshly boiled sheets in hand. There was no possibility she was domestic help because she had too much poise and class. She wasn't exactly beautiful. That wasn't the right description. She was highly attractive. She was arresting, with eyes of bluish-gray. "Tommy used to work for me," he said. "He's a friend," he added, realizing it was true.

"I'm his doctor," she said, shifting the sheets to one arm and offering her hand. "Charity Werthing."

Howerton accepted her hand in his and held it a moment

before shaking. It was tempting to turn it slightly and kiss it, doctor or not. "Gregory Howerton."

"I've heard your name mentioned," she stated evenly, withdrawing her hand from his grip.

"And I'd heard doctors had come."

"My brother and I traveled from Philadelphia, but he had to return."

Howerton glanced at Tommy. "Has he revived at all?"

"No."

"Is there any hope?" he asked more sharply than he'd intended.

Her eyes flashed with irritation. "As a matter of fact, everyone here has hope."

She was a fighter, he realized. She had class and style, but she was strong willed, too. He looked at the IV bottle. "What's in the bottle?"

"Essential fluid and nutrients."

He looked at her.

"Did you mean specifically?"

"If you don't mind."

She turned and set the sheets down, then folded her arms defensively. "Twenty ounces of water, fifty grains of sodium chloride, three grains of potassium chloride, twenty-five grains of sodium sulfate, twenty-five grains of sodium bicarbonate, two grains of sodium phosphate and two drachms of absolute alcohol."

"You could have skipped that last one. He's not much of a drinker."

"We're battling dehydration, electrolytic depletion, acidosis and nitrogen retention. Each of the ingredients is important."

"Pretty impressive. Having that formula in your head."

"It's not impressive, it's memorization. I've prepared it many times."

He grew somber. "Is he going to live?"

She studied him a moment and then uncrossed her arms. "I hope so."

"As a doctor, I'd hoped you'd know."

The defensiveness was suddenly back. He could see it in her posture. "I'm a physician, Mr. Howerton, not a fortune-teller."

"How long can he hang on like this?"

She didn't answer right away. "Another week. Maybe two. Maybe longer. I don't know."

"I suppose I appreciate your candor."

She didn't seem to know what to say to that. "If you'll excuse me," she said.

She started to turn away, but he spoke again. "A doctor is an unusual occupation for a woman."

She lifted her chin slightly. "It never seemed so to me."

He looked at her left hand and was pleased to see there was no ring upon it. "Really."

"Yes, really. My father was a physician."

"But not your mother?" he asked with only a trace of a smirk.

"No, but she could have been. She certainly never discouraged my calling."

"I need a doctor at the ranch."

"Right this minute?" she asked calmly.

Her eyes were a clear, sparkling blue-gray, like a lake on a cloudy day, and there was definitely a modicum of amusement in them. Or perhaps sarcasm. And spirit and intelligence. "On staff," he clarified. "The town needs another, as well, but I plan on hiring the best available. The town can borrow her in her spare time."

"I wish you luck with that. My plan is to return home."

"I'd like a chance to change your mind."

Her color flared and her eyes flashed again. Like a burst of unexpected heat lighting on a summer day. "Based on what? You don't know a thing about me."

He shrugged. "I know what my gut says, and my gut is never wrong."

"That must be very nice for you."

"Surely, you're a woman who investigates her opportunities," he challenged.

"I *am* generally a woman who investigates my opportunities. And *you* are a man accustomed to getting his own way. A man who's probably used to having people fall at his feet because of his wealth."

Her spirit was refreshing. Hell, it was downright intoxicating. "Which won't be you, because you come from wealth." She drew back slightly, disconcerted that he'd guessed correctly? "You've lived a highly privileged existence, unless I miss my guess."

"Which you never do," she retorted sardonically.

He nearly smiled. "I hazard a wrong guess from time to time. I said my *gut* was never wrong. I have an instinct for people. Like Tommy here," he said, glancing down at him. "Everyone thought one thing." He shrugged. "I knew they were idiots. I know quality when I see it. I know it in horses and I know it in people."

"I have an instinct for people, as well, Mr. Howerton. Most of us do."

"Tell me, Doctor, do I rub you the wrong way?"

"Because of your arrogance, you mean?"

"Confidence," he corrected.

"No. You don't . . . rub me the wrong way, but I do have things to attend to."

Her color was quite high, her eyes glistening and her respiration significantly increased. All good signs. If he didn't miss his guess, she was every bit as intrigued by him as he was with her. "I won't keep you, then. For the time being," he added because he couldn't stop himself. He waited for another flash of her eyes before speaking again. "Do you know where Emeline is?"

"She's resting," she replied curtly. "One hour a day. Doctor's orders."

He nodded and looked at his hat. Looking back up at her, he asked, "Is she alright?"

She hesitated and looked away from him. "She's been better, as I'm sure you can imagine." She looked back at him, having willed some steel into her spine. "But she's strong. Generally speaking, women are as strong as we're required to be."

"I'm of the same opinion," he stated earnestly. She frowned slightly as she studied his expression. He recognized that he'd thrown her off balance, but, then again, she'd done the same thing to him. He didn't remember the last time his blood had surged this hotly. The last time he'd wanted something quite so badly. "When she wakes, she'll want to know that Blue and Mitchell are dead."

She blinked, startled by the words. "I'm sorry?"

"Blue was the one that did this," he said, motioning to Tommy. "Although Mitchell was really responsible. Plus, he killed another man. Shot him in the face."

She absorbed the news in silence.

"Mitchell was Tommy's brother, but—"

"Yes, I . . . I know."

"I probably should be going, myself. It was a pleasure, ma'am. Or do I say Doctor?"

"Either is fine."

"Or might I say Miss?"

She crossed her arms tightly against herself. "I'm not terribly particular, Mr. Howerton."

"In that case, it was a great pleasure, Doctor Charity Werthing. I'm sure I'll see you again soon." He started for the door, passing mere inches away from her. Close enough that he heard her intake of breath. He'd just reached the door when she spoke again.

"How?"

He turned back to her. "How . . . will I see you again?"

Her cheeks reddened and her eyes blazed. "How did those men die?"

He put his hat on his head. "At the well-deserved end of a rope," he replied, tipping it to her before walking on.

Charity stared in disbelief even after he'd gone, then stepped back, shaking her head. A tremor passed through her and she turned to look at Tommy before walking over to sit in the chair beside his bed. After all she'd heard about Mr. Howerton, she'd expected someone wholly different. She'd heard 'successful' and 'full of himself.' She rubbed her arms, disturbed by the sensations flooding her system. She hadn't been told he was handsome and vibrant. *Forceful.* That's why he was so successful. "So that was Mr. Howerton," she murmured. She took a breath and exhaled, determined to get her pulse to slow and her face to cool. "Oh my," she whispered.

Chapter Fifty-One

Em had never been one to enjoy naps because they made her feel so sluggish afterward. That's how she felt now, curled on her side, not asleep but not quite awake. She gasped softly as she felt movement inside her. She looked down at her bulging midsection and felt thoroughly shaken by how large she'd grown. She put a hand to her swollen abdomen and felt movement. She heard footsteps, rounding the bed, and looked up to see Ben—which meant *she was dreaming*.

"I think it's time," he said with a smile.

"Time?" She struggled to sit up and that's when she noticed Tommy on the other side of her. The sight was so jarring, she woke. "Tommy," she whispered. She sat up and looked down at her stomach. It wasn't bulging, of course. Not yet. That had been pure fancy, but the rest of the dream had meant something. Either that Tommy was about to wake or—

She got to her feet and left the room but, outside, nothing seemed extraordinary or even different. She could see the men working in the fields. Doll was on the front porch peeling potatoes. Queen Pretoria, the cat that had recently adopted them, sat curled at her feet.

"Did you have a good rest?" Doll asked.

Em felt light-headed because everything had changed, only no one seemed to realize it. Tommy was either gone or he was awake. She was sure of it. "I had a dream."

"A good one, I hope."

Em lifted her skirt and broke into a run. She had to get to Tommy.

"Em?" Doll called.

The windows in the dining room were all open and a breeze made the curtains billow inward. Em heard footsteps coming her way and stopped, knowing Charity was coming to give her news of her husband. Em reached out to brace herself against the wall. *I'm not ready,* she thought.

Charity appeared, breathless and crying, and stopped short when she saw Em. "I was just coming to—"

Em squeezed her eyes shut and shook her head. She wasn't ready to hear it. She wasn't ready to lose him.

"His eyes are so blue!"

Em's eyes flew open, and Charity was nodding fervently.

"What is it?" Doll asked from behind her.

"Go," Charity said in a thick voice.

Em walked blindly, dizzy as could be, one arm stretched out. She stopped before she reached his door, terrified it wouldn't be true. But she grabbed a breath and rounded the corner into the room to see him sitting up, looking at her. She burst into tears and ran to him, and they held each other and cried. When she pulled back, it was to stare at him. He was looking back at her, but she still couldn't fully believe it. "Oh, Tommy."

The bell began clanging outside, and she went right back into his arms.

* * *

In the fields, the men all straightened. Wood swallowed hard, knowing it would be news about Tommy. One way or the other, the fight was over.

Em pulled away and then she leaned in and kissed him. Her heart ached to see the familiar expression on his face, as if he couldn't look at her hard enough.

There was a shy knock and she turned to see Charity standing there with a tray. "I hate to interrupt," Charity said. "But we've got to get some food in him."

"Yes, we do," Em agreed, smiling tenderly at her husband.

Charity walked over and put the tray in front of him. "We're going to start light, with some broth. And please don't feel shy about letting your wife help." Besides a bowl of rich broth, there was bread, a thin wedge of cheese, a bowl of strawberries sprinkled with sugar and a glass of water. "Eat what you can," Charity continued. "Your stomach will have shrunk, but you need nutrients."

"Thank you," he said weakly.

Charity beamed a smile. "You're so welcome." She turned and left again.

"I didn't even think to introduce you," Em said as she reached for the spoon.

"She did."

She brought a spoonful of broth to his mouth and he took it. "Doll has toiled over a fresh batch of broth every day," she said.

"How long have I been out?"

She bit on her bottom lip, hesitant to answer. She brought another spoonful to his mouth. "Everything is fine," she said soothingly.

"How long?"

Her gaze connected with his. "Nine days."

"Nine days," he repeated under his breath. He looked down at her stomach. "Are you alright?"

Her eyes welled with tears. "I am now."

"The baby—"

"Will be fine. Charity examined me, and she said everything is fine." She fed him another bite. When he'd finished all he could, watching her warily the whole time, Em picked up the glass and brought it to his lips. His hand closed around hers and he drank. Em had just set the glass down when Doll cleared her throat from the door.

Em grinned at her. "Come in."

Doll came forward, her hands clutched together. "Honey, you are a sight for sore eyes."

"It's good to see you, too," Tommy said.

Doll leaned down to press a kiss to his forehead, swiped at her eyes and started to leave, but there was now a small crowd at the door.

"Tommy!"

"I can't believe it," Wood said as he pushed his way through the others. "You look good!"

"What do you mean you can't believe it?" Tommy teased weakly.

Laughter rang out and Wood grabbed Tommy's hand in both his.

"It's good to see you, man," Hawk said.

"You look great," Jeffrey added.

The other men hung back at the door. They were part of the crew, but not part of the family yet and they felt it.

Wood pulled up a chair next to the bed. "We won't wear out our welcome or nothing, but I just got to look at you for a minute." He shook his head. "It's so good to see you."

"How do you feel?" Jeffrey asked.

"Puny," Tommy admitted.

"I bet," Wood said.

"You been out a long time," Jeffrey said.

"We should send word to Emmett," Em said, directing her words to Wood.

Wood nodded. "And to Howerton," he said.

"I was going into town tomorrow," Hawk said. "But I can go today."

"Tomorrow will do," Doll said.

Tommy looked confused. "I don't even remember what happened."

It grew quiet.

Tommy looked at Em. "Last thing I remember . . . I was worried about you. It felt like you were in danger."

"Damnation," Wood exclaimed. "It just occurred to me that she was, too. Okay, nobody ever, *ever*, questions Tommy's instincts again."

Charity eased back into the room. "That's enough excitement, I'm afraid. We need to let him rest."

There were good-natured complaints, but everyone passed on words of encouragement and quickly filed out. Charity was the last to leave, shutting the door behind her.

"It was Blue who shot me, wasn't it?" Tommy asked quietly, as if just recalling what had happened.

Em nodded.

Tommy was quiet for a moment. "Why?"

Em sucked in her bottom lip, worried this was too much, too soon. She picked up a strawberry and fed it to him. "It was an accident. He was up to no good, but he didn't mean to shoot you."

"Why am I in the bunkhouse?"

"So everyone could help watch over you." She reached for the bread and pinched off a piece, which she fed him.

"Did the tobacco all get planted?" he asked after he'd swallowed.

She laughed quietly and then shook her head. "Yes. Everything's fine. Even the men you hired for the planting—they've worked out fine, Wood says."

Tommy thought about it. "Malcolm, Davis, Joey and Edward," he recalled slowly.

Em nodded and smiled. His mind was fine. It was just fine.

He reached out and put his hand on her stomach again. "Did we pick out the baby's name?"

She shook her head and fought tears. "No. Not yet. We still have to do that."

An hour later, Tommy and Em walked into the dining room. He moved haltingly, leaning heavily on Em for support. Charity's jaw went lax.

"Oh, I like this, seeing you on your feet," Wood exclaimed, clapping his hands and jumping to his feet.

"'Fraid I'm going to hurt Em," Tommy worried in a raspy voice.

"You're not," she assured him.

Charity watched in astonishment. Naturally, he was weak, but he was so much better and stronger than she'd expected. Brain damage had seemed a good possibility given the injury, but he'd escaped it. And to already be on his feet? It was astonishing.

"Not to be unsociable," Em said, trying to sound casual. "But we're going home now."

Everyone burst into renewed applause and Tommy and Em both laughed.

"Can I help?" Wood asked, stepping next to Tommy. "I know you want to do everything all at once, but—"

"Yes," Tommy replied.

"I can help, too," Jeffrey offered enthusiastically.

"Not a chance," Em laughingly exclaimed, before the three of them moved on.

"Hey, Tommy," Doll called, "can I interest you in some apple cobbler for supper?"

"Yes," five voices sang out at once.

The screen door bounced shut.

"And you," Doll said, directing it to Charity. "You get anything you want." She shook her head in wonderment. "We will never be able to thank you enough for all you've done. You and Jack. Never."

Charity smiled and ducked her head, more emotional than was reasonable. "It has been a great pleasure to be part of this," she said when she could trust the strength of her voice.

"This is a great day," Doll rejoiced. "I just wonder if we shouldn't let the others know right away. I know I said tomorrow would do, but—"

"I could go to the ranch," Charity offered with a small shrug. "And let Mr. Howerton know."

"Now, that is a good idea. Then he can send one of his men into town to tell Emmett, who'll pass the good news on." She nodded, liking the plan. "I'll have one of the boys hitch a wagon for you."

"No, that's alright. I think I'll ride."

Doll considered her and then gave a smug smile. "You do that."

Charity left with a light step, buoyed by the thought of a trip to the Triple H. Her pleasure was all due to Tommy's recovery, of course. It would be a thrill to pass on good news for once.

Tommy leaned back against a mass of pillows. He was in his own bed in his own room, where he was supposed to be, and Em sat facing him. "This is better," he sighed.

She nodded and tears glistened in her eyes.

"Lie next to me," he said, patting the bed. "I need to feel you next to me." She slipped off her shoes, letting them drop, and then stretched out beside him, clinging with a strength he wished he had. Nine days. He'd lost nine days. He couldn't fully grasp it. "If the baby is a boy," he said quietly, "let's name him Ben."

"I'd like that," she murmured. "Do you want a boy?"

"I want a life with you. It doesn't matter to me if our baby is a boy or a girl."

Her grip tightened. "Me, too," she whispered.

He relaxed and then jerked his eyes back open, having started to doze.

"It's alright," she said as if sensing his fear. "Don't fight it."

"I don't want to sleep," he murmured thickly, although he was already being pulled away.

"I'll be right here with you. We'll nap and we'll wake up together."

"Promise?"

She kissed his stubbled cheek. "I just got you back, Mr. Medlin. I'm not letting you go anywhere without me."

Chapter Fifty-Two

As Charity rode into the Triple H, it appeared to be quitting time. The hands, making their way to the bunkhouse or chow hall, watched her with unabashed interest. Gregory Howerton emerged from the house, and he looked pleased to see her. "Is there word on Tommy?" he called.

She smiled, but didn't reply.

He hurried down the steps. "He came to?"

She reached the house. "Yes. He is awake and he was on his feet before I left."

Howerton huffed in surprise. "On his feet." She dismounted and he took the reins from her. "What about his—" He paused and tapped his head.

His eyes narrowed with concern and she noticed the crow's feet. He really was a very handsome, compelling man. "There's no brain damage," she assured him. "I believe he's going to heal completely."

Howerton smiled broadly and then looked around before calling out, "Tommy came to! He's going to be alright!"

A cheer went up and echoed again and again as the news spread, and Charity smiled along with Howerton.

"Come have a drink with me," he said to her. "We'll have champagne."

"Is there anyone you could send to town to tell Emmett?"

"Who wants to go into town?" he called.

More than a dozen affirmatives came at once.

"Go! You can all go. But, first thing when you get there, find T. Emmett Rice and tell him about Tommy."

"Yes, sir!"

Given the rush of activity and excitement, she guessed going into town on a weekday was not a common occurrence.

"Think she can take a look at Coy, sir?" someone asked from behind her.

Charity turned and saw three men coming toward them. She looked at Howerton.

"One of my men is down," Howerton explained hesitantly. "Gored by a bull a couple of days ago. Caught it in the back-side."

"How badly was he hurt?"

"Bad," he replied grimly. "I wanted to send for you but, you being a woman and all, he felt more comfortable with Doc Simmons."

"So the doctor did see him?"

"For all it was worth. Doc claimed he was lucky because the bull missed his spine, but Coy's got a helluva lot of pain and this swelling in his gut."

Foreboding filled her. "That's infection."

Howerton nodded slowly. "That's what the doc said yesterday. He already said nothing could be done." He glanced at his men. "They're just hoping for a miracle."

"I'll certainly take a look at him."

Howerton shifted on his feet and didn't reply.

"You don't want me to?" she asked, surprised by his reticence.

"He's going to die soon," Howerton stated quietly. "There's nothing to be done or I would have already seen it done."

"She is here, though," one of the men said. "What could it hurt?"

Howerton looked up at the men and then waved them on. But not unkindly. It was apparent he cared.

"They have a point," she said after the men had walked on. "I can, at least, make sure his pain is being managed."

Howerton sighed with reluctance. "I don't want this to be the first thing you do here. As it stands, it's on the other doc. I mean it was accident and all, but—"

He was trying to *protect* her. She felt dumbfounded and strangely flattered. Perhaps vaguely insulted, as well, but there was no time to sort out conflicting emotions when a man was injured and possibly suffering. "I'm here and he's injured. Take me to him. Please."

He gestured toward the bunkhouse and they started toward it. "I don't have my bag," she realized as they walked.

"Why don't you take a look at him? If you think you need it, I'll send someone for it."

She stopped and looked at him. "You really think there's no hope."

He nodded slowly and seconds of silence elapsed.

"What's his name?"

"Coy Jones. He's only eighteen, maybe nineteen. I just hired him at the beginning of the season. Good kid. Good worker."

"I have to see him."

"I know. I get that. You came how far when you learned a man had been shot in the head? You had to know there was a good chance he'd already be dead by the time you arrived."

"Of course."

"But you came anyway. Dropped everything, left your life and traveled . . . what, four hundred miles to save the life of a stranger if you could. Knowing he might already be dead or, if he wasn't, he probably soon would be. Who survives being shot in the head?"

"People can survive all manner of illness and injury. It happens. Since we'd had a similar tragedy befall us—"

"Your father."

She nodded.

"I heard as much at the farm." He sighed. "I truly do admire your passion to heal, but I'm pretty damn sure Coy is past saving. But . . . we'll see what you think." She nodded her agreement and they began walking again. Howerton took a quick step to reach the bunkhouse first. Opening the door, he called, "There's a lady present," before opening it wider for her.

A lady. A woman. They didn't forget what she was for an instant. Gender was so much more distinct and primal here. She followed Howerton inside, but stopped abruptly when she saw Coy Jones. His color was dramatically off and he appeared to be in great pain. The few men sitting around Coy stood.

"Coy, this is Dr. Werthing," Howerton said. "I want her to take a look at you."

"Why?" Coy asked in a breathy voice, as if it hurt to speak. "Doc said it's over."

"You're still breathing, aren't you?" Howerton asked. "Dr. Werthing here just brought a man out of a coma."

Charity gave Howerton an accusing look. She had not brought Tommy out of a coma, nor was she a miracle worker, and he knew it. He had just built her up and given this young man false hope. Shrugging off her frustration for the moment, she stepped in closer and felt the young man's head. He was burning with fever.

"I said we should get his fever down," one of the men said. "Dunk him in a tub with ice from the ice house."

"Fever actually serves a purpose," she replied as she pressed her fingers against Coy's carotid artery to determine the strength of his pulse. "The body heats when it's trying to burn off an infection. May I?" she asked Coy as she took his bedcover in hand.

He gave a brief nod.

She pulled it back and saw that his abdomen was distended. "I need to take a look at the wound."

Coy looked up at Howerton as if to plead for help.

"Gentlemen," Howerton said.

The men quickly filed from the room.

Howerton sat in a chair beside Coy's bed. "Listen to me, Coy. She's a doctor. She's seen more naked bodies than we've got cattle grazing. Just turn over and let her see you. If I need to make that an order, it is one."

Coy gave in with a grimace. He sucked in a breath as he turned, obviously in agony.

Charity bent closer, pulled off the bandage and inspected the wound, already knowing the swelling in his abdominal cavity indicated a massive infection. The horn of the bull had likely punctured part of the bowel. Gut instinct warned that he could not be saved, and yet her mind raced through options. She straightened and looked at Howerton before squatting to address Coy face-to-face. "I want to be honest with you, Coy. It's not good. I think the horn of the bull punctured part of your intestines."

"Can you fix it?" Coy whispered. It hurt too badly to speak louder.

"I can try," she said hesitantly. "But infection has already set in and there's nothing much we can do for that."

"Try," he grunted. "Please."

She squeezed his arm lightly, and then stood. Howerton rose at the same time. "I need my bag."

He nodded and started out, walking quickly.

"Do you have any medical supplies here?" she asked, following him.

He turned back. "Like what?"

"Carbolic acid?"

"No."

"Chloroform? Ether?"

He shook his head again. "No."

"Does anyone have any laudanum or morphine?"

"Not that I know of. But I'll ask."

· "Did the doctor leave no pain medication for him?"

"He gave him some morphine, but the pain got worse, and it's gone."

"I need my bag," she said urgently. He nodded and hurried out, his expression grim. She walked back to Coy, pulled a chair close and sat, leaning forward to touch his cheek with the backs of her fingers. He was a fair-haired young man with a youthful face.

"I wish I'd seen you in the first place," he whispered. A tear slipped out the corner of his eye and ran down the bridge of his nose. "Mr. Howerton wanted me to."

"The important thing is to stay strong and hopeful," she gently returned. "Can you do that?"

"It hurts," he breathed.

"I know. And I'll give you something for the pain as soon as I get my bag. It won't be long." A soft grunt was his only response. "I'll be right back," she said softly. She stood and left the bunkhouse, then leaned against the side of the building, dazed at what she'd just committed herself to. Howerton was already coming toward her, his stride long, his expression somber. "Someone's gone for your bag," he said. "And we're looking for laudanum. Maybe one of my maids." His gaze raked her face, and there was concern in his eyes.

"I don't think I can save him," she admitted just above a whisper.

"I don't think so, either," Howerton replied. "He's too far gone. It goes to show why we need you, though. You'd have at least found the problem and tried to save him."

"I don't know that he could have been saved," she objected with a slow shake of her head, "and quite frankly, I have never done what I'm about to do."

Howerton gripped her arms. "You'll be fine."

Perhaps it was meant as nothing more than a show of support, but it was too much like an embrace. It was personal and possessive. "I appreciate your support, Mr. Howerton," she murmured, stiffening.

"Greg."

Her throat felt too tight to speak for a moment and she was painfully aware that her face had flushed. "I'll need a place to operate," she said as she sidestepped, forcing him to relinquish his hold. "Somewhere like a kitchen, where the surroundings can be made as sanitary as possible."

"I'll see to it."

He turned and started back to the chow hall, and she took a deep breath and went back inside, still feeling warmth where his hands had been.

The kitchen had been scrubbed clean and then wiped down with vinegar. The sharp tang of it hung in the air. Charity looked over her surgical instruments, which had been laid out after being boiled. A pile of clean rags was at the ready as was silk suturing, which had been soaked in carbolic acid. A dozen fat candles lit the area from the chandelier above the table. It wasn't dark yet, but they couldn't risk losing the light.

"Are you ready?" Greg asked from the doorway.

"I'll need a few people to assist throughout the surgery, and Coy will need to be carried over here once I've put him under."

"Done."

She picked up the bottle of chloroform and a clean rag and started out, trying to look all business, although he could tell she was having second thoughts. He fell into step beside her. "You don't have to do this."

"I have to try," she said, looking straight ahead. "He asked and I said I would."

He nodded in acceptance and opened the door of the bunkhouse for her, not even bothering to announce her, since the men were expecting her. As they walked through the long room, men stood. It was hushed, the atmosphere somber. They all knew this was an exercise in futility, but he respected that she needed to keep her word. She needed to try. She sat in the chair beside Coy's bed, while he went to the other side.

"Are you ready?" she asked.

"I feel kind of funny, being naked," the kid whispered back.

She smiled tenderly. "I know, but you won't for long," she said, hefting the bottle of chloroform. "I promise." She unscrewed the lid.

"Thank you," he bit out.

She nodded. "When you come to, you'll have discomfort. Remember that you can take the laudanum. You can sip a little directly from the bottle if the pain is bad, or you can have it diluted in water."

He nodded.

She doused the rag in the chloroform, set the bottle down and transferred the rag to her left hand before bringing it to Coy's mouth and nose. "Just breathe normally," she said in a soothing voice. "You'll slip into a deep sleep and not feel any more pain for a while." His gaze was locked on hers, and she gently smoothed his hair back with her right hand. Soon he wasn't able to keep his eyes open any longer, and yet she still continued holding the rag close and stroking his hair. Howerton was moved by the gentleness of her touch. He pictured her tending to their young son flushed with the fever of a minor ailment.

"I'll need assistants," she said.

Several men spoke up, volunteering.

She locked gazes with Roger, one of the younger men, who was standing close by. "Just like I'm doing, you'll hold a rag near his mouth and nose once we get started."

"Yes, ma'am."

"And I'll need one more."

"I'll do it," Max Jordan offered. "He's a good friend of mine. I'll do it."

"Thank you." She straightened and rose. "You can take him," she said to the men waiting to transport him.

Howerton watched as they lifted Coy onto the stretcher. Charity recapped the bottle of chloroform and followed them outside. In the yard, men stopped what they were doing and now watched. Most took their hats off.

"Good luck, Doc," someone called.

In the kitchen, Coy was laid out on the table and positioned on his stomach, per her instructions. She walked over to the stone sink and washed her hands well and then dipped them into a bowl of vinegar before drying them. As she walked over to Coy, Howerton rolled up his sleeves and followed her example.

She doused the rag in chloroform again and showed Roger how closely to hold it over Coy's mouth and nose. She then walked over to the makeshift operating table and looked at Greg as he joined her. "I'll need rags throughout."

He calmly nodded.

She looked at Max, who was standing against a far wall, awaiting instructions. "What's your name?"

"Max."

"Max, as you can see, there's a pot of water boiling and there are tongs over there. When I ask, come get whatever instrument I hand you and put it into the water. It should boil for a few minutes, then pull it out and let it cool on the towel."

"Yes, ma'am."

"While it's boiling, wash your hands well with soap, rinse them and then stick them in the bowl of vinegar before drying them off. This must be done before handing me any clean instruments."

He nodded quickly.

"Can all of you tolerate the sight of blood?" she asked, looking first to Howerton, who gave her a short, confident nod.

"Not a problem," he assured her.

"Yes, ma'am," Max said. "No problem for me, either."

"I can, Doctor Werthing," Roger said.

"Don't get too close to the rag," Charity warned him. "What's your name?"

"Roger West."

"Roger, if you begin to feel faint, please speak up and let me know."

"Yes, ma'am."

She pulled the blanket off Coy's body. "Max, will you set this aside?"

"Yes, ma'am."

She peeled off the bandage and dropped it on the floor before irrigating the wound with a solution of carbolic acid. She picked up a small, knifelike instrument. "This is a scalpel," she said, linking eyes with Howerton. "I have another right there."

He glanced at it and looked back at her with a nod.

She took a deep breath, exhaled slowly and made an incision, extending the length of the wound. Foul-smelling fluid seeped out. "Rags," she said calmly.

Howerton handed them to her. "That's a lot of pus."

"Sepsis," she murmured. "Max, boil this, please," she said, setting the scalpel down.

He retrieved it, but it slipped from his hands and clanked on the floor. "I'm sorry," he apologized.

"It doesn't matter," Charity replied reassuringly. "Boiling kills the germs. But be careful, the edges are sharp."

Once again, Howerton experienced a flash of image. Of her, talking to their sons. Patiently instructing them. By God, he wanted her. He wanted to marry her. He wanted her to be the mother of his sons.

"The wound is four, maybe five inches deep," she said before she reached inside her patient, working partly by sight but even more by feel. She pulled a slimy, pale mass of intestines toward her.

"Oh, geez," Max muttered from the stove.

"So, don't look," Roger snapped.

"Scalpel," Charity said, holding out her hand, which was covered in blood.

Howerton handed it to her carefully. "What are you going to do?"

"I'll attempt to cut away the damaged section of intestine," she said slowly as she did it. The room was silent for several seconds. "Then I'll sew the good ends back together. I'll need the silk suture. With the needle. It's already threaded."

"She's going to sew his guts up," Max said softly.

"You shouldn't talk," Roger chastised. "You're going to bother her."

"No, it's fine," Charity said in an even voice. "I talk all the way through procedures. It's . . . calming."

"So, talk," Howerton said. "Is there any medicine for the infection he's already got?"

"No," she said regretfully.

He grunted. "There ought to be."

She set down the scalpel. "Max," she said. She held out her hand to Howerton. "Needle."

He handed it over and she bent closer and began sewing the ends of the intestines together with a deft touch. "There are herbs that help," she said as she worked. "And ancient remedies that ought to be researched and developed, perhaps implemented again."

"Is that so?" Howerton asked conversationally.

"As a matter of fact, ancient Roman medicine was quite

similar to the medicine we practice today. Most people don't realize that."

"I sure as hell didn't know that," Roger agreed.

Howerton offered more rags.

She glanced up at him with appreciation. "Extract the excess and then just drop it on the floor."

He did it, clenching his jaw. "How was it similar?" he asked, keeping his eyes on her hands.

"The practice of medicine was split among different specialties," she replied as she continued to sew tiny stitches, "and all surgical tasks were only performed by appropriate specialists."

Howerton reached for another rag and used it to sop the blood and pus from around the wound while trying to keep out of her way.

"Can I ask a question?" Max put in as he set a freshly boiled scalpel down.

"Of course," she replied without looking away from her task.

"Do you ever think about what you're doing? That your hands are in a man's guts. His insides."

"I think of it clinically. There's damage here that needs to be cut away and the good ends sewn together. The body is a rather miraculous machine. I work on one small part and focus only on that."

Greg glanced at her, impressed by her concentration. Her voice was even, almost a monotone, but the answers intelligent. She was able to do what few could, two things at once and equally well. "You were talking about the Romans?"

"They had very similar instruments to what we use today. They used painkillers and believed in taking sanitary precautions that we've only just recently returned to."

"So, obviously, we didn't keep building on their knowledge," he mused.

"No. If we had, there's no telling where we'd be."

"So what herbs could help him?"

"Deer velvet, garlic, rosemary, sage, eucalyptus, those are several that can be helpful against infection." She bent closer and inspected her work, then glanced at Roger. Her gaze sharpened with concern. "Max, take over for Roger, please."

Greg glanced over and saw how pale Roger was. Max hurried over and took over his job.

"Roger, go sit against the wall," she said.

"Sorry," he muttered. "I just . . . got . . . kinda . . . woozy."

"It's fine. Just sit on the floor. You'll be fine."

She glanced at Greg. "Can you irrigate for me, please?"

He picked up the bottle of carbolic acid. "Just pour it?"

"Yes. Where I'm working."

He did, frowning in concentration.

"Thank you."

He glanced at Max to make sure he was keeping a proper distance from the chloroform; they couldn't function properly with another man down. Max was keeping well back from it as he reached for another rag and stayed at the ready.

For the next hour, Charity worked in silence except for calling for irrigation or a rag or finally the scalpel, which she used to cut the thread before carefully putting the intestines back in place. "If Roger is well enough, he can go and ask for some of the others to come for Coy."

"I can," Roger said.

Howerton looked at him. He was still pale, but he'd make it. "Tell them to stay right outside the door until we call for them."

"Yes, sir," Roger said before starting to his feet.

After Coy was taken back to his room, and only the two of them were left, Charity went to wash her hands. "You will stay the night?" Howerton inquired as he followed her. He stared at the pink suds that formed as she scrubbed. "You'll want to be close in case he needs you."

She rinsed and reached for a clean towel. "I suppose whomever you sent for my bag explained the situation?"

"Of course." He moved in to wash his hands, and his arm touched hers. "They know where you are. Why don't we go have that glass of champagne? Or something stronger. Then we'll have some dinner."

"I don't have a change of clothes," she replied, stepping back from him.

"Doll sent something. Along with word that Tommy is just fine." He glanced at her to judge her reaction, but she only looked tired and somewhat wary as she offered the towel. He took it and dried his hands. As they walked back to the house, he considered offering his arm. In fact, it took restraint not to, but he sensed she needed a certain amount of space and control. "Does it seem too quiet here after the noise and bustle of the city?"

"No. I love it. Especially the fresh air."

He was delighted to hear it, but refrained from showing any reaction. They walked up the steps and he opened the door for her.

"This is lovely," she commented as she walked in.

"It could use a woman's touch, I'm sure."

She gave a small shrug. "I think it suits you perfectly."

He heard the housekeeper's footsteps and looked over at her. "Dinner in an hour, when Doctor Werthing's had an opportunity to change and rest a little."

"Yes, Mr. Howerton."

"If you could see to it that a bath is prepared."

"Right away, sir." She turned and left.

"I'll give you a little of the tour on the way to your room," he said as he led her down the corridor. "Care for a drink?"

"No, thank you. I'd best keep sharp."

He led the way into his office, announcing it perfunctorily, and poured a glass of scotch, which he offered her. She looked at him quizzically. "Yes, I heard you," he said. "But is there anything else to be done?"

She hesitated, and then accepted the glass.

He poured another. "There's not one chance in ten he'll recover," he stated. He turned and found her gaze riveted to his and in it was a touch of hurt. And stubbornness and a ferocious hope. "That's no reflection on you."

She turned away from him and sipped.

"Tell me, do you get emotionally involved with most of your patients?" he asked as he walked around to face her.

"Who said that I do?" she asked coolly.

He smiled.

"Oh," she said. "Those instincts of yours. Those instincts that are never wrong."

"Something like that."

She shrugged. "I suppose I do."

He came closer. Too close for propriety, although he didn't give a damn. She looked at him defiantly and held her ground. He liked that. "Like I said, there's not a chance in ten he'll survive," he said softly. "And I don't want you to be hurt by it."

A myriad of expressions crossed her face and then she lifted her chin. "You needn't worry about me, Mr. Howerton."

"Greg," he reminded her.

"I believe you said you were showing me to my room?"

He grinned and gestured her onward.

A quarter of an hour later, Charity opened the door of her room and peeked out into an empty hallway before hurrying to the bathroom at the end of the hall, where a hot bath was waiting. She was wearing only a robe, which felt wrong. And pleasingly wanton. What thoughts she was having, all the fault of Gregory Howerton and the way he looked at her, not even attempting to conceal his desire. It was as if he'd made up his mind to have her, which was . . . *what?*

She wanted to fill in the blank with *insulting*, but that wasn't true. She wasn't insulted. She felt an attraction to him. No, that wasn't accurate, either. She was drawn to him, like a moth to a flame, which was what she felt herself resisting. She had worked too long and hard to control her own destiny to fall for a man like him.

She stepped inside the bathroom and shut the door. This room, like every other, had been built for comfort and practicality, designed and decorated by someone with money and good taste. She slipped off the robe and climbed into the tub with a heavy sigh. For a few minutes, she relaxed and it was wonderful, but thoughts of Coy started her anxiety rising.

Not one chance in ten was right, and yet she'd opened him up anyway. The bloating and distension of his abdomen had clearly indicated the bowel had been punctured, the intestines had leaked and infection had set in. Barring a miracle, it was too late. And she'd opened him up anyway.

Had it been hubris on her part? She could have provided comfort and pain relief until he slipped away, but no; she'd cut him open. She leaned forward and hugged her knees as tears snaked down her face. She wiped them away with dripping, wet hands. It was infuriating. You wouldn't catch Jack soaking in a tub and crying after operating on a patient. You wouldn't catch one in ten male doctors doing such a thing.

She shook her head and exhaled forcefully. This was fatigue talking. She had tried to save a man, despite the odds. It was not ego; it was that she wanted a miracle. For him, not her.

Charity walked into the dining room, dressed in a simple, coral colored gown, and Greg stood. "Feel better?" he asked, despite her red-rimmed eyes. She'd cried.

"I do. Thank you."

He walked over to pull her chair back for her. "I chose a Bordeaux, but if you'd prefer something else—"

"Bordeaux sounds wonderful."

He seated her and walked back to his place. "You were magnificent today," he said, raising his glass to her.

"You're kind to say so." She sipped and nodded her approval.

"You enjoy wine, then?"

"Very much. This is delicious." She took another sip. "You were very helpful in the operation. Thank you for that. It's rare for a layman to be so calm under those circumstances."

"Tell me about Tommy. Who was with him when he came to?"

"I was."

"What did he say?"

She shook her head. "He said his wife's name. He just wanted Em."

"I can't imagine coming to after that many days. You wouldn't know which end was up."

She nodded in agreement and drew breath to reply, but refrained when the housekeeper, Janice, entered with a tray.

He'd ordered that they go right to the main course, prime rib with sautéed squash, onions and mushrooms. "I had them skip the soup," he said. "Unless you want it?"

"No. This is perfect."

Janice put plates in front of them, refilled wineglasses and left. They began eating and the food was delicious.

"I sat him up," she continued, "and helped him to drink. The IV and catheter bothered him—"

"I can imagine," he interrupted.

"So I removed them before going to get Em. But she'd had a dream and was coming to him. We almost collided in the hall. I swear she . . . knew. She knew something had happened."

He nodded. "Some people are meant to be together. And they are."

She nodded.

"Tell me about your life in Philadelphia. Did you work in a hospital?"

"I do," she said lightly, correcting the tense. "At Preston Retreat, a hospital for the care of indigent married women of good character," she finished with a wry lift of her brow.

"Which part do you take issue with? Married or good character?"

"Both, in this case. Medicine should be provided to those who need it, when they need it. Character and marital status should have nothing to do with anything."

"If you don't like their rules, why not go elsewhere? I'm sure there are plenty of other hospitals in Philadelphia."

"Oh, indeed. Twenty-three hospitals within the limits of Philadelphia, not to mention thirteen dispensaries, where treatment is provided to the poor at no cost. Unfortunately, most of them don't employ female physicians."

He reached for his wine and sat back. "I know a place that hires female physicians. Pays well, conditions are comfortable, there's always something to do and good wine to enjoy. Oh, and the air is fresh."

Her cheeks took on a definite pink glow.

"There are many benefits to life in the country," he continued. "By the way, we're not far from a decent little town. There's really not much that you could need or want that can't be had. And if there is, we take a trip to New York or Chicago. Or Philadephia."

"Are you from this area?" she asked with a polite coolness.

"No. I'm from New York, but I have no intention of returning. This is home now."

"Dinner is delicious," she said before taking another bite. "You have a wonderful cook."

He got the picture. He was pushing too hard. She was changing the subject. Not that he'd stop.

When Janice entered with dessert, freshly baked oatmeal cake with a coconut glaze, she offered tea or coffee, which they declined. When she left, he pushed his dessert away. It held no appeal. "May I ask your age?"

"Almost twenty-eight. Entirely too old for mar—" She broke off in mortification and her face flamed. She pushed back her chair and stood.

He did the same, concerned by her distress. He'd wanted to push and prod, but not to scare her off.

"I'm sorry," she breathed. "I need some air. Will you excuse me?"

She started for the door, but he moved into her path, stopping her. "Entirely too old for marriage?" he said, finishing the statement for her. "I disagree."

"Please let me by," she said, trying to maneuver around him.

He grabbed hold of her arms. "Charity—"

"I don't know what made me blurt such a—"

"You said it because I've asked you to stay. Because I want you to stay. And because you sense I have every intention of making you fall in love with me. Which is true. I want you to need me. I want you to stay with me."

"Let me go. Please. I need some air."

"You said I was arrogant once, and maybe I am. I'm a man who goes after what he wants, and I make no apologies for that. Perhaps when women adopt the same strategy, you'll be hired wherever you damn well want to be hired."

She huffed in objection. "I have *always* gone after what I wanted, thank you very much."

"What about now?" he asked, eyeing her lips. He wanted

to kiss her and he suspected she wanted it as much. He felt her trembling.

"As I already said, I need some air."

"Alright. Done. We'll take a moonlight stroll. My lady's wish is my command. I'll just say one thing more. I've observed more than a few doctors at work, and you are as good or better than any of them. That's why I want you working here. It may even have a little to do with why I want you to be my wife."

She yanked back. "You don't even know me!"

"I don't know you as well I will, but I know you. Somehow." He moved closer. "A year from now, when someone asks me about my wife, because they've never met you, I'll say she's lovelier than you can imagine, with a mind that astonishes me. Then I'll probably add that I don't care in the least that she's outspoken, stubborn and willful."

For a moment, she suffered from a loss for words. "You truly are—"

"Tough," he interjected. "Arrogant at times." He shrugged. "I've worked hard to get what I have. But I've got a heart, too. I protect what's mine. I care about the people that work for me. I'd be a damn good husband . . . and father." He paused, but she didn't speak. She was shaken, but in a good way. "I think you know, too, that I won't take no for an answer when my mind is set on something. I want you. In fact, I'm not about to let you go. Not when you're the best thing that's ever walked into my life."

He pulled her into his arms and kissed her. One hand gripped the back of her slender neck, the other caressed the small of her back. When he released her, he studied her flushed face. "I'll never hurt you, Charity. And I'll never see you hurt."

"I'm going to my room now," she said, stammering slightly.

"What about that walk?"

She hesitated.

"If I promise to behave?" he added.

She turned her head, battling something within herself. "Good night," she said as she started from the room.

He watched her go, and it occurred to him how wonderful it would be to have a daughter. He'd always wanted sons, sons that looked, thought and acted like him, but the mental picture of those sons, once so distinct, had suddenly and irretrievably altered. They suddenly had lighter hair than before and blue-gray eyes. They were more thoughtful now. Still strong and fine looking and passionate about the ranch, but they also had an excellent grasp of medicine and the ancient Romans. He turned and went for his wine with a smile on his lips.

Chapter Fifty-Three

Although it was early, Tommy had bathed, shaved and eaten breakfast. He'd used the outhouse on his own and now he sat on the porch, getting some air. Em brought him a cup of coffee, kissed his temple and sat next to him. He'd asked for the whole truth about what had happened and she'd resisted and hedged, but it was time. "Tell me."

"I was in the outhouse, sick," she reluctantly began. "I heard you yell as I was coming out, and then I saw Blue. He came from behind me. He had a gun and he fired." She swallowed hard. "And you fell." A tear rolled down her face and she quickly wiped it away.

"I'm sorry for what you went through," he said, leaning over to take hold of her hand.

"I'm sorry for what *you* went through. I don't know why people can't just leave us alone."

"He got away, I guess?"

She shook her head. "Mr. Howerton and his men went after him."

Tommy waited.

"They . . . they hanged him."

Tommy looked out to the fields. "Did Blue say why he came?"

"His intention was to take me back to Mitchell."

Tommy looked at her sharply.

"Apparently, Mitchell blames me—"

Tommy nodded as he absorbed this. "I guess I shouldn't be so surprised." He paused. "As soon as I'm strong enough, I'm going to find him. And I'm going to kill him."

"You can't. He was arrested in Roanoke."

"For killing Johnny Macgregor? He was the one who did that?"

She nodded. "Yes."

"Did . . . did they hang him, too?"

She hesitated and then nodded. "I'm sorry."

"At least it was the law," he said quietly. "Otherwise, it would have had to be me."

"It wasn't the law," she said haltingly. "The judge let him go because there wasn't enough evidence. It was Mr. Howerton and his men."

Tommy looked back to the green fields, saddened and relieved at the same time. Or maybe he still wasn't thinking altogether straight. He glanced up and noticed a stain from a leak in the ceiling of the porch. "It looks like a rabbit," he said, vaguely recalling that he'd noticed it once before.

Em looked, too, and then smiled. "It does. I never noticed."

He sipped his coffee and began to rock. Maybe his thinking was just fine, after all.

"Blessed," Em said.

He looked at her. "What?"

"We are so blessed," she said, reaching out for him. Their hands connected and held tight. "Too often I've feared I was cursed . . . with bad luck. But we're not. We're the opposite. Bad luck comes looking and it's turned away. Because we're blessed."

Slowly, he smiled. And nodded.

* * *

Charity woke the next morning, aware that someone was in her room. She was confused for a moment as to her surroundings, but everything came back to her quickly. "Good morning," she said in a raspy voice.

"I'm sorry, miss," the young woman in her room said. "I didn't mean to wake you."

"No, it's alright," Charity said, sitting up. "What time is it?"

"Nearly eight. Mr. Howerton said to bring a fresh pot of tea at eight."

Charity blinked as a ray of light lit the silver teapot on the table across the room. There was also a bowl of fresh cut flowers and a small basket containing freshly made bread of some sort, judging by the scent. She was ordinarily up by now, but the day before had not been ordinary by any means and she had not been able to sleep for half the night thinking about it.

"Shall I bring your breakfast?"

"I think you just did," Charity replied with a smile. "It smells wonderful."

"Cinnamon rolls. It's a specialty of Mrs. Deckling. But I can get you some eggs or fatback or—"

"No, what you brought is perfect. Thank you."

The maid left and Charity rose. She poured herself a cup of tea and walked over to open the curtains. Marveling at the misty mountains in the distance, she tried to prepare herself for seeing Coy. Not one chance in ten was probably right, barring a miracle, and there was nothing left to do. Nothing but to face the inevitable.

She thought of Greg Howerton. Of the kiss. Of the feeling of his arms around her, then gave a quick shake of the head, trying to push the suddenly crowding thoughts away. It wasn't right to think of that now. She set down the cup of tea and went to get ready. Action was the key; it was always the key.

She stepped from the house and saw a man breaking in a wild horse in a nearby corral while a few others stood back and watched. In the distance, cattle grazed and men built fences. Life here was so different from the city. A warm breeze blew and yet she experienced a shiver at the unbidden thought that she could be happy here. She swallowed hard and walked on, shaken by the thought. Had her entire world just shifted on its axis? Because of a man? Because of Gregory Howerton?

She reached the bunkhouse, and hesitated. She knocked lightly and then opened the door slowly, fearful of catching the men by surprise, but there was no one in the room except Coy and a middle-aged man who sat by his bed. The man stood at once and she walked closer. Coy looked worse. She felt his head and pulled back the covers to see the condition of his abdomen. It was grossly distended, worse than before. The infection was too far progressed. The surgery had been for nothing.

"Hurts," Coy whispered.

She glanced at the bottle of laudanum she'd left. Not much was left.

"Not that," he bit out. "Knock me back out, Doc. Till I'm gone. Please."

Her eyes filled and spilled over. Crying was not professional, and she detested herself for the weakness, but it couldn't be helped. She nodded.

"Here you go, ma'am," the other man said, offering her a chair.

She sat and opened her bag with trembling fingers. She pulled out the bottle of chloroform and a rag, then looked at Coy, wanting to express how sorry she was.

"Thank you," he mouthed. "I found out—" he whispered.

She leaned closer. "What?"

"It's not so bad," Coy finished. "Dying. It's not bad."

She shook her head. "No, it's not bad," she managed. She poured chloroform onto the rag.

"You're a good doctor," Coy said. Every word was work, his pain excruciating.

"Bye, kid," the man said.

Coy nodded once.

"I'll tell everyone you said so long," the man added. "And, hey, we'll be seeing you on the other side. Right?"

Charity put the rag close to Coy's mouth and nose, wishing she were tough enough to stop crying.

Coy held her gaze for a moment and then closed his eyes. She brought the rag closer, determined to leave it there until he was gone. It was time to end his pain. She looked away, willing the ache to stop, but it didn't. Had she done the right thing in operating? She'd wanted him to live. She'd wanted another miracle, but she'd known the odds. She looked again at Coy and then noticed the other man had left. She was alone in the room.

She moved over to sit next to Coy on the bed, felt for a pulse and discovered there wasn't one. She set the rag and chloroform aside and allowed the quiet of the room to press in on her. The moments following a death were important. To reflect on the gift of life, the fragility of it, the *magic* of it, was important.

Minutes later, Greg Howerton stepped inside. She didn't look over but she was acutely aware of him walking toward her. He sat on the chair facing her. "No more pain."

She shook her head and wiped her face, still avoiding his gaze.

"Are you alright?"

She nodded, but didn't trust her voice to speak.

"Look at me," he said gently as he took her hands in his.

His were strong and callused. She liked the feel of them. She liked being held by him. She liked his strength. She had worked long and hard to accomplish all that she had; why did allowing herself to love a man diminish any of it? She looked into his eyes.

"We all knew he was going to die when his gut puffed up like it did. That was before you got here. What you did was to give him hope when he needed it. And, somehow, you made him realize it was okay to die, too."

"You give me too much credit," she said in a thick voice.

"I don't think so." He stood, pulling her up with him. For a moment, they just stood there and then he enfolded her in his arms. She didn't resist this time. It was exactly where she needed to be.

Chapter Fifty-Four

December 28, 1882

Wood leaned back in his chair and watched Tommy pace. "You might as well play a hand or two," he commented. "Make the time go faster."

"I'm not playing cards while my baby is being born," Tommy stated.

Wood shrugged. "Suit yourself, Papa."

"Deal already," Joey complained.

Jeffrey, who was shuffling, gave him a dirty look. "So I don't shuffle good as some of you. I'll deal 'em when I've shuffled 'em."

"Geez, Louise, my grandmother shuffles faster. And she's got them knotty fingers."

Tommy went for his coat.

"Son," Wood said. "Emmy's got Doll and Fiona and Charity over there with her. What do you think you're gonna go do?"

"He's anxious to see if his baby is pretty like Em or pretty like him," Hawk teased from his seat at another table, where he was engaged in a chess match with Ed.

"Hey, Ed," Wood said. "Why don't you get your guitar and come strum a tune to soothe Tommy."

"Ed's busy contemplating his next move," Hawk rejoined.

Tommy shrugged on his coat and left the bunkhouse. Em's pain was unnerving, but he had to be there.

The black sky was spitting snow again and the frozen ground crunched beneath his feet. He put his collar up and balled his fists in his pockets. He hadn't gone a dozen paces when a shooting star caught his eye. He stopped and smiled; it felt like a good omen. He hurried on, but when he stepped inside the house, it was too quiet. There was no screaming or crying out from Em, nor was there a baby crying. His stomach was tight with fear as he took off his coat and tossed it over a chair. He started toward the room, but stopped short when Doll emerged crying. "What is it?" he asked breathlessly. "Is Em alright?"

She stuck her hands on her ample hips and sniffed. "Tired is all. Good and tired. And, honey, you have got yourself a beautiful baby girl."

Tommy blinked, hardly daring to believe it. "Is she alright? The baby?"

"She is the prettiest little thing I have seen in my whole life. She cried for a moment and then she settled right down to sleep."

Tears filled his eyes and he laughed with sheer relief. "Can I—"

"Get on in there! Go see your wife and daughter."

Daughter. He had a daughter. What an astonishing thing. He went into the room, and Fiona passed him on her way out. "Congratulations, Daddy," she said, patting him on the back.

"She's fine," Charity assured him from Em's side. "Mother and child are both fine."

He walked forward, his gaze locked on Em's. She smiled, although she looked worn to a frazzle.

"Catherine?" Em asked.

He nodded and carefully sat on the bed, peering into the blanket at a small, dark-haired babe. He reached out and touched her clenched fist with his finger. She was so tiny and yet so real and whole. He looked into Em's face. "You still have any pain?"

"No. I'm just tired. And shaky. And sore."

He leaned forward and kissed her.

"I'm not sure how many times I want to do this," Em said warily.

He smiled and kissed her again.

"Do you want to hold her?"

He hesitated a moment because she was so tiny and fragile, but then he reached for his infant daughter.

As Fiona, Charity and Doll finished bundling up, the clock on the mantel in the parlor chimed eight times. They opened the front door and saw that it was snowing harder than before. They braced themselves and dashed out into the cold night to go share the joyous news.

Inside the bunkhouse, Wood finally won a hand and stood up cheering. The other men commented loudly, although everyone shushed when the door opened and the women came in. "Boy or girl?" Wood asked, turning to them.

"I'm telling you, it's a boy," Jeffrey stated.

"I say it's a girl," Hawk said.

"Well, do you want to hear?" Doll asked. "Or do you want to keep running your jaws about what she might be?"

Wood laughed and clapped his hands. "It's a she?"

Doll grinned back at him. "She's a she. Name's Catherine Anne Medlin."

The cheer that went up was loud and joyful.

* * *

At the Triple H, Greg Howerton paced the floor, waiting for Charity's return, but on his tenth trip to the door to peer out at the worsening conditions, he decided to go after her.

In his law office, Emmett heard the clock chime and knew it was well past time to call it a day. He glanced out the window and then experienced a sharp thrill out of nowhere. "I have a feeling we're going to have a new little soul with us soon," he murmured. Perhaps it was foolish to speak to Ben, but sometimes he felt him so keenly. "If it weren't so dad-blamed cold out there—" he muttered, as he rose.

In the parlor of the bunkhouse at the Martin-Medlin farm, Edward strummed "Greensleeves" as everyone sipped hot mulled wine. A fire crackled in the hearth and added to the pleasant glow in the room. When the door opened, and Greg Howerton stepped in, Charity smiled because she'd known he would come. She rose and walked over to greet him.

"The baby?" he asked, locking gazes with her.

"A girl," she replied with a smile.

He returned the smile and started to pull off his gloves.

"Come on in," Doll called to him. "We're celebrating."

Before he could even take off his coat, Charity leaned in and kissed him. "I love you," she mouthed.

"I know," he replied quietly. "I got those instincts, you know."

As snow blanketed the ground and split rail fences and roofs, Catherine Anne Medlin's eyes opened, revealing startling blue irises and causing her father to laugh even as his eyes filled. Cradled in his arms, the baby's face puckered as she began to cry, and Tommy and Em exchanged a look of complete and utter love before moving in closer to comfort her.

If you enjoyed visiting Green Valley,
read on for a preview of *Spirit of the Valley*,
coming this November!

Jeremy lifted his hand to knock on the door of the Greenway cottage, but lost his nerve. Lightning flashed in the night sky and he looked around at the wildly blowing trees. He'd chosen a lousy evening, but here he was. After thinking of little else but the very pretty Mrs. Carter for three weeks straight, it was the moment of truth. He blew out a breath and knocked. With the racket the wind was making, he had no idea if she'd hear it. After long seconds with no response, he raised his fist to knock again, but the door opened and she was standing before him, the wind buffeting her, ruffling her clothes and blowing back her hair. His heart began thudding faster.

"Yes?" she called to be heard over the wind.

"I, ah—"

He moved back as she opened the screen door to better see and hear him.

"I apologize for showing up so late in the evening," he said loudly, "but I thought you might need some help," he said, leaning forward slightly so she could hear him.

"Need some help?" she repeated, confused by his meaning.

"Around here. You know T. Emmett Rice?"

She nodded.

"He . . . suggested you needed some help with the place."

She blinked in surprise and clutched at the front of her shirt to keep it from blowing open. "I'm sorry," she said, "but I'm not in a position to hire anyone," she replied haltingly. "Mister?"

"Sheffield." He took off his hat. "Jeremy Sheffield."

The rain suddenly let loose, falling hard at an angle, bouncing off the porch floor. It had been raining off and on for two days and it didn't seem like it was going to stop anytime soon. "Please, come in," she said, opening the screen door wider. "You'll get soaked."

He stepped inside, barely avoiding brushing against her, and the savory scent of food assailed his senses. His mind raced for what to say next, but the little girl suddenly appeared in the hall, providing a distraction.

"Go finish your supper," Mrs. Carter said to her, seeing her at once.

"I am finished."

"Rebecca," Mrs. Carter said in a tone that apparently meant business, although the girl gave Jeremy a decidedly suspicious look before walking away. Mrs. Carter turned back to him with an apologetic expression. "I'm sorry you came on such a miserable evening." She held herself stiffly, her hands clutched tightly together.

"I don't mind bad weather. I usually work in a hole where there is no weather."

She looked puzzled.

"I work in a mine," he added.

"Oh. I see."

"Like I said, I heard you could use some help."

"I won't claim it's not true," she began slowly. "Unfortunately, I'm not in a financial position—"

It was dim enough in the small parlor that he couldn't see her face clearly, but it was better that way. Easier. He'd come this far. "Well, ma'am, there's other ways to pay a man," he said quietly. Other than a noticeable intake of breath, she made no sound or movement. He opened his mouth to say something else, but shut it again because he hadn't meant to put it that way exactly. Or had he? "I mean to say there's other arrangements that could be made." She still didn't respond. "Like how some people barter?"

"I . . . I'm not altogether certain what I have to barter with," she replied hesitantly.

He shifted on his feet. "The food smells awful good."

She exhaled, relaxing slightly. "It's stew. In fact, why don't we go into the kitchen," she said, stammering slightly in her nervousness. "We have plenty to share."

"That sounds good."

"Mama," a child called from the other room. "There's another leak."

Mrs. Carter made an onward gesture and then led the way, although she'd only reached the hallway, when she turned back to him, a decidedly conflicted look on her face. Because she wanted him to leave. He held a breath, waiting for the words.

"Mr. Sheffield."

She looked so uncomfortable and he had taken her by surprise, which wasn't fair. "Would you rather I leave?" he asked quietly. "It's alright."

"I . . ." She stepped over to the lamp on the wall and turned it up before turning back to him. There was a blush on her face and her arms were folded. "I'm not sure I believe you wanted to barter for . . . food," she said softly.

He nodded slowly as he struggled for a response that wouldn't frighten her away. "I didn't have any one particular thing in mind," he said, keeping his voice as low so the children wouldn't overhear. "And that's the truth. I wanted to help. I knew you couldn't pay. I'm not trying to trick you or anything."

"I didn't mean that," she said quickly.

"I can tell you this much," he said. "I didn't have any one thing in mind. And I'd never ask for more than what you'd want to give. If that's a home-cooked meal or two, I'll take it."